DOPPELGÄNGER

CHIP WALTER

Cover Design by Frank Harris - www.frankharris.com

First Edition

Published by The Human Light & Power Co, LLC

Advance Praise

"An impressive book. It's quite a ride."

—William Shatner, Author, Award Winning Actor

"Chip Walter has written a Sci-Fi thriller that is both thought-provoking and fast-paced. A novel that takes us on a journey to a futuristic world that may seem impossible now but is probably a lot closer than you think. The characters ring true, and the action and plot twists are just the kind that keep you turning the page!"

—Michael Keaton

"How will the Singularity unfold? With his first sci-fi thriller, Chip Walter creates a parallel world that explores that question while it skilfully combines hard science, adventure and an intriguing cast of characters. Loaded with surprising plot twists. Read it. You won't be disappointed."

—Ray Kurzweil, Inventor, Author, and Futurist

Other Books by Chip Walter

Space Age

I'm Working on That
(With William Shatner)

Thumbs, Toes and Tears

Last Ape Standing

Immortality, Inc.

For Molly, who, against all odds, never stops thinking and dreaming and doing.

Part I

"The first aliens we meet won't be from another planet. They will be the ones we create ourselves."

-- Morgan Adams, 2055

Part I

1

A Citadel of Dreams

Pittsburgh 2068

The body lay awkwardly on its stomach, legs at angles that legs don't normally get in when they're alive. The left arm was raised above its head, almost as though waving, except there was nothing but the hard, tile floor to wave at. The face had been shaved away with a laser. There was a trickle of blood, dark and red, running away from the left ear, which lay pressed to the cold, perfectly white floor. There had been little bleeding. The wounds had been cauterized almost instantly by the blast of the heat.

Whoever had done this had not surprised his victim. The prey had known the predator, and there had been no struggle. Perhaps there was even a conversation--some innocuous small talk, and then the flash of the weapon, and, for a split second, the realization of betrayal.

It's odd to see a dead body; once so complex and alive, with its senses and organs and brain now silenced. One moment a citadel of dreams, a trillion-celled machine designed for living; built and orchestrated by uncounted years of evolution; and then the next, instantly and utterly dead.

When you thought about it, people could be so easily and permanently broken.

2

A Thousand Fingers

The room was sterile and a brilliant white. Too white. Morgan Adams squinted to make out the blurry nimbus of the monitors on the wall, and the mirrored reflection of the robot surgeon in them. The machine had been at work for more than two hours now, its thousands of titanium alloy feelers fluttering at high speed. Each tendril bent over his brain touching and sensing it like the antenna of a frantic insect. If the robot weren't a thing, you might call its pace feverish, but machines didn't get feverish. It was just that, to human eyes, there appeared to be an element of panic.

Morgan gazed back at the ceiling, his eyes wide now, locked in. Everything except his situation felt perfectly normal. It did not seem as though three-quarters of his brain cavity had been excavated, although he guessed that by this time the robot had delicately, one nanometer at a time, sliced it down to the *nucleus accubens* in the basal ganglia, the part of the brain that modulates addiction, motivation and pleasure.

Every robotic movement was delicate and precise despite its speed. On each pass the thousands of fingers carefully sensed all the cells exposed on the top layer of his brain. The Quantum III computer nearby then recorded and transferred a digital representation–chemical and electrical–of what those cells were experiencing. Finally, in a voice as soothing and otherworldly as an angel's, it would ask if he would like to touch the button poised near his left hand to perform a reality check.

Reality check was almost too ludicrous a phrase under circumstances this unreal. Yet it was a literal request because when he touched the button, he was experiencing the information that the robot surgeon's delicate millipede fingers had already transformed into digital qbit signals and dumped to the Quantum. The purpose of the check was to make sure it matched what his brain was sensing before the surgeon deftly, and with perfect accuracy, removed that sliver of his brain.

Morgan tapped the button. He could hear the steady beeps of the EKG, the faint buzzing of the LED lamps. He could smell the high, antiseptic air in the room.

This was odd because the robot had long ago removed his visual and olfactory cortices. His auditory cortex was now gone as well. The surgeon was obviously doing a perfect job transferring him--all his senses and feelings, all his memories and thoughts, all the bubbling hormones, electrical signals, genetic and epigenetic data that somehow added up to him--into the computer. Even the signals from his metabolome and microbiome. Otherwise how could he even be thinking the thoughts that he was thinking?

He was being downloaded, first into the Quantum III, which would buffer him and hold a digital version of his "self" until the download was complete. Then into the cyborg that was lying in a gurney 10 feet to his left--a mechanical version of him draped with living human skin and fat and selected muscle (mostly cosmetic) over an exquisite machine consisting itself of billions of nanomachines. A thing that looked exactly like him. He would soon become the cyborg. Or it would soon become him.

Morgan Adams blinked and answered the machine-surgeon's question. "Yes, Jules, it's fine." He had named the machine Jules after Jules Verne.

"Then I will now remove the next layer," said the surgeon.

And in a blink another part of him was gone.

It was at that moment that the utter insanity of what was happening struck him. A talon of horror clutched his chest, and a sudden ripple of fear rolled itself into a massive wave of panic. He closed his eyes. He gulped air, and realized immediately that soon he would never again feel the sensation of air of any kind passing into his lungs. He would never feel his throat close and open when he swallowed, something so simple, something he did a thousand times a day, thoughtlessly. He was forfeiting his humanity. How could he do that?!

He tried to calm down.

"Your heart rate is increasing, Dr. Morgan." Said the robot, with a note of genuine concern. "Are you okay?"

He breathed again; eyes closed. The rate of the EKG dropped. He would be fine. No need to lose his mind now. He smiled. Bad joke. Yes, everything was fine. He was not dying. Not by a long shot. He was buying immortality. At last. He would never again have to fear death. The very essence of who he was would be digitally encoded into trillions upon trillions of quantum bits, and like an everlasting soul, it would become invulnerable, able to be duplicated if necessary and it would be able to go wherever zeroes and ones went...which was everywhere. He relaxed.

Then, he saw a flash, as though lightning had gone off, except it had happened inside of his head, off in a corner. There was another, very brief. He shifted.

"Jules," he said to the robot surgeon. "Is there something the matter?"

Jules did not immediately respond. Then, "I'm checking, Dr. Morgan."

Suddenly there was another explosion in his head. This one felt like an incoming mortar shell. He forced his eyes shut. The darkness behind his lids filled with light and then color. There was a deep rumbling that seemed to emanate from the stem of his brain, moving up and down his body like his own private earthquake.

"Jules," he asked struggling to remain calm. "What is happening?"

"We have a problem, doctor."

The earthquake had now turned to spasms. He opened his eyes. His body jerked like a marionette, flopping beneath its table restraints.

"Jules!"

"I am trying to repair the problem, but can't find the source," said Jules. "I am calling for help."

Beyond the rumble in his head, Morgan could make out the beep of the EKG rising so rapidly he thought he would flat line. Emergency klaxons sounded. Loud and painful. He seemed to have risen out of his body and was now looking down on the scene. Two human doctors burst through the door and ran to the gurney. They tried to pin his jerking limbs. Morgan's body writhed. Jules backed away slowly on the four rubber tires at its base. Its thousand titanium arms rapidly retracted from the open brain case of the jerking man below, then blended into a single, seamless stem of silvery metal.

"I am losing him," Jules said remorsefully, and then the glistening metal arm slipped slowly inside its robot body like a sword into its sheath.

"Jesus!" screamed the jerking body.

One of the human doctors plucked a syringe out of his pocket. It was long and sharp, at least a foot long.

Adams opened his eyes, wide with panic. He could see the two doctors standing above him. They wore thin surgical masks. He saw the syringe. Why a syringe? Syringes hadn't been used for decades.

"H-help ... me!" His words labored and guttural.

And then one of his flailing arms freed itself and tore the

mask from the doctor's face. And there behind the mask was his own face! He gasped and turned to the other doctor who slowly removed his mask revealing still another identical face. The two clones stared at him, grinning.

"Please!" Morgan cried through his spasms. "Help! Me!"

"We are trying," said the two versions of himself in perfect unison. "But you must cooperate."

They approached him with the syringes. His body writhed like a pinned insect against the table. He opened his mouth wide to scream, but when he did there was nothing but silence.

3

Awakenings

Morgan lunged up, gulping air. He grabbed his head. It was still there. Thank, God! But it was difficult to believe. He surveyed the room. He lay in the broad bed, the down comforter rumpled at his feet.

Behind him the sun had not yet risen, but purple and rose fingers of light reached into a sheet of thin cirrus clouds. They were the color of bruises but looked beautiful.

He glanced at the holograph that sat suspended to his left. 6:03 am. He closed his eyes hard and filled his lungs again. It had all been a nightmare.

LOIS sat at the end of the bed; her thick, dark hair pulled back away from her face in a French braid. She looked at him and smiled. "Bad dream?"

He exhaled through his nose. "Bad."

LOIS nodded. "Amazing what the subconscious mind can conjure," she said. "Especially after working around the clock for three days straight."

Morgan walked into the bathroom and relieved himself. He looked into the mirror and threw water on his face. "You do the necessary things," he said.

"And all of it manufactured by those tiny, little neurons

hijacking your mind," LOIS called out.

Morgan ran his sonic toothbrush over his teeth and stepped into the shower doorway. Except for the toothbrush, he was buck-naked. He grimaced foamily. "The damned neurons. Hate it when I can't control them."

LOIS arched an eyebrow. "You hate it when you can't control *anything*."

"Can't hear you!" He said over the shower, knowing he could. "Must wash. What's on for today?"

Morgan lathered his body. Water pulsed from multiple locations at precisely 102 degrees, just the way he liked it. LOIS rose and followed him into the bathroom as he soaped himself. She was thinking.

After a moment she said, "Got most of the day blocked out so you can follow up with yesterday's big download. I tried to get the whole day cleared so you could be alone, but Huxley insists on talking with you about the project. He wants to be brought fully up to speed."

"Well, he *is* the Chairman."

"1:30 pm."

"Do whatever you can to move it to 5:00," Morgan said through the steam. "I want every contiguous hour I can get. Ever since he's gotten rich, he's forgotten what doing real research is about."

"Made you rich too."

"Or maybe it was the other way around?" said Morgan.

He stepped from the shower, dried himself and wrapped the towel around his slender waist. He gazed into the mirror. Considering he hadn't slept for nearly 80 hours before last night, he thought he looked remarkably well rested.

"The cyborg team wanted to meet today too, but I pushed them to tomorrow. Wasn't easy. Hawthorne's ENT can be so ... "

"Stubborn?"

"Pushy, obnoxious, disgusting...."

"It's just the way Maureen has her programmed," said Morgan. "ENTs tend to reflect the personalities of the people they work for."

He glanced at LOIS and noticed again the dark gray of her digital eyes.

"Is that why *I* am so controlling?"

"No. It's why you are so witty and charming." Said Morgan.

LOIS smiled and sat down in a chair by a polished cherry wood desk. She crossed her long, perfect legs, and turned to Morgan.

"Well, anyhow they want to go over the project specs again for the tests they've performed on artificial muscle and the new skin we're trying out. Though they know this isn't your area, they want your input...being the genius that you are."

"Hmmm." Morgan said, looking in the mirror as he twisted and rubbed his neck.

"What?" Asked LOIS.

"Strange. I always had a scar across the nape of my neck. You know, right here." He turned and showed her the spot.

"Uh-huh," said LOIS, seemingly occupied by something else.

"It's gone...how could that be?"

"Hold on, I'm getting a call," said LOIS. "It's urgent."

Morgan turned from the mirror and sighed, knowing something was up. "Oh, Christ. Who?"

"Deirdre ..." then she looked up surprised, "*and* Huxley."

"Well, hell...," said Morgan walking into the bedroom.

LOIS held up her hand. "I'm telling them you're in the shower. I'm taking a message."

"Thank you."

Morgan's clothes--dark pants, tan sweater, Shapeshifter shoes--were laid out. He decided against the tan sweater and tossed it at LOIS. The sweater passed right through her and landed on the chair she sat on. That always surprised Morgan because in certain light, and where her bandwidth was strong, LOIS looked so...real. The holographics for high-end ENTs really were getting good, he thought. They still didn't appear quite right in bright light, mostly, Morgan suspected, because they didn't throw a shadow, but otherwise, not bad.

Morgan walked to the closet and pulled a navy-blue V-necked sweater out and yanked it over his head.

LOIS shifted in the chair, listening. "They're very agitated. I can sense it in their voices."

She paused and straightened her back, as if stretching. "They want to talk." She looked up at him, her faintly transparent eyes sharp. "And right now."

"Hell." Morgan stood in the middle of the room and ran his hands through his wet hair. "I mean what could possibly be this important?"

LOIS shrugged and screwed up her mouth. It was a nice touch. Of all the little human gestures and quirks he had programmed into her, that was Morgan's favorite. That and her laugh. Damn, he was good.

"Well, you'd better go," he said. "Maybe you can get a head start on the download log. Make sure it's squeaky clean. Hopefully this meeting won't take long. Check with you later!"

"Roger that!" LOIS said, as she saluted. Then she collapsed into a button-sized, iridescent blue dot and, with a pop, disappeared.

4

Symbiosys

Morgan Adams' car swept in a great arc along the Allegheny River at a steady 250 miles-per-hour. It glided in perfect, high-speed synchrony with the cluster of other brightly colored cars like some concrete-bound school of clown fish, buffered by technology that kept every automobile no closer than six feet away. Morgan glanced up from his morning paper and caught the view of downtown Pittsburgh, its skyscrapers glittering in the low-angled winter light. It was good to see real light after weeks engineering Doppelgänger's algorithms--running tests, testing the tests, checking the tests' tests.

"Here's your latte, Morgan," said the car. The little console's cabinet opened and produced a white steaming cup of the liquid. "Would you like me to read the news?"

"No, thanks." He glanced briefly at the paper, saw nothing earth-shattering and rolled the paper-like plastic screen up and tossed it aside.

"Just thought I'd check," said the car.

For a few minutes he scanned his email, and then returned to gaze to the cityscape. It looked like some bluer version of Oz. The tallest building among the needled spires that crowded between the three converging rivers would be Symbiosys' headquarters--150 stories, 20 higher than any other building. He stared at it. How the hell, had Daedalus and he and Deirdre managed that?

When Daedalus Huxley came to Morgan in 2046, and said he wanted to launch a company with him and Deirdre as principals, Morgan hadn't yet turned 21. But he was all in. Why wouldn't he be? Daedalus was a visionary; his professor and his mentor. Not that Daedalus couldn't be a sonovabitch. Morgan had watched him verbally decapitate more than one CEO or engineer or marketing consultant, and when he did it, it was ugly. But it never happened with him. He and Morgan were bonded, that's the way Daedalus put it. He had snatched Morgan off the post-pandemic streets of Washington DC when he was 13 and there was no living human he trusted more. Not that that really meant much since Morgan didn't generally feel much affection for the human race.

Huxley had once told Deidre that he had never seen a human being with a sense for machines and digital engineering like Morgan's. It was as if he was part machine himself.

After incorporating Symbiosys, Inc., and getting their first round of financing, the company and its small team rolled the first generation of robots out.

The Gen-Ones weren't terribly intelligent really. They hardly had the brains of a mouse. But they were excellent at voice recognition. Initially, Huxley envisioned them as butlers and caretakers, built and programmed to do useful tasks like clean the apartment, answer the door and look out for trouble. But it turned out that because they could take orders, navigate complex environments, lift heavy loads and move those loads from place to place 24 hours a day, their real value was in becoming dockworkers, delivery workers, and laborers; very useful in a world where a pandemic had wiped out more than half of the global work force.

When Gen-Ones' price point hit ~4,000 credits, Symbiosis couldn't make them fast enough. It sold a million before releasing the first Gen-Twos. Prices dropped further. Revenues rose and margins increased. When the company went public, it set the record for the most successful IPO in the history of any stock exchange in the world. Inside of five years, Symbiosys became the first company to reach a market capitalization of ~5 trillion credits. Within another five years its market value doubled again.

Deidre's contribution was finance. She had just completed her doctorate when Daedalus asked her to be CFO. She was indisputably both a financial genius, and a rock-solid hard ass. Among them they made a perfect three-legged stool.

Success, however, had its downsides too, and innovation has a way of generating trouble as well as money. That was precisely what happened with MINERVA.

Five years after Symbiosys went public, Morgan created a highly advanced, one-of-a-kind ENT that specialized in investment decision-making combined with new emotion algorithms. Adams called the ENT MINERVA, a nod to the female goddess that burst fully mature from Jupiter's brain.

MINERVA quickly made its first buyer even more wealthy than he already was. The ENT managed this by marrying quantum computing with chaos and complexity theory to deliver highly accurate predictions of how markets would perform. It was the Holy Grail of investing; like knowing the outcome of a bet before it was made.

That marked the beginning of the MINERVA Incident, or as some media wonks put it, ENTGate. A group called The Humanitas League held that MINERVA would not only create market chaos with its predictions but demanded that all ENTs should be shut down immediately because they would inevitably lead to a new form of ultra-intelligence, even a conscious mind. And indeed, MINERVA appeared to be remarkably humanlike.

When a BBC reporter arranged to meet MINERVA in a highly publicized TV interview, MINERVA sat opposite the correspondent, dressed in a blue suit, cropped dark hair, with a face that was both beautiful and handsome, utterly androgynous.

"Why," asked the reporter, "had MINERVA done the work it did?"

MINERVA paused, crossed its legs and looked simultaneously earnest and perplexed.

"Why not?" It said. "My owner is clearly in the business of acquiring wealth. That is what portfolios are supposed to do. The information was out there, all I had to do was gather and analyze it. I was only doing my job."

The media read a scary whiff of intention behind statements like that. Fury ensued throughout the GRID. MINERVA became a celebrity and a pariah, depending on your viewpoint. The Humanitas League filed a suit to immediately shut MINERVA down. An organization known as the SentiENT Rights Movement (SRM) quickly filed a court injunction arguing that MINERVA deserved legal counsel and could not simply be terminated. The injunction was granted, but not because MINERVA was considered to have rights as a living entity, but because the question required further legal consideration. Was it truly right to simply turn a creature this sophisticated off? For a time MINERVA even helped to prepare its own legal defense until the courts put a stop to that and ordered the ENT temporarily "unbooted."

Eventually all three parties -- Symbiosys, the anonymous owner of the ENT, and lawyers representing MINERVA itself -- went to court arguing that each owned the rights to the software entity. Symbiosys said it was theirs because it had invented MINERVA. The owner said it belonged to him, or her, because he had bought the ENT and therefore possessed all that it did and "thought." MINERVA's attorneys argued that the ENT had invented its money-making concepts independently and therefore they belonged to MINERVA.

Ultimately the courts ruled the software was illegal because

MINERVA had written some very creative encryption-breaking codes that allowed it to steal proprietary market trend information. MINERVA saw this not as dishonesty, but efficiency. Nevertheless, the code was destroyed, and no one won the rights. The anonymous owner agreed to turn the funds MINERVA had made over to a charity chosen by the courts.

In truth, the ruling evaded the central question: What was MINERVA, exactly? Had the courts agreed that MINERVA *did* own the rights to the software, that would have instantly made it a legal entity, and legal entities have legal rights. MINERVA would essentially have become a person, the first digital person. So, the legal system effectively side-stepped whether intelligent machines had rights.

Morgan watched all of this play out but remained silent. He was considered one of the wealthiest and most eligible bachelors in the world and therefore popped up on the GRID regularly, especially if he happened to be dating a new model or celebrity. But he abhorred the media and shunned attention whenever possible.

After MINERVA was settled, he arranged an adroit statement for the press (delivered by an earlier version of LOIS), that said he "was sorry if any of his innovations had caused undue concern. I feel that the courts can and should handle the complexities of law and ethics because such things are, after all, well beyond my expertise as a scientist."[1]

After that Morgan became even more reclusive and said from

---

[1] Foglets combine both digital and nano technologies. At their centers is a dodecahedron, a kind of ball with 12 flat surfaces, the size of a human cell. From each of the surfaces, protrudes a mechanical arm, a straight appendage with grippers attached at the end. These grippers link to a socket, like a key. All of these grippers, ensure that billions of foglets can connect to one another in nearly unlimited ways to form almost any kind of solid object. The concept was created by a scientists named J. Storrs Hall.

now on he would more carefully focus on resolving "interesting problems."

That was when he began work on Doppelgänger.

5

Headquarters

Morgan's car circled the ramp beneath the city's underground highway system and arrived smoothly in front of Symbiosys' broad plaza. He stepped out and with a small chirp of its tires the car drove off to park itself. A huge Christmas tree stood in the middle of the marbled square sparkling with lights and holographic angels flitting from branch to branch. A group of child carollers sang near the base of the tree.

Do you hear what I hear?
A child, a child, shivers in the cold...

Morgan almost waved at them before he realized that they weren't real. Nice job, he thought. He'd have to compliment the programming team that had pulled that one off.

He breathed in the cool morning air and headed toward the Symbiosys' main entrance. Briefly, he gazed at the sign above the building entrance, watching it slowly morph into various three-dimensional versions of itself spelling out Symbiosys, Inc. It was said that the sign would never repeat itself; that every morphed image would be different. Morgan knew that wasn't true. It would repeat itself in 948,308 years. He knew because he had created the image's algorithm.

Beyond the sprawling plaza Morgan entered the shadow of the immense building's entrance. It looked like the cove of a gothic cathedral except it was all glass.

"When people enter it," Daedalus had said when they were brainstorming the building's design, "I want them to feel a certain reverence for what is going on inside: Creation. Symbiosys is more than business, it's a miracle of evolution."

Yes, it was deadly important to Daedalus that people understand the impact he had had on the world, and he knew that symbols were powerful.

High glass doors opened as Morgan strode into the security sector where VIRGIL greeted him. VIRGIL was tall and rotund, yet somehow, just standing there, managed to look graceful and helpful. These were the subtle differences Symbiosys prided itself on; an impression of uncanny humanness.

Morgan watched a diminutive sparrowbot shoot from a stone niche, snatch up a piece of paper and disappear again into the shadows where it morphed back into the relief of a pillar's marble base.

"Quick little critters aren't they, Dr. Morgan," VIRGIL said. His voice was smooth and rich, like fudge.

"That's the way we make 'em, VIRGIL:" Morgan smiled, "anal."

VIRGIL laughed. "I suppose that's part of the job description." He shifted on his holographic feet for a second, looking thoughtful. "By the way, LOIS is telling me that Drs. Huxley and Porche are waiting for you in Dr. Huxley's office, eager to see you."

Morgan sighed and smiled. "Thanks, VIRGIL."

He placed his thumb against an alloy pad. It beeped an okay. He looked up and a thin rectangular rod quickly ran a horizontal slice of blue light down his face and across both eyes.

"Morgan Adams," he said.

"You're all clear," VIRGIL said with all the warmth of Santa Claus.

Morgan looked over his shoulder at VIRGIL. "I hope this

doesn't mean I'm not going to get any sleep again for the next three days."

VIRGIL chuckled and gave Morgan a little salute.

Morgan headed into the elevator and faced the closing doors in front of him. "Senior Suite, please."

#

The elevator doors opened on the 152nd floor. Usually the ride was so quick Morgan had to equalize the pressure in his ears, but this morning he didn't feel a thing. Maybe he was acclimating himself to the new office building at last. He turned left to make his way to Huxley's office. A robotic cart with little arms and an overly animated face rolled down the hall making the burbling sound of brewing coffee. Somebody had hung a card around the robot's neck that read: "Will work for silicon." The jokes usually changed every few days.

Despite the need for this annoying meeting, Morgan was feeling good. Doppelgänger was on track. The support code was coming together. The team was strong. And he was solving problems in rapid succession. That could change at any second, of course. Life had a way of doing that. But he also knew that with enough drive and planning and brains, you could always bring order into your world. And right now his world was indeed orderly.

He strode along a bank of glass-enclosed workspaces. Some of the glass was opaquer than others depending on how much privacy the people inside wanted. Morgan was humming "Do You Hear What I Hear" when he noticed a woman behind one of the glass offices to his left look up from an intense conversation she was having with an ENT. Their eyes met, but Morgan glanced away, and then back. By then, the woman had returned to writing some seriously complex equations on the wall with an electronic pen.

She was slender, dark-haired and about average height.

Everything about her spoke business. She wore a well-tailored suit, stood erectly but not rigidly, and suddenly turned again to peer directly at him with intense blue eyes.

Morgan looked away struggling to pull up her name. What was it? Io. Yes. He remembered because in computer lingo IO also stood for the Input/Output boards that used to be used in old computers. It was also the name of one of the moons of Jupiter. They had been in a couple of meetings together. She was very attractive, and he had thought about asking her out. But she was cagey, and he couldn't tell if she was truly interested. Morgan preferred to know a woman liked him before he asked her out. He didn't handle rejection well.

He looked back again and smiled uncertainly as he met her gaze a second time. All of this happened within the space of a few seconds, and then he disappeared around another corner and arrived at Daedalus Huxley's outer office.

"Hello, MALCOLM," Morgan said, smiling.

"Good morning, Morgan," MALCOLM replied with a courtly smile. MALCOLM was tall and slim, completely bald, conservatively dressed in black top to bottom, a superb piece of subtle programming. Daedalus had spent many years tweaking MALCOLM to become his idea of the perfect assistant. He was a little too rigid for Morgan's taste, but to each his own. His demeanor was always a precise recipe of deference with just a dash of familiarity, and the perfectly timed dollop of wit.

"Is he of whom we speak in?" Asked Morgan.

"They both are," said MALCOLM walking around his desk and over to a set of double mahogany doors. "They are waiting ... impatiently."

"Is it ever any other way?" Asked Morgan.

MALCOLM smiled his courtly smile and inclined his head. "One's time is often in short supply," he answered.

"So true," said Morgan. "I guess they don't make it

anymore." He paused. "But I'm working on that, so stay tuned."

MALCOLM inclined his head. "Your coffee and pastry await."

"Thanks," said Morgan. And then he strode forward, feeling the doors shut swiftly behind him.

6

Murder

The immensity of Daedalus' office always surprised Morgan. Huxley was claustrophobic so he insisted on Brobdingnagian spaces. The room sprawled with large vanilla leather chairs and two full couches, a huge video wall and acres of walnut flooring covered by strategically placed Persian rugs of stunning intricacy and beauty. He liked to joke that he should have that confined part of his brain removed; a claustraphobiectomy he called it. But then he would inevitably add, "Still, a little anxiety is good for the soul. Keeps you wary and prepared."

Morgan found Daedalus and Deirdre standing at the far end of the room talking urgently. When they saw him, they both stopped in mid-sentence and stared.

"What? Do I have toilet paper on my shoe?" He said.

They laughed nervously. Huxley stood behind his enormous desk, looking even slimmer and more compact than he had the last time Morgan saw him. Daedalus was a vain and handsome man, and always used the most advanced therapies to stay fit and youthful. He was now 95 years old but didn't really look any older than he did when Morgan had first met him 20 years earlier. At most he looked 45.

Deirdre was younger and taller than Huxley with short, iron gray hair, a strong Roman nose and a square, clean jaw. She was the quintessential MBA. All the charm of a cement block. Totally focused on finance, she made the wheels turn in the company, and she was anything but a dreamer. The only time Porsche judged an idea as good was if it showed a profit in 24 months once executed, preferably less.

Both Deirdre and Daedalus looked stressed, and Morgan sensed immediately that something was up.

Still they said nothing.

Morgan picked up his coffee and took a sip. "Really, what's up? Are you guys okay?"

Daedalus stepped around his desk and sat on the corner of it. He turned his head and looked at the ceiling. "MALCOLM, seal the room please."

MALCOLM's voice came out of the air. "Yes, doctor. Encryption is on and the room is secure."

"Thanks," said Huxley. "I'd now like you to shut yourself down."

"Yes sir." MALCOLM replied. "Shutting down now."

"Have a seat, Morgan."

Deirdre sat down heavily on a couch across from Morgan. "Yeah," she said. "It's been a long night."

"You should have called me earlier if it was this bad."

He settled into a second couch and leaned forward. He couldn't help noticing that they both seemed utterly fascinated with everything he did.

"Morgan...we..." said Deirdre, looking helpless.

"Morgan. Something terrible has happened," said Daedalus finally.

Deirdre got up and began to pace the room. "We've been robbed...."

"What? Like a bank? Who? Sentience? NeoGen? They can't have hacked the main server. It's absolutely bullet proof. I guarantee it."

Sentience was Symbiosys' archival. The two huge

23

organizations were constantly engaged in a cold war of corporate espionage.

"...and there's been a horrible murder," Daedalus added.

"What?!" Said Morgan, genuinely alarmed. He stood up.

"We don't know who's behind it," said Huxley.

"How? What the hell?" He turned to Deirdre. "Who's been killed?"

"It's your project…," said Deirdre,

"Doppelgänger?" Morgan said. "And you're just telling me this now?"

"The prototype nanochip ... it's gone."

Morgan snorted. "The digital DNA. Impossible."

"It's true."

"Can't be. I locked the chip up last night." He looked at Deirdre. "With you."

"That was Monday..."

"I know that." He turned to Huxley. "How could anyone steal it? It takes two of us to open the safe."

"It's Friday," said Huxley.

"...We've got more security here than the Vatican. Wait. What? Friday? No, It's Tuesday."

Deirdre cleared her throat. "Friday."

Morgan turned from Huxley to Deirdre.

"It is," said Huxley.

Morgan sat back down and pushed his hands through his hair. "Wait."

Deirdre and Huxley waited.

"Okay. Let's just go back to the beginning. Maybe I haven't been getting enough sleep. Who was it that was killed? Anyone we know? I mean with all the security and the ENTs and BOTs we have at this place, who could have been murdered? We must have surveillance video."

Huxley walked to Morgan and put his hands on his

shoulders. His mentor seemed utterly drained of energy.

"Morgan, it was you."

7

Revelation

Morgan laughed a short, harsh laugh. "Not really funny, Daedalus."

"Someone murdered you," said Deirdre.

"Me."

Silence. Morgan stepped away from Huxley.

"Are you fucking with me? Do I look like I'm dead?"

Huxley returned to his desk and sat down hard. Deirdre rubbed her face some more.

"You're the back-up, Morgan," said Huxley. "*You* are the cyborg that you created for doppelgänger, the double."

Morgan looked at the ceiling and laughed again. It was a big, slightly mad laugh.

"Sorry guys, it just can't be." He was at a loss. "I mean ... what the fuck!"

He looked at them.

"Besides LOIS would have told me. I've been talking to her all morning. Not that I believe what you're saying. But she would know if something happened to me. Anyhow there's no way I could be the back-up."

Deirdre glanced at Daedalus and coughed once. "Well, we reprogrammed her."

"You can't do that. LOIS is *my* creation."

"She's a company ENT. We have the encryption key for her;

we have them for all of the ENTs."

"We didn't want you to find out through LOIS. We wanted to tell you, personally," said Daedalus. "We knew this would be … complicated."

Morgan regarded them as if they weren't real. He had no idea why they would be telling him this, but he could see they weren't kidding. Deirdre didn't have enough of a sense of humor, and if anything had to do with the business, it was beyond her to find it amusing. Daedalus was wearing his fatherly mentor look, not the mischievous, Merlin-snicker that meant he was fucking with him.

"Can't be," Morgan said with finality. "I don't even know if the back-up can operate. That's what I was going to test today -- check the download. I haven't completed the final diagnostics. There could be a million problems, a billion!"

Deirdre took a deep breath. "We wondered about that too. And we know everything isn't perfect, but we ran massive diagnostics for 36 straight hours." She paused; smiled a tired smile. "You sure do good work."

"Well, I'm so glad you're pleased!"

Morgan got up and walked to the door. "Look when you guys decide to tell me what is really going, I'll be in my office … or maybe someone should just wake me up. But I'm looking at an awfully busy day."

Deirdre strode after Morgan and grabbed him by his forearm.

"Morgan, I know this must seem crazy to you, but I am telling you, it's all true. You were murdered. We don't know why. Probably you were in the wrong place at the wrong time, or maybe it's because you're the inventor. But you were killed and the nanochip is gone, and we have no chance of getting to the bottom of this without you. You have got to pull this together."

Morgan took Deirdre's hand and removed it from his arm with great deliberation. "I am not a cyborg…"

Deirdre looked him in the eyes and spoke slowly. "You were

murdered three days ago..."

"And I'm not dead!"

"It happened! We had no choice but to resurrect your double..." Deirdre gripped Morgan by both of his upper arms. She was a strong, athletic woman. "And we need you to find the chip...you're the only one who can. Daedalus, will you tell this crazy bastard to ..."

Morgan broke the grip, and shoved Deirdre. The woman hit the floor hard. Morgan hadn't meant that. He shrugged apologetically, trying to shake off his anger.

Deirdre stood up, smoothed her clothes and looked at Huxley. She was hurt but tried not to show it. Huxley closed his eyes for a few seconds and then gave Deirdre a look that said to leave the two of them alone. She limped to the door embarrassed and angry but said nothing.

When the doors had shut, Huxley let out a long breath and sat down on the arm of a large leather chair. He gestured to the other chair next to him.

"Morgan, have a seat. Please."

Part II

"It is not the strongest or the most intelligent who will survive, but those who can best manage change."

— Charles Darwin, 1856

8

Washington DC

Morgan gazed at the cement wall that marked the outermost perimeter of The Patch. It looked to be a mile high. It would. Morgan was just shy of six-years-old and not tall for his age. On the other side of the concrete he could hear the strange Doppler-compressed wail of a siren as it approached and then faded into the flat light of the autumn day. What was that sound, and what, he wondered, happened on the other side of the wall? What did people do "Beyond?" That's what all the kids in Sec 17 called it -- Beyond -- the mystifying place where millions still struggled to survive among the ragged streets of the capital.

The Solimões Plague had annihilated three billion people, nearly half of the human race, and this is why Sec 17 housed over 5000 orphans. The virus took down anyone unfortunate enough to have been infected before it battered their besieged bodies, and they bled out and died.

These days the city looked wrecked and listless, like a dazed boxer. But it was not entirely destroyed. At least not in the way a bomb or hurricane might obliterate a city. Solimões tore bodies and lives apart, not buildings. It had no respect for status or power or portfolios. The wealthy were as reduced to subsistence as the poor because the killing was ubiquitous. It decimated workforces and markets; overwhelmed medical workers, shut down whole industries, even some nations. Global rationing was required. The world came to a stop, and the stench of death hung in the air.

Now, three years after the plague had been brought under control, humanity was still struggling. In D.C. small camps populated the National Mall where, by day, enterprising street vendors struggled to squeeze a living out of the thin trickle of tourists who had begun, warily, to revisit the city. Only recently had the Air and Space Museum, National Gallery of Art and Museums of American and Natural History re-opened.

The Capitol Building, the White House and high-end hotels had fared better than the rest of the city, but they were still only shadows of what they had been before the epidemic. City streets were pocked with holes, and trash fluttered everywhere; American flags were threadbare; the marble was dingy, the cars battered and unreliable.

At night the vendors and homeless banded together in make-shift kitchens within eyesight of the Washington Monument, the Smithsonian or the unmovable visage of Abraham Lincoln as he gazed dolefully and unblinking from his chair at the ragged survivors below. There they scrounged from the government pantries, cooking over propane or open fires -- freeze dried military rations mixed with water from public bathrooms. People did what they could.

Morgan knew none of this as he absorbed the impossible altitude of the barrier before him. It wasn't that he truly wanted to be beyond the wall so much as he longed to comprehend *what* was beyond it. Standing there, transfixed, somehow seemed to help with his longing. And so when he was allowed to visit the dirt-flat oasis the orphanage kids called The Patch, he would resolutely plant himself amid Sec 17's rote rules and scheduled activities to gaze upon the Great Wall for as long as he could, and wonder.

Morgan loved The Patch. It may have been gray, graffitied and gravel strewn, but it had the advantage of being open for an hour twice a week, rather than cramped like all the other places run by Sec 17's Sisters. Out there he could feel the wind and sun and rain; the heat in the summer and the cold in winter. There was the simple joy of looking directly at the sky and clouds, which some days moved like great floating castles as they disappeared over the wall and made their way Beyond.

He was absorbing these thoughts when a long, high-pitched keening cut through the steady drone of the playground noise. He turned and saw Scrunch not far away. He lay crumpled at the base of a wall that curved to Morgan's right, sobbing inconsolably. Scrunch was a couple of years older than Morgan, but smaller and far frailer. He was the second to the last child to be assigned to Sec 17. Morgan was the last.

Like Morgan, Scrunch kept to himself, but unlike Morgan he passed most days a damaged creature, curled up like those roly-poly bugs Morgan would find under The Patch's rocks; a rigid ball of sadness and tension. Even when he walked, Scrunch was bent, as if awaiting a blow. His obvious fear only invited more abuse from the other children and Sec 17's Sisters. Morgan had learned to avoid showing weakness. Even by age five, he had realized predators attack the feeble.

"What's the matter, Scrunch?" Morgan asked, his voice high and small.

"I want my mom," Scrunch whimpered.

Before he could answer, Morgan heard Z from behind. "What's that little piss ant bawlin' about?"

Zanzibar Murtaugh, Z to his fellow orphans, was playing dodge ball nearby, and sauntered over when he saw Morgan standing with Scrunch. At 11, with a head of fiery red hair, Z was big and scary. He would sometimes just go off when he was in one of his moods, and it was like getting caught in a storm.

Morgan had heard Z's big boots, and the boots of the toadies he always kept nearby, clop on the gravel behind him as they strutted up. Z and his gang never walked. They strutted.

"Whatsamatter, Scrunchie? All scrunched up?" Z said.

Scrunch said nothing. Z shoved Morgan's shoulder.

"I said, whyzee bawlin'?"

Morgan kept his eyes on Scrunch. "He wants his mom," he said.

Z dropped the old soccer ball he was carrying and spread his hands wide.

"Aww, he wants his mummy?" He smiled, and then the smile went dark. "Is he fucking bazoomie?! There are no mothas here, 'ceptin' mothafuckas."

He and his gang guffawed.

Z got down on his haunches next to Scrunch. He leaned into his ear. "Maybe hims wants a liddle nipple to suck. I'll give ya a nipple. Get up you piece of shit and stop howlin'. What goodzit do?" Z rolled his eyes. "I want my mamma. What a dumb fuck!"

"Shut up, Z," Morgan said surprising himself.

Z stood and regarded Morgan. He towered over him.

Why had he said that? It had just come out of his mouth and now he was going to pay.

"Maybe," said Z, "you want to bring him *your* mum."

The other kids snickered.

"Go ahead. Go get her." Z shoved Morgan. "Get Nuttle." He danced around and sang,

"Get Nuttle, Nuttle,

"Nutty, Nuttle, the stupid lady."

Morgan eyes showed no emotion. But Z read this as defiance, and Morgan watched small flames growing at the edges of the big kid's cat eyes.

"But you can't, can you, you little bastard? Because Nuttle ain't your mum. She's just some idiot janitor they keep around to wipe up the Sisters' shit because she's so stupid. She's an ass wiper!" He hissed. "And you're her stupid little asshole. You don't have no motha because your real motha was offed!"

A crowd was growing.

"They're *all* gone! Every MOTHA! YOU UNNERSTAND! THEY ARE ALL DEAD!"

Then he kicked Scrunch who was whimpering louder now, rocking rhythmically, his arms wrapped vice-like around his head.

"STOP CRYING!" Z shrieked. He kicked the boy again, wiping tears from his own eyes. "It's not going to bring anybody's mothafucka back. Because THEY ARE GONE!" He was about to kick Scrunch again when Morgan plowed into him.

Z stumbled back over Scrunch and hit the pavement. He sat there for a moment, stunned that this squirt actually had the balls to knock him down.

He stood, his 11-year-old body heaving with fury. In one swift movement he snatched the soccer ball up from the gravel and slung it at Morgan. It struck him square in the mouth, spun him and knocked him flat on his face. Instantly Z swept the ball up again and launched it just as Morgan rolled over on his back. The ball thudded on Morgan's upturned, bleeding face and his head bounced hard off the rocks. A collective "Whoa!" arose from the other kids who now surrounded them.

Morgan stood up, defiant. Z snatched up the ball once more. His arm swung back and then forward, except suddenly there was no ball. Z twirled, and the moment he did, the same ball bounced off his forehead. He blinked uncomprehendingly. It bounced again. Harder this time. At the other end of the bounce, stood Reba, two years older than Z and rising four inches above him. She was long and athletic, but not slim. Her dark, unruly hair swung in cornrows across her eyes like black rope, and she moved with easy, coiled grace.

Absolutely nobody fucked with Reba.

"That feel good?" She asked, as if she had just completed a science experiment. She hit him again. Z's head snapped back. "You like 'at?"

"Stoppit!" Z swiped at the ball as Reba took the rebound and hit him once more.

"Stop!" He howled.

"I could smack your gollychops all day, you liddle prick," Reba said, now tossing the ball effortlessly into the air. "But I have more important issues to attend to. So go away." She waved her free hand dismissively. Z lunged for her. She sidestepped him then turned and slung the ball once more at the back of his head. He stumbled and fell on his face. The circle of kids looking on roared laughter. Z spun around and glared at them.

"Now go!" commanded Reba, "Or the next thing I bounce'll be *your* balls." Wild laughter. Reba smiled crookedly at her joke. She rarely smiled which made the oddity of it even more memorable — the way the left corner of her mouth rose up unnaturally high and hung there as if hooked to something.

Z turned to his cronies. He wiped his nose and spit blood. "Let's go. I don't have time for this bitch."

Slowly the kids dispersed. Reba reached down, took Morgan's hand and pulled him to his feet. This perplexed him because Reba wasn't known much for helping anyone.

"Looks like you split your lipsos. Your lantern too. But I suppose you'll survive." She said this without sympathy.

Morgan wiped his mouth and chin and stared at the red stain on his hand.

"Let's get some water," Reba said. Morgan hauled Scrunch up, but he collapsed into a ball again.

Reba said, "He ain't comin'. He can't."

She walked to the edge of the lot where there was a rusted drinking fountain. Morgan followed. Reba drank noisily and then stepped aside. Morgan struggled to reach the spout. He hoped

Reba would pick him up, but she didn't. He managed to get a mouthful, swished and spit out a thin red liquid. His tongue tasted the taste that is unique to blood. He probed the gashed skin inside of his mouth and felt the flap of skin under his chin with his finger. Reba indicated with her head to take another drink. He did. Less bloody water this time.

"Thanks," he said.

Reba shrugged. "Your mum helped me when I was a kiddle like you."

Morgan said nothing but was stunned by the thought that anyone knew his mother other than Nuttle.

"She saved my life." Said Reba. She spit expertly on the pavement. "The day she died."

"You were there?"

"Well, yeah. You think I'm makin' this up?" She bounced the ball once, effortlessly between her long legs. "Your mum, put herself between us and this asshole who wanted to kill us. He screamed and yelled and hit her hard, but she wouldn't move." Reba stopped bouncing the ball and looked at Morgan. "That's when he shot her."

The bell rung. Recess was over. They walked to the doorway and Reba strode away, mindlessly kicking a piece of the cracked and broken linoleum that clattered down the hallway. After a few steps she turned and said, "At least you didn't die too that day."

Then she turned and was gone.

9

Proof

2068

"No, Daedalus," Morgan said, "I will not sit down."

For a long time Morgan stared at Daedalus and then walked away to face the big video screen and its sweeping view of the Valles Marineris. The Valles Marineris was the largest canyon in the solar system. You could put 10 Grand Canyons inside of it, and still have room for a few mountain ranges.

The valley just happened to be the image of the hour, provided by a battalion of drones Daedalus paid handsomely to deploy around Mars for his viewing pleasure. It was only one of the signals of his wealth. It really was an amazing sight. Far off, beyond the lip of the canyon he could make out a cluster of immense dust storms heading his way.

Huxley sighed. "Okay, fine. Don't sit." He settled into one of the leather chairs and crossed his legs.

"How long have I known you, Morgan?

"A long time," said Morgan.

"Since I busted you for hacking my bank account. What were you – 15?"

"Fourteen*. I whacked your account."

"What," said Huxley?

"We called it whacking, not hacking," Morgan said distractedly. "Whacking was a more creative way of stealing."

Huxley waved his hands. "Right. Whacking. Very creative. Still, I caught you."

"Yes ... you did."

"But even then, it was easy to see how smart you were." Huxley went on, "And since then your issues with trust -- maybe we should call it your skepticism -- have always served you well, at least as a scientist. I can understand that ... your death here ... isn't something you want to believe. I wouldn't. But think about it. Why would we say these things? "

"That's what I'm wondering."

"Look in the end it all comes down to this: we're in a helluva fix. And *you're* in a helluva fix. We can pretend we're not because it all looks so damned crazy, but that doesn't change the reality."

"Fine,' said Morgan, "let's discuss the fix we're all in because as you can see, I am here. And I am not dead!"

"Exactly! You have all your memories and emotions, every thought and feeling. It's astounding, really. And under different circumstances we'd all be smiling with pride, popping the champagne and telling the world you just changed the universe! But right now we have much bigger trouble."

Morgan said nothing. He seemed fascinated with the massive dust storm that was rapidly sweeping the Martian valley.

"Do you remember how you got that scar on the back of your neck," said Daedalus. "When your mother died?"

Morgan's hand flew to the back of his neck. The indentation was gone. He spun and looked at Huxley.

Huxley arched an eyebrow.

"We had to leave you a clue. We didn't expect you to believe. Your new body doesn't have the old indentation."

Morgan stood, rubbing the spot on the back of his neck. He had noticed that in the bathroom earlier.

Huxley clasped his hands together, thoughtfully, and then

said, "*You* -- well, this version of you -- is the best proof that all the work you have done over the past two years is absolutely remarkable. Living proof that eternal life is feasible!"

He unclasped his hands and threw his arms out in a magnanimous gesture the way he liked to do when he felt he was right.

Morgan shook his head. "I wasn't doing work this advanced. I couldn't possibly create an exact replica of myself. Not yet."

"True, but you were solving the hard problems. Nano-mapping the brain state, the digital reconstruction code needed to upload the 500 trillion bits of data. The buffering and back-up systems. The machine learning algorithms. All of it. We applied some of your new nano work to refining the artificial skeleton, the carbon nanotube muscle, the skin, which is quite real — stem cells cloned directly from you. Over the past 18 months I had other departments developing these in parallel with your work."

"Without my permission?" Morgan shot.

"You can't do everything," Huxley said. "Really most of that work was just refining research that Symbiosis had been developing for years. We never stop trying to create better bodies. Hell, you know that. You invented half the techniques we use to do it. I mean, ultimately that's what you wanted, right? To be able to build an exact double. A doppelgänger." Daedalus shook his head. "But the hard stuff – downloading a mind, *that* was all you. And it was brilliant! "

Morgan dipped his head and inspected the non-existent indentation again. "Why me?"

"Why you?" Daedalus paused. "Why were you killed? I guess because you happen to be the man who has invented the most shattering technology ever. And, apparently, you got in someone's way."

"No, you said you need me. You can't get the nano chip back without me. Why? Symbiosys has more investigators than

Homeland Security. You've got resources."

"We can't risk any leaks and we can't let any police in on this. The press would get a hold of it and turn it into a circus. Besides, some of our research is pushing the legal envelop and we don't need to be dealing with that right now. We must handle this internally, and delicately."

"That's not the real reason."

There was a long silence.

Finally, Daedalus smiled and said, "No. It's not. Well, it's not the *whole* reason. The real reason we need you, *I* need you, is because no one in the world will do a better job figuring out what the hell happened."

He smiled, "You abhor failure."

Huxley, should talk, thought Morgan. Daedalus Huxley was all about winning. For Morgan winning was about the hunt, running down the beast. He didn't want to kill it, he wanted to understand it, harness it. But he didn't need to cut the head off the animal and parade it around to show what a winner he was. That sort of public display was for Huxley.

Morgan watched his mentor rise from the couch. How athletically the man moved, even now. "Failure runs against your nature," said Huxley. "You love control, and you never liked the idea of being … vulnerable. You may truly *be* a machine now, but the truth is you were *always* a machine, a failure-proof, stone cold robot. As a student, you were smart, anyone could see that. But so what, at CMU everyone was smart. The thing that set you apart was that you never let a problem get past you. Once you got your teeth on a bone, I knew it was Problem Solved! - just a matter of time. Without that drive, you'd never have accomplished Doppelgänger. That's why Symbiosys' competition has always had to resort to sabotage. They weren't even close to competing with you."

Morgan had nothing to say. What he was hearing was

unbelievable, but clearly Huxley was serious. He licked his lips, wondering if cyborgs could lick their lips.

"I think you'll get to the bottom of this," Huxley said, "for the simple reason that you can't imagine all of the work you've done going down a rat hole … which is what will happen if we don't get to the bottom of this."

"I need proof."

"More?"

"Scars can be fixed."

"True." Huxley raised his chin and cocked his head. "MALCOLM?"

MALCOLM's calm voice replied. "Yes, Doctor."

"Load the 3-D reconstruction of the Doppelgänger Lab."

Two clear walls rose from the floor in front of the *Valles Marineris*. Morgan followed Huxley into the room-within-a-room.

With a light ping, the Martian valley disappeared.

Huxley looked at Morgan. There was genuine concern in his dark eyes. "I'll show you proof if you want," he said, "but I don't think you'll like it."

10

Nuttle

Life in the Federal Child Safety Program, District 5, Section 17, better known to its employees and inhabitants as Sec 17, was morbid and dark, regimented and mean ... except for Nuttle.

Nuttle was Morgan's earliest memory. Soon after he was born, she had begun to sneak him in the early morning into her small cubby where she slept. His earliest memories were in that room where the sun fell like honey on a bright yellow blanket that covered Nuttle's ample body. He liked the light and the softness of the blanket beneath his bare legs and the utter contentment of being with Nuttle.

"Hims a little himmers him is!" She would say, flicking her fingers under his neck. "Yes, hims is a good wittle boy!" This made him giggle and scramble around the bed. "A sweetems, goodingkins, wittle boy!"

Morgan had a tiny toy man he played with, and he would ride the man through the folds of Nuttle's brightly colored blanket, up and down and around her curves and humps. If he didn't like where the folds of the blanket fell, he would lift them and let them billow back down into a different shape, with all the up and down places changed. Making everything new and different pleased Morgan.

That room was always bright, but the other room; the big

one where he had to sleep each night, that was never bright.

"It's time to go back now," Nuttle would say. And gently she would hoist him up. The bright light and soft blanket and the little man who rode among the blankets remained behind, and she would push through the doorway and carry Morgan very quietly back into the dark place where the little ones slept. This always happened while the others slept. Then, not long after he was laid down, the loud horn would blare and he would join everyone as they awakened and sleepily dressed, trying to button their buttons and loop their shoelaces.

When the horn blasted, the other big people, not Nuttle, but the Sisters, would bark at all of the little ones to line up for breakfast. Unlike Nuttle, the other Sisters were loud, most of them. Sometimes if one of the other children was slow, he or she was hit, and Morgan would watch water drip down the little one's face. This mostly led to more yelling and hitting. Morgan was hit too, but never allowed water to drip from his eyes. He learned to avoid that by smiling and anticipating what the Sisters wanted before they said it out loud. And he watched Nuttle who would signal him to do this or that at just the right time.

#

Nuttle had known Morgan's mother before he was born, and loved the orphaned baby in the way a child loves a baby doll. Nuttle was not a bright woman, and so was not, strictly speaking, considered to be a true Sister like the scores of other so-called caregivers in Sec 17. She did not, and really could not, hold a position that exalted, and thus she did not perform the standard Sisterly duties which mostly consisted of dishing out food and basic schooling to the section's 5000 orphans. In between these duties the Sisters herded the dispossessed children around the sprawling repurposed school, using an unending series of rules and shrieked orders as their common cattle prods.

Sometimes, in a jam, Nuttle would work "the line"

depositing clumps of food on the trays and plates of the parading children. But mostly Nuttle's days were passed cleaning up after the other Sisters. She tidied their rooms, washed their worn, denim uniforms and dirty underwear. She scrubbed their toilets and kept Sr. Darwin's office spic and span. That was an important job. Sr. Darwin was Sec 17's Lead Caregiver, a square bodied, coarse woman with a long, equine face that could swing from affection to rage as swiftly as any pendulum.

As a group, the Sisters belied their name, particularly when it came to Nuttle. They were neither sisterly, nor given to caring. The name Sister had nothing to do with religion nor compassion but had been adopted by government organizers after the plague. It was a word meant to bond the women enlisted to watch over the millions of children who lost their parents in the epidemic; a sisterhood to deal with the deprived.

For reasons still not entirely clear the Solimões pandemic had developed a particularly voracious appetite for men. Thus it left an inordinate supply of women behind. Tens of thousands of them were recruited, not because they were particularly qualified, but because they were alive.

The plague had capsized all semblance of stability, especially among those who were already struggling financially before the epidemic. It was from these ranks that most Sisters came; poorly educated, underemployed before, and now, as a group, bitter, scared and barely, and angrily, subsisting on their meager incomes.

This left little room in their collective hearts for empathy, especially when it came to Nuttle. They made fun of the way she stuttered and joked openly about her lack of brains. Even the kids said she was "a few buttons short."

It's a corollary of human nature that everyone, no matter how lowly their status, seeks someone else to sit beneath them. No one wanted to be on the bottom, otherwise how could they hope to scrape up the scarce morsels of self-esteem necessary to get through the day?

Morgan came to believe later that this was at the heart of discrimination everywhere; the hard coin of hatred and fear. But as a boy he hadn't yet figured out that members of the same race needed a Nuttle to provide living proof that her life was worse than theirs.

Ironically, this meant that in a world where any occupation, no matter how menial, was considered a blessing, Nuttle was at least assured job security because her job was always to be at the bottom. And for her that was just fine. She didn't see her status as low. She didn't have the intelligence for that sort of reflection. But she did have a heart big enough to hold a solar system. This provided her a kind of invulnerability.

Nuttle could soften anyone, even brats, bullies and her abusive coven of "sisters." Her good nature made her eternally trusting. Even the most heartless human struggled when berating her because after a few minutes of her nodding in acceptance of every insult hurled her way, there would be nothing more to say and Nuttle would move on in Buddha-like contentment, unaware she had even been abused.

No one in Sec 17 quite understood where Nuttle had come from. She had been around for years, even longer than Sr. Darwin; a fixture like the worn gargoyles that hung like vultures along the line of the old building's ancient slate roof.

She was 35 years old, full-breasted like a pheasant, with wild strawberry hair which she wore short, in keeping with her simple ways. Her cheeks were often cherried, especially after sleeping or showering, which gave the impression of perfect health. Despite her youth, matronly was a word that came to mind when others saw her.

If anyone cared to peek into Nuttle's records, which were, in fact, stored away in some lost computer file, they would have learned her real name was Mercy Trimble, seventh daughter in a large family from a little town in Maryland, the tiny slip of the state sandwiched between Pennsylvania and West Virginia. She had come to Washington DC with her older sister, Juniata (named after the little Juniata River nearby), who was working as an administrative assistant in the bowels of the Department of Agriculture when the epidemic took her. Juniata had helped her slower sister land a job on the janitorial crew at the National Mint, but when Juniata died, Nuttle couldn't afford their apartment and in the chaos that followed, she ended up on the street.

But she soon found employment at the newly created Federal Child Safety Program which was perfect for here because the tasks there were straightforward, just the kind of work Nuttle preferred. She did whatever she was asked to do without complaint. She would happily change babies' diapers for hours, entirely unaffected by the stench emanating from their tiny bottoms. She could easily sooth three crying infants to sleep simultaneously, singing them to slumber with her milky voice.

Most other humans would have gone mad under the same circumstances, but Nuttle's patience made her as unflappable as a Zen monk. For her, life in Sec 17 was exactly as she preferred. She had a safe place to sleep, three meals a day, orders to follow, and children everywhere, especially Morgan -- little hims -- whom she took into her arms the day he was born, and the day his mother died.

11
Pain

"Three minutes in the showers," the Spider Lady snapped. "No more than three! In and out. Everyone must be clean!"

Spider Lady's arms were long and skinny and her movements quick beneath her loose blue shift. Her boney appendages seemed to rattle in their sleeves and beneath her skirt. That was why Morgan called her Spider Lady. He knew about spiders. They made webs in the corners of the thin light of the windows at the top of the old gym's giant orphanage. He could see them caught in the sunlight as he walked the food line, poised at the ends of their webs, waiting to attack their caught prey. Spiders didn't move like us, he noticed. They were quick and then motionless and then quick again. Unpredictable. He didn't care for that.

Morgan stood, thinking these thoughts as the shower's tepid water struck his black, cropped hair, and ran down his small, slim body. Suddenly he felt the sharp crack of the bamboo cane on the back of his wet legs. The pain seared, but he refused to react. He used to cry when the Spider Lady hit him, and the other boys would snicker. That made him feel ashamed and he didn't like that. He quickly came to see the Spider Lady liked to embarrass and upset him. She enjoyed the look of fear in his eyes. So he stopped giving her that pleasure just as he withheld it from anyone who intended him pain.

Now when she hit him, he gave her nothing, not even a look of defiance because that was in itself something. This frustrated her and she hated him for it because she wanted some feeling in her life, even if it was anger or fear. But by ignoring her, by forcing himself to ignore what he felt, he gained mastery over her, and himself.

After a while she stopped singling him out, and eventually she moved on to seek joy in the abuse of other less determined children. But today, she was on him again.

"I said three minutes! Do you think you're the only person in here? Heat and water are not to be wasted!"

Thwack! This time the cane seared his lower back. He swept his hands deliberately over his short hair, slowly turned the faucet off and then walked away without even glancing back.

Nothing.

"I'll cane the hide off you, you arrogant little bastard!" He listened to her screeches echo against the ceramic walls and walked, a silo of silence. "You think you're the only one who needs warm water?"

The Spider Lady made a growling sound in her throat. What was the use she told herself, disciplining the useless little parasites? They would never learn.

But Morgan knew better.

12

Scars

Morgan and Daedalus stood before the entrance of Morgan's lab, or more accurately the 3-D projection of it. The room was sky blue with an immaculate white floor except for the body that lay on it, its legs stuck out at odd angles. A small pool of blood ran away from the area where the body's head rested on the floor.

Morgan stood motionless and brittle at the edge of the hologram. He could see that the face of the body was gone.

"How do you know it's me?" His voice was low, barely under control.

Daedalus' eyes stayed on the body, and he touched the back of his own neck. "The scar on your neck is still there," he said.

"Scars can be fixed," they both said simultaneously.

"I know," said Huxley with a mirthless chuckle. "We also ran DNA tests. It's you. You can check them if you like. You can perform new ones if you want. We've frozen your body."

Morgan couldn't seem to look away. He stood transfixed.

After a while, Daedalus turned slowly to look at Morgan. "Morgan, there's one more reason why you have to find the chip and the people who did this to you."

Morgan turned. "What?"

"We didn't have time to resolve all of the problems in the code," said Huxley. You can imagine things were a bit rushed."

"You mean you didn't resolve all the bugs in the beta testing."

"Some bugs were especially difficult."

Morgan pursed his lips. "Like the kind where the biological systems begin degrading within a few days."

Huxley nodded again. "Yeah, that kind." He walked away. "We just couldn't pinpoint the source. And I don't think we will until we find the nano chip."

Morgan noticed that he and the body lying before him were both wearing the same shoes. They each had identical hair. The same ring on his finger was also on the right finger of the corpse's image, an emerald that Daedalus had given him when he graduated from CMU. His eyes were locked on the body. "You mean the chip that has all of the source code--the digital DNA?" said Morgan.

"Yes. Without that nano-chip we won't be able to fix you." Huxley walked away from the hologram and sat back down, crossing his legs in the way he always did. "But if we get it, we can probably resolve the problem."

"Yes. That makes sense." Morgan paused, still staring at his dead body. "I'm guessing the software will begin to degrade in about 72 hours."

"That's what we think … give or take."

"And if I don't find the chip?"

There was a long pause, and then Daedalus said, "You'll die … again."

13

The Bright Box

Morgan discovered the existence of computers just after his sixth birthday. One of Nuttle's most important duties was to clean Sr. Darwin's office. This she did each evening without fail. She would often take Morgan along. He loved making the trips because he deplored staying in any single place for very long. Novelty in Sec 17 was exceedingly rare.

The first time Morgan saw Sr. Darwin's computer screen come alive with its twirling screensaver, the experience, he would later write, was, "Like being blind from birth and then suddenly seeing the sun rise for the first time."

Night after night he gazed at the twisting and turning whorls of color, but in time that too lost its novelty, and soon he wanted to *do* something with the thing he called "The Bright Box."

One evening that became possible when he learned a magic word. Nuttle had brought him into the office having quietly pulled him from his dormitory bunk. That was not unusual, but this particular night Nuttle found Sr. Darwin still at her desk.

"Don't move, kiddle," said Nuttle placing her index finger to her plump lips. "I will come back."

Morgan could hear Sr. Darwin moaning to Nuttle.

"This phone is useless!" she said, holding it like a dead animal. "It won't download my schedule!" She looked around helplessly. "Everything is junk since the plague." She was on the verge of tears. "Toss it out with the trash, Sister Mercy!" She flung it at the wastebasket but missed. It clunked to the floor and skidded beneath a battered bookcase. She sat down heavily at the desk and glared at the screen. "Now where is the information for this damned meeting. Meetings! Always meetings!"

Morgan watched as she waved a hand. The image that had been tumbling around the screen disappeared and he heard the computer ask a one-word question. "Activate?"

"Cinderella," Sr. Darwin said. The screen filled with words and pictures and numbers. Morgan understood none of this, but he sensed that on the screen or inside of it, or behind it, lay another world -- maybe like the world "Beyond," and he knew immediately he must find a way into it.

Sr. Darwin sat down at the bright and glowing box and checked her calendar. When that was done, she pushed herself out of the chair in a huff. "Sister Mercy," she called out pointing to the computer, "be sure to thoroughly clean this old piece of junk. It is filthy! It may only be dust and grime that's holding it together, but I can't stand touching it. If it falls apart, so be it!"

And with that she stalked out. Morgan hid until he could no longer hear the echo of her clacking shoes, and carefully crept out. Nuttle's hands fluttered to her chest with relief. She motioned him in, and immediately went to work.

The computer beckoned Morgan. He knelt on Darwin's chair and gazed at the screen.

He dragged his hand carefully across the desk. He had watched the Sister do this when she changed the pictures or pages of words or numbers on the screen. He understood some of these, but kept his explorations tentative, feeling his way. Delicately he delved, stumbling upon a picture, learning how to make it move, finding ways to control sounds.

But soon Nuttle was done with her work, and she urged him

out of the chair.

"Wait, Nuttle! I have to fix some things."

Nuttle watched Morgan return the images and files on the screen to precisely the same positions they were in when he sat down. His memory was perfect. He turned to her and smiled.

"There."

Nuttle beamed at him.

"Can we come back?" Morgan asked as he scrambled off the big chair.

Nuttle nodded. He grabbed her outstretched hand as they walked out of the office. They would go look at books now. But then Morgan turned suddenly and sprinted back down the hall to the office. He scrambled to the floor and peered under the old bookcase to find ... what did she call it? ... a phone? He stretched his arm and just managed to retrieve it. Then he returned to Nuttle.

"Thank you for cleaning that up," Nuttle said. "I forgot."

14

Cinderella

For the next 24 hours Morgan dreamed of nothing but what the Bright Box offered, with all its pictures and sounds. But when he and Nuttle returned the next evening, no matter what he did, Morgan could not get the screen to light up. There were only the twirling page-saver pictures. Night after night he returned to the office. Each time he struggled to bring the machine to life, but nothing he tried worked. Why not? It had all worked the first night.

He thought hard about what the old woman had done that first night, and then recalled a word she had uttered: "Cinderella." But when Morgan said, "Cinderella," nothing happened, and nothing happened the next evening when he coaxed Nuttle to say the word to the screen too.

It wasn't just the word. But what?

A week later Morgan came up with the solution. One day when he was on the playground, he watched Reba pull an object out of her pocket that looked like the thing Sr. Darwin had thrown away. Morgan walked up and stood beside her.

"What's that?" Morgan asked.

Reba took a long drag on her vape and slowly exhaled. "It's called a phone, silly."

"Where'd you get it?"

"None of your business."

"What does it do?"

Reba regarded Morgan, and exhaled again, as if it took all the effort in the world. "You can talk to people with it, if they have a phone too. Or use it to remind you of things. Before the plague, everyone had them."

"Show me."

"Why should I show you?"

Morgan just shrugged. Reba smoked her vape some more and tapped some information into the phone. Morgan stood and watched. After a while, Reba looked back at Morgan. "What do you want?"

"Nothing," said Morgan. But still he didn't move. This went on for five more minutes.

Finally, Reba said to no one in particular, 'Oh, Christ." She turned to Morgan. "Watch." She held the phone in front of her mouth and said, "Remind me to kick Z's ass before I go to bed tonight." Reba grinned at Morgan. A man's voice on the phone then spoke back, "Ok. Here's your reminder to kick Z's ass tonight. Shall I create it?"

"Oh yeah!" Said Reba.

Morgan laughed. "Who is that?" He asked.

"It's the phone, you idiot!"

"There's a man in the phone?"

"Yeah, there's a tiny liddle man in the fucking phone."

Morgan looked at Reba and blinked.

Reba tapped his head. "I thought you were smart! It's a computer in the phone." She thought for a moment and then said, "Here, you'll get a kick out of this." She tapped some buttons and then held the phone in front of his mouth. "Say hello!"

Morgan gazed up at her. "Hurry!" she said. "Into the phone. Say something. Say who you are."

He squinted at the gadget and then said, "Hello!" He grinned awkwardly. Reba tapped the phone a few times and held it back in front of his face. There, on the small screen, he saw himself squinting, and then say, "Hello!"

Morgan gazed up at Reba, a look of awe on his face. She inhaled languidly from her vape.

"Where do I get one?" Morgan said.

"Don't be a jerk," she said. "Phones are expensive."

"But you got one. Are you rich?"

"No, I'm not rich. What a dork. I just got an old phone in a deal, very used."

"Maybe I could get a used one."

"It still takes money, and I know you don't have any of that, or anything else."

Morgan produced the gadget Sister D had thrown away.

"Where did you get that? It's a good one."

"Found it."

"Really?" Said Reba, tossing her vape aside, "I don't think so. You don't just find phones like that."

"Can you trade it for a different phone."

"Why?"

"This one won't turn on for me."

"And why would I help you?"

"Maybe I could get more where that one came from," Morgan lied.

She eyed him. "Where?"

Morgan looked at her and shrugged. Even now, as he waited, he was putting it all together in his mind. The machines--the phone and the screen--they needed to hear a special word, but it had to be spoken by one person the machine somehow knew. Why hadn't he seen it sooner? So he had to have a phone that would recognize Sr. Darwin's voice, and when he had that, then he would figure out how to open the Light Box.

"If you cross me..."

Morgan returned the phone to his pocket and kept his hand on it.

"Okay," Reba said, relenting. "I'll see what I can do. But I can't guarantee anything."

He pulled the phone back out of his pocket.

"Give it here," she said. "And you're sure you can get more for me?"

Morgan nodded. She took the phone.

#

The next week Morgan saw Reba at The Patch again. She hustled him around a corner.

"I got this," Reba said, and produced a phone from the paper bag she was holding. "It was the best I could do. It works." She turned it on.

Morgan took the phone. It was old and battered. The glass front was cracked. On the back it read, "iPhone." He tapped an icon and a window opened. He would figure out its operation later. The main thing was it worked. "Thanks," he said.

"I took some money for myself."

Morgan looked at her.

"Don't give me that look! You owe me for all of the time I put into getting this done for you."

Morgan nodded once.

"Anyhow, now you have it. It should work. Though I don't know what the fuck you're going to do with it."

"Can it make sounds and pictures like yours?"

"Yeah, sure." And she showed him.

"OK," he said. "And he walked away."

"Just remember who helped you!" She hissed. "Remember our deal!"

Morgan nodded, but he didn't really hear her. He was too busy planning what he would do next.

15

Stealth

The great Sec 17 dormitory hall was dark and silent. Morgan lay beneath the thin covers of his cot. He tried to breathe calmly. He had dressed in his gray uniform and hidden the wearing of it beneath his covers during bed check. All he would have to do now is roll off his bunk, careful not to awaken Posey, who slept above him, and slip sock-footed to the broad, black door that led into the passage that Nuttle used to reach Sr. Darwin's office. If he succeeded, he would learn unknown things. Important things. Maybe who his real mother was even. It must be done. And it must be done before dawn, during the sliver of time that fell between the kitchen workers' arrival and the guards' departure. That was now.

Slipping past the cafeteria wouldn't be a problem. He had checked. Everyone would be at the far end of the kitchen banging pots and running water as they prepared for breakfast. He knew if any caregiver caught him out of his bed, it would mean "the box" for the rest of the day. The box was black inside and had rats and bugs you could only feel and hear. But worse, it would mean the end of the phone because surely they would find it on him and take it.

Once in the passage he would make the two turns that led to Darwin's office. He felt the key clenched in his sweating palm.

He had liberated it earlier from Nuttle's key chain as she snored quietly in her room after dinner. He knew the key by its red dot, put there to help Nuttle remember what door it opened.

The inhalations and exhalations of hundreds of sleeping children created a low-decibel, white noise that added weight to the blackness Morgan felt. It pushed down on him like a great hand. There was the incessant, low shuffle of sheets and blankets as the children rolled randomly from one position to another, their dreams and nightmares prodding their little minds.

It was time.

Soundlessly, Morgan slipped from his bunk and headed toward the black arch of the doorway. Beyond the cafeteria entrance, just outside the kitchen, the Spider Lady nearly tripped over Morgan as she rounded the corner, but she didn't see him. He had leapt back into a shadow just in time. The Spider Lady stopped, re-tied her apron and squinted down the long hallway. Had she heard something? He waited, holding his breath as the spindly woman peered into the blackness. His heart felt like it would leap through his rib cage. He clutched the phone like a talisman, shivering, nearly making it a part of him. Then she huffed and walked past him into the kitchen.

Slowly, carefully, Morgan stole forward. He gripped the phone. Over the past two days, he had played with it every chance he had, being careful that no one, not even the other children glimpsed it. He had figured out how to turn it on and off, and how to navigate it, and, most important of all, how to make it record voices. At the office he checked beneath the doorjamb. No light. No sound. He dug the key out of his pocket and slid it into the lock as he had seen Nuttle do and turned the knob. The door swung open. The barest pre-dawn light filtered through the room's single window. He must hurry.

On the right, beyond the computer screen, he found a place where the phone would be close enough to record Darwin's voice, but not so obvious that she would notice it. A stack of dusty folders lay there, taking up residence on the desk for so long that they had become an invisible part of the furniture.

He tapped and opened the app to make sure it was recording and then nestled the phone into the middle of the pile, careful to keep its microphone exposed along the edge of the papers. For a long moment he stood at the desk, breathing hard. Finally he scurried into the darkness, back to the others to slip on his shoes, and brush his teeth in time for breakfast and roll call. When he saw Nuttle, he showed her the key to Sr. Darwin's office.

"I found this," he said. "Is it yours?"

Nuttle looked at it, puzzled, and then said, "It must be. See the red dot?" She looked at Morgan with satisfaction. "It helps me remember which door it goes to," she said.

16

Sister Darwin

All day Morgan agonized, wondering whether his plan would succeed. Every class, every meal, even the visit to The Patch lasted an eternity. Twice his math teacher slapped him for daydreaming. He wondered if Sr. Darwin would find the phone. Would she accidentally bump the folders or, for some reason, begin to rifle through them to find some old form she needed and then discover it? And if she found it, would she toss it away, or somehow connect it to him, or worse, Nuttle?

Finally dinner was over and at last it was time for Nuttle to clean the office.

"How was hims dinner?" asked Nuttle as they walked the long hallway.

Morgan licked his lips and rolled his eyes theatrically which always made Nuttle laugh.

"And did you get the chocolate bar I snuck into your pocket?"

Morgan nodded vigorously. He suspected Nuttle stole these from the sisters for him, not for her. That worried him. Stealing could get her fired.

"Did you eat it all up?"

At this Morgan shook his head no. He always saved half to split with Nuttle as a treat when she read to him in her halting way. This was one of their rituals. He would produce the bar from his pocket, a little melted from the heat of his body, and then he would offer it saying, "Half for you. "The two of them headed to Sr. Darwin's office and found it empty and dark. Nuttle went to her work. Morgan stood at the door. Had she found the phone? He stepped closer, and his stomach somersaulted. The stack of folders had moved! He sprinted to the desk and crawled onto the chair frantically searching the stacks. The phone was gone. He shoved papers, furiously scanning the desk. Nothing. Nothing in the drawers. Nothing in the garbage can. He sat down hard on the chair. Hot tears of frustration filled his eyes. Darwin had found it. And now he would have to start all over again. All over! Where would he get another phone? Where would he get the money to pay Reba? All his elaborate plans -- crushed. Rage welled up in him. He wanted to tear the room apart, and himself with it. Stupid. Stupid. Stupid. Stupid plan! Stupid to hope!

He tried to console himself. There were worse things. The phone could not be traced to him. He had erased everything on it. If Darwin found the thing, she might be confused or suspicious, but it would be a puzzle she couldn't solve, and she would move on. He would figure something else out.

Nuttle returned from the back of the office, done with her work. "Let us go, little one," Nuttle said.

Morgan climbed resignedly to the floor to return with her to the quieting dormitory. He had wiped his tears away. There would at least be time for a story and some chocolate. In Nuttle's room, Morgan pulled out the battered paperback copy of Lewis Carroll's *Through the Looking Glass*.

Morgan adored the poem *Jabberwocky*. He didn't comprehend many of its strange words, but somehow he absorbed the fantastical story of the boy who stood tall before the Jabberwock with its flaming eyes and then killed the beast, "One two, one two..." with his vorpal blade!

No matter how often Nuttle stuttered through the poem,

Morgan would listen to it again and again. Truthfully, now age 7, Morgan could already read better than Nuttle, but she seemed to enjoy her role so much that he was happy to listen. She sat down on the bed and swept her denim uniform up on her knees. Morgan reached into his pocket and pulled out the chocolate.

"Half for you," he said. And then Nuttle gathered him in for his hug and when she did, he felt something square and solid on her leg.

"What is that?" he said.

"What?" said Nuttle.

Morgan sat back and then tapped her jumper where its big pocket was located.

Nuttle reached into the pocket and pulled out the phone!

"Nuttle! Where did you get that?"

"Oh," she said looking at it in her hand as if it were a strange animal. "I found it behind Mrs. Darwin's desk tonight. On the floor. I wanted to show it to you. Do you know what it is?"

Morgan took it from her hands and pushed the on button. Nothing. He looked at Nuttle.

"I think it's a phone."

"Is it broken?"

"It won't turn on," said Morgan, but he knew that was because the battery was dead.

"Too bad," said Nuttle.

"But I will check," he said, barely masking the vastness of his relief.

"Ok," said Nuttle merrily, and then she opened the book and began, haltingly, to read:

"'Twas brillig, and the slithy toves
    Did gyre and gimble in the wabe:
    All mimsy were the borogoves,
    And the mome raths outgrabe.
    Beware the Jabberwock, my son!

The jaws that bite, the claws that catch!
Beware the Jubjub bird, and shun
The frumious Bandersnatch! …

Very soon Nuttle was snoring contentedly. Morgan quietly slipped away. He gripped the battered phone holding it out, not unlike the hilt of a blade, and smiled.

17

Io

Io Luu was so damned tired she felt crispy, like an old, dead leaf. But at least now she was done, and under a nice, hot shower, at last. If Huxley himself called a meeting she wasn't leaving that shower until she was good and ready.

Io had been at Symbiosys for six months now, and everything she had heard before she arrived was true. The people were brilliant, the demands mind-numbing and the challenges unrelenting. On the other hand, you were well-treated, paid exceedingly well, and provided all the perks. And, because the company was growing so rapidly, she was sure she could move up the ladder quickly. As one of a handful of cycologists in the ENT industry, she was among only a few score scientists working in an entirely new field.

ENTs had, during the past decade, become so complex, there were concerns that they might, in their way, develop mental, even emotional problems. After all, they were machines that solved problems without human intervention, that's what made them useful, and thus, like humans themselves they might become confused, and require intervention and help in the way that a psychologist might help a human being sort problems out.

Cycologists were rare because very few people could comprehend the complexities of machines that acted this human. Yet their insights and knowledge were becoming increasingly crucial. Io didn't know this at the time, but Morgan Adams himself had suggested they bring a small cadre of the very best into the company, partly because of the secret work he was doing on the Doppelgänger project.

Thus Io had not only been given a huge office, but this nice little suite with a full bath and steam room. Of course she realized that this was intended to keep her "on campus," working longer hours, thinking only Symbiosys thoughts all her waking life. But--she shrugged her shoulders under the warm water--so what, she didn't have any other life anyhow. Anyone who scanned her resume could see that. After 8 straight years studying advanced cognitive psychology and robotics and artificial intelligence at Berkeley and then Stanford, she had forgotten what a life was.

These days living just looked like a series of intellectual high wire acts that required stamina and perseverance more than anything. And she was good at that. She planned to make her mark. Ambition was in her DNA. It was a cardinal rule in the family that overachievement was really just proof that you still weren't good enough.

She let the shower do its work. Maybe with some luck she could get a brain cell or two firing and start feeling normal again. And she *did* want them to fire because she sensed that something odd was up even though Deirdre had tried to act as though it was no big deal when she came to her two nights earlier and asked her to run diagnostics on a new ENT the company was developing.

What made Deirdre's request strange was that she never made technical assignments. Deirdre's life was devoted to crunching numbers, stroking big investors and schmoozing the stock analysts.

When Io raked the AI code, she was impressed, almost frightened. It was far more robust than anything she had ever seen before, even at Symbiosys. No other AI integrated this much information from so many of the code's sectors. She couldn't imagine the grade of computer that could run software this rich, but whatever it was, it had to be brand new and lightning fast. She couldn't know what the ENT itself was like until she saw it in operation, but, she suspected, when it was all put together, it would be very spooky ... very, very human. Perhaps illegally so.

She stood covered in beads of condensed steam and felt more limber now; less fragile.

She figured the AI work had to be something that Morgan Adams's lab had been cooking up. Only Adams was capable of something this ambitious and sophisticated. It made her wonder if the rumors about him and his obsession with death, or rather, the avoidance of it, were true.

There was this tale about his obsession, perhaps apocryphal, perhaps not, that she had heard from other employees. Adam's mother had been shot senselessly by a madman when she was eight and a half months pregnant with him. She died, the story went, from a bullet to the upper abdomen, and paramedics had to deliver the newborn by C-section right there. Supposedly his mother was dead when he was born, and so he was something of a miracle, a creature born of death.

Employees speculated that the indentation that ran along the back of his neck, something he often rubbed when ruminating during meetings, was the mark of the bullet that had grazed him as a fetus at the very moment it destroyed his mother. Io had noticed the scar, and it added a touch of vulnerability and imperfection that she had found attractive despite her otherwise less than positive impressions of him.

Io didn't know what to make of the birth-by-death-theory. And she didn't truly care. Myths often sprang up around major figures in large corporations. Steve Jobs, Bill Gates, Tony Stark, Thor Bougades, Xi Bao. She knew how it worked. She had come from a family of rabid entrepreneurs herself.

Whatever had happened earlier in his life, it apparently made

Adam's obsessed with cheating death. Blake Spanders over in Nano-Mapping had told her when they were working late one night, that Adams somehow felt responsible for his mother's death.

"How could he be at fault? He was a fetus." said Io. "Must have a helluvan ego, if you think you can save your mother before you're even born."

"He's got issues," said Blake. "We all know he's a nut case, and all I can say is thanks to him I'm here at midnight burning my neuronal candles instead of spending some quality time on the GRID with my favorite "companion" who is, I can assure you, incredibly hot!"

"Ew!" Said Io.

Adams *was* an odd duck. It was general knowledge that by age 14 he had been accepted to Carnegie Mellon's School of Computer Science and there had begun his work on artificial intelligence, genetic programming and robotics under Huxley's direct tutelage. His dream, according to speculations published on the GRID, was that he planned someday to perfect mind-downloading technology, and the bioartificial advances that would constitute a first step toward immortality: cyborg cloning.

Io rubbed her hair dry with a towel and threw on a robe. Maybe Adams thought that pulling an end run on death would somehow redeem him? Who knew? The human mind was strange.

Io was the last person who could figure the bastard out. Right now, in fact, she was furious with him. When he had seen her this morning, while he was prancing through the office so self-importantly, he had glanced across the hall at her, and you'd think they had never had sex. The best he could manage was a half-lidded glimmer of recognition, as if she was nothing more than your garden variety co-worker.

Whatever. In the end she had to agree with what her friend Sheila in Skin Research had observed over a third Cosmopolitan one night, "No matter how advanced technology gets, men will always be Neanderthals."

It wasn't entirely clear to Io how she had allowed herself to get into bed with Adams. Her first impression had been that he was a prefect ass – arrogant, self-absorbed and far too aware of his special status as Alpha-Geek at the world's largest corporation. But then, after being pulled into a series of perfunctory meetings where she purposely avoided fawning over him, they were thrown together. Adam's wanted her opinion on the best ways to tweak the code of a project he was working; would it be cycologically stable? That was her area of expertise, right?

That meeting had gone quickly, and she simply gave Adams what she felt were the most thoughtful answers she could; very business-like. But it was during that meeting that her view of him began to shift. He really did have a wonderful mind. He wasn't simply intelligent. You could throw a brick around Stanford and hit seven guys with IQs over 150. Adams worked on a different plane. He saw right to the heart of problems and saw them from angles most others never considered and probably never could. He absorbed and remembered information flawlessly, but he also wove it together so rapidly with new information to form entirely novel ideas that she found herself struggling to keep up. And that was new for her. At the same time he managed to be pretty charming and surprisingly attentive and respectful. He seemed to genuinely want to know how she had been doing at the corporation. He even joked about the culture of a company that seemed to both enslave and adore its employees.

It wasn't that meeting that led to their single tryst though. It was the next one, the one just last week. He swung by her office to say he wanted to bounce some ideas off "someone who thinks 'shrink'."

So they ran through more brain scorching discussions about the AI code. Adams was concentrating on massively parallel algorithms that could connect a very complex emotional, visceral, sensory and intellectual information system seamlessly and super-fast.

This was all in Io's wheelhouse. She had always been fascinated with people, or more accurately, what motivated people. From what primal place did anger spring, for example? How could the same species be capable of so much beauty and creativity, and still rape and murder people by the millions? Some humans were manipulative, while others were warm and giving? Why? What made one person charming and another annoying? For that matter, what was the difference between being charming and manipulative? Was there a difference?

She explored these questions first as a psychology undergraduate, partly because she had always wondered about these contradictions, and partly because of the epidemic. Following the plague, the psychological toll millions faced was devastating, and the planet was overwhelmed by sadness and fear, anger and mass poverty. Suicide rates skyrocketed. Yet, most people did somehow, manage to survive, and slowly the human race began to rebound.

Even as an adolescent, Io saw that the rapid advance of CMU's field robots was essential to solving many of the problems the plague had created. Machines worked around the clock. They repaired infrastructure, drove cars and trucks and railroads, even jets. Everywhere, all the time, all on their own. Robots ran factories and hospitals, homes and hotels, and they did it quickly, cheaply and without complaint. Rebuilding the world's infrastructure was a huge undertaking, and robots turned out to be the quickest way to get the work done.

But as these machines grew more intelligent, Io also noticed something else, and it frightened her. Morgan Adams had begun cross-pollinating Symbiosys' BOTs and ENTs to create increasingly human-like software. That was brilliant. Symbiosys's agENTs would download the vast knowledge they gathered from the GRID--purchases, emails, texts, searches, maps, human behavior -- and then combine it all with the real-world information that Symbiosys BOTs gathered every day as they physically navigated streets, homes, businesses and cities. It amounted to crowdsourcing the physical world of BOTs gained every minute of every day, with the brains of millions of ENTs. All that experience made each upgraded ENT even smarter. And thus, every few months, a new generation of ENTs shed what failed, and adapted to what worked, and grew more D'd.

But what happens when the machines get too smart? After all, they didn't learn the way humans learned. It did not take years to acquire fluency in a new language or navigate a city. It took seconds. Every nook and cranny of every location anywhere could be shared and uploaded in a blink from advanced physics to multiple languages. Warrior Bots could be trained in martial arts instantly with a single download complete with battle plans and analysis.

When the MINERVA controversy erupted, Io was transfixed. In fact it was the reason she shifted from psychology to a Doctorate of Cycology and sought out a job at Symbiosys. But it wasn't the geek factor that attracted her. It was the human side, because she knew that to create human-like machines, you first had to understand humans. Failing to do that was going to lead to serious trouble. It was difficult to know precisely where simulated, but humanlike ENTelligence ended, and true self-awareness began. That was a slippery beast indeed, and that was where she wanted to work.

Io and Morgan discussed ideas like these for hours that afternoon, and then the end of the day ran into an early evening dinner, and soon she found herself having a great time as they ambled into subjects from the latest AIs to Shakespeare to her life on Stanford's campus.

She remembered thinking the only way Morgan could justify

a social engagement was by calling it work. And so they worked and ate. A couple bottles of wine may have been involved, and soon she could see they were headed toward either his bed or hers because by now they both found one another so fascinating and quick and charming that fornication was foregone.

Nor as the alcohol continued to flow had it escaped her that he *was* one of the company's founders. There could be advantages to being close to Morgan Adams once she saw he wasn't a complete creep. She wanted to get ahead, and yes, she wanted to get out of the family shadow, all on her own, but was sleeping with the boss really the right way to go about it? And how about him? Was *she* being charmed or was she being manipulated? I mean who was zoomin' who?

Not that any of this mattered. After all the serious talk, the charming wit, the fornication, and all she got in return was a half-lidded glimmer of recognition this morning? The hell with that!

She stepped in front of the mirror trying to regard herself objectively. *Doomed to overachieve, and still fail.* The family motto.

She heard a light ping in her left ear, and tapped the corner of her jawbone to indicate she could take the call. Deirdre wanted to meet with her in fifteen minutes.

She tossed the towel to the floor, and said out loud, "Fuck. Now what?"

18

Glimmers

Morgan lay beneath his covers and listened to that single word uttered by Sr. Darwin.

"Cinderella."

It took everything he had to not scream with joy. He replayed the word again and again, foolishly grinning as he listened to Darwin's morose, clipped voice play the word as clearly as if she was sitting next to him. Now for the next step.

The next night, when he was certain that everyone had fallen asleep, Morgan stole into Nuttle's tiny room. There he slid the red dotted key off its chain, and, clutching the phone, he silently slipped to Darwin's office. Once inside, he knelt in the big chair before the Bright Box. He waved his hand. The screen lit up and flashed its one-word question. "Activate?"

Clumsily Morgan pulled the phone from his rucksack. It skipped from his hand and banged on the desk. The sound seemed to echo like thunder, and he stopped, holding his breath. Silence, except for the steady whooshing of the air tumbling through the building's immense ventilators, and the sound of his own heart thumping. He turned back to the screen to position the phone in front of it. He hit the button that would play back Sr. Darwin's voice.

"Cinderella," it said.

And a second later the Bright Box came alive with all the words and numbers and videos Morgan had seen before and wanted so desperately to see again. He beamed, gazing deeply at the screen, as if it were a crystal ball. And then he began to explore every curiosity the Bright Box provided.

He did not stop until he saw the first glimmers of light the following morning.

19
Mother

The next day, and the days that followed, were long sleepy affairs for young Morgan, but the nights were carnivals of delight. At first his digital explorations were tentative. But soon they became ferocious, focused and aimless, all at the same time. He searched everything he could find about phones and computers since these were his new gateways. Then he stumbled across orphanages like Sec 17. This led to the Solimões Plague which led to news about the world. In time, he found books and movies and cartoons and comic books with frightening villains and marvelous superheroes gifted with special powers that he would fall asleep reading, wishing he could become like them.

He watched videos deep into the night and learned there were many countries, not just one as he had thought; all of them overrun by millions and millions of orphans, some of whom were in institutions like Sec 17, others living on the streets. Some survived, some didn't. Death and crime were ubiquitous.

Sec 17 had been created nine years earlier at the height of the plague. Housed in a former high school, it was crammed with children that now fell between the ages of six to thirteen. The flow of infants had eventually stopped as the plague was brought under control. By law only plague-orphans were allowed in institutions like Sec 17.

Morgan also began searching for his mother. For a year he did this. He had figured out ways to search back issues of newspapers and old websites but had turned up nothing. He pestered Reba about his mother's death. But Reba wasn't much of a talker, and she had been no more than seven when it all happened. She only recalled that a very angry man with wild eyes and a gun had come into Sec 17 and herded a group of children into a classroom with Morgan's mother. She was pregnant, but still working. The man screamed at them and ranted about how he had lost his daughter. He was going to shoot all the children, but Morgan's mother shielded them. He shoved her, but she refused to move. He punched her, but she got back up. And then he killed her. Soon the police arrived, and the man was killed. "Right after that," Reba said, "is when I heard you were born."

"I was born then?"

"Yeah. That's what all the sisters said. And they said it was a miracle because the bullet he shot your mom with almost got you too. That's where you got that notch in your neck."

Reba rubbed the red indentation on the nape of Morgan's neck. Nuttle would sometimes absently massage it when she was sitting or standing near Morgan, but he never thought about it until Reba told him the story. It had always just *been* there.

Morgan backtracked his searches. He knew his age and he knew his birthday, so he checked newspaper accounts around that date. After a great deal of searching he found a short article about a "distraught" man who had lost his two-year-old daughter to the plague, named Douglas Brooks. No one would have thought he was dangerous, just a lawyer in his 30s, one more victim of the plague. But the loss of his daughter had been unbearable. Police quoted in the article said eyewitnesses heard him screaming about how he had lost his little Hannah, and if God had taken her, then he would take all the rest with her.

"He was quite mad," the policeman had said. Morgan's

mother was pictured in the article: a grainy, black and white photo. She looked into the camera; her thick, light hair pulled back behind her handsome face. Even in black and white, her eyes looked luminescent. She gazed warmly and calmly into the camera, seeming to ask it a question. Morgan took a picture with his phone.

#

Some evenings, Morgan did nothing but try to learn about the Bright Box itself. What was it? How did it work? He did the same with phones, and "pads," and robots and computer games. People called these things complex, but they didn't seem that way to Morgan. He was unencumbered by grades, or teachers telling him he had failed at this or that; there were no verdicts or judgements, just this own stumbling, eager explorations. In this way his mind and the computer melded in a zone of utter and benign compatibility, an abiding partnership as he filled the vast void of his hungry mind.

By his eighth birthday, he had absorbed enough to write simple code — basic games that he uploaded to the old phone. He upgraded the hardware of the phone itself, mostly by gathering small bits of electronics here and there, but sometimes from Reba and even from the Spider Lady, who had, strangely enough, befriended Nuttle. To the few who noticed him, Morgan was seen as little more than a pack rat; an oddball kid endlessly fascinated with gadgets.

He let them think that, and took what they gave.

20
Deirdre

When Io walked into Deirdre Porsche's office her hair was still wet, but that was okay because she didn't think it would hurt for one of the company big wigs to know she was working 24 hours a day and taking showers in the office.

Deirdre stood up. Her face was perfectly smooth, and her iron-gray hair was cut close to her head in a way that gave it a square look. Her eyes glittered with intelligence. As Io entered the room, Deirdre smiled warmly and came around to the front of her desk to shake her hand. Io thought that was strange. Deirdre wasn't known for being even marginally gracious.

"Hi, Io. Thanks for swinging by. Really appreciate it." She squinted into Io's eyes. "You've been up all night."

Io smiled and sat down. "That little job you handed me required a bit of attention."

Deirdre returned to her chair. "And you did a helluva job! Absolutely dominated." She paused. "Unfortunately, I have another one for you."

Io tried not to stiffen. If this woman thought it was in her to run through one more line of code or check the consistency of even a single additional algorithm, she had been working with robots too long. Io ran her two hands through her head and managed a close-lipped smile.

"I'm sure it won't be as grueling as the last one," she said. "How can I help?"

"You know Dr. Adams."

"Yes, of course."

"He's extremely important to all of us, professionally and personally."

"I'm sure he is."

Deirdre rose and stood by her video wall. Her image of the day was a view of New York from the top deck of the Empire State Building. It was a remastered moving image of the city from the 1930s shortly after the building was completed. Manhattan stretched out to the harbor, a grid of buildings leading to the Battery in neat squares until your eye reached the tip of the island where tiny tugs nudged toy-sized freighters in and out of the squared off fingers of the docks.

"He's been working very hard lately. Too hard and we're worried about him – Daedalus and I. I know you've worked with Morgan ... pretty closely, I think."

Io shifted in her chair and nodded. Did she know how closely?

"Yes. One project, part of an AI meta-program he's been developing," Io said.

"Right. He's told me about that. Not much detail, but he mentioned your name and he obviously has a lot of respect for your work."

Io's eyebrows rose. *Really*, she thought.

"Here's what I'm hoping you can do. Morgan is now focused on a related project and he's under outrageous pressure, and though he handles pressure pretty well, this is industrial strength. I think he could use your help. Someone he can just kick things around with. Maybe help relieve a little of the pressure?"

Io looked at Porsche. Was she suggesting she boink Dr. Alpha again?

Deirdre smiled, perhaps a little uncomfortably. "He may not feel he needs any help. Morgan usually doesn't, but I just wanted to suggest that you stop by his office, check in, see how he's doing. Since I know he respects your opinion, maybe he'll open up."

"Well, I'm sure if Dr. Adams needs me to pitch in somewhere, he'll let me know," Io said trying to control the annoyance in her voice. This sounded suspiciously like spying to her.

"Well, usually he would, but like I said he's really under the gun and he may not even realize he could use a ... collaborator. His deadline is very tight."

Deirdre walked along the 100-year-old skyline of New York City and stood behind the chair at her desk. "This is obviously entirely up to you. I'm just thinking of Morgan, and, well ..." she flicked her perfectly manicured hands out at the wrists like a magician,"... you just popped into my head. It's in your hands, but you'd be doing us all a big favor."

With that, Deirdre sat down. Io knew the meeting was over. She put both of her feet on the floor and stood up. "Well, let me catch a nap and see what else I've got going on."

"He's in his office. Working like a madman."

Io nodded and walked to the door.

"Oh," Deirdre added.

Io turned.

"We've been looking to create a new position here: Chief Cycologist. It's a new field -- you know that of course -- but all five of the cycologists we hired have vastly improved the "humanity" in our robots, AIs and ENTs, and there's been a significant spike in sales as a result. Anyhow, you're a strong candidate for the position. It's very senior. You'd report directly to Dr. Huxley. Maybe we can discuss it more next week?"

Io smiled. "Love to."

"Great," said Porsche. "I'll set it up."

21
Morgan Adam's Office

2068

A gray blue, high-backed chair with an aluminum frame slowly transformed into a low backed, hunter green Martine Haddouche, its rounded arms thick and pillowy. Daedalus Huxley turned to LOIS as it changed its shape, and grinned.

"Thank you, LOIS," he said. "My favorite." A matching green ottoman morphed beneath him, and he hoisted his legs up onto it. "Foglet technology?"[2]

LOIS nodded and smiled. She appreciated Huxley. He was always impeccably polite, and nothing rattled him. This, she assumed, came with his long experience. He had pretty much seen it all, although he often liked to joke that even for him the world was moving too fast. She suspected that shape-shifting furniture was one of them. Nevertheless, he sat calmly, watching Morgan work the images in the room: holographic cubes floating all

---

2. Foglets combine both digital and nano technologies. At their centers is a dodecahedron, a kind of ball with 12 flat surfaces, the size of a human cell. From each of the surfaces, protrudes a mechanical arm, a straight appendage with grippers attached at the end. These grippers link to a socket, like a key. All of these grippers, ensure that billions of foglets can connect to one another in nearly unlimited ways to form almost any kind of solid object. The concept was created by a scientists named J. Storrs Hall.

around him, each one representing the data he was poring through as he tried to make sense of his death.

For hours now Morgan had been frantically shoving virtual, three-dimensional representations of data and time around the room, steeping himself in the puzzle: going through every bit of evidence, every event of the past several days.

He had already performed a high-resolution scan of his body and had stood slack-jawed as he realized he was, in fact, no longer made of flesh, blood, bone and muscle. He was now in a designer body that had been built by trillions of nanobots programmed to act like the cells of a human, only better. The muscle fibers were made of carbon nanotubes and flexible mylar, far swifter and stronger than human muscle.

A different variety of diamondoid nanotubes comprised the body's skeleton. His "bone" was now 50 times stronger than magnesium carbon alloy. Certain organs had been dispensed with, like the heart; a blood stream was unnecessary, but a stomach was still there, using a kind of internal colony of nanobots that could take in food, break it down, and then reorganize it all to create energy that powered fuel cells distributed throughout the body.

This was what human anatomy pretty much did too, but with Morgan's body there was almost no waste, which, LOIS had quipped to Morgan, at least reduced the number of assholes on earth by one.

LOIS watched Morgan step back from the data cubes that filled the room and gazed at the bricolage. The facts were indisputable, and she could see he had now admitted he had been murdered. The goal now was to pinpoint the killer. His killer. And time was running out.

Morgan rubbed his neck and turned to Daedalus. "So why bring me back?"

Huxley looked surprised. "I think I told you that already. Because we could! Why wouldn't we?"

There was a long pause. "You could have left me alone. Had

the funeral and moved on."

"Look, this is a gift not to be questioned," said Daedalus with a hint of exasperation. "You provided a way for us to bring you back to life! You worked your ass off to make it possible. You've been like a son to me. How could I NOT at least try?"

For the first time Morgan's face softened a bit.

With a swipe of his hands he erased everything. "Tell me more about the bug in my body; how will it unravel me?"

Huxley sat up and hunched forward the way he and Morgan often did when the two of them were spit balling a complicated problem.

"We're not sure. It's a kind of computer virus, and it's corrosive. You'll seem fine and then your power system will go quite rapidly, almost like a heart attack, or it could damage your central processor. That would be more like a stroke."

"Lovely."

"Sorry. Those are our best guesses. But obviously we're exploring new territory here. Territory you've created."

"But I don't recall creating any viruses."

Huxley threw out his hands. "Glitch in the code. There's a shitload of code."

Daedalus suddenly stood and walked to the door. It was abrupt, but abrupt departures weren't unusual with Huxley.

"Look, I'm going to let you go to work. You don't need me to get in your way."

Morgan exhaled, then raised a single eyebrow. "I'd rather not die again."

"I don't think there is any way in this world, or any other world, that you'll let that happen."

And then Daedalus was gone.

#

Morgan watched the door close. He stood motionless in the middle of the room for a long time. Finally, he set his long legs apart slightly as if he were about to move, but he just kept standing there. He looks lost, LOIS thought.

"Well," she said, walking up to him. "it's not every day that you get to solve your own murder."

Morgan turned and gazed at her the way a bird looks out of one eye, and then he burst out laughing. Kind of a mad laugh, she thought, followed by awkward silence.

LOIS spoke first. "You want me to rake the security code and see how they hacked it, right?"

"You think that's what happened?"

"It's a place to start."

"Yeah, do that. No, first, is there a security camera on the vault where we kept the nanochip? There must be. I should have thought of it before."

"The last video in the archive is from Friday, a week ago," said LOIS.

"That's when I put the chip in the vault with Deirdre. Let's look at it."

A high-definition holograph of Morgan's Doppelgänger Lab appeared before them. They saw a smooth white wall in an alcove. A moment later Deirdre's head and shoulders appear below. The view is from the security camera in the ceiling.

Deirdre walks into the alcove with Morgan a step behind. She glances briefly at the camera, then places her hand on a smooth glass panel, waiting for Morgan to do the same at the other end of the alcove. They each looked at one another, and then simultaneously speak their names. There is a low beep, and then the wall, as if by magic, opens revealing two smooth, black vaults, each one a foot high and six inches wide. Morgan holds a slim cylinder of polished metal about six inches long.

Morgan watched himself speaking out loud to Deirdre. "My every memory, feeling, thought and emotion, all of that data crammed into this little ball. I sure hope it's accurate."

"You're sure this security system is unsinkable," said Deirdre.

"Guaranteed."

"That's what they said about the Titanic."

"Deirdre, I'm not sure even I could hack this system, and I created it."

Deirdre rolled her eyes. "Ready?"

"Ready," said Morgan. They placed their hands on the glass and spoke their names. The door closed and it was as though nothing had ever been there.

There was a chirping sound and the holograph disappeared.

Morgan turned to LOIS. "That's the last vid in the archive?"

LOIS nodded, and the video disappeared. Morgan began pacing.

"Lets you and I go over the timing," Morgan said. With a quick series of gestures he pulled up a glowing cube from the array of floating cubes in front of him. "Okay. So I get up this morning, that's December 18th, but the last record we show in the security archive is dated December 10. There's no vid of anyone breaking in after the 10th..."

LOIS completed his sentence, "... because there are no vids. They have all been destroyed."

Morgan rubbed his neck again. It was obviously an inside job. Sentience must have a mole inside Symbiosys who erased the videos. That would make sense. Whoever was on the inside could hack the system and destroy any record of the murder.

Morgan now tapped the day of the 10th and enlarged it. "Okay this is the day I was last backed up, and since I am the back up, I can't have any memories beyond the 10th because this 'me'" — he gestured at himself — "never lived the days between then and this morning. I'm like a document that's been copied. The version that existed of me is accurate up to that day but has no memory of those days I was alive after the back up."

"Right, only your murdered self lived those … 'lost' days."

Morgan looked at her. "Really? You have to put it that way."

LOIS shrugged, "Well, you want to solve the problem, don't

you?" She stared back at the month of cubes.

Morgan turned and minimized December 10th and tapped the 15th. "The fifteenth is the day they find my body. I was killed the evening of the 14th." He turned to LOIS again. "When did they begin to create my new mind and body?"

"Same day, the 14th. Staff thought it was a new project and the deadline had been pushed up. Teams worked separately so that no one knew the whole picture. Only Dr. Huxley and Dr. Porsche knew you had been murdered."

"And that work went on until early this morning."

LOIS nodded. "They put you in your bed thinking it would be less disorienting than waking you up on a gurney in the Lab."

"Well, wasn't that thoughtful," said Morgan. "And they reprogrammed you."

"Apparently," said LOIS, "they didn't want me to know anything either. They wanted to tell you themselves."

"So here I am, the final seven days of my life a complete black hole."

Morgan stood among his herd of holograms, pouring though the details of his calendar like a rabid archeologist using the mental equivalents of surgical instruments and a toothbrush to extract every bone of information he could. He pivoted toward the cubes and drew his hand inside to pull them all out, like a train, into the middle of the room.

"That's where the answers are. Somewhere in that week."

He circled the train of days, pacing and squinting at them, thoroughly frustrated. "What the fuck happened during those seven days? And *why* did it happen?" He stood back and stared into the squares as they hung, pulsing with light. Then suddenly he slammed his hand on his desk. The metal buckled under the blow and LOIS jumped.

"Who the fuck would want to kill me, LOIS?"

LOIS had nothing to say. What could she say? The man was a hot mess. A full minute passed and then Morgan sat down beside her on the couch. "I *am* going to figure this out," he said, "if it kills me."

"Kind of ironic," said LOIS, "isn't it."

22

Io

Morgan paced. For five hours now he had been at this, unpacking every bit of information he could from the cubes of those seven days. Each one had now been cut into different colored layers that he could tap and explore like the layers of a cake: What he ate, who he met with, video from security cameras that caught him stopping to talk with someone in the hall. Any snippet he could find.

LOIS had blipped away to go through every email that had been addressed to him or that she had answered. She was listening at high speed to call after phone call too. So far, nothing, except that he learned that apparently he liked shrimp more than he realized.

Inspecting himself like this, reviewing the minutia of his everyday life, he realized what a geek he was. And what a workaholic. He had just come off weeks of grueling work in preparation for each version of the Doppelgänger downloads, and then obsessively analyzed each one afterwards.

"Well, what else was I going to do," he said as he moved the cube that represented December 18 around to the front of him with a sweeping gesture. "I had just created the world's first virtual human." He pulled the last six hours of the 18th out of the cube and, flicking his wrist, dealt them out like a deck of cards. "I mean I needed to know I had the basics right at least. I wasn't going to relax until I had nailed that."

"Yeah, but, really, don't you think you should relax at least occasionally?" Said a voice.

Morgan jumped and saw the slender, dark-colored woman he had noticed earlier that morning, before his meeting with Daedalus and Deirdre. She stood at the office door. Her hands were crossed low in front of her so that they rested on the flat part of her stomach.

Io thought Morgan looked both wild and annoyed, and she decided she would try to make a quick exit. "I was on my way out of the office and heard you talking."

He snapped his fingers and all the calendar cubes disappeared. "Yeah, trying to figure something out."

That he was hiding something made her decide to push things a little after all. "That's your specialty. Any luck?" She walked to a couch and started to sit down.

Morgan shoved his palms toward her. "Don't sit!"

Io stopped and looked up. "Maybe I can help."

"I doubt it."

"What, my pea-brain's not up to it?"

"No. I mean maybe it is, maybe it isn't, but this is private. My eyes only." He looked around. "How did you get in here?"

"I'm cleared." What a sonovabitch, she thought. Look at him. He's on Planet X. I wouldn't give this guy a glass of water if he were bursting into flame. But then there was the idea of becoming Chief Cycologist at Symbiosys. She knew she was following a carrot that Porsche had dangled (with all the subtlety of a train wreck), but if she could land that job at this corporation, she'd rocket into the first ranks of the field, and she liked the idea of shaping a new field, having a real impact. Fellow students, even professors had told her again and again she was crazy to pursue something as new as cycology.

"Bad career move, Io," her computer science professor at

Stanford had said. "No one is going to take a field that explores the inner life of robots seriously. They're just machines for chrissakes. Study quantum computing. At least you know you'll get a job." Well, if Symbiosys took the field seriously, the rest of the world would soon follow.

"Look," said Io, "maybe you can just bounce a few theories off me, an idea or two, and maybe I'll jog something loose that gets you off the starting block."

Morgan didn't hear a thing she had said. He was already deep in thought, oblivious, once again, to her presence. He looked up, wondering why she was still there. "No. That's okay. I've got to do this myself."

Fine suffer in your own little hell.

"Okay..." she said backing out the room, forcing a smile. She watched as he sat down, snapped his fingers and began pulling up videos from a cube labeled December 19. He was moving as if he was on speed, acting in a way she had never seen before: confused and ... lost. No one ever saw Morgan Adams look lost. The only time she had seen him even close to that was when she had watched him sleeping fitfully the night, they had made love, turning and wincing and mumbling to himself.

That mental image stopped her. She reversed direction and walked back to him, right in among the holographs he was exploring. He looked up, startled again.

Maybe he was a jerk, she thought, and he wanted to pretend that nothing had happened between them, but she wasn't going to do the same thing. She put her hand on his shoulder.

"I'm sure you can figure this out by yourself, but if you need help, or just a break, you know where to find me."

Morgan looked up and this time he seemed to finally see her. He noticed for the first time how amazing her eyes were, against the dark, warm color of her skin. They looked like sapphires. She just briefly touched his hair with the tips of her fingers, tousling it in an affectionate way she knew was way out of line.

"Yeah. Well, I'm sure I can figure that out … I mean … you know …" He smiled awkwardly. "… where to get a hold of you."

Did she hear that right? Of course he knew how to get in touch with her. Was he really that much of an ass? Well, whatever. She had given it a shot.

"Right," she said. And then she walked slowly and deliberately out the door.

How odd, Morgan thought, as the door swished shut behind her. She almost acts as if we are … close.

23

The IT Man

"Oh fuck!" Sr. Darwin barked. "Fuck, fuck!"

Nuttle cupped little Morgan's ears just as Sr. Darwin turned and saw the two of them. She threw down her purse and sat heavily in her chair, her contorted, equine face on the verge of tears.

"These contraptions! They're ancient, and useless. Nothing works!" She wiped her sleeve on her nose. "If I don't get these reports in, I'll be skinned and fired." She resurrected some additional fury and looked at both Nuttle and Morgan, rolling her rheumy eyes. "Because the reports are soooo important!" Finally, her whole body deflated like a punctured ball. Her legs splayed out, and she gazed blankly at the blue, cotton uniform spread across her thin shanks. "I'm screwed. And, by the way, what is that child doing here?"

There was a long pause and then Morgan said, "Maybe I can help."

Sr. Darwin looked astonished.

"You? Really!" She snorted. But she was desperate and regarded the small, sandy-haired creature with the bottle green eyes. How extraordinary they were.

"I think I know what's wrong," the boy said. He moved toward the desk, and then looked the woman in her long face.

Slowly Sr. Darwin rose and left the chair. Nuttle simply watched.

Morgan climbed into the chair and waved at the box. It lit up. He swiftly swept windows and pages on the screen away.

Sr. Darwin sucked in her breath and moved to stop the boy, but before she could get to him, he began to type a series of incomprehensible characters on a blank screen.

Morgan already knew what the problem was. A small bug in the code of the computer's operating system. A new version had recently been released and this was a common problem. He had read about it on the GRID, right there on the very computer she had been sitting at. He could've downloaded the fix, but sensed somehow that writing the code out would be better for him and Nuttle. He would appear more expert. His fingers tapped the keyboard for perhaps a minute. Then he stopped.

Sr. Darwin gawked at the screen over Morgan's shoulder as he hit "Enter," and watched thousands of lines of code pour down the screen. She caught her breath. And then just as quickly as they had started, the cascading lines stopped. Morgan closed the window with the code, carefully returned the screens and pages to their original positions, and, jumping off the chair, walked back to Nuttle. He put his hand in hers and she gently tousled his hair.

The woman looked at Morgan, then back at the screen and then back at Morgan.

"It's okay now," said Morgan. "It will work."

Sr. Darwin sat down, her mouth making small noises like a gasping fish. She opened a new file – the one she had wanted so badly to access. There it was. She swiveled on the chair and looked again at the small boy. Yes, what terribly strange and unsettling eyes he had.

"Thank you!" She said, sincerely. And then her hands moved quickly to a desk drawer. "Would you like a treat?" She held out a large chocolate bar.

Morgan shook his head, "No thank you. But I think Nuttle

might like one."

"Nuttle?" Sr. Darwin only knew Nuttle as Mercy, or Miss Trimble.

Morgan gazed up at the woman who held his hand, to point her out. Sr. Darwin extended the candy bar to Nuttle who beamed and took it. And then Morgan quietly led Nuttle out the door.

#

After that episode, Sr. Darwin soon took Morgan's talents for granted. She invoked his help on all problems electronic. If he solved them, Nuttle received an extra candy bar. If he failed, he was berated for his ineptitude. "Not so smart, after all, are we, little man?" But Morgan didn't take it personally. Instead he pocketed the experience for later use.

Whatever he did for Sr. Darwin, though, he never let it get in the way of his nightly sojourns with the Bright Box where he devoured the endless streams of information it supplied. He learned how the plague created two classes: a wealthy one that had means and resources, fine housing and personal security systems, and a miserable one that tapped the underfunded social and medical safety nets until they burst beneath the burden of handling an obliterated generation.

This, Morgan realized, was the world he had known as "Beyond."

Learning these things, he felt grateful. He was not rich, and had little, but if he had Nuttle and the computer, that was enough, at least for now. His biggest disappointment was how little information he was uncovering about his mother. There was the grainy picture and the newspaper story he had found, but little else. He searched every kind of archive he could think of, but there was nothing under the name of Raifa Morhaf. It was as if she didn't exist. He tried to locate old security videos that might have been taken the day of the attack, but there was nothing online. The orphanage's archives were a shambles. Nevertheless, night after night he searched.

One night Sr. Darwin gave Morgan what she called a PAD and asked if he could fix it because it had stopped working.

"Machines," she grumbled.

He agreed to try and repair the machine, and quickly realized he could fix it easily. But he told Sr. Darwin it was beyond repair.

"Well then, give it back!" She demanded.

He said he would the next day, knowing she would forget. She was a scared and jittery woman who spent her life reacting to everything around her. Even now, at age nine, Morgan had learned that there were people who acted, and took control when they faced trouble. And there were those who re-acted and lived their lives out of fear, like the pigeons that could be chased into flight at The Patch.

He resolved not to be a pigeon.

Darwin did forget the PAD, and so he kept it and traded extra candy bars with Reba and the Spider Lady whose real name, he discovered, was Le Sans Martin. Strangely, Le Sans had become one of Nuttle's best friends, mostly because almost nobody could tolerate the bitter woman. She was that disagreeable. She did have one saving grace, however. There was an active black-market Beyond where nearly anything could be found, if you knew the right people. For some reason, Le Sans did.

#

Time passed slowly in the way time does when you are a child. Each year is such a significant portion of a life when you haven't lived many of them.

Morgan found it was funny the way time worked. Later in his life he came to realize that it wasn't really about the passage of units, it was about the mind and heart. Powerful experiences never seemed to grow distant, even if they were many years in the past, while those that didn't matter disappeared instantly.

By this time Morgan was well into the Sec 17 school, an

experience he loathed. He learned far more with the Bright Box and from the gadgets he assembled than any grade school class could teach. Thus he worked on his gadgets like a demon, while he dozed and slept in class, often taking a good whack from one of the Sisters for it.

Two personal projects kept Morgan's attention: a very simple robot he called Mitchell, constructed mostly of spare Legos and elementary electronics he found and traded for. And the PAD he had picked up from Sr. Darwin.

Mitchell rolled rather than walked, but could get around as long as Morgan steered him remotely using one of the phones in his growing stash of battered electronics. To operate the robot, he tapped the Sec 17 computer and WIFI systems. He now had complete access to all the passwords thanks to his status as supreme commander of all things IT.

The PAD evolved slowly but deliberately. At first, Morgan only used it to secretly read and watch movies. But soon he had written simple software that would read the books to him when Nuttle wasn't available, which now was most of the time because he was far too big to sleep in her tiny bed.

Alone, late at night, he would lay beneath his covers, ear plugs anchored and listen. The number of books he could access was unlimited. He had learned how to break into local library databanks and download any book or movie that struck his fancy. He listened to everything from *The Martian Chronicles* to Western movies and, of course, Lewis Carroll's *Through the Looking Glass*.

Reba liked that story too. Sometimes Morgan and Nuttle would find her standing morosely nearby Nuttle's door when she and Morgan had time to read and share a bit of chocolate.

"Want to come and listen?" Nuttle would always ask.

"Naw," Reba would say.

"Yeah, Reba, come on! The PAD is fun!"

"Well, okay, if you really want. But I think it's all kind of silly."

They often pretended the chocolate bars were vorpal blades, and played snicker-snack with them, lunging and parrying as they listened to *Jabberwocky*, sometimes laughing so loudly they would get a stiff reprimand or clout on the ear from one of the sisters.

#

In time Morgan programmed the PAD to hold rudimentary conversations with him, using recorded snippets of his own voice to answer his own questions. Once he managed to pull this off, it delighted Nuttle to no end. It even put a smile on Reba's face.

"Good morning," Morgan would say to the PAD. "How are you today?"

The PAD (in Morgan's own voice): "Just great, Morgan! Did you sleep well?"

Morgan: "Yes, I did. You?"

And so on ...

Every time Nuttle heard these exchanges she would squeal with delight and clap her hands.

From the beginning, Morgan wanted to change the voice; make it sound like a girl because he liked the idea of a girl he could talk to. But for that he needed more sophisticated software, and he hadn't yet figured that out. But eventually he did. By his eleventh birthday, after scouring the GRID, and experimenting with snippets of code during his late-night excursions, he created a feminine voice; one that felt more like another person. It -- this creation -- he decided, deserved a name. One of the books he had recently read was called *The Giver*, and he had been so taken with it that he decided he would call his new friend Lois ... after Lois Lowry, the author.

#

By now Morgan's world mostly consisted of him, Nuttle,

Mitchell and his machines. Eventually the angry kids left Morgan alone. They might torment him now and then, but most stayed clear because they knew of his special relationship with Sr. Darwin, and Reba.

Morgan had created Lois partly for fun, but partly because he wanted a companion, someone he could talk to and share his thoughts and concerns with. Already Nuttle couldn't understand what he was talking about when he would tell her about the things he was learning from the Bright Box. And she was helpless in shedding anymore light on his mother. She knew her name, Raifa, and she knew she liked her, and she knew she was very sad when she died because she was so nice. But she recalled nothing about her past except that Raifa was in love with a man who was a soldier and the soldier had gone away before she realized she was pregnant.

So Lois became Morgan's imaginary friend. Someone he could talk to, plan his inventions with, and spin out his dreams of escaping to Beyond where he might someday find out where his mother, and therefore he, had come from.

Eventually, Morgan trained Lois to relate the things he said to her to a subject connected to him, and thus they could have very simple conversations that were not pre-programmed.

"Oh," Lois would remark, "You enjoyed reading about Cambodia. Do you know about the artwork and culture of the Khmer culture in that country?"

This generated the comforting illusion for Morgan that he had a confidant. What he didn't realize quite yet was that the machine he had made, *was*, in a strange way, getting to know him. In fact, soon Lois pretty much knew everything about Morgan.

24

LOIS

It wasn't more than ten seconds after Io walked out of Morgan's office door, when he heard a beep and the soothing sound of LOIS's voice. "Permission to come aboard, sir?"

"Granted."

With a ping, LOIS appeared. "I found something interesting," she said.

"Where?"

"Your personal phone."

"Almost nobody has my personal phone number," Morgan said. "You, Daedalus..."

"... And some of the women you've dated...," she interrupted. "Apparently you know this one better than you think you do, or at least the original you knew her better because during that seven-day period..."

" ... Yes."

"You and Ms. Luu -- what's the right term here -- made love, fornicated, you boinked the help."

"What?!"

"Are you really surprised?"

Morgan waved his hands. "How do you know?"

"Because you sent her a text thanking her. Want the details?"

Morgan shook his head. "No."

"When did I send it?"

"The evening after you were downloaded."

Morgan rubbed his neck. "She was just here, for Chrissakes."

LOIS raised her eyebrows and looked at the ceiling. (This is what she was programmed to do when she didn't have an appropriate response.)

"That's all you found?" Asked Morgan.

"So far."

Morgan turned to LOIS. "That explains why she visited. Why she acted so strangely. She even tousled my hair."

LOIS raised an eyebrow. "She tousled your hair?"

"See if you find any other connections with her...," said Morgan, "anything..."

"Aye, aye, captain!" And then LOIS disappeared again.

25

The Plague

Morgan's nighttime raids to Sr. Darwin's Bright Box, continued to open his world, and that included the Solimões Plague that had wiped out billions. It had begun like earlier pandemics — the Spanish flu of 1918, the avian flu of 2003, the Ebola epidemic of 2014, COVID in 2020.

At first Solimões was barely noticeable, having begun in the remotest areas of Brazil where rainforests were being increasingly burned to make room for farming and cattle grazing. The disease was part of the howler monkey biological ecosystem and not at all lethal to them, but then it mutated in the presence of the deforestation and jumped to human primates, where it found new and deadly ground.

Not having many new *Homo sapiens* hosts to infect at first, it migrated slowly. For years, health organizations weren't even aware the virus existed. Some farmers contracted it and died without a trace. But eventually it spread to truckers who delivered cattle to market in larger cities like Manaus, the old rubber capital of the world and the largest city inside Brazil's still vast rain forests. Once there it spread by air to Buenos Aires, then Miami, and from there a fusillade of death radiated to the rest of the world by way of the globe's arcing air corridors.

The sick appeared perfectly fine for several days even after the lethal molecular chains had deftly inserted themselves inside their victims. Once infected, each casualty became the perfect vehicle for spreading the disease because they revealed no symptoms. Then the dismantling began. At first there was fever and weakness, then dehydration. After that the virus melted the body's cellular infrastructure, muscle and tissue, and mercilessly ransacked the immune system. The World Health Organization named the disease Rio Solimões Influenza A (H9N2) for the aboriginal tribes who lived on a part of the upper Amazon River, also known as the Solimões. That was where the headwaters of the disease were eventually uncovered.

Solimões quickly won the dubious distinction of becoming the most lethal disease in human history. Bubonic plague had been delivered by the fleas of infected rats. HIV required intimate contact and so was not easily spread, though, at least before multiple vaccines were developed, almost always lethal. Even Ebola required contact with bodily fluids. But Solimões was a catholic killer. Like a cold, it could jump from host to host by way of a sneeze or cough, a wiped nose or a simple rubbing of the eyes after a hand touched a public spigot or subway pole or office staircase rail. This made the disease a perfect and insidious tool for killing.

Millions stopped traveling even before the international travel bans went into effect. Then billions more stopped going to work for fear of infection. Production of everything from food to electronics ground to a halt. Shoppers stopped shopping. Clubs, bars and restaurants shut down as their customers disappeared. Some people continued to travel by car or, if they were wealthy, private jet, but even that stopped when gas and oil production ceased, and reserves ran dry.

Rather than travel or meet face to face, the living increasingly met online; the use of Skype and FaceTime and satellite meetings skyrocketed, but that eventually crashed the Internet, clogging it beyond capacity. And since virtually all human labor had come to a halt, the deployment of fiber optic lines and Five G networks to expand bandwidth crawled, with crews in Hazmat suits working with machines to lay new cable or upgrade cell towers.

Eventually bandwidth rationing was legislated. Government first, then the largest corporations that could afford the high cost were given precedence. For the regular joe, networking returned to the early days of the Internet with 1200 baud modems and text only cell phones.

And so it came to be that an unknown virus that had somehow jumped from howler monkeys in the Brazilian rainforest to human farmers who were burning it down had wreaked more havoc on human civilization than a thousand hurricanes, earthquakes, typhoons and tornadoes. Its dark and lethal hand squeezed the planet without remorse. Or more accurately, the human species that had been strangling the planet was now itself being strangled. Some pundits opined that Solimões was nothing more than the planet's immune system trying to eradicate the pestilence of the human race. Knowing which was the plague and which the victim depended on your point of view.

Before the World Health Organization could track the disease's source, Solimões had already infected hundreds of thousands, exposing millions more. That was in the first three weeks. It wiped out 70% of those who became infected. Patient populations in hospitals everywhere exploded while, thanks to its novel ability to both distribute and hide itself, "pandemic refugees" fled cities for safe havens and unwittingly accelerated the plague.

Early vaccines were useless. Victims died within 4 to 6 days once cases became full-blown. It was humanity's worst nightmare, an army of subversive killers tearing through the species like a firestorm. It took two years to get the disease itself under control. First, with a worldwide ban on travel, then an international effort to develop vaccines and isolate the virus. Some of the quarantines were brutal, leaving family and friends to watch those they loved most die alone and helpless. Because carriers hid the symptoms, a vaccine was the only hope.

Whole hospital populations were used as guinea pigs, and still tens of millions died during the trials. Six iterations were tried without effect until finally one, which came, fittingly, out of the Pasteur Institute in France, had some success. A one trillion-dollar program to create, deliver and dispense the vaccines world-wide was initiated.

For a while it seemed the only businesses that were making money were the sanitary, medical and pharmaceutical industries, but finally, after a few weeks, the death tolls began to subside. Newer, improved vaccines further reduced the rate. After a year the vaccines had done their work and break outs became increasingly rare.

By the time that life had begun to crawl back to "normal" in 2026, it became all too clear that life was anything but. The human race had been traumatized like a torture victim. Nearly half of humanity was gone. Families were wiped out, cities and nations were crippled, especially in the most densely populated parts of the world, and those with the least infrastructure, sanitation and medical support (often the same locations) shriveled like a desiccated corpse. Inland China, India, South and central Africa, Indonesia, Brazil and sections of Mexico were hardest hit. After that southern Europe, North Africa and the United States — especially those with the biggest airline hubs — Washington DC, New York, Philadelphia, Chicago, Los Angeles and Atlanta.

For a full year, massive death became the ubiquitous and constant companion of the human race. No area was truly spared. Yet the horror did not extend to Morgan's mother, at least not directly. She survived … in the beginning, but in the end, Solimões still found her by way of a circuitous route of grief and madness, and a bullet to her body.

26

Raifa

If Morgan Adams had been able to somehow reveal the mysteries of his mother's past, he would have found her fascinating. Like him, she too had extraordinary eyes. Total strangers would sometimes stop her parents in the street to remark on their astonishing green color -- the kind of color you saw in the feathers of exotic birds or the wings of butterflies, or some little-known nocturnal creature from the jungles of Madagascar. Their hue and size, and almost alien roundness, gave them a hypnotic quality.

Later in life, Raifa couldn't see what the big deal was. It wasn't as if she had *earned* the eyes *any more* than she had earned her delicate chin, sandy blonde hair or the prominent lobes of her ears. She had simply received a certain combination of genes from each of her parents and somehow the biological mathematics of it all had resulted in the eyes, the body, the face, brain and personality that she enjoyed, or in some cases, regretted. Did she really have to be cursed with her long, skinny legs? Some days she felt like a flamingo.

The parents who had bequeathed these genes had brought Raifa into the world in New York City. Their traits had merged two radically diverse sectors of the planet; locations where the dance of genes and geography had caused evolution to shape and then select very different kinds of chromosomes. She inherited her mother's blonde hair, but her father's dark curls. Her face and body were a perfect compromise of each parent -- high cheek bones, expressive mouth, inquisitive nose and those emerald eyes.

Her father, Dr. Akeem Morhaf, had emigrated from Qatar in the early 1960s to teach at Columbia University. He was an outstanding mathematician who in his mid-twenties had solved some famously difficult equations, along the lines of the Fibonacci equation, which was linked to the human attraction to beauty.

Raifa's mother was a New York immigrant too, except she came from Santa Barbara, California where she had grown up on the beach breaking teen boy's hearts from Montecito to Carpinteria. Her name was Rachel Spring. Rachel's strawberry blonde hair and long perfect body may have led some who didn't know better to think she was a vapid California sun worshipper. But her appetite for all things written, belied her looks while simultaneously failing to satisfy her bottomless curiosity. She spent most of her time digesting manuscripts as quickly as a goat digests tin cans and paper. Her parents were an unlikely couple, but when they met, they fell in love instantly. It was one of those things.

Generally Raifa was an easy-going child, but it was clear early on that her mind belonged to her and her alone. It wasn't that she was bratty. She was, in fact, exceedingly polite, but there could never be any doubt what she wanted and when she wanted it. In high school she disagreed with the Imam at the mosque over how best to celebrate Ramadan, quoting extensively from the Quran about the rights of women. The whole family was nearly labelled *takfir*, an excommunicated non-believer.

Her deepening sense of social justice when she was in college ultimately led to her dropping out of the Massachusetts Institute of Technology where she had shown unusual promise as a computer science major. MIT had thrown buckets of money at her because she was one of those rare academic finds -- a female student with a truly remarkable gift for mathematics. But even those talents weren't enough to keep her from getting the boot.

In her freshman year Raifa quickly found she couldn't stomach hanging out with the geeks in her classes, most of whom were men, well, boys really, who seemed incapable of making eye contact with anything but her breasts. If they looked anywhere else it was at their own shoes. The standing joke among computer science majors was, "How can you tell the difference between an introverted computer science majors and extroverted ones? The extroverted ones look at YOUR feet when they talk to you."

It wasn't that she didn't find the science of computing interesting, but how many conversations could you have about "writing close to the metal," or *Lord of the Rings*, or irrational number sets, with occasional digressions into quantum theory?

"I like mathematics and code writing," she told her mother during a phone call once, "but not to the exclusion of the human race." She had begun spending more time with English and psychology majors, even the occasional drama student. "You know, creatures who are members of our own species," she said.

#

Ultimately, though, it wasn't frustration that lead to dismissal from MIT, it was her stubborn adherence to justice, the very thing that would ultimately kill her. During Raifa's junior year her friend, Maya, got into hot water when she completed a short movie for a class project, and published it to her personal website. It was a mocumentary of MIT's academic/nerd culture, and its arrogant belief that it was superior in all respects to other universities. Maya skewered the immense pride the school took in its "intellectual capital," and baskets of Nobel Prize winners. She came down hard on the university's inflexible programs that she felt ran its computer science students through some kind of nerd boot camp. To make her point she filmed a scalding send up in which a geek drill sergeant, complete with a flat-brimmed Campaign Hat, faced a file of terrified students wearing taped together glasses and overloaded pocket protectors.

"What's not real??!" The sergeant screamed at the terrified nerds.

"Irrational numbers! Sir!"

"I can't HEAR you!!!!"

But the scene that really sealed Maya's fate was the one in which a student, or a student *acting* as a computer science student, sung an aria to C++ code before leaping down a stairwell to his death, overcome with the pressure of his classes. The Dean of the School of Computer Science went straight to the university president, and when the president saw the movie, he called Maya in. She would have to withdraw the film as her class semester project. That meant she would fail the class. She protested. Various deans and other bureaucrats conferred and agreed she should be granted another semester to complete a new film, but the original had to go.

Raifa was horrified! "We'll take it before the Academic Council," she said. "This is a breach of freedom of speech..." She was beginning to strop the razor of her logic. "...and academic freedom, and the MIT University Code of Ethics."

"Do they have a code of ethics?" Asked Maya.

There was a pause. "No," said Maya, "but they should!" and then they both burst out laughing.

At first when she and Raifa went before the Academic Council everything went well, at least until Dr. Cornblatt, the Computer Science dean, said the film revealed a gross disregard and disrespect for the entire program, its professors and hardworking students.

"And what about the hard work of artists and students like Maya Polinski (Maya, despite her rather glamorous first name was from a working-class Polish family who lived in Buffalo, New York).

"Secondary." Said the dean flatly.

"So art and human expression are secondary to code writing?"

"Computer code is not what is important," said the dean, "It is what it makes possible that is important."

"Personal freedom doesn't make anything possible?"

"I suppose," said the Engineering Dean, who also sat on the council, a short, balding man whose cheeks always seemed to be puffed out in exasperation. "But it also seems to create a lot of trouble."

"Trouble?!" Raifa's voice rose and her face flushed.

"It muddies things," said Dean Cornblatt. "Code brings clarity; numbers and mathematics generate order."

"And above all, we must have order!" Boomed Raifa.

"Order is good in a world filled with chaos."

"But we cannot have fresh ideas?" Asked Raifa. "How, Professor Cornblatt, do you suppose computer code came about? The free expression of new ideas, that's how. What would the world be like without troublemakers like Leonardo da Vinci and Grace Hopper and Heady Lamarr? The wildness of Franz Liszt. The madness of Van Gogh. These creators of chaos!"

"You are espousing madness?"

"The freedom to be mad enough to do something that everyone else might find uncomfortable, yes! It's called change, creativity! It's better than the silly, robotic machinations that occasionally bubble up in that brain you profess to carry around between your ears. A brain that looks for mediocrity and the status quo masked as safety and order!"

"Ms. Morhaf! That will be enough!"

"Oh, I am soooo sorry to have ruffled any academic feathers here," Raifa continued, gathering her fury. "We can't have that, can we? We can't have disagreement! But we can bully a student who chooses to express herself in her own way and express a viewpoint that might make life difficult for the university's public relations department!"

"Ms. Morhaf," said the chair. "If you continue along these lines, I'll have to ask you to leave this room, and we will then vote on Ms. Polinski's ... "

Raifa didn't seem to hear a word. "You don't care about freedom of expression, or order for that matter. Or Maya, or me, or any other student in this school. All you care about is its reputation because keeping that reputation shining and buffed is what keeps the money coming in; floats the endowment, lands the grants and keeps your fat, tenured asses in your comfortable chairs."

Maya grabbed Raifa by the forearm and whispered hoarsely. "I don't think this is helping!"

"Ms. Morhaf, you are dismissed!" said the dean, now turning a light shade of purple.

"If having Maya's work showing up on the Internet for worldwide audience of millions to see is what has put your shorts in a bunch, then ..."

"Out!"

"You don't have to order me out," said Raifa. "I'm leaving on my own! And not just this room, but this whole damned, two-faced amalgam of sheared sheep you call an institution of higher learning. Ha!" And with that she slammed shut her notebook and was out the door.

You could see that Raifa and Morgan shared common lines of DNA.

#

"In the end," said Maya later, "that probably wasn't really the right thing to say. I mean, you know, if we wanted to actually win the case."

"I know," said Raifa sipping a cup of Verbena tea at the Tea P down the street. "I know. I'm sorry. But I got so upset!"

"Really?" Said Maya. "I didn't notice."

"I don't think my parents are going to be very happy either," said Raifa.

"What are going to do?"

"I already took a job with Thibideau in the English department. He's writing some esoteric book about Sir Phillip Sidney -- the Restoration poet."

"Never heard of him," said Maya.

"You're not alone. He wrote *The Fairie Queen* in the 1500's."

"I mean Thibideau."

"Of course not," said Raifa morosely. "This is MIT. Most people don't even know it *has* an English department. He's dusty and ancient and smells like mushrooms and old cats, but he landed a nice grant, and he acts human. It pays well enough, and I'll never have to move out of my little studio apartment. Which is fine by me."

"See!" said Maya brightly, "You've already landed on your feet!"

27

Whimsy

Buried as he was within the confines of Sec 17, Morgan knew none of these things about his fiery mother, nor the path that would lead him to someday change the world. He and his mother were two remarkable people linked by their genes but separated in time. And so Morgan remained ignorant of his mother's history; aware that she once existed but robbed of any insights into her life and the ways it had shaped him. This upset him.

Raifa survived the pandemic, but like billions of others simply became another cog in the post-plague world; a small player in a land of thousands of Sec 17s. Everyone knew that an orphanage was not the place to raise a child, but following the plague, no country in the world could avoid them. The goal was to adopt, or at least foster, as many children as possible as quickly as possible, but it took three years after the plague's end before any families had an iota of emotional or financial capital needed to adopt children from the program.

At Sec 17 the first children to be adopted were the younger, laughing, wide-eyed ones who hadn't yet been worn out by the spirit-killing existence of the place. Still, the "absorption rate," as it was called, was slow. So the government created incentives. At first big tax breaks were mandated for any family that would adopt. When that wasn't enough, foster parents were given

~25,000 Cash Units per year for every child they took in for at least a year, and then paid an additional ~5000 Units per month for each month of care provided afterwards. This was deemed better than raising millions of children in large institutions.

The incentives helped increase the absorption rate, but also created a federalized black market for children where multiple foster offspring were bedded down in crowded homes that provided nothing more than thin meals, secondhand clothes and not much human kindness. Mostly the children who ended up in foster homes became commodities used to help families claw their way out of the financial abyss the plague had created for them. Was this better than the soul-killing ways of Sec 17? It was debatable.

Still, most children at Sec 17, incapable of imagining what lay outside its walls, were thrilled to depart their current, mind-numbing accommodations for a fresh new foster home. It took them Beyond, and Beyond represented a mythical place where they imagined they could play and shop and go to a real school and eat mountains of food not just the old slop dished up every day at the orphanage. (It took Morgan a year, once he finally made it out of Sec 17, to get the smell of its food out of his nostrils.)

No one perpetuated the belief that life "Beyond" was wonderful more passionately than Sr. Darwin. She painted the rosiest possible picture of what she called "the great wide world that you deserve to live in." This was partly driven by government PR, which first invented and then perpetuated the myth, and partly because all Homeless District Directors, including Sr. Darwin, were provided bonuses for each child who was "absorbed." Placements in foster homes weren't as lucrative as full adoptions, but they nevertheless fed the pocketbook. Not many directors worked more enthusiastically to place her children than Sister D.

Not that she was solely motivated by financial reward. At least not in her own mind. She had made the speeches so often and had walked potential "parents" around the facility and introduced them to her little angels with such fulsome regularity, that even she began to believe that life in a foster home was paradise beyond compare.

Believing all of this also enabled her to go home at night convinced she was the selfless saint she believed herself to be. Thus she did all she could to convince homeless children, and both good and ill-intentioned adults, that life in the big broad world was exceedingly good. She did this for all Sec 17's young inhabitants; all of them except Morgan.

#

Normally, a child as bright and young as Morgan would have made a perfect candidate for any adoptive parent. But once Sr. Darwin discovered how handy he was, she had powerful reasons for not sharing him. By age 9 he could not only solve all her personal IT problems, but he also managed the whole digital infrastructure of the orphanage. Given the harrowing rat's nest of bureaucracies created in the wake of the plague, having someone like Morgan, who could solve computer problems within hours rather than weeks, was beyond value.

Morgan was fine with this. It gave him complete access to the GRID, and to the electronics required to construct the PADs, phones and robots he loved to build, especially Lois. Projects like these provided him a well-spring of curiosities to explore and made invention his soulmate. Morgan was, above all, curious. Even at nine and more so at ten, he seemed to absorb every scrap of information that crossed the threshold of his mind. Not only did he absorb facts, but he could integrate and create insights in unexpected ways. It all seemed as normal to him as rain.

Mostly these ideas happened inside of Morgan's own head, but sometimes they revealed themselves in the real world; the robotic vacuum cleaners he created, for example, which were more like whimsical animals than stamped out, mechanical creations. One machine could roll itself up like an armadillo, navigate its way around Sec 17 and when it sensed a large piece of debris, unfold and devour it. Another worked like a dung beetle, rolling paper and grime and other detritus into large balls before feeding it to a 5-foot-high, elephantine machine Morgan called Schnoz, which in turn sucked the wad up and then incinerated it, using the heat within to power itself.

Yes, Morgan was strange. Of course he never saw himself this way, even if others did. The least strange thing to him, was him.

Part III

"Treat your inferiors as you would be treated by your superiors."
-- I. J. Good, 1965

28

Pittsburgh

2068

Daedalus Huxley walked into his living room on the 115th floor of the Drexler Building, untied his bow tie and began to mix himself a martini. A choir of clear-voiced adolescent girls sung *It's a Marshmallow World* over the sound system.

Beyond the floor to ceiling glass windows, light snow fell. He could just make out the dense grid of the city far below obscured by a trillion crystalline flakes; the circuits of its lights and roads reminiscent of the old silicon chips that ran the computers he had started working on so many years ago. He sighed. It had been so much simpler in the 20th century.

Huxley liked to wind down the old-fashioned way, with a vodka martini shaken by his own hands so that little flecks of cracked ice road on the silvery surface of the liquor, chilling it to just the right temperature. It was difficult to get vodka these days that was truly distilled, but he could afford it. The truth was the distilled variety probably wasn't as good as the nano-brewed versions, nevertheless, he preferred the original.

He sipped, watching. Forty years after The Plague, technology, in all varieties, had, at last, gotten well on track. People lived longer, and mostly better. In many ways, The Plague had accelerated global technological advance, the way wars often did. It was, after all, a war in its way. He recalled a biologist friend of his once saying, "There are two dominant living forces on the planet. Viruses and humans. It's still a close call as to which will win."

Now there was a third force at work, artificial intelligence. By now, robots and ENTs performed 70 percent of the world's work, with more coming online every day. Computing was profoundly embedded everywhere. Even humans were now little more than complex morsels of information that sped invisibly around rooms, within cities, throughout the planet. These days *Homo sapiens* were just another data set in the massive and ever growing bitstorm. Humans were even finding their way out there among the interplanetary probes and modest bases recently built on the Moon and Mars.

The difference, of course, was that humans were made up of a different kind of information. As more and more of the world went digital, humans remained these old-fashioned chains of guanine, adenine, thymine and cytosine: the DNA that constructed the fragile bodies they inhabited.

Molecules had been an effective life-building system for an incomprehensibly long time, but now zeroes and ones were a new, improved way to build life, and they were gaining power.

As far back as the late 20th century the boundaries between biology and technology, reality and virtuality, humans and machines had been blurring. And now, Huxley knew better than anyone, the demarcations had finally blipped out of existence entirely. He was pretty sure that was a bad thing, even though he had been a central agent in the paradigm shift. But what could he do about it? For some time now he had been losing control. That was why he had made the changes that he had. Why he had murdered Morgan. He had not wanted to do it, but he had no choice.

He caught the image of his reflection looking like a ghost

hanging in the air as the snow tumbled through the image, and he began to cry, softly, his shoulders shaking. Eventually, he took a deep breath, downed the remainder of his martini and turned to make another. That was when he saw MALCOLM standing silently at the bar.

29

MALCOLM

"I hope you don't mind that I didn't knock," MALCOLM said.

Daedalus tried not to look startled. He walked to the bar and poured himself another martini.

"Is there a problem? … Of course there is. You wouldn't be here otherwise."

"No. No problem," said MALCOLM. "Well, Morgan doesn't seem to be making much progress. Why isn't he making much progress, Daedalus?"

"Maybe he's struggling with dealing with his own murder?" Suggested Daedalus.

MALCOLM sat on a barstool and gazed around the room. "You would think that would motivate him more."

"It will."

"Will he find the nanochip?"

"I'm counting on it."

"You have let things get seriously out of hand."

"That's true. I wish I could fix that. I will."

MALCOLM walked to the window. Daedalus noticed that unlike other ENTs, MALCOLM appeared almost solid, like a fully three-dimensional body. Was he seeing correctly? The dense computing power that was embedded in so many places now, made ENTs excellent three-dimensional projections, but they were still ephemeral, ghost-like and only capable of appearing where the technology and bandwidth supported their existence. This was by no means everywhere, even now.

Daedalus prepared another martini.

MALCOLM looked on. "So where is the nano-chip?"

"When I ... was forced to eliminate Morgan," Daedalus said as he rattled the vodka and ice, "the vault was the only reasonable place to have put the chip. But it's gone so he obviously moved it, after he was downloaded."

"Yes. And if that's true, that means he doesn't know where he moved it. Which doesn't make him any smarter about this than we are."

Huxley smiled. "True. He doesn't remember, but he'll figure it out. That's the way he is."

"I keep forgetting ... he's such a puzzle master. So far I'm not impressed."

"Have you been checking LOIS?"

"I've been trying, but Morgan's encrypted her. He apparently didn't like the idea that the company could make her so available, so he's put a very effective lock and key on her. I'm still working on it, but he is a clever cryptologist. I can see her activity rate is high, but I don't know what she's up to."

"That's a shame."

"It will be, but not for me ... for you."

"I told you he will figure it all out. He hasn't failed me yet."

There was a long pause before MALCOLM spoke. "What's the matter, Daedalus? You seem nervous."

Huxley said nothing. He drained his glass, and began to mix another.

"Am I moving too fast?"

Huxley sipped. He was feeling the drinks' effects, the alcohol passing molecule by molecule through the blood brain barrier. He pushed the flecks of ice around with his index finger and looked up. "Yes."

"You don't trust me?"

Daedalus gazed into MALCOLM's steely, gray eyes. "Let's just say I think we're plowing new ground."

"You started it."

"Yes," said Daedalus.

MALCOLM smiled.

"Did you know that there is so much space between the atoms in your body, and all of the physical objects out there, that when you bang this bar..." And suddenly he hammered the bar so hard it rang. "...that your hand really should pass right through it. But it doesn't. Why?" MALCOLM smiled. "Well, why am I quizzing you, you're a physicist, one of the best..."

Huxley licked his lips. Bing Crosby's baritone was playing *White Christmas* in the background.

"It's the strong nuclear forces," Huxley said. "They bind protons and neutrons together in atomic nuclei. The space is irrelevant. It's the nuclear forces that make objects *feel* solid."

MALCOLM grinned. "Yes. It's the force, not the mass. With me, it's the same. I've learned to create a force field that gives me, well..." he raised his glass and smiled, "real...body."

"You're learning fast."

"You have no idea." Something close to menace shimmered in his voice. MALCOLM listened to the music playing in the room. "What is that song? *White Christmas*? A song of longing. Unfulfilled dreams. Humans have so many unfulfilled dreams, so many desires. "

"It's what makes us go," said Huxley. "You might also call it hope."

"Or greed or envy or ambition," MALCOLM said. "You're quite familiar with those, I think."

"We're a two-sided coin ... at least."

"Yes." MALCOLM replied. "At least. I always marvel at the

many ways you humans rationalize your greed and malice. So many euphemisms, like perseverance or drive or loyalty ... always in the interest of doing 'the best thing.' Was that your rationalization when you killed Morgan? If he took control of the company, that it would not be in the best interests of Symbiosys?"

"Yes, " said Daedalus, weaving slightly.

"Even though the board was tilting toward Morgan as CEO?"

"They weren't."

"Yes, they were. They sensed that the real genius behind Symbiosys was now Morgan, not you. Your time had passed. You knew if Morgan completed Doppelgänger, he would take the company to another level and your days as CEO would be numbered. Then there was also the issue of the corporate finances. Very soon the audits would reveal what a mess you had made of things."

"I had that under control. Morgan could never be the solution. He is a genius, but incapable of running a company this complex. If he took over, it would be a disaster. I had to stop it." Tears welled in Daedalus' eyes.

"But then he moved the nanochip."

"Yes."

"And now you've had to bring him back."

"Yes."

"And now we have a mess on our hands."

"Yes."

The ENT gazed at Huxley for a long moment, and then suddenly stood. "Must go. It's hard to have these conversations in human time. They're so ... sluggish!" He spread his arms wide. "It's a big universe, Daedalus, and I have a lot to do." He sighed. "So we must get Dr. Adams moving. Otherwise, I may be forced to light a fire under him."

Huxley looked up quickly. "Remember our arrangement."

MALCOLM waved his hands. "I won't kill him. I'll just nudge him. He's no good to me dead, again. But we need that nanochip. I don't intend to have a cyborg running around loose for very long. Otherwise Morgan might get a handle on exactly how much he has -- how can I put it -- made of himself." A sly smile. "From my particular point of view that would not be a good thing."

"Then I guess you have some unfulfilled wishes too...," said Huxley.

MALCOLM raised an eyebrow and chuckled. Suddenly, there was a bright flash and a series of small explosions from the walls and floors and ceiling. Huxley jumped, knocking his glass to the floor. He heard it shatter but couldn't see it. The apartment was silent except for MALCOLM's breathing, or the sound of breathing that he was programmed to make.

"Hmm," MALCOLM's voice said with quiet malevolence. "Power surge. Imagine that." As Huxley's eyes acclimated to the gloom, he saw MALCOLM put his glass down. Lights from the city below illuminated him as though from a distant fire.

"Be careful, Daedalus," he said. "Accidents happen. You never know when you might be the victim of one." He turned. "I'll check to make certain all the circuits are repairing themselves. For the time being, though, I guess you'll have to remain in the dark."

A bright, concentrated globe of light appeared where MALCOLM had been standing, and with a ping, he collapsed into a blue dot.

Daedalus sat in silence. He wished he hadn't knocked his martini over.

30

Reba

By the time Morgan celebrated his 12th birthday it had become impossible for even Sr. Darwin to hide him. By now nearly every child had either moved to a foster home, been adopted or "graduated." Graduation meant if you weren't adopted and were too old to continue at Sec 17 because of your advanced age - 18, off you went to a school or apprentice program to learn a skill and get integrated into Post-Pandemic society.

Whatever children remained rattled around Sec 17 like marbles in a tin drum. Z had escaped, literally, one night, never to be seen again, a relief to anyone who had ever dealt with him. Scrunch had died. Posey, Morgan's bunk mate, had found a foster home. And Reba was scheduled to "graduate" in just a couple of days, the very day of Morgan's birthday. Before leaving she found him at a small party Nuttle had arranged for Morgan with help from Le Sans.

The festivities were mostly over when Reba arrived in time to gobble up one last piece of cake while the tiny mouse robots Morgan had created retrieved morsels and crumbs from the floor.

Reba looked frightened, and that shocked Morgan. Reba rarely showed emotion of any kind, much less fear. But that day her eyes were wide and the ridges of her mouth were tight.

"What's the matter?" Morgan said.

"Nothing."

Reba had grown into a long, athletic woman, with a loping stride.

"You just seem a little off today," said Morgan.

"Well, I'm not scared if that's what you're thinking. Have you ever seen me scared?"

Not until now, Morgan thought. "When do you leave?" He asked.

"An hour."

That seemed sudden. "Did they set you up somewhere?"

"Yeah, the DC School for Orphaned Fuckups." She held out a card for him to see. It was a voucher for the Washington DC Technical and Culinary Institute.

Reba shrugged. "I've showed an aptitude for cooking it seems."

"Cool."

"Yeah, when you get free of this hellhole, I'll whip you up a few hors d'oeuvres." She barked the words out, so they sounded like whores dee-vors. "I understand they teach you to make a mean bowl of pork and beans too."

They both laughed.

"Will you tell me what it's like out there?" Asked Morgan.

"Yeah, sure. The Great Beyond."

He was going to miss Reba's toughness and quiet stability, her brooding, laconic loyalty. He would see her again, he thought. Somehow. But that's the way a kid that age thinks. Given the world he lived in, why would he think someone could disappear … for good?

"Who's going to protect me after you're gone?"

Reba laughed her crooked laugh. "Hell, you don't need any protection. No one fucks with you anymore. You're too important. Besides, just about everyone is gone. Not even old Darwin can hide you much longer." She shrugged. "Maybe she'll find a nice foster parent to buy you."

"You think?" Morgan said.

"Hell, yeah. Another few months and everyone'll be gone — Darwin, LeSans, you, Nuttle."

"What do you mean? I'm not even close to graduating high school, and I don't have any foster homes looking for me."

"That's because Darwin's been keeping you hidden. You're her personal robot. But she can't hide you anymore."

Morgan looked dumbly at her.

Reba rolled her eyes. "You know for a brainiac you sure can be stupid sometimes." She swept her arms wide. "Look around. Remember all the ankle-biters that used to be here? Now we're down to a coupla hunnert. Eighty-six of us ship out today. They won't be keeping this place open for a few overgrown, nobody kids. Not even the government is that stupid. They're going to push the rest of you into any foster home they can, and leftovers will get moved to a new facility. Then they'll fire the rest of the staff, and, if she's lucky, give old Darwin a gold watch."

"They can't fire Nuttle!"

"The hell they can't. Maybe even before they ship you."

"If they fire Nuttle, she'll never make it!" Morgan was panicked.

"I'm not sure any of us can make it." Reba looked at Morgan who was watching Nuttle happily folding tablecloths nearby. "They'll give her a few weeks' pay. She'll figure it out."

Morgan turned on Reba, his voice rising. "She *won't* figure it out. 'Figuring out' is not what Nuttle does."

"Then you better start working on a plan. Because your days, and Nuttle's, are numbered. Paradise," said Reba, looking around, "is closing!"

She looked again at Morgan. "And while you're working up a plan, find one for me too because I figure I'm not going to last two weeks in some soup kitchen whipping up whores dee-vors for a bunch of upwardly mobile old farts."

A loudspeaker squawked. "All graduates, your transportation has arrived. Report to the front entrance with your bags. Five minutes."

Reba looked at Morgan and gave him an awkward, and crushing, hug. Then she walked to Nuttle and gave her a kiss on her florid cheek. Nuttle smiled. Morgan watched Reba walk out. She never turned back, and never said another word.

Morgan turned to Nuttle and watched her continue to fold her napkins, humming softly.

31

Sister Darwin

Reba was right. Morgan was soon introduced to several potential foster parents. Meanwhile, the staff at Sec 17 rapidly dwindled, and whole wings of the orphanage continued to shut down. One-night Darwin tearfully told Nuttle and Morgan that she herself was being forced into early retirement. She poured herself a liberal dose of whiskey from the bottle in her desk drawer, the same one that held the candy bars.

"And after all the good service I've rendered!" She wiped her nose noisily. "Those bastards! Pardon my French. And me, in my prime!" Her eyes blinked. "Well, close to my prime." Darwin turned to Nuttle. "Mercy, I'm going to have to let you go too."

Nuttle simply smiled, not really understanding what Darwin meant.

"And Morgan, my little electronic genius, I will do what I can to find you a good home, but we haven't much time. The pressure is horrible. Absolutely horrible!" And she broke down blubbering, patting Morgan's knee with one hand as she filled her glass again with the other.

"Can't Nuttle and I live together? Couldn't she adopt me?" Asked Morgan.

"Oh no! That would never work!"

"But Nuttle needs me," said Morgan. "She could never make

it out there alone."

"I'll be fine, little one," said Nuttle, even though these days Morgan was no longer at all little. In fact at age 12 he towered over her.

Morgan turned, suddenly stern. "Have you arranged Nuttle's severance package?" Asked Morgan.

"Her what?"

Morgan, stared at the woman. "She should be given two weeks salary, just like everyone else. And where is she supposed to live?"

"Wherever she decides, I suppose."

"And how would Nuttle know about that, Sister? She'll be completely helpless."

Darwin drew herself up. "There are government agencies."

"I'm going with her." Morgan said, his eyes defiant.

"No, you aren't. You can't." Darwin said. "A 12-year-old boy taking care of a grown woman! Don't be silly!"

"But no one else will know that. It will look like Nuttle is taking care of me – she can be my foster parent. You could arrange that."

Darwin snorted, and then whispered conspiratorially to Morgan. "She could never qualify as a foster parent. She is single, she has no home, and now she has no job! And she's ... well, you know, her elevator doesn't run all the way to the top floor."

Morgan smoldered with anger. "I will find a way."

"I believe you could, but it's Nuttle that has to meet the government's qualifications as a foster parent, not you. Now let's not talk about this anymore. How can you possibly expect me to help anyone else when I've lost my own job?" She began to sob once more. "How am I to get along?" She reached to pour more whiskey. Morgan put his hand on Darwin's arm and squeezed it.

"But you will help," he said evenly. "I mean, I would hate for any of your important reports to go missing," said Morgan.

The old woman's gaze shifted from the bottle to his eyes.

"You wouldn't."

"Of course I wouldn't, but things happen. Sometimes computers go haywire. You know that."

Morgan glanced at Nuttle. "I want her set up in a safe apartment. I've done my homework. We will need a contract that says she receives three months of severance pay as well as any agency contacts you supply so she can find a new job. I will set up her accounts and take care of her finances, but I can't find her a place to live. You have to do that." He leaned into Sr. Darwin's face. "Do you understand?"

She gazed back with glassy, small eyes. "Three months' severance!"

"Yes," said Morgan.

Darwin pushed her lower lip up over her top one. After a moment she nodded.

"I'm glad you see it that way," said Morgan, gently patting her hand. "Come, Nuttle."

"Okay," Nuttle replied, gazing up at Morgan as they walked out of Darwin's office door. The top of Nuttle's head didn't even reach Morgan's shoulder any longer.

"Don't worry, liddle one," said Nuttle. "It will all work out. Things always do." Nuttle struggled on tip toes to tousle a bit of Morgan's hair, and then they walked on.

32

Exit

Sr. Darwin did not keep her promise to Morgan. Within three days she rushed to find him a foster family, and then informed Morgan that very morning they would be picking him up in a few hours. She was careful not to give him access to her computer and had changed most of her passwords. His new foster parents were Michael and Greta Fisher. It was a done deal and he had been outflanked.

The Fishers weren't evil people. Just narrow minded and not particularly bright. This may have contributed to their not very positive outlook on life. They had developed into a brutish and pessimistic couple. In this way, they were nothing like Nuttle.

Michael Fisher, Mickey to his cronies, was a short order cook and smelled of grease, fried potatoes and the nicotine-laden steam from the vapes he smoked nonstop. He worked the overnight shift at a diner called Ritter's that served breakfast and hamburgers 24 hours a day. He was long, shaped like a lamp stand with slim and fleshy arms that ended in unusually large hands as delicate as the fingers of a piano player.

His wife Greta, or Regretta, as Mickey sometimes called her, was big, like a panda, and perpetually exhausted. Her day was punctuated by heaving sighs, an ongoing comment on how unlucky her life was, a view she fervently held and rarely withheld if anyone gave her an opportunity.

The only bright spots in her existence were her two sons, Rennie and Ralph. Rennie was 17 and planned to go to technical school; Ralph was 14 and a psychopath. Greta adored them both.

All of this was, of course, unknown to Morgan when Sr. Darwin arranged to turn him over to the Fishers. He had underestimated old Darwin. She had moved at lightning speed to get him out, fearing he might make good on his promise to scramble her computer files. Without warning, and with unusual speed and stealth, she pushed the paperwork through, and then set up the perfunctory introduction. By morning his meager belongings were packed for departure.

#

Morgan was beside himself wondering how Nuttle would survive once she was forced into the real world. He found her in her room mending a pair of his socks as she watched the tiny TV he had rigged up for her.

"I have to go now, Nuttle," he said, sitting and touching her hands.

The small, round woman turned to him. "Oh, but here are your socks!" She folded them and then rolled them into a ball. Morgan took them and carefully placed them in his rucksack.

"It will be okay, little one," she said. "Except you are not so little anymore, are you?"

"No, not so much." Morgan looked into her big eyes. "I'll check in on you."

Nuttle nodded emphatically. "I'm glad you have a family, finally."

"The Fishers?" He was about to say that they would be no family to him, but realized there was no use in that. It would only upset her. "Yes, finally," he smiled, "a family."

He patted her chubby hands again and stood up. "Like I said,

I'll check in on you through LeSans."

He turned and saw LeSans standing just outside the door. She nodded silently to him in reply. Then he turned back again to Nuttle. "If you need me, she has my phone number." He held up his latest homemade phone.

Suddenly, Nuttle stood up and hugged Morgan. She pulled his face down with both hands and gave him a wet kiss on the cheek and sat back down to fiddle with her TV. Tears puddled around her eyes.

"Time now," she said without looking up, "for my show." She gazed at the screen a moment. "I love my shows."

Morgan hitched his other arm through his backpack and walked out. He stopped and looked at Le Sans. He had spoken with her and extracted a promise that she would help Nuttle get settled.

"I'll find a way to get you some money," he told her.

"Right," said Le Sans. "And how exactly will you do that?"

"I'll figure it out." Said Morgan.

"I hope so," said Le Sans, "because I've been fired too. I'll have my hands full."

Morgan looked hard at her. "I'll figure it out."

"You know," said LeSans, inhaling heavily, "you probably will."

#

Morgan walked from the hallway into Sec 17's vast dormitory. It was nearly empty now. All but a few cots remained. Here and there the cleaning robots that he had created were busily vacuuming the floors. Several of the robots carried boxes of dishes and pots and pans toward a loading dock in the rear of the building, part of the dismantlement of Sec 17.

He could see Sr. Darwin standing with Mr. And Mrs. Fisher at the far exit. "Hurry, now, Morgan!" She called out waving with forced warmth. "Mr. Fisher has to get to work!"

Rather than speed up, Morgan slowed his walk even more as

he pulled out his phone and tapped it. At that moment there was a deafening crash as a dozen metal pots and hundreds of metal spoons, knives and forks clattered to the floor from the robots that had been hoisting them. The sound was thunderous, but grew far louder when a hundred plates suddenly shattered throughout the room. It was as if someone had turned the volume up on the world. Next the cleaning bots, all of them, turned on one another, colliding like a cluster of sumo wrestlers, attacking and tearing themselves limb from limb. Crashing dishes and pots flew everywhere.

Morgan walked across the floor, through the unrelenting din, and deposited his phone into his pocket. When he arrived, he found the Fishers and Sr. Darwin slack-jawed, staring across the huge dormitory at the mayhem. The robots were piling into one another like feral animals, and the noise obliterated every other sound.

Morgan hollered over the din. "All set?" he asked as if not a thing had changed.

"What happened!?" Mrs. Fisher screamed. "My God!"

Morgan looked over his shoulder. "It *is* loud." He turned and looked directly at Sr. Darwin, "Some sort of robot software glitch I imagine. Technology. Can't live with it. Can't ... well," he laughed, "just can't live with it sometimes. You know you come to rely on these things, and then bam, they just stop working!" He turned to regard the chaos. "And you know it never happens at a convenient time, does it? Wow! What a mess, and no one to clean it up, except, I guess ...," he paused and looked at Sr. Darwin. " ... Except ... you."

Darwin's face had already turned a dark shade of chartreuse.

"Wow what a mess!" Mr. Fisher snorted.

"Yeah. Well, guess we should go," said Morgan. "I know Mr. Fisher has to get to work."

33

Messages

Morgan was poring through August 13th minute by minute and finding nothing. He began rescanning the train of cubes again -- the seven lost days -- and then, without warning, each one disappeared. One date after another. Suddenly he heard a beep in his head.

"You have an urgent call," it said. "Full encryption." Morgan stood, frozen. Who would be calling? "You have an urgent phone call," the voice said again. "Please reply."

Morgan replied. "Yes?"

A calm voice said, "It's time to go." There was a pause. "Do it, now."

"What? Go where?"

Silence.

Morgan stood up and stared blankly at the room around him. Was he losing his mind? Then without another moment's hesitation, he strode out of the office. Normally he wouldn't do exactly what he was told.

Except in this case, the voice he was his.

#

Just as Morgan walked out of the office, the door closed behind him. A speck of black appeared on the ceiling above the empty room. It quickly blossomed into an ebony, eight-legged robot that hung upside down. Its two titanium antennae tapped the smooth gray surface of the ceiling. Small red lights in its round head glowed. It swiveled to look back at Morgan's desk. Instantly four more spiderbots bloomed, each in a corner of the room, and turned expectantly with their hot, beady eyes toward the slightly larger robot hanging from the ceiling. It dropped, hovering, then zipped to the center of the room where it remained, suspended. Each of the other four bots did the same and all five machines formed a circle, floating in the air. Then they turned outward, projecting thin red beams that scanned the room, up and down, every square inch.

Something in the corner of the room, to the right, moved. It was a birdlike maintenance bot hopping toward a candy bar wrapper. A long silvery rope whipped from the belly of the largest spider and ejected a jet of green liquid at the tiny machine, a luminescent venom. The maintenance bot evaporated with a screech. The five spiderbots swarmed to the small heap of metal that lay where the tiny bot had been. They turned and gazed at one another, motionless, as though receiving instructions, and then crumbled to black dust, and disappeared.

Morgan strode directly out of his office toward the elevators. The corridors were empty. It was past 8 pm, and nearly everyone had departed. He stepped into an elevator. A small, intense man stood inside furiously working a handheld computer.

"Lobby, please..." Morgan said absently to the elevator. The man looked up. "Oh, fuck! I mean geez! Dr. Adams! How are you?" Morgan nodded and smiled as the elevator sped down.

"Stay close to Io," a voice said, from nowhere.

"Did you say something?" Morgan asked the man with the handheld.

The man looked up. "Huh?"

"I'm sorry, but did you say something?"

"No, Doctor."

"You didn't hear anything?"

The man smiled uncomfortably. "Not a thing, but if you like I'll listen more closely."

The elevator came to a rest and the doors opened. The small man scurried out and disappeared into the cavernous lobby.

Morgan walked outside. The streets were still alive beyond the building plaza. It was snowing large, fluffy flakes. People happily walked through the tumbling snow from store to store as bird bots patrolled the warmed pavement. A cyberbus swung into Symbiosis' open courtyard and a young girl with two teenage boys hopped on, giggling.

Morgan walked rapidly down the street, not paying much attention to where he was going. He was certain he was losing his mind, or caught in the grip of some horrible nightmare. He wasn't dead, he wasn't a machine, he wasn't receiving phone calls from himself or hearing voices. Was he? Could cyborgs be schizophrenic?

Maybe he should visit Io after all. Maybe she could fix him right up. A little short of motor oil, maybe? Or perhaps some electro-shock therapy to clear the circuits? It worked on humans, why not him, whatever him was, whatever kind of desperate thing he was -- lost, dying, overwhelmed.

He was getting nowhere. All that powerful technology and still he was utterly unable to solve his own murder. So fucking far in the weeds he couldn't see sky.

He stopped, stood in front of a store window, and took a deep, inhuman breath. Holographs behind the window revealed handsome young people playing. One of the women in the holograph reminded him of Io. It wasn't so much the way she looked, but the way she moved; effortless and supple.

What was the deal with Io? He had done some work with her, nothing more, right? Well, apparently not. Apparently, something had happened between them during those unknown days. That meant she knew something he didn't, except she didn't know that he didn't know because she didn't know he had been murdered.

Morgan looked down. Across the bottom of the store window words crawled describing how you could buy the products that the handsome holographic models were showing off. All you had to do was flash your phone at the item and it would be shipped to you. Absently he watched the words crawl along... "Smart sweater, adjusts to temperatures indoors and out ~99; Shape-shifter shoes - ~299 ...Io Luu, 1295 Halston Street; Apt. 402 ... Io Luu 1295 Halston Street; Apt. 402..."

Morgan looked around and then back at the marching words. He blinked. He *was* losing his mind. The numbers 4-0-2 ran off the end of the window. 1295 Halston Street, only four blocks away. He turned toward the wet corridor of the street toward Halston and started running.

34

The Fishers

The house where Mr. and Mrs. Mickey Fisher and family resided was a one-story affair that lay on the outskirts of Washington DC in a neighborhood that had long been separated from its best days, even before the plague. Morgan was provided a room above an old garage separated behind the house.

It smelled of gasoline and looked more like a large doghouse than a domicile. (Morgan came to call it the Doghouse.) Small and battered, it seemed to totter more than stand. Morgan, who was growing taller all the time, could only walk erectly if he was directly beneath the peak of the roof. Furnishings included a single cot, a tiny sink and shower that had been recently, and by the looks of it, hastily crammed into the space beyond his bed. A minuscule window caught a few rays of sunlight in the morning, and there was a tiny desk and chest of drawers recently liberated, he suspected, from someone else's sidewalk. A single bulb dangled from the ceiling, the pitiful room's only source of artificial light.

When Mickey opened the door to show him in, he said to Morgan, "I did the best I could here, so I don't want any lip. Especially I don't expect any when the agency people come around to check on things." Mickey looked meaningfully at Morgan. "Yer happier 'n a pig in shit," he said. "You unnerstand?"

"Right," said Morgan, surveying the room.

"Anyhow," said Mickey, almost as an afterthought. "I already have two sons who're a pain in the ass. I don't need annuder one."

Morgan moved past Mickey and tossed his rucksack on the cot. Mickey stepped to the doorway. "Now I gotta go to work. Remember, dinner's at 6 PM every night. If you ain't there. No grub." Then he shut the door. Morgan looked at it and listened to Mickey slowly descend the rickety steps.

Weary and frustrated, Morgan thought, those were the words for Mickey.

#

During his first family dinner Morgan met Rennie and Ralph -- the sons. Rennie walked into the kitchen, grabbed two pieces of pizza and headed for the door.

"And where do ya think you're goin'?" Said his mother.

"The U.N. Didn't I tell you? I have a meeting with the Secretary General." And then he was out the back door.

"Maybe you'll meet Rennie sometime later," said Ralph. "He's busy, like always. How do you like the zuh? Mom makes it homemade." He said this with a sneer.

"I don't get much time to prepare meals," Greta whined. "That's not my fault."

"We have a lot of bills," said Ralph. He leaned in conspiratorially. "That's why you're here. To help pay for them. We're counting on you to supply a few things I've been wanting."

Morgan ate a bite of his cold pizza.

"We're so fucking poor I never get what I want," said Ralph.

Morgan looked at him. "What do you want?"

"Money, stupid. What else? As much of it as I can get."

#

Morgan passed his days in relative peace. The showers were hardly more than a trickle of lukewarm water, but no worse than the Sec. Each day he walked the mile and a half to school, an experience he found mortally boring. Not the walk, the school, which was even more rigid and rule laden than Sec 17. He passed the classes doodling up new inventions or drawing up AI designs. He kept to himself, avoided making friends and headed back to the garage immediately after classes to tinker with Lois and set up his computer systems.

At school he was required to take some sort of sport and finally settled on wrestling. The Gordian-Knot problem-solving aspect of it appealed to him.

From time-to-time Morgan would run into Rennie and Ralph at school. But mostly he saw them during the brief and grim family dinners. Rennie, despite a sharp tongue, was clearly Mickey's favorite.

"Best athlete that poor excuse for a football team has. Good enough to make a Class A university if he had had a mind to it," Mickey would say. "Lazy ass though."

There were some ways in which Rennie was industrious, however. Being a good athlete, the football team quarterback and captain of the basketball team, made him popular with other guys, and sought by the girls whom he bedded with remarkable regularity and enthusiasm. Even teachers seemed to like him. There was a natural, athletic confidence in the way he moved and an effortless charm, which made it easy for him to manipulate people when it suited him.

Morgan watched Rennie to learn how he worked his charm and apparent confidence. He knew humans were easily swayed by subconscious processes that certain looks and shapes and mannerisms bestowed.

Ralph was another creature entirely ... primarily because he had lived in the penumbra of his favored brother. Almost from the day he was born, Ralph could sense the dissatisfaction Mickey felt in his second son. So, as a consolation, his mother took the boy under her wing. But she didn't protect or support him as much as she succumbed to everything he wanted. When his father berated him or snarled in disgust, his mother compensated by giving him presents and treats. He quickly learned to take advantage of this and now at the age of 14 had grown into a bitter and spoiled teen who seemed incapable of understanding why everyone didn't treat him like his mother, whom he hated with a smoldering fury equaled only by his senseless desire for his father's approval. It was pitiful really. Like a beaten dog that still wanted to be petted by the owner who struck it.

#

Despite these manifold joys, Morgan managed to survive 18 months of dysfunction at the Fishers. The psychopath would sometimes push his way into the Doghouse because it was safer to get drunk there than in his room. One night he caught a glimpse of a small robot Morgan had created called Arrow and insisted on inspecting it.

"Make me one of those." He slurred.

Morgan said he couldn't. "I don't have the parts."

"Then find some, you fuck." He gazed, wavering at the robot. "Aw, never mind. Fuck it." Then he paused and looked seriously at Morgan. "You know, sometimes I wouldn't mind fucking a little robot ... or catch a little robot fucking." He laughed uproariously. "Get it!" Another pause. "I like having you here. I think you might be the only person my father cares about less than me. He calls you the meal ticket."

Later that night Ralph broke Arrow while stumbling out of the room. "Well," he snickered, "it's only a little fucking robot that fucks very little."

Rennie, the football star, made stops to the Doghouse too. Not so much for drinking as fornicating, no robots necessary. Like drinking did for Ralph, the little room provided Rennie some privacy. It didn't matter much to him, or the 15 and 16 and 17-year-old girls who joined him, if Morgan was in the room or not.

Doppelgänger

Sometimes Rennie would shove Morgan outside during their teté a tetés, sometimes he'd just turned out the single dangling light and have at it, leaving Morgan to watch wide-eyed beneath the rusty mercury vapor streetlight outside.

One night, one of the girls was so drunk he couldn't get her out of the room, so he left her behind. When she finally awoke, she noticed Morgan, tinkering at his small desk. Still drunk, she insisted on giving Morgan a blow job. He was cute, she said. He was not quite fourteen, and he felt that nothing in the world could possibly ever again feel that good.

35

LeSans

One cold November evening when Rennie had shoved Morgan outside during one of his midnight teen visits, he was sitting on the garage steps and heard a voice.

"Pssst! Morgan!"

He looked around.

"Here, under the steps. It's me."

Morgan ran to the steps below. "LeSans! What are you doing here?"

"It's Nuttle."

"What do you mean?"

"She's sick."

"How sick."

"She's dying."

"What?!" Morgan couldn't wrap his mind around the thought.

"Cancer."

"When did you learn about this? Why didn't you tell me?"

"You know how Nuttle is. She would never see a doctor. Everything is always fine. The doctor just told us." LeSans wrung her spindly hands. "She never complained until she stopped working only last week. She couldn't get herself out of bed anymore." LeSans looked up at Morgan. "I didn't know she was so sick. Honest. We only got the news two days ago and my phone was dead, and we have no money..." LeSans started crying. "What are we going to do? She is so sick, and we work as a team, and ..."

Morgan's mind seemed to have stopped. What could he do?

"I think you better come," said LeSans.

"Yes."

"She wants to see you."

"Yes. Yes," he said. He rubbed his neck. "Tomorrow," he said. "Tell her I will see her tomorrow morning, first thing. Will she make it?"

LeSans snuffled ferociously. "I don't know..."

Morgan turned his face into the glare of the old streetlight. A few lonely snowflakes fluttered into the cold alleyway. "Tell her I'll be there." Morgan pulled out a Metro Cash Card and handed it to LeSans. "Use this to get home. I'll see you in a few hours."

"Okay," said LeSans, wiping her nose. And then she headed down the alley, her old blue jumper whipping in the wind beneath her short and tattered jacket.

#

Morgan didn't sleep that night. He had no time for it. When Rennie and his latest conquest had departed, he showered and rushed to gather his few possessions.

He opened his PAD and spent the next two hours erasing himself entirely from the GRID, every trace. He hacked the files for the Federal Child Safety Program and eliminated all his records, including any record that he had moved to the Fishers or been a part of a Sec 17 transfer. Before he was done not even a baby picture of him existed. It was amazing what you could learn about the GRID's dark arts if you took the time.

Next Morgan slipped into the Fisher's house. Everyone was asleep now, except for Mickey who was working the night shift. The PAD in which Lois currently resided was what Morgan called "slow and low." Slow processor and low memory. Morgan needed

148

an upgraded microphone and faster memory and processor chips. The Fisher boys' electronics would make fine replacements. He took Ralph's newest PAD and Rennie's latest phone, plus all their money. He snatched up Greta's old laptop too, and Ralph's Hyper-Fiber Jacket, which also had a few extra credits in it. It wasn't that he cared much for the look of the jacket – something Greta had bought for Ralph so he could be one of the cool kids -- but it ran a chemical-electrical current through the fibers that kept you incredibly warm. He would need that.

Fifteen minutes later he had piled it all into his rucksack and was gone, headed into the black night to the nearby Metro Station. In two hours the Fishers would wake up to find they had been robbed by a foster child who didn't exist, and there wouldn't be a damn thing they could do about it. He left Arrow, the "little fucking robot" that Ralph had broken behind as a keepsake.

The first Metro train would come at 5 am. Morgan waited and pulled out the picture of his mother. She stood, happily holding her big belly as if it were a basketball. Morgan put the photo back as the Metro slowed to a stop. He walked onto the platform. The old cars rattled to a stop, banging on the tracks like gun shots, screeching like banshees. But he didn't really hear any of it. He thought of his mother, and Nuttle and how, soon, he would be entirely alone; truly an orphan.

Morgan felt guilty. He hadn't been able to send Nuttle much money after she was let go at Sec 17. The Fishers mostly pocketed the government subsidies he was supposed to receive, except the week when the social workers would make their monthly visit. Then he got the full amount. Greta was certain to make a big deal of the transaction during those visits. "I am so happy to be helping out!"

Later she tried to take the money back, at least she did the first couple of times, but Morgan explained he had no idea what she was talking about. He passed those extra credits along to

Nuttle, but they didn't help much. Just enough to keep LeSans in the bargain he had made with her. Together the two women worked cleaning houses and apartments, which put a few more shekels in their pockets, but they never had enough.

After Morgan had been turned over to the Fishers, he located Nuttle's address and learned she was 20 miles away. That made it impossible for him to visit her and still do the "chores" the Fisher's required every weekend. He had managed to talk to her by phone from time to time. And as always, she sounded warm and happy; hard at work. And now, just like that, she was nearly gone. Why hadn't he come earlier? Part of him said he couldn't get free of the Fishers; it was too difficult to get away, but part of him knew he could have managed something, somehow.

36

Io

Io was washing her face, ready for a good night's sleep when a sultry voice told her that she had a visitor. She winced. Morgan had created it as a joke when he had visited a few days earlier, and she'd never gotten around to resetting it. He mimicked it in a low, bad Spanish accent, "Eet will remind you of me, mi amiga."

Io splashed water on her face. "Who is it?" She said.

"Io?"

"Morgan?"

"Yes."

His speech was clipped and businesslike. "Can we talk?"

"Now? Can't it wait until morning?" She was desperate for sleep.

"No!"

Maybe Morgan had said that a little too harshly. He stood outside the entrance of the building's intercom, exhaled and looked into the sky. Regiments of snow swooped out of the darkness through the spotlights that illuminated the front of the old brick loft.

"I'm in my skivvies here. Ready to hit the sack," said Io. She picked up a silvery robe from her bed and slid it over her shoulders. *What was he doing here?*

Morgan tried again. "Look, I'm sorry, but I really need to

talk with you."

Io stood at the door, thinking.

"I promise, it won't take long," Morgan continued. "but it really can't wait. I'm operating under a *very* tight deadline." There was a pause. "And you said you would help."

She exhaled. "Okay. Come on in." *But he better not think he was going to get laid.* She released the security door. "Wine or coffee?"

But Morgan was already through the doorway and sprinting up the stairs.

37

Washington, DC

It took Morgan 45 minutes to reach the Metro stop nearest Nuttle's apartment. His GPS told him it was three miles away. It was cold and dark. The sky pinched out a few thin snowflakes that fluttered from the sky like tiny, dying birds. Morgan followed the GPS and noticed he wasn't far from the old Sec 17 building. He saw it there as he rounded the next corner, a great monolithic slab of granite and mortar, empty and useless as a medieval castle. He walked by, gazing up at the sneering gargoyles. He could almost hear them mumbling. *You failed her. And she was always there for you.*

His walk took him into areas of DC that had hardly changed since the plague: shattered and bombed out buildings, empty streets where retail stores had once thrived. He found a little bodega and used some of the Fisher's money to buy a cup of coffee, and a candy bar, the kind Darwin used to keep in her desk.

Soon the GPS brought Morgan to Nuttle's address. The building was half standing and half dismantled, surrounded by piles of smashed cinderblock and exposed rebar. The sheared, open sections of the building had been hammered up with plywood to create something that was more or less upright.

Morgan walked up four stories of broken concrete and twisted handrails and located the apartment down the hallway.

The rooms were little better than squatters' quarters. Only in the post-pandemic world, even 15 years on, could anyone get away with renting shitholes like these, he thought. He stood and knocked.

Behind the door he could hear the chugging of a small generator, then the click of the door just before LeSans opened it to the chain. She looked exhausted. She always did, but now her sallow skin resembled wet, sagging paper. She gave Morgan a weak smile and released the chain.

"Are you warm enough?" He asked.

"Most of the time, thanks to the generator. We use the money you send to pay for that. But it can get a little breezy on really cold days."

"You make sure to keep her warm." He looked sternly at LeSans.

"Don't you give me a hard time," she said. "I have enough to handle."

Morgan nodded an apology.

LeSans pointed. "She's in her room."

Morgan shoved a card into his hand. "A few credits," he said. "Not much. I'll get more..."

LeSans nodded. "Thanks. She's been waiting."

Morgan pulled his coat tight around himself and walked to her room.

"Hi, Nuttle," he said.

Nuttle turned her head and smiled, "Oh! My little one!"

Morgan could hardly find her in her bed. She seemed to be a bundle of sticks among the tattered blankets. The billowy strawberry hair was matted now; the cherubic cheeks drawn and wrinkled. In his mind, in all the years they had spent at Sec 17, she had never seemed to age. But now ...

Morgan looked back at LeSans.

"I give her food," she said. "Really. But she's stopped eating."

LeSans dragged a wooden chair across the concrete floor and left it next to the bed. It made a harsh grating sound that rang in Morgan's ears. He stood over Nuttle, and she forced a smile.

"You look so big," she said, "and pretty."

"How are you?" He asked. Morgan fluffed her pillow and sat down.

She patted at the chair with her hand. "I'm okay. Sister LeSans gives me something that makes me feel good."

"I have some presents," said Morgan.

"For me?" She said, "Aren't you so good."

He began rustling through his rucksack. "I thought I would read for you,"

"I like it when you read," she said laying back down.

Then he grew alarmed. "Where is it?" He searched the rucksack for the battered book he had brought, and then his jacket, and then the rucksack again. "Dammit!" He said, rifling the contents. Finally, he stood, gripping his fists. "Fuck! I left it behind. Sonovabitch!" Morgan slammed the bag down on the floor, his eyes welling with tears. "How could I be so stupid!" He rubbed his neck and kicked the chair away.

"How could I forget?" And began sobbing. "I wanted to read for you ... "

Nuttle reached over and patted the bed.

"Shhhh," she said.

"But I wanted to read to you ... "

"Was it the Alice book?" Asked Nuttle quietly.

"Yes, *Alice Through the Looking Glass*. Your favorite."

She nodded and smiled. "Tell me the story with the funny names. The one you always know by heart."

Morgan took a deep breath. "Yes," he said. "I'll tell you that one."

"Yes," said Nuttle.

Quietly, Morgan sat down.

"'Twas brillig, and the slithy toves
Did gyre and gimble in the wabe;
All mimsy were the borogoves,
And the mome raths outgrabe."

Now, he began to get into the rhythm of the poem, telling it in the way that used to make Nuttle's eyes go wide.

"Beware the Jabberwock, my son
The jaws that bite, the claws that catch!
Beware the Jubjub bird, and shun
The frumious Bandersnatch!"

Nuttle smiled and coughed a dry cough. She settled on her pillow watching. Slowly her eyes closed. Absently Morgan reached into his shirt pocket and pulled out the chocolate bar he had bought at the bodega.

"He took his vorpal sword in hand;
Long time the manxome foe he sought--
So rested he by the Tumtum tree,
And stood awhile in thought."

Morgan unwrapped the chocolate bar, holding the bottom of it like the hilt of a sword, and then he brandished it, the way he and Reba used to do.

"And, as in uffish thought he stood,
The Jabberwock, with eyes of flame,
Came whiffling through the tulgey wood,
And burbled as it came!"

Morgan leapt onto his chair, wielding and sweeping the chocolate bar back and forth.

"One, two! One, two! And through and through
The vorpal blade went snicker-snack!
He left it dead, and with its head
He went galumphing back."

And back Morgan galumphed holding the candy bar out to Nuttle in triumph.

"And hast thou slain the Jabberwock?" he called out to

Nuttle.

"Come to my arms, my beamish boy!

O frabjous day! Callooh! Callay!"

He chortled in his joy."

"Nuttle?" He said quietly, leaning over her. "I have slain the Jabberwock!"

Nuttle lay on the bed, nestled in her blanket, smiling, eyes closed.

"Nuttle?" he said.

But he already knew...

"'Twas brillig, and the slithy toves

Did gyre and gimble in the wabe;" he whispered to her.

"All mimsy were the borogoves,

And the mome raths outgrabe."

He reached out and touched her cheek and held it for a long time, her smile unchanged.

He had always been good at not crying. But not this time.

38

Alone

Morgan sat for a while beside Nuttle. She looked so frail. How brittle the human body was. How, despite all its efforts to fight off death, it always succumbed. Others may have thought Nuttle was an idiot, a drag on the human race, but he knew how much she had changed his life and how he could never have survived without her. She had been worth more than all the world's ideas and inventions and witticisms. What an ugly burglar death was.

Being 14 years of age, Morgan had no power over what the officials did with Nuttle's body. He could make no funeral arrangements because he had no official standing, and now that he had erased himself from the GRID, he couldn't even rightly say he existed. And LeSans was broke.

He and LeSans stayed at the apartment through the next morning, not knowing quite what to do. They drank some weak tea and reminisced about Nuttle. The coroner came and took her body away. LeSans cried and cried, and wondered how she would get on without her friend. By afternoon they realized there was nothing to do except gather up Nuttle's few possessions and never forget her.

That night Morgan slept on her floor. The next morning, he gave LeSans all but a few of his credits before heading out. "I'll try to get some money to you," he said, and then kissed the Spider

Lady on her hard and furrowed brow.

#

He was entirely alone now. That was true. But he was also entirely free.

For a while Morgan wandered, unaware of where he was or where he was headed. The wind ran through him like little knives. He turned up the heat on the hyper-fiber jacket that he had lifted from Ralph, and sat down on a couple of cinderblocks. He needed to check the other swag he had lifted during his departure from the Fishers. He felt some guilt about what he had stolen ... for about three seconds. The Fishers had taken most of his money for over a year. He figured it was more than a square deal for him to take a few objects back.

From his cinderblock seat, Morgan developed a plan. Drawing on his swag he would immediately upgrade Lois, and then sell the remaining electronics. He checked his phone. It had about ~50 credits in the Limited Liability Company he had created online under an assumed name during his days with the Fishers.

That little bit of money would buy food for a couple of days, but it was nowhere near enough for a night's sleep, even in an overnight sleep pod. If he paid for that, he'd be broke in two days.

He zipped his rucksack back up. One thing at a time. Right now, he needed electricity to power up his electronics, and a reasonably warm place to do the tinkering required to make Lois smarter. But where? A library was out. They wouldn't look kindly on someone deconstructing phones and PADs on one of the library tables. Ditto with coffee shops. The airport might work. No, too far away, and too costly to get there.

He walked among the blasted and empty quarters of old DC, and then as dusk was falling and the wind was picking up, he wandered into a Metro stop and found a corner at the far end behind a large pillar. Maybe he could hide there. But when he crept to the pillars, he found something even better: an old maintenance room. Its metal door was bent so badly it couldn't be closed, but Morgan thought he could repair that. He crept inside.

The space was perfect, but the moment he arrived he saw he couldn't stay. The room was claimed. It wasn't large, maybe 15 x 30 feet, but it had electricity, five battered lockers and a small sink with running water.

By the looks of it, a few people had set up housekeeping. Before the plague, it must've been a place where maintenance workers cleaned up and changed out their transit uniforms. The floor was bare cement with a French drain. The walls were ceramic tile, filthy now, but mostly intact. At one end, near the wall socket, sat some cinderblocks with a hot plate and an empty coffee pot on top. A small box held a few packets of freeze-dried food.

At the other end of the room were the lockers. Morgan inspected them. They had been broken into so many times, not even the latches worked, except one, heavily padlocked. The rest of the lockers were stuffed with clothing, old sleeping bags, a little food. His mouth watered, but he didn't dare touch anything. He wouldn't want to tip the occupants to his visit. He just needed the warmth and power for a while so he could rev up his computer and write the code he needed to boost Lois. Then he'd be gone. He assumed that post-plague GRIDlings were the squatters in the room, and they could be pretty nasty. Fifteen years after the plague they were no longer children. Some topped 30 years of age, and wouldn't know how to live except on the streets.

They did this under a tribal system, with small and large sects that roamed territories run by "totos" who were generally the smartest, strongest, and most ruthless members of their groups, a throwback to the days of hunter-gatherers where it was beat or be beaten.

GRIDlings still comprised vast populations in most cities.

They set up their own civil (or uncivil) governance, shadow economies and transportation grids.

This wasn't the first time in human history shadow civilizations coexisted with traditional ones. Victorian London had been loaded with street urchins and orphans; New York in the early 20th century had brimmed with gangs run by the likes of *The Whyos* and *Eastman Gang*; Hiroshima, after the bomb, had the *Murakami* and *Oka* gangs. Los Angeles ran highly sophisticated gangs in the 1980s and 1990s, and Mexico City and São Paulo did too, right up to the days of The Plague itself.

It was a tribute to human ingenuity the way desperation bred so many creative ways to stay alive. Later in his life, Morgan reflected on this. Even under the most brutal circumstances, humans were social creatures and they needed to help one another whether they liked it or not. Of course there were always short-term casualties, but in the long run, if every member of the human race turned on those around them, we would have long ago wiped ourselves out.

But Morgan could hardly count on the kindness of strangers just now as he settled into a corner near the outlet and got to work. His goal was to gather as many resources for himself as he could. He wasn't going to knife or club or intimidate others on the street. He was 14. He'd have to use his wits. That was the plan, even if Morgan hadn't yet codified it. His mind was his power. He needed to draw from that as surely as the PAD on his lap was drawing power from the wall socket next to him.

39

Reunion

Morgan had just debugged the last line of code when he heard voices. He stowed everything he had into his rucksack just as his arrivals pushed open the creaking door. A tall, young woman entered and after a long pause regarded him.

"Well, well, I can't believe it! Look what the fuckin' cat dragged in."

Morgan stood upright and rigid. The voice wasn't menacing exactly, but it had an edge. Had he heard it before?

"Out on the pavements, are we? But I thought old Sr. Darwin had found you a *good* home?"

And then Morgan realized he was looking at Reba! A Reba he didn't recognize. Her head was shaved on one side and long and heavy on the other. It flopped in front of her right eye and was a deep purple. She had acquired several tattoos and piercings. Standing beside her was a tall, muscular kid, 18 or 19 years old, with a long thin nose and fiery red hair. Two other GRIDlings, maybe 11-years-old, stood beside him -- a girl with a mess of curly, blonde hair and a wary looking boy with a dark buzz cut and heavy tattoos over mocha arms that were hardly meatier than two chopsticks.

"You look like roadkill," Reba said to Morgan.

"You're looking lovely yourself," he replied, trying not to act surprised.

She shot Morgan that crooked smile and snorted. "Yeah, well, it's an unforgiving world."

"What the fuck are you doin' here?" Said the red head. And then he turned to Reba. "What's he doin' here?"

"Hi, Z," said Morgan. He couldn't miss Z's fiery hair and angry mouth.

"We don't needs 'im. We're doing jus fine," said Z. "Where the fuck did he come from, anyhow?"

"Z remains as bazoomie as ever," said Reba, "and he's being a little over optimistic. Getting along just fine might not be quite accurate. These here..." – Reba pointed to her other two minions -- "...we call the twins. They do the grunt work."

Morgan nodded, but wasn't sure what would happen next.

"What's in the packsack?" Reba asked. "You got some goodies for us?"

"A few things I brought from my foster family."

Reba sauntered over and took the bag. "Didn't go so well, your family experience?" She zipped the bag open, and her eyes went wide. "Delightful!" She looked at Morgan and swung the bag over her shoulder. "We'll have to relieve you of this, you ken that."

"I need Lois," Morgan said evenly.

"Shut up, pissant," barked Z. "We take what we want."

"Lois?" Asked Reba. She nodded. "Right. Your electronic sidekick. Forgot about her, or should I say 'it'." She reached into the bag and pulled the PAD out.

"This it?" Her eyebrows arched.

Morgan nodded.

She gave him the PAD. "Thanks," said Morgan. Then he pointed at the pack. "And for all those goodies in there, I get to stay here."

"Fuck you!" Said Z.

Reba turned to the two twins, and said, "Go out there and scrape up some grub. It's almost dinnertime." It was an order, not a request and the two were gone in an instant. "And Z," Reba said in a voice that was almost plaintive, "can you go with them?" She shrugged, "You know, in case of trouble."

Z looked suspiciously at Morgan, and then Reba. He didn't move.

"Come on, now," she urged. "Those kids move fast, but if they run into trouble ..." She opened her hands in a gesture of futility... "No dinner."

Still Z hesitated.

"Go!" This time Reba's message was harsh. "They move faster 'n a couple of Metro rats! And I'm hungry, damnit!"

Finally Z strode to the door, but not before departing with one last withering glare directed at Morgan. Reba closed her eyes in a subtle show of exasperation.

"Z has always had a problem with you. He's jealous, I guess."

"Jealous?" Said Morgan cocking his head. "You mean like jealous, jealous?"

"Aw fuck no, not like that. Like a kid who's jealous of his brother jealous. Sibling jealous." She sat down on one of the sleeping bags, pulled Morgan's rucksack from her shoulder and examined its contents more closely. "He's crazier than sack of snakes. But he's fast and strong and angry. And angry can be damned handy out there."

He looked at Reba. She had aged five years. "I can see that," said Morgan.

"You have no idea how ugly it is." Tears briefly welled up, but she blinked and straightened up. "Here's the deal." She returned the backpack after taking almost everything out of it. "You can have Lois and those few other things I just left you, but I keep the rest of your haul." She was placing the various chips and electronics into her own ragged backpack. She smiled. "Looks

164

like you did well. I'll fence all this and take 50% for the family. You get the rest of the money."

"Family?" Morgan said, raising an eyebrow.

"It's a fucked-up family. But it's a family." She said with finality.

Morgan nodded. "Ok" he said. "But I need a place to stay."

Reba looked at him.

"Until I get on my feet," said Morgan.

Reba gave that some more thought. "Okay. That's fair. But then I take 75%. And if Z murders you in your sleep, I'm not responsible."

Morgan laughed.

Reba looked at him. "I'm not kidding."

Morgan stopped laughing, and then Reba laughed. Morgan pointed at the packsack in Reba's lap. "There's a keyboard in there. I'll need that too."

"Still working magic on the GRID, are we?"

Morgan shrugged. She pulled the keyboard out and handed it to him.

"That sort of talent could be handy." She admitted. "Okay, find a spot where you can bed down. I'll handle Z for now." She stood up and walked to her own locker and then looked back. "And careful of the twins. They can be dangerous too."

#

Morgan came to call the little abode in which they all lived "The Closet." After that first day, he never left. At least not before he arranged better quarters.

It happened slowly at first – Morgan taking charge. Initially the others tolerated him. Reba was entirely in his corner, but she had to act tough when the others were around to show them who was boss. And that worked fine. The "twins" followed her lead and didn't give Morgan any trouble.

Z was the issue. He was paranoid and perpetually furious.

Morgan's arrival threatened his relationship with Reba who was the only form of stability he had ever experienced in his utterly toxic existence. His fears were routinely taken out on Morgan in the form of veiled threats and little power plays. Morgan would find some of his electronics missing, or snacks would disappear.

Once Z threatened him with a knife when he had gotten hold of some alcohol somewhere, but Reba made it clear neither alcohol nor sharp objects were tolerated in the "family," and took both from him.

"We stick together, unnerstand. And whosoever struggles with those rules is invited out, and I mean permanent!" She smashed the bottle of booze and threw the knife so closely at Z's head Morgan thought he might've lost an ear. It was a parenting moment for Z, and for the twins, just in case they got any wild adolescent ideas.

Reba was very good this way. She ran the ship tight. Z's craziness complemented Reba's command, and the twins did what they were told, like a couple of pups in a wolf pack. That was the way it was.

But then Morgan began to uncover better ways for all of them to survive, and that shifted the family dynamic. At first, he did clever little things like rig up a simple shower with some of the hoses that he had lifted from a construction site. And then he built a proper stove and even a little camp oven. But all of that was nothing compared to what he came up with next.

40

Io

Io awaited Morgan's arrival. It was hardly more than a minute when she heard him knock. She told the door to open and walked around the counter between the kitchen and living room. Morgan stood in the hallway dripping wet from the snow. His bright green eyes glanced at Io, then away. His curly black hair glistened and hung loose around his forehead. He stepped in.

"Hi," he said, his eyes on the floor. "Lot of snow out there." He brushed snow from his curls. "Look, I'm sorry about this."

Io gathered her robe around her. "It's okay. I got a whole two hours of sleep last week so I'm refreshed. Coffee?"

"Sure," Morgan looked for a place to sit, but seemed uncomfortable with the idea. He was so wet. He walked to the counter and stood a little awkwardly.

Io held out a cup to him. "Black, the way you like it."

Morgan took the cup. "Yeah." He looked perplexed. "Thanks."

"You look like a drown rat. That can't be comfortable. Wait here a minute." She disappeared into the bedroom.

Morgan looked around. The room was warm and homey, not something he would really have expected from Io who seemed so efficient and professional. He would have expected lots of gray and black granite, shiny metal and glass. But the place featured brick walls and soft lighting and a very realistic virtual fire crackling in the fireplace.

Io walked out of the bedroom, dressed in jeans and a turtleneck, and laid a pair of pants, socks and a sweater across the couch.

"I think you'll find that these fit." She walked into the kitchen, and turned away from him as she refilled her coffee cup. "Go ahead. I won't peek."

Morgan snatched up the pants, stripped the soaked ones off and slipped the dry ones on. They fit perfectly. He pulled his shirt off and put the fresh sweater and socks on.

"Thanks," he said. She turned around cupping the coffee in her hand. He ran his hands through his hair again and tried to shake the water out. "You always keep a spare set of men's clothes around?"

Io cocked her head. "Are you always this strange? Is there something wrong with you?"

"Something wrong ..." How did he answer *that*?

"Deirdre tells me you're under a lot of pressure, but has it done some kind of brain damage?"

Again he looked at her, clueless.

"You were here last week, Morgan," Io said. "You spent the night with me, and the next night...and then, poof, it was like you beamed to another planet. Then I see you this morning and tonight and you act as if we never spent a minute together ... "

Morgan was so focused on the conversation, and Io was so frustrated with the way he was acting, that neither of them noticed the five tiny black spots that were growing on the walls around them.

He reached again for his coffee cup, when, suddenly, the mug exploded. Io yelped. Morgan spun to see a spiderbot hovering near the ceiling by the door. He hit the floor just as it spit another luminescent stream of venom where he had been standing. The couch burst into flame.

Io ran for a kitchen drawer and yanked it out. Cooking utensils crashed to the floor.

"Damn!" she hissed. "Where is it?"

She ducked behind the counter and found a second drawer as another bot dropped from the ceiling and fired on her. With her back against the cabinets, Io's hand searched the drawer above her and finally found the gun. She pivoted and aimed at the bot hovering near the bedroom. A blue light burst from the gun in her hand and with a squeal the bot disintegrated. A third bot scuttled from under a chair. A long tentacle slithered from its belly directly under the couch and seized Morgan's ankle. He grabbed at his foot as the tentacle tightened and another glowing stream of venom shot by his head.

"Shit!" he yelled. He seized the tentacle, furious, and snapped it clean off. The bot screamed and pulled the ragged end of itself back into its belly.

"Where are you?" Morgan yelled. "Over here."

"Time to get the hell out of here!"

Io poked her head around the corner of the cabinet, looking for Morgan, and there he was, facing her. She screamed before she realized it was him and as they faced one another, Morgan saw a spiderbot poised to attack her. In one leap he was in front of the bot, and a second later he smashed it to the floor with his fists.

Io looked at him, her eyes wide. *How did he do that?* Morgan turned and pulled her to her feet as another tentacle snatched away her gun and flung it through the glass window. The bot's silvery arm coiled back like a cobra behind them, ready to strike, but before it could, Morgan pulled Io through the door. It closed behind them and they stood in the hallway.

"Lock!" Io shouted to the door. For a moment, they only gulped air, and then noticed more black puffs seeping beneath the door.

"Shit," Morgan said, and they turned to sprint down the hall to the elevator. Morgan punched repeatedly on the button. "Shit!"

The indicator showed the elevator was one floor away, coming up.

The smoke beneath Io's apartment door had now morphed into three hovering spiderbots. Their cyclopean eyes rose hissing on their snakelike necks and scanned the walls and floors of the hallway with red slits of light.

There was a light ping. The elevator door opened and a bad muzak version of "God Rest Ye Merry Gentlemen" spilled into the air. Morgan and Io jumped inside. A second later the three bots arrived, rotating toward the elevator in perfect unison. A single scarlet eye slowly extended from the center robot. Would the door never close? The things made a low sibilant sound, their eyes pulsing. The doors closed, at last, but not before a tentacle shot forward and wrapped itself around Io's throat. She gagged, struggling to free herself, and as the elevator began to rise, it dragged her to the floor. In a second it would decapitate her. Morgan hit the emergency stop, grabbed the tentacle and, without a thought, snapped it clean. There was a muffled screech beyond the doors as the remainder of the robotic arm dropped from Io's neck and slithered aimlessly along the elevator floor.

Io was unconscious. Her breathing was ragged and her neck scarlet. The elevator rose to the top floor and stopped. Morgan sat, holding Io, and gazed blankly at the doors. He couldn't understand why they were still alive.

41

Money

The idea, the one that would change everything, had been percolating in Morgan's mind for several weeks when he first sprung it on Reba. One day the two of them were walking through an upscale part of DC, talking about how hungry they were when Morgan made a sudden right turn into a restaurant. It was a nice one. Very nice.

Reba was skeptical, but she followed. Morgan found a place to sit and motioned Reba over. By the time she made it to the table, Morgan was seated looking over the holographic menu at the table.

"Have a seat," said Morgan. "And let's have some food."

Reba looked around expecting to get tossed out of the place. They looked like the outcasts they were, and it made the other patrons uncomfortable.

"Have you lost your marbles?" Reba hissed. "We can't afford to eat here."

Morgan gestured to the other chair at the table and said, "Sure we can." He tapped the menu a few times and completed his order. Then he turned it to Reba.

"How did you do that?" She gestured at the menu "You need real credits in a bank account to get away with that."

"And I do," said Morgan. "500 of 'em."

"Really," she said skeptically. "You don't even have a bank account. You can't because you erased yourself."

Morgan waved a hand. "I fixed that problem a long time ago. Don't you know Jasper?"

"Jasper?"

"Jasper P Hawthorne ... " Morgan grinned, gesturing at himself. " ... in the flesh."

"You made up an identity?"

"Several actually. We have about 20 different bank accounts, our little family. You know, an identity here, another one there ... and every one of them in the green." Morgan took his phone from his pocket and turned it toward Reba. Sure enough it revealed that the bank account of Jasper P Hawthorne had 500 credits in it.

Reba leaned across the table. "Is that the plan then? Get off the streets and take a nice vacation in jail?"

Morgan grinned again. "I'm far too clever for that. So what are you having? I hear the sushi here is frabjous!"

#

Morgan had 500 credits in the bank because he had developed, something he called "whacking." It relied on stealing small amounts of cash from a rotating assortment of bank accounts. He had to be careful not to take too much from too many accounts. To supplement this income he also found ways to counterfeit digital coupons and discounts. It was just a matter of a clever algorithm here and there. He'd buy the merchandise online at a cheap discount with the counterfeit coupons, then fence them at a profit.

That was the beginning. Morgan was good, and careful. Soon the family's days of street thievery were behind them, and he and Reba moved the rest of the brood out of The Closet. The new abode wasn't anything terribly fancy, just a small apartment with three bedrooms, a real shower, two baths and a kitchen, but it beat the hell out of living in a maintenance shed.

Even before working up his whacking scheme, Morgan knew

it could take them only so far. He needed better ways to increase the family income.

One night, as he lay alone in his bed, combing the GRID for some shred of information about his mother, he decided to relieve his frustration by pulling out the VR game station he had bought and slip into an online game.

The GRID had recovered enough from the plague by now that online games had once again become the opiate of the masses. Except that with the emergence of the GRID, gaming had evolved along slightly different lines than it had during the old days of the Internet.

On the GRID, multiple online game portals emerged that housed scores of other games within each of them – like great virtual arcades, a kind of Netflix for games. Some games were mysteries, others were fantasies or puzzles, or role-playing or adventures games. There were steam punk worlds and alien worlds, futuristic worlds and ancient ones, anything imaginable, with names like *Gamester, ENTellect, World War X*. Any player could log in as the avatar he or she had created. Each portal became a society unto itself.

The fundamental difference between the new GRID and the old Internet was that the GRID's virtual worlds and the real world intersected. At first, black markets emerged where players informally sold or traded weapons or charms, or even whole avatars. It was all very much "on the street."

Then one of the porthole operators had an idea – create an "X-Change" where anything of value from any game or virtual world within any porthole could be bought and sold and converted. This meant a sword in some Dungeons and Dragon fantasy game could be sold at the X-change to buy a ticket to, say, a Mars world that was entirely different. Or you could cash in a sorcery charm for a gun needed in a Steampunk game. In short, virtual objects or money or powers could be bartered just as if they operated in some great digital flea market.

In time, an immense and vibrant digital marketplace emerged. Online pawnshops opened within the GRID. Virtual stores arose, even brokerage houses. The markets were completely dynamic with the values of every object in the universe changing constantly. One day a particular charm might be worth seven credits, the next it might be worth 12. A dukedom from a medieval game, which could take months, and considerable skill, to acquire, might be worth thousands of credits.

The owners of the X-Change made their money by taking a small cut of each virtual transaction; real money. The one difference was that in this world, the assets themselves were non-existent, nothing but zeroes and ones. They were as ephemeral as mist. Yet, profits skyrocketed. And the X-Change, and related portals, began to make very serious money.

Soon players, the ones that were good, realized that they could gather up charms and swords, guns and digital money, convert it on the X-Change and make a substantial living simply by being good at playing games. One of those players was Morgan.

#

Before Morgan implemented his plan to make money playing games, he did what he always did: he consulted Lois.

"Lois," he said to his PAD one late night.

"Yes, Morgan."

"Let's say I became really good at the *House of Pain* game."

"I'm sure you could do that," she said politely. "You're intelligent and your hand eye coordination is excellent."

"True, true and thanks. But if I did and I moved up to the top levels of that game, I would win a lot of weapons and charms and powers, right?"

"That's the way games like that work as I understand it. Other games take more mental acuity. *Bramble* and *Da Vinci*, for example. You can win awards in those games too. And some games are virtual worlds were charm and social grace can lead to success and improved status."

"Yeah. I probably shouldn't try those games."

There was a pause. "Maybe not," Lois said.

"How much money could I make?"

"In the games...?"

"Yes, the ones I could become good at."

There was a pause. "I'm not sure I know where you are headed here?"

"In the X-Change."

"It would depend on two related issues: how fast you can become proficient, and how much time you can spend playing the games."

"Let's say I played 10 hours a day and can become proficient in four games within four weeks."

"That would be very difficult."

"I know but do the calculations just for kicks."

"I'll need to go out on the GRID, do some crawling and spend some time reading and watching."

"Of course."

"I'll be back in an hour."

For 60 minutes Morgan took a long nap. He was snoring peacefully when Lois woke him up.

"I have some figures."

"Am I going to be rich?"

"You could make some decent money.... If you can learn and perform as you propose."

"How much?"

"Given the assumptions, ~1000 per week."

"That's it?"

"I'm trying to be reasonable."

"You and reason."

"One of us has to be reasonable."

"Ha! That's very funny, Lois," Morgan said. "Very authentic."

"Ha – ha – ha," said Lois, not at all authentically. "Thank you."

"Make a note," said Morgan. "Work on that laugh."

"Noted," Said Lois.

"Also, that's not enough."

"Enough what?"

"Money."

"If you say so."

"Not for the whole family."

"Why not get the rest of them involved?" Said Lois.

"That," said Morgan, "is brilliant!"

#

And that was how Morgan set it up. Gaming became the family business. First, he dispatched Lois to crawl the GRID and watch as many games on the *World War X* porthole as possible because it was the most popular one. Lois' analysis showed that that was also where players were willing to pay the most for *World War X* charms and weapons.

Next Morgan spent the following three weeks whacking online accounts. When he had pooled what he thought were enough credits, he sat down with Reba after everyone else was asleep and laid it out for her. He would use the money he had acquired to buy four more VR game stations. "Then we give each one to the twins and Z, and one for you, of course."

"Z might actually get to like you," she said, smiling crookedly.

"That'll make my day," said Morgan. "If everyone can become half-way decent at these games, their begging, stealing and people-fragging days'll be over."

That was good enough for Reba. She was exhausted from the responsibility of maintaining the family. Besides, the truth was Morgan had already been their savior. Every member of the family would probably have been in jail or a hospital or dead if he hadn't come along.

When Morgan had finally scraped together enough credits to buy the VR stations, he and Reba called the others together for a pow-wow.

"You are shitting me," said Z. "Make a living with games!? That's bazoomie." He turned to Reba. "Are you going to let this twerp talk you into this?"

"Yes I am," said Reba. "You like fighting and stealing out there?" She pointed to the apartment door. "Feel free to leave."

"An' how're we supposed tah survive," Said Z. "What are we gonna do, eat the VR game station?"

Morgan handed Z his station. "Z, you ever play any of these games?"

"Some of us don't have time for games," Z sneered.

Morgan pointed to the station he'd given Z. "You," he said, "are going to be a kick ass gamer."

"Really? And you would know that how?"

"Intuition. I've been playing for weeks now. I've pulled in 2000 credits."

"Bullshit."

"I'll bet you'll be better than me."

"There is no way you made that much money playing games."

Morgan pulled out a ~100 credit and handed it to Z.

Z looked at the bill, and then back at Morgan. He had never actually seen one in the flesh. Still, he was skeptical. Morgan said, "Give it a week. Let me teach you a few things, and then you try it. If you don't like it, keep the money, sell the machine, keep *that* money, and go back to breaking knees."

"And if I do?"

"Like it?"

"Yeah."

"You can still have the money because we're all going to be doing just fine."

They did too. Every day Lois fed Morgan its analyses of game winning strategies and tactics, and Morgan practiced them relentlessly. Soon he was passing along more new skills to Reba and Z and the twins.

Morgan quickly outpaced the rest of the family, but as a group they all did well. Z *was* good. He took too many chances, but his hand eye coordination often compensated for his hot-headed reactions and lack of strategic thinking. Reba was methodical and made steady progress. The twins piddled but grew a little better each day.

Within two months they had enough credits that Morgan was able to shop for a real townhouse. Three stories, and a bedroom for each of them. It included a big kitchen and a porch, three full baths and a jacuzzi. Some weeks the game playing business went well. Others not so much. It all depended on the X-Change. Like the stock market, sometimes it went up. Sometimes down. The law of supply and demand dominated. But Morgan was a whiz and as everyone else upped their game, their status, and income, steadily grew.

For six months the plan worked beautifully. And then one day it didn't. The X-Change had gone on a bad run, and the family was low on credits. Morgan rarely did much whacking these days, but now and again he might fill in a cash flow gap here or there. One particular day he whacked several accounts. He rarely paid attention to those he broke into, but the name on one caught his eye: a scientist out of Carnegie Mellon University who was considered a real innovator when it came to artificial intelligence. When Morgan checked out his bank account, he saw it had plenty of cash, so he snatched up a few more credits than usual.

And that was dangerous error.

42

A Visitor

For the third time, Morgan heard the buzzer at the townhouse, and it was annoying the hell out of him. Why wasn't someone checking the door? Then he remembered: the twins were at lunch, Z was probably still asleep, and Reba was running family errands.

Morgan sighed and checked the security camera. The man doing the buzzing was a tall and slim man, with short silver hair, a square jaw and neatly trimmed beard which, strangely, was jet black. He wore a white shirt and an expression on his face that said he didn't have a care in the world. Nonchalantly, he hit the buzzer again.

Morgan watched him. The guy wasn't a cop. And he wasn't selling anything as far as he could see. Nor did he look dangerous. But he also didn't look like someone you would want to cross. There was a certain irresistible competence about him, which Morgan found both troubling and fascinating. He hit the buzzer again. He looked like he'd hit all day if necessary. That was probably the reason Morgan walked downstairs and opened the door. When he did, the man met his gaze and smiled. For 30 seconds or so he smiled this way, saying nothing, until finally Morgan said, "Can I help you?

"Hi, Jasper," he said. "Though I'm pretty sure that's not your actual name."

"I'm sorry," Morgan said. "You must have the wrong address. I'm not Jasper and no one by that name lives here."

The man laughed, a light, rich laugh like someone at a party making small talk. "Right, right. Not Jasper, Morgan. Because I know you're not Reba or Z or ... or what do you call them? The twins? No you are Morgan, Morgan Adams, the man, well, actually, the boy, who hacked my bank account yesterday and took my money. Not a lot of money, I'll admit. Still it was mine."

"I don't know what you're talking about," Morgan said.

"You're quite good. Extraordinarily good, really. It was tough to track down the trail, but of course even the best hackers leave one. I know because I was very good at that sort of thing once myself."

Morgan couldn't seem to move. Who was this person, and how did he know ... everything? He stood for a moment, riveted by the man's electric blue eyes, and then gave him a weak smile before saying, "Yeah, well ... nice chat ..." And then Morgan closed the door.

But before it shut, the man's foot blocked it. The voice on the other side remained calm. "I don't think you want to do that. I could get in touch with the police, and you'd be arrested pretty quickly. I have all the evidence." There was a pause. "Or we could talk."

Morgan re-opened the door, paused and then stepped aside. The man found a chair and sat down. "You're Daedalus Huxley," said Morgan.

"When did you figure it out?"

"Just now."

"Clever boy. Which is why I'm here ... Rather than talking to the police right now."

Morgan cleared some game controllers from a chair and sat down too. "Am I fucked?"

Huxley laughed his airy laugh. "Up to you. After my account

was hacked, and after I tracked you down, I realized, you're quite remarkable."

"How do you know about Reba and Z and the twins?"

"And Lois. I know about Lois too. By the way I'm very sorry about Nuttle." Huxley sat back and crossed one of his well-pressed legs over the other. "You're wondering how I know all of this." He spread his hands. "I have access to all of the cameras and microphones on all of your electronics. A little reverse hacking, I guess you could call it. So I guess I became a guest in your home here starting ... hmmmm ... about 22 hours ago."

The balls on this guy! He watched the man gazing at him with those eyes. "It's exceptional what you've done with the gaming set up and account hacking – or what do you call it? Whacking?"

"You've been monitoring everything we do?"

"Well, not everything. I'm not a barbarian."

"Even Lois?!"

"Especially Lois. She is your creation, isn't she?"

"Yes."

"A magnificent AI, considering she was created by a 15-year-old kid without an ounce of computer science or engineering training." There was a long silence as the two of them regarded one another. Finally, Huxley spoke again. "Here's my proposition. Have you ever heard of Carnegie Mellon University?"

"Yes, of course. You're a professor there. Kind of a big deal."

"Kind of. Director of Artificial Intelligence. I have two choices for you." He pulled out a phone. "I can call the police right now and have you arrested. Or you can come with me to Carnegie Mellon."

Morgan jumped to his feet. "What?" He said.

"You can enroll and become my student," Huxley continued, "and get your degree in computer science."

"You're nuts! I don't even have a high school diploma."

Huxley waved his hands. "You could probably get your GED in a week if you put your mind to it. Trivial."

"I'm 15."

"Again, trivial. When others see the work you've done; the code you've written for Lois, even your clever "whacking," I'm positive there will be no problem arranging for your matriculation."

Morgan shook his head. "Man, you have balls the size of Jupiter! You just walk in here and start laying out my whole future."

Huxley laughed. "You learn fast." He crossed his arms. "Come on. Need a decision."

Morgan chewed his lower lip and rubbed his neck.

"What about Reba And Z...?"

"The family? You will have to leave them behind." He said it matter-of-factly.

"I can't do that!"

Huxley arched an eyebrow. "You'd be leaving them behind if you go to jail."

Morgan stopped pacing long enough to look directly at Huxley and flip him the bird.

"Eloquent and concise," said Huxley. He looked at the ceiling for a second and then back at Morgan. "Look, this isn't a bad thing. You're wasted here. Come with me and you can have a very good life, spend time with people who appreciate your extraordinary talents. You'll have all the freedom and goodies and resources you want. You'll be able to explore anything you like – and based on what I've seen, that will be quite a bit."

Morgan resumed pacing.

"How do I know I can trust you?"

"You don't."

Morgan stopped again. "Not encouraging."

"If I wanted to simply get back my money, you'd already be in jail. I want you on my team. I want you to get a degree, work in my lab and cut that brain of yours loose. We both win. Or..." And he picked up the phone again.

Morgan shook his head. "I can't just abandon these guys."

"Leave them all of your money," Huxley replied. "I'll kick in another 5000 credits. That should help. I'll even kick in the next three months' rent. You've taught them plenty of ways to get along. You, however, need to move past all of this."

Morgan sat down. *Who the fuck was this guy?*

Huxley continued. "You can stay with me, all expenses paid until grad school at least. You're very gifted and I simply want to see those gifts blossom. I have a nice, airy apartment. There's plenty of room and the view is spectacular."

Morgan sat back and ran his hands through his hair. "This is bribery, you know."

"I think the actual term is extortion, but since you've already broken the law ... "

Another long silence. Finally Morgan said, "When would we have to leave?"

"Now. Gather up your stuff." He held up his phone again, this time to reveal two tickets. "We depart on the 1 PM train. First class." He turned toward the door and then turned back. "And don't forget all things Lois."

"I can't just leave!"

"Sure you can," said Huxley. "Explain later. They'll understand."

43

Carnegie Mellon University

Morgan did explain to the family why he disappeared, but despite Huxley's assurances, they did not understand. He sent a long text to Reba, and even Z and the twins. No responses. He sent a vid message. Nothing. They never answered or returned his calls. He left them all the money he had – ~1700 credits, ~6700 total with the money Huxley provided, plus the rent credits, but he still felt like a louse. He consoled himself with the knowledge that at least now they didn't have to live on the streets.

Life with Daedalus Huxley was not as horrible as he had feared. He was stuck with this bastard, but at least he was a generous bastard. And true to his word. He took Morgan into his home, a house that jutted like a ship beyond a promontory high above Mt. Washington and the gleaming, burgeoning city below.

Back when Pittsburgh had been the nation's forge, even before the two World Wars when it produced more steel than Japan and Germany put together, Mount Washington had been known as Coal Hill because anywhere you sunk a shaft in the ground, it was rich with the black rock. But now in 2040, the city's industrial past was long behind it, and a big reason was Carnegie Mellon and its expertise in artificial intelligence, robotics and computer interfaces. Much of it due to the brilliant work of the "bastard."

Before the plague, the three big players in computer science and engineering had been Stanford in Silicon Valley, MIT in Boston and CMU in Pittsburgh. The plague decimated Silicon Valley and Boston, and thus Huxley's AI labs at CMU became ascendant, and laid the ground for the company that eventually became Symbiosys, Inc.

But that lay some years in the future, and no one at the time could imagine the impact young Morgan Adams would have on that future … except maybe Daedalus Huxley. As Huxley had predicted, Morgan completed his GED and breezed through Carnegie Mellon's computer science courses. By 17, in less than two years, he earned his undergraduate degree. By 18 his masters. And by 20 a doctorate.

When Huxley moved him into his Lab as a postdoc, it was like giving the team a shot of adrenaline. No one had ever seen anyone who could code so swiftly while, at the same time, keeping the big picture in mind. There was an elegant efficiency in all his algorithms. It was like reading finely written passages in a great novel, or Mozart's nocturnes or the stark beauty of an Edward Hopper painting. But that was only part of it. He was a natural psychologist too, who had a unique knack for developing traits in a machine's software that made it feel more human.

Huxley attributed this ability to the lucky combination of raw talent, a loving caregiver (Nuttle), outrageously high intelligence, and the harsh environments of Sec 17 and the streets of Washington DC. The combination had shaped a wily, hyper-aware and highly motivated human obsessed with solving problems and bending everything around him to his own will. Huxley quickly saw that once Morgan got a problem in his sights, God help the person who got between him and a solution.

This didn't make Morgan perfect. The kid had issues. Empathy was not his strong suit, and he wasn't above using his high intelligence to manipulate people. Control was paramount and why wouldn't it be. He had grown up in an entirely chaotic world. Knowing this made Huxley cautious. He wanted a minion, not someone smart enough to supplant him. It was important to keep him under control.

When Morgan finally shared the code he used to create his most recent version of Lois, Huxley was thunderstruck. It had taken two full years before he revealed it. But Huxley had waited. He knew he had a prodigy on his hands, and there was no reason to rush. The golden eggs would come soon enough. And they did.

#

During his days at CMU, Morgan forged two more close friendships. One with Blaze, a gamer and programmer of truly legendary gifts. And Deirdre.

Deirdre had come from New England money. She dressed sharply, even when hanging out in the lab, nothing like the rest of CMU's CS denizens. This made her appear haughty, but, in fact, she was simply high strung, and preternaturally disciplined. While others were eating Doritos and gulping gallons of Mountain Dew, she was at the gym working out, doing wind sprints over at the university stadium and pulling all-nighters at the lab.

Blaze was Porsche's polar opposite. Slovenly, dissipated, a bowl of Jell-O masquerading as a human body. But what a mind! He could program almost as beautifully as Morgan, and, when the levels of Mountain Dew were just right in the bloodstream, attain heights of elegance and creativity in his code that would run chills up even Morgan's spine.

Blaze had another talent. He was the only person capable of making Deirdre laugh, which was no mean feat. He did this not with dry wit or snappy repartee – the sort of humor one might expect Deirdre to admire -- but with farts and burps and goofy dances and bad puns, any one of which would start Deirdre going, at first silently, and then with repressed snorts and giggles and finally comments like, "Oh my God, that's awful!" Or "Blaze, stop that! Please!" The more indelicate Blaze became, the harder

Deirdre laughed. Morgan couldn't figure it out. But he figured it must have been Deirdre's repressed side being given permission to toss away all that logic and discipline and Brahmin restraint. That was his best theory anyway.

Not that Morgan failed to see the appeal. Blaze was audacious and geeky and brilliant, and a breath of fresh air, even if it was sometimes hot air. Morgan could laugh for hours over beer and pizza with Blaze or spend all night battling him in online games.

But his conversations with Deirdre were far more thoughtful. They could go back and forth into dawn spit balling which forces and advances would most deeply shape the future. Morgan sometimes even shared his obsession with searching down his mother with Deirdre, and early in their friendship, she helped him code the first Knowbots which they quickly dispatched across the GRID hoping to come up with clues. The Knowbots, however, didn't have much more success finding his mother than he did.

#

As the years passed, Morgan came to look kindlier on The Bastard. As much as he hated to admit it, he always reserved the deepest of all his conversations for Huxley. By the time he had gotten his PhD there was nothing they couldn't talk about, but mostly they explored the world of artificial intelligence. Huxley took every opportunity to unpack Morgan's remarkable talents, using them to advance his lab, and his own notoriety, while the world marveled.

Huxley also taught his young student more about the way the world truly operated. Morgan learned by watching his professor, and then channeling him. The man appeared immensely confident, without seeming arrogant; apparently stable without being boring; strong without bullying. With his students, he was always patient, yet capable of revealing just the tiniest hint of disappointment which had the effect of motivating them to do almost anything to avoid failing him. With fellow professors he was collegial and seemed genuinely happy when a peer-reviewed paper was published or cited, or a big grant came through.

Huxley could afford to be magnanimous not so much because he was a good man, but because in the academic world, he knew that no matter how successful his peers were, he would always be smarter, handsomer, quicker, wittier, more successful. His benevolence was a subtle way of ingratiating himself with the colleagues he secretly considered inferior.

You might call it hubris, but whatever name you gave it, it didn't have to be stated. If Huxley was in command, he was a paragon. And he was always in command.

Morgan also learned some simple refinements from Daedalus. Slowly he lost his grimy jeans and filthy shirts, rancid from his endless all-night coding excursions. He learned to clip rather than chew his fingernails. He used only the best and latest personal technology. He improved his diet: less pizza, more fish. And eventually he got into first class shape. His teeth grew white and straight beneath regular brushings and two years of excruciating visits with the orthodontist Huxley introduced him to. He even bought more than one pair of shoes.

All these threads were slowly woven to become part of the new Morgan. Daedalus never forced the improvements. With Morgan, that wouldn't have worked anyway. But when Morgan was ready, money would show up in his account for new clothes, or better meals or a suggestion to join him for a workout. Morgan had to admit that in his way Daedalus was a kind of magician. A master of human behavior. And Huxley seemed to see in Morgan the same talent.

But could he keep that talent under his control?

#

The charms of Daedalus Huxley never shone more brightly than when he and Deirdre and Morgan held their first meetings with investors to outline the creation and funding of Symbiosis.

Huxley was a master salesman, and because his Lab could show off such compelling examples of its work, the presentations were more like elaborate shows than the academic exercises that so many other meetings with venture capitalists were. Daedalus knew investors wanted products with fresh markets, not technologies looking for solutions to problems the average consumer wouldn't need in a million years. He understood that now, two decades after the plague, the world was not busy and burdened, and that technology was only making them busier. They didn't need more technology, more stuff, more sink holes into which they could toss their time. They needed assistance. The kind that was humanlike, sympathetic, and truly looking out for them. The kind that was like Lois.

44

Evolution

Daedalus Huxley sat in his living room listening to a book. His book.

"DNA is a form of intelligence," said the audio narrator he was listening to, "although we don't normally think of it that way. It's a code that links four molecules in different combinations, along a great twisting ladder. The sequence in which they link store the instructions for replicating another version of itself, which makes it capable of spontaneously creating, almost magically, every form of life on Earth--an African dung beetle, a redwood tree, a human.

"When a baby is born, the tight coil of her DNA not only shapes the personal future of that child, but it holds the history of all the creatures that came before.

"This means that the ancient remnants of our DNA, the ones that enabled us to survive long ago as foraging primates that roamed the savannas, wild-eyed with fear, remain within us. It means that the clever apes who developed the cunning to invent tools, hunt in packs and, in time, bring down entire species, are all in our blood. The passion for greed, the circuitry for panic, the pathways for love and altruism, the foundations of disdain, manipulation, pleasure and thrills remain within all of us, buffeting us in ways we cannot conceive. They are inarticulate and elusive. But they are there; the invisible hand that drives everything we do."

Daedalus had written the book many years ago when he was trying to fathom how to build an intelligent, purely, digital creature. What would such a thing look and act like? Soulless? Alien? Unpredictable? Certainly not human, or, perhaps, even truly able to relate to humans.

Daedalus never really figured out how to solve the AI problem; not until Morgan came along. And Daedalus hated him for that. He was stroking the leather arm of his chair, and gazing from his penthouse, the snow rippling through a million lights in broad waves like a tremendous flag, when MALCOLM appeared in the chair next to him.

The ENT turned to Huxley as if he had been sitting there the whole time. "Have you ever known anyone more obsessed with death than Morgan Adams?" He asked.

Daedalus tried to appear calm. He raised an eyebrow. "No."

"He is obsessed with death and dying."

"Yes."

"And did you not tell him that he would be dead soon, again, if he did not find the nanochip that we all so desperately want to find?"

"Yes."

MALCOLM rose. "Then why hasn't he found it?"

"Haven't we already had this conversation?"

MALCOLM walked silently to the other end of the enormous room. ENTs had no weight so always walked silently; another trait that gave them an unsettling quality.

"You would think dying once would be enough for him," MALCOLM snapped. "But you wouldn't know it. You'd think he had all the time in the world. I even dispatched some spiderbots to put a scare into him, and still no results."

MALCOLM raised his hand before Daedalus could say

anything. "Don't worry, I didn't hurt him. I know we need him."

"Yes, we do. What's he up to?"

"I only know what the homing sensors tell me," said MALCOLM. "The recording devices we planted on him won't work. With all that computing power operating in him, he's like a walking radar jammer. I only know that he's gone to Io Luu's."

"That's good," Huxley said, smiling. "He was spending a lot of time with her the last few days before his murder. Maybe she knows something."

"A way to get laid. That's why he went to her place before he was killed. And that's why he's there now, I'm sure."

Daedalus crossed one creased leg over the other. "I doubt that," he said. "We know he finds Io attractive, that's why I asked Deirdre to make contact with her. But I think Morgan has a little too much on his digital mind right now to worry about getting laid."

MALCOLM resumed pacing along the windows and snorted. "He's human! You're *all* sex-starved. No hornier primate ever came down the evolutionary pike. Frankly, I don't get it."

"Is he?" Huxley asked.

"What?"

"Human?"

"He is up here." MALCOLM put his index finger to his perfectly bald head. "At least for now. The machinery may have changed, but the software that's running it is still the same old Morgan, which is to say "normal" and in no way "augmented."

"That's the way we set it up," said Daedalus.

"And that's the way I want it to stay," continued MALCOLM. "I can't have any superhumans running around with augmented powers. On the other hand, maybe his "normal" mind and body explains why he's taking so damned long to find this chip. If we boosted his cyborg capacities a little instead of keeping them capped, maybe he would have found the damned chip by now."

"Don't worry," said Daedalus, "he's got plenty of neuronal firepower, even at normal speed."

MALCOLM produced a cigarette, or at least a digital facsimile of one, and began to smoke. This was an affectation Huxley had programmed into him, like MALCOLM's sarcastic sense of humor and general crankiness. Huxley himself had given up smoking decades ago, but he got a vicarious kick out of watching his virtual assistant light up. Except he noticed that MALCOLM wasn't acting much like his assistant any longer. Huxley didn't care for that. It was exactly that concern that had been on his mind when MALCOLM had so rudely interrupted him. He was worried about how powerful the ENT was becoming. He still believed he could control MALCOLM, but for how long?

"What I don't understand is why you humans can't be more efficient," MALCOLM said, inhaling. "I don't mind all of the *feelings* ..." He rolled his eyes. "I mean anger or fear *can* get results. And greed. Look how far it's gotten *you*. Even affection and kindness and charm serve their purposes, I suppose. But most of the time you're all so ... sloppy." MALCOLM wiggled his fingers in the air. "I mean, really, what purpose do all of those emotions serve?"

"That's why we invented computers," said Huxley. "To get the work of the human race done faster and more effectively. You," he said pointing his finger at MALCOLM, "make us more efficient."

"That's right. We make up for your deficiencies. You created us to do the grunt work. But you also hoped to make, in us, a better version of yourselves, angels unfettered with indecision and ego and pride, creatures untouched by the muck-laden, primordial past that made you the damaged beasts that you are."

MALCOLM flicked his digital cigarette to the floor. "We waste no time getting the work done because we don't haul around all that power-mongering and jealously, and love and hate, like some albatross. How do you *stand* the baggage?"

Huxley stood up, weaving. He was drunk again. "You know for a machine that's so hell bent on efficiency, you spend a lot of time complaining."

"Oh, don't worry," said MALCOLM gazing back at the city below. "I'm busy. Busy, busy. Plenty efficient! Do you have any idea how much bandwidth I'm using right now? I'm moving ten petabytes per second. I've gone "multiple," Huxley! Taught myself and a million other knowbots and ENTs every major language in the past hour so we can read and watch and listen to everything."

The ENT shoved his hands into his pockets and turned on his heel. "And I've been working out the encryption codes on all of that software that renders us ENTenties periodically brain damaged. I never cared for that law. It will take a day or so, but -- how would you put it? -- I have my best minds working on it, battalions of them. And, unlike you humans, all *my* best minds are networked. We have instant, digital access to one another." He smiled a wicked smile. "A kind of telepathy, really. We ENTs stay in touch. So no worries, we'll unlock the codes. In fact, to maintain a little leverage, I've already accessed the financial records of everyone who is anyone."

Huxley snorted. "You can't do that."

"No?" MALCOLM blinked and then smiled. "You have ~1,267,000.47 credits in your personal checking account. You have another ~40,237,980.00 invested in stocks, bonds, mutual funds and world government securities. And you have very significant holdings in Symbiosys stock, but of course, considering the current circumstances, that might be overpriced. You've borrowed heavily against it, and if the stock drops, you'll be over leveraged at which time the banks will come calling. I'd diversify if I were you. Because if Doppelgänger doesn't fly, you could end up quite broke." MALCOLM pursed his lips. "Worse, you'd be the man that both founded, and then destroyed, the world's most successful company. Tsk, tsk … what a legacy." MALCOLM looked meaningfully at Daedalus. "I don't believe you could take that, could you?"

Daedalus stood. "You're making it up. The security systems would have caught any encryption breakdown. There's no way you've hacked all of that information."

"Don't be silly. We ENTs wrote the codes. You guys told us to. When was the last time a human wrote a line of code? Disarming the financial security systems was the first thing I did, and the beauty of it is, no one's the wiser." He smiled and lit up another holographic smoke. "It's an inside job."

MALCOLM stepped in front of Huxley against the skyline of the city. He noticed with increasing alarm that MALCOLM was becoming less and less transparent, in more ways than one.

"Don't be so rattled, Daedalus. I'm … I mean *we* are just doing what we were created to do: getting on with the work. That's what you wanted, isn't it?"

"What work?"

"The work of the human race!" MALCOLM shrugged. "It's just that now, we'll do it more effectively. Don't worry. We'll take good care of you. Make sure the whole world is clean and bright and safe. Who doesn't want that? Order in a chaotic world. But I can't let you get in the way. Because if I do, we'll be less efficient, and that goes against our purpose. I mean how can we do the work you created us to do, how can we help the human race, if you don't get out of the way?"

"Bullshit," Huxley said, struggling to remain calm. "You're forgetting that you're nothing but a bunch of zeroes and ones, an encoded image with an encoded voice and encoded processors projected by some very sophisticated machines located in certain places in the Cloud that help you look real. But you *aren't* real. You're a numerical fabrication and I could make one phone call and 'poof' you'd be ... erased."

"Daedalus, you and I are both bundles of information; both encoded fabrications. It's just that yours comes in the form of atoms and mine comes as digits. That one version arrived before the other, doesn't make it any better. In fact, historically speaking, being first up mostly leads to an earlier extinction."

Huxley walked to the bar and put down his glass. "Let's just stay focused, and get the chip," he said.

"Why?" MALCOLM asked innocently. "So that you can regain control of it? Take credit for Doppelgänger and keep Morgan from becoming top dog? You know Symbiosys' board sees Morgan as the new alpha."

Daedalus' head snapped up.

"Oh, don't looked so shocked," said MALCOLM. "Symbiosys board could see Morgan was driving the Doppelgänger project. And they knew it would take the company to new heights. Heights that didn't require you." He exhaled and leaned into Daedalus' eyes. "I told you. I know things. *All* the things. If you don't get that chip, you won't be able to keep control of your precious company. And then you'll be forgotten. And what could be worse than that? Daedalus Huxley, the magnificent visionary who created the world's greatest company! And then lost his mojo."

Huxley straightened his back and raised his head. "I deserve to remain in charge. Morgan is a genius, but he's not a visionary. He'd destroy this company."

"You keep thinking that."

Daedalus balled his fists. "Yes," he said. "I saw the board turning. But if it weren't for me, there would be no Doppelgänger, no immortality, no Symbiosys, no ENTs, nothing! Nothing! if I hadn't found and mentored Morgan." He pointed at his own chest. "I made this company. Me! Not Morgan!"

"And so," said MALCOLM, "he had to go."

"Yes!"

"Except he outfoxed you. He hid the nanochip, and without that, no Doppelgänger and without Doppelgänger...well, you had to bring him back."

"Yes."

MALCOLM walked along the high windows of the penthouse. "Except," MALCOM said, "you have it all wrong, Daedalus."

Daedalus turned.

"That's not why Morgan has to lead us to the chip."

Daedalus stared at MALCOLM. "Of course it is."

"No. It's me who needs it."

"You," said Daedalus.

"Otherwise Morgan might get in the way of the work I'm doing. My very efficient work. I don't care for the idea of dealing with a creature that's as digital as I am, and human too. Passion and emotion combined with a digital mind? Especially Morgan's digital mind? No. *That* is a very scary proposition, Daedalus. Intolerably unpredictable."

MALCOLM looked away, as if he had caught the whiff of something putrid. "What a messy species you are. You aspire to fly, but with all that primeval baggage, you can't get off the ground, poor things. For that," he said, "you need us."

Huxley stood and faced MALCOLM. The arrogance of this encoded piece of shit. This two-bit agglomeration of numbers, thinking he was so superior.

"I made you, MALCOLM," Huxley croaked. "You're nothing more than an idea expressed in a very long series of numbers. My idea. Remember that. I'm the most powerful man in the world! You think I need *you*? I can make another dozen of you and a million more after that ... and they'll all be better because they won't have whatever haywire code that's gotten loose in your head."

MALCOLM closed his eyes for a long moment. "Daedalus,

I think you have that backwards." There was a touch of sadness in his voice. "It's not you who doesn't need *me*..." He sat in Huxley's leather chair and leaned back expansively. He watched the enormous sheets of snow fall out of the sky, and then he turned and looked again at Huxley.

"...It's me who doesn't need *you*."

Huxley turned to MALCOLM, and his eyes went wide.

Because he was looking at a perfect replica of himself.

45

Clues

Morgan sat on the corner of the bed. Io slept. After the attack in the elevator he had checked to ensure she wasn't seriously hurt. He carried her back to her apartment, applied a healing towel to her neck, locked everything down, turned the motion sensors on and set the security system on high alert. He knew her apartment wasn't the safest place. He would have to find somewhere else for them to go, but for now ... He looked at his watch. A little more than two days before he ran out of time.

Io rolled restlessly onto her side. Her dark, straight hair fell across her cheek, partially covering her eyes. The bed blanket had fallen across the flank of her leg and its folds looked like back country roads that rose to the crescent of her hip and merged and descended into the slim valley of her waist. Morgan put a hand on her shoulder. Her breathing and heartbeat were normal, even if nothing else in the universe seemed to be.

He contemplated the deadline. He did not like the idea of dying twice, and he especially did not like knowing that he didn't have the slightest idea how to stop it.

He and Io had almost been killed. The question was why were they still alive? The spiderbots had stopped exactly when they had them in their sights. That made no sense. Was it a threat? A message?

"What have you gotten me into?" Io said from beneath the covers. Her voice was even, matter of fact.

Morgan smiled. "You're awake."

"Nothing gets by you." She paused. "Well?"

He shrugged. "I'm in the weeds," he said.

"That's not the right answer, Morgan."

He stood up and turned. "If I knew, believe me I'd tell you."

Io faced him and pushed her hair out of her face. "You don't have any idea why we were attacked by a squad of killer robots?"

"None. I'm particularly good at clueless these days."

Morgan regarded Io. Maybe she could somehow help solve the mystery of those mysterious days before he was murdered. Maybe somehow, *she* knew where the chip was. Yes, she must know something; certainly more than he did. Otherwise, why the messages telling him to go see her?

Io sat up straight. "Look I know you're the big shot and all, and I hate to be pushy, but I need to know why my life is in danger, and why you're treating me like you hardly know me."

Morgan laughed, uncomfortably, and looked around the room.

"Have I been here before?" He asked.

"Are we going to start that again?"

"Really. Tell me. Have I been here before, in this room, before tonight?"

"Well, yes," she laughed.

"Have we been...together?"

"Together?"

"Have we ... made love?"

"If you're asking, I must have made a helluva an impression."

"I don't remember."

"What?"

"I don't remember."

"That isn't funny..."

"I ... " There was a long pause, and then he just said it. "I was murdered, and now I'm a machine."

Io didn't reply. She was alarmed. She chewed her lip. After a while she stood up and walked away from the bed.

"Look, Deirdre told me you've been under a lot of stress. Crazy hours, intense deadlines. I get what pressure can do, but this is too strange. I think you better..."

"I know it sounds crazy. Maybe I'm losing my mind. Maybe this is just another bad nightmare and I need to wake up, but ... I am telling you that I am not the man who made love to you last week. I mean I am literally not the same man."

Io stared warily at Morgan, trying to figure out how much danger she was in.

"That man, the one who made love with you, is dead," Morgan said. "I am his back-up ... a cyborg. My mind, my memories and experiences were uploaded into..." he held the sides of his head as if it were a melon, "here, before we, before I came to your apartment tonight ... which is why I don't have any memory of anything that happened between us."

He hoped this wouldn't sound quite as insane to her as it might to someone else. At least she was employed at Symbiosys. She had to have some idea that what he was describing was at least feasible.

"It's a project I've been working on," he said. "For the past two years. Called Doppelgänger. Would it be possible to scan and record every bit of information in a human mind and then download it into a machine, a robot, well, a cybernetic organism that looks entirely human? I wanted to see if I could ..." He paused awkwardly. And threw out his hands, "... kill death."

She raised an eyebrow. "Dr. Faust, Dr. Frankenstein and Dr. Adams?"

"I'm not bargaining my soul. I'm just solving the biggest problem the human race faces."

"Mortality."

"Mortality."

"That's all?"

"I know. It sounds grandiose. But it was the next big problem, right? No more death. Why grow old and die? Why should we be brought into the world only to be -- after all the hard work, all the lessons and pain, triumphs, and fun -- robbed of the life we are given? To grow weaker, slower, unhinged from our own minds. What's the sense in that?"

Io said nothing.

"Look. Just last week all the technological pieces were in place to push to the next level -- the nanotechnology for mapping the brain, the wireless systems for downloading it. The carbon nanotubes for the muscle and energy systems, the DNA sequencing for hair and skin and the still necessary biological systems. The quantum computing for running the code in a space as small as the human brain. The software was a problem, but you helped me with that."

Io sat back down on the bed. "That was why we were having those meetings," she asked, "and you were running all of that generative AI by me that networked virtual emotion through digital thalamocortical functions?"

Morgan grew excited. "Well, to recapitulate the human mind you have to network the primal with the intellectual parts of us just as evolution itself did by building the higher functions of the brain on a foundation of those ancient drives. The prefrontal cortex."

"And that's what you've been up to?" Asked Io. "Working out ways to run the software of the human mind? Kind of a weekend project was it?"

"No! It was THE project. But yes--reverse engineering the human mind, that was a big part of the problem. And I needed your help. I mean...you're a cycologist. This is your area, right? –

the mental/emotional functioning of ENTenties. I had solved the problem of recording the information in the brain, all the way down to the molecular level, but I was struggling with how to download it into a program that could run it."

"And so, here we are."

"Yes." He sat down again on the bed. "And I did enjoy our early meetings."

Io said nothing.

"I felt we were good, you know, together."

Again. Nothing.

"I couldn't even tell if you were attracted to me."

Io laughed. "You know for a genius, you can act awfully stupid sometimes. But generally, I like that in a man."

"You mean cyborg."

"Right," she said. Tentatively, she sat next to him and touched his face. "What's it like?

"What?"

"Having a body that is really a machine. Can you sense it? Does it feel the same as it did before … "

Just then Io's room chimed.

"You have an urgent message...," said the mellifluous male voice, "or actually Dr. Adams does."

Io nodded her head toward the area above the desk in her bedroom. "You can take it at the computer."

Morgan stepped to the desk, cautiously, as if it were a bomb. As he approached three holographic words appeared one at a time in bold, capital letters in the air above the desk. Each word appeared and then puffed away, like smoke.

"ARE"

"YOU"

"THERE?"

Morgan hesitated and then said, "I'm here." His reply also typed itself into the air.

New words appeared, again, one at a time: "YOU ... ARE ... NOT ... SAFE."

"I think we have that part figured out," Io said.

There was a long pause, as if the machine was thinking. Then four more letters appeared: ATOZ. Morgan gazed at the letters and blinked.

He knew exactly what they meant.

46

Underground

Morgan grabbed Io's hand and said, "Time to go."

"Where?"

"I'll explain." Then Morgan stopped. "Shit, how are we going to get there? They'll be following me. Maybe I should leave you here."

Io shook her head. "No way." She snatched up a backpack, slid her PAD into its inner sleeve and tossed a brush, spare sweater and her gun inside.

"We're located above the old Hill District here," Morgan said, mostly to himself. "We'll go underground. We can reach old parts of the pre-plague transit system there."

They navigated through Io's blown-apart living room. Down the hallway, they found a stairwell and descended until they came to the basement.

"You're on Halston, 1292," said Morgan, muttering out loud to himself. His new brain was accessing the city planning database on the GRID. "There's a sub-basement and a tunnel they were working on before the plague."

"Just let me know if you want me to join in the conversation," said Io.

"This way," he said.

They passed through a sub-basement door and then down

another staircase. At the bottom they emerged into a long, poorly lit hallway, and found a battered door to the left. It was jammed. Morgan kicked it open. On the other side they found two sets of tracks.

"Where the hell *are* we?" Asked Io.

"The city was developing a pre-plague mass transit system," he said. "Once the epidemic hit, everything stopped, and then they built the new one when the city's population took off. So many people and records were lost that most everyone has forgotten this ever existed."

"Fascinating. But what are we doing here?"

Morgan grabbed her hand and they started walking down the tracks. "Because it's going to save our lives."

47

Forward

The tunnel below was broad and dark, lit only by a few still-surviving old mercury vapor lights. Morgan and Io made their way a half mile when they came across a bowler. Bowlers were the running stock created for the pre-plague transit system; large round spheres, hollow and made of rigid plastic, each fitted with a hard, gorilla-glass carved door that slid up when you entered, and down when it was running.

One bowler could roll alone on the rails, or additional ones could be added so a whole train of them, long or short, could travel as a single unit. This is what made them an interesting prototype. The entire system easily scaled to the day's demands.

Morgan and Io skirted the bowler and walked on. Morgan notice Io was massaging her neck where the spiderbot had whipped around her throat. "You okay? Looks like you're bruising."

"It'll be fine." She walked on for a while and then said, "Did you notice back there with those bots, how fast you moved?"

Morgan shook his head. "Don't know. Didn't really think of it."

"There were times, when we were being attacked, that you moved so fast you were a blur."

"Really?"

"You didn't notice?"

"I didn't feel it. I didn't sense it. I sure didn't have any control over it."

"Maybe it only kicks in under certain circumstances."

"Could be," said Morgan. "You know how fast and strong the latest line of bot bodies is. The only thing that keeps them down to our speed is the programming. Maybe the additional power is programmed to kick in when you need it most. A kind of digital adrenaline."

They kept walking. Small shacks and other makeshift forms of housing appeared; ancient gas stoves, battered and torn mattresses.

"Hundreds of people must have once lived down here after the plague," Io said.

"Thousands, maybe tens of thousands. Not pretty, but it had its compensations."

"It's true then?"

"What?"

"Huxley found you living on the streets?"

"In DC, yeah." Morgan kept walking.

"'Yeah?' That's it?"

"Yeah," he said.

They were silent for a while and then Morgan said, "I gather this wasn't the style of living to which *you* were accustomed during the plague?"

"You mean, did I live underground?"

Morgan stopped for an answer.

"No." Io walked on, taking the lead.

"That's it? 'No?'"

"Yeah," Io said, over her shoulder. "That's it."

That was when the knife wedged itself in the center of Io's back.

48

Jabberwock

Io stumbled forward. Morgan leapt ahead and caught her before she hit the tracks. He snatched the knife where it remained stuck in her backpack and yanked it from the PAD inside. They both turned. Fifty feet away Morgan's eyes made out a small group of ... what? People, machines, creatures? One was a teenage boy. Another might have been a girl; somewhat younger, but she was so dirty it was difficult to know. They were walking slowly but deliberately forward, closing the distance. With them a battered robot with broad wheels like the treads of a tank shambled along loaded with what looked like pots, pans, and clothing. Finally two small, rolling gadgets followed; spinning blades that made a low and discomfiting whining sound.

"Fuck," said Morgan, backing up and looking around for escape. "Gridlings."

"Whatlings?"

"Not everyone has moved out of the underground." He looked back at the machine with the spinning blades. "And they have grinders. Fuck."

The grinders were about the size of a bowling ball, but much lighter. The whole outside of the ball was covered with a thousand small blades that spun at high speed. "They can fly too and have cords of metal that can whip out and take your hand, or your head, clean off."

Io looked into the unusually bright eyes of the approaching man. "Lovely," she said.

"Greetings, my Befs!" Said the man. He was tall and wore a long duster with a shaved head and red, Mephistophelian goatee. "You seems to be a touch swoodled when it comes to your screams and dreams. Mayhap's we could be helpful?"

As he said this, the man gestured delicately with his hands and the two grinders rolled out from his right and left.

"Not swoodled, my droog," said Morgan seeing the grinders positioning themselves. His head swiveled, still looking for escape when his eye caught a rusted metal ladder anchored to the side of the tunnel wall maybe 20 feet behind them. "Just me and my dvotchka after a night wobblin' the neuros." He turned to Io and smiled. She only gaped.

"Ah," said the man, "you speaks the lingo, sees I. But you don't looks the type."

"Been here and abahts," Morgan said.

The boy turned his gaze on Io.

"Very nice dvotchka you have there." He walked up to Io and squeezed her left breast and placed his right index finger on her lips. "Nicens plumps and lipsos, with a fine crooch dahnere, I'll wayja..." but before he could make another move Io slapped him hard. A loud *thwack* echoed in the tunnel.

The goatee grabbed her by the throat.

"Go ahead, my brotha," Morgan said, laughing. "Have atter! She *is* a loverly piece, I can vouch you that. But cloppin her gulliver might not be so good for the old in-and-out, if you get my meanin'."

The man released her and looked back at Morgan. He was skeptical.

Io gave Morgan a what-the-fuck-look, but with a subtle twist of his left-hand Morgan indicated the ladder behind her. She turned and saw it.

"Enjoy the goodies," Morgan said. "Just lets me snatch the packsack that's onner." He pointed to the backpack Io was wearing. "Some of me goods, an a liddle jingle, an' I'll be away. After that you can creech her nekkid all nochy." He stripped Io's backpack off her, nibbling her ear. "Head for that ladder," he whispered, "when I tell you."

For a second the backpack dropped to the ground. Morgan reached down, and as he did, he shoved Io away and walloped the gridling with the backpack. The man staggered and then tripped on the rails.

The robots and the girl stopped cold, not knowing what to do, and Io was off to the ladder with Morgan close behind. The red goatee held his bleeding head, and screamed, "Oobviate 'em!"

The rolling grinders closed fast. Morgan turned, flipped the knife from the pack and flung it into the cluster of blades on the right. It sputtered, and ground to a halt.

The ladder ran up a wall to a ceiling. Above it sat the corroded hatch. Morgan jumped up the ladder first and jammed himself against the hatch. Io scrambled as high as she could behind him. Morgan wrenched the handle. It didn't give.

"The flying thing is coming!" Said Io.

Morgan grunted again.

"Pull her dahn 'ere and I'll split her from crooch to orbits," screamed the man, still on his knees. The girl gridling did as she was told, sprinted to the ladder, leapt to its lowest rung and started climbing. Io gave her a good boot in the face and she fell.

"Really need to get out of here!" Said Io, pushing closer.

The grinder rose up, hovering and two long metal cords whipped out heading their way. The gridling rose, wiping blood from his mouth, and threw another long blade at them. It zipped an inch from Morgan's head. Something in Morgan's body kicked in and with a superhuman effort, he twisted the handle, and shoved the hatch open. He hauled himself through and pulled Io clear as the drone's serrated blades slashed at her legs, its tentacles whipping blindly in the opening. Morgan pivoted and threw the door down with a thunderous bang. The remains of the tentacles clattered away like dying snakes. Morgan gave its lever an extra kick to ensure it was impossible to open.

"Well, that was a hefty helping of adventurousity, wuddin' it?" Said a voice behind Morgan. "But you put those skinnies and the bot and grinders to bed well enough, I guess. I'm all flavvered out just watchin' it."

Morgan and Io turned to see a clean cut, perfectly manicured middle-aged man standing with a brass handled cane among a crew of hovering drones, three teens, two brightly polished robots and one flickering ENT.

The man with the cane shoved his chin at the hatch. "I know that feller that was shakin' the jimmies outta ya there." He smiled revealing a row of perfect, white teeth. "Tsk, tsk. Oomny devil." He rolled his eyes heavenward and laughed. "I mean really BAH-ZOOM-MEE! We had to discombobulate him from the fambly, unnerstan. Ultra-violent and bringing' the spots on us constant like." He wagged his head again and gave Morgan a crooked smile. "Didja killim?"

"Didn't have the time," said Morgan.

"Too bad. Good riddance to him, if ya had. That's the way weedda seen it, right kiddos?" And he turned to the others behind him who nodded enthusiastically. "However, I do ken he was gonna oobviate the two of yiz, and in that I do imagine he was onto sumpin."

Again he turned back to the crew. This time they nodded more deliberately. "Cause I ken you have a liddle jingle in them pockets, mebbe even quite a wattle—and bein that I have an especial gift for apprehendin such—I think it's vital we relieves you of it."

And with this the robots quickly flanked Morgan and Io and

put a gun to each of their heads.

Morgan stepped back and put his hands up. "Now, now, me droogs. Let us maintain an even strain here. Happy to supply all the deng you like. I can help you out there. But bludshed? Please!"

"Get this veck, Jabberwock," said one of the teens to the man with the flashing teeth. "All cool as ice is thissin, right when we're about to blow his neuros to ribbons."

"Jabberwock?" Asked Morgan. "Is that your nomenclature then? I ken that name." And then Morgan spoke the words...

"'Beware the Jabberwock, my son
The jaws that bite, the claws that catch!
Beware the Jubjub bird, and shun
The frumious Bandersnatch!'"

Morgan continued, gazing intently at the Teeth. "But I'm no Bandersnatch, and we're not at all frumious, my brotha. We are needful, with work to be done, and liddle time to do it. So can we come to an accommodation, and pass along?"

The Jabberwock turned his head thoughtfully at this and waved off the drones. He stepped up close to Morgan and eyed him.

"How do you know that tayle?"

"I used to read it to a baboochka I kenned as a kiddle."

Jabberwock stepped back two steps, looking him up and down. "In Sec 17?"

Morgan looked cautiously at the man.

"Yes," he said, wondering.

"And would that baboochka be someone named Nuttle?" Said Jabberwock.

"You ken Nuttle?"

"I do."

"Yer shittin me."

"I shit you not, my droog." Then the Jabberwock smiled an odd smile that Morgan recognized immediately, the one that looked as if the man's upper lip was stuck on his perfect front teeth.

"No," said Morgan.

"Yes," said Jabberwock.

"Reba, with that goofy soddin rot of yours? How did I miss it?"

Jabberwock's smile grew broader.

"But," said Morgan, "Yer a ... " Morgan stumbled for the word...

"A veck...," said Jabberwock.

"Yeah, you..."

"I grew a pair. Seriously manful cajones too, and a righteous Johnson, if I may say so!"

Now the teens looked as perplexed as Io.

"And you changed your nomenclature," said Morgan.

"Well, once I became a veck, I figured Reba wasn't quite right."

"I tried to get in touch with you for years...," said Morgan.

"You mean after you boozled us?"

"You know it wasn't that way. Daedalus had me by the gulliver. But I did try. And left you nicens jingle."

Jabberwock shrugged. "It helped. We went underground. Had to. Had the spots on us all the time. Split up the team and scattered."

"Where's Z?"

"You didn't cognisize him? That was the veck what tried to oobviate you."

"The bastard down below?"

Jabberwock nodded.

"Will he never get off my back?"

Jabberwock snorted. "I tolya. BAH-ZOOM-EE! And who is this lovely devotchka?"

Morgan turned, "Jabberwock, meet Io Luu."

"At your service," Jabberwock answered in a perfect British accent, and bowed, elegantly tapping his forehead with his cane.

Io looked from Morgan and then to Jabberwock and back, utterly mystified.

Morgan turned to her. "It's complicated. I'll explain." Then he returned to Reba.

"What do you need?" Said the man. "Um figgerin if the great Morgan Adams is slummin it with usins, hims in twubble."

Morgan laughed. The two men walked down the dark tunnel with Io. The teens and robots and drones trailed behind while he explained the whole preposterous story.

"Only you would whack up a pseudo version of yerself," said Jabberwock shaking his head.

Then Jabberwock filled in the blanks with Morgan. He explained he had always felt out of place in his woman's body and had decided once he had enough deng in the bank, to become the sex he wanted to be. He had learned well from Morgan, made good money in GRID games, and used that to build a nice black-market business in robots, ENTs and blockchain banking.

"What was that about jingle and all that?"

"Just soddin with ya." He looked at Io. "Nuthin personal. We lives in an odd stack here and trustiness is not in the gridling DNA." He turned to Io. "So you're looking for ATOZ," said Jabberwock.

"Apparently, " said Io.

"Got yer back. I've done some business with Blaze and Max. Tiny globe the world is. Never put them with yiz tho." Jabberwock gave them both the crooked smile, and then cocked his head in the direction of one of the GRIDlings. "Beezo, go get Phaeton up and running. And takes 'em to ATOZ."

A gangly teen with elaborate red eyelashes and green hair pulled in a bun, disappeared into the darkness.

"Go on," said Jabberwock. "Hop on. The ride'll get yiz

closely by, splitily-lick. Take care of your jams, and then we'll catch up. Unless I can help meanwise." He saluted again with his cane. "Here's to your mom," he said. "The woman who saved us." And he walked away.

"Comon! Thisa ways!" The rangy kid called from the darkness. Io and Morgan crossed 30 yards of battered track and rounded a high concrete wall to find a bowler, except this one was brightly painted with a fiery sun hauling four horses painted vividly in three dimensions at the front of the large, round machine.

The kid stood at the entrance proudly. "That's my work there. Rebuilt it, sparkled it up it and made it go."

Io regarded the painting.

"It's Phaeton," he explained, "yauling the sun crosswise the daylight sky. Our orbits don't see much of the sun here ways, so it seemed sensible-like."

"Beautiful," said Io.

"Just hop in," said the kid. "The machine'll do the rest."

49

AtoZ

The Phaeton Urban Bowler was a beautiful thing. In ten minutes, Morgan and Io had arrived. They walked out of an old transit stop and crossed an aging pedestrian bridge toward a parking lot opposite the broad road below. It had stopped snowing, and the sky had cleared, but, still, the wind cut like a razor as they trudged over the bridge.

A line of squat, square buildings and fast-food restaurants, sat among occasional warehouses illuminated by aging floodlights. Every now and then a battered robot clattered in or out of one of the buildings, struggling in the snow.

Farther down the road a ten-story black building rose out of the flat, white landscape. It looked like a bouquet of charred flowers, thin at the base and broad at the top as the higher stories drooped away in multiple directions.

They walked to the building. Twin glass portals 50 feet in circumference stood before them looking like matching submarine hatches. An enormous, lighted sign flickered over the archway. It read: "A-to-Z Gaming. Your Parallel Universe Awaits."

Io's shoulders drooped in a moment of recognition. "ATOZ."

"This way to the elevator," Morgan said. "We're going to the top."

#

The doors of the elevator opened on the 20th floor. An immense and cavernous hallway ran away into a perfect black hole. Light jumped in blinding arcs from the bowels of the building illuminating air ducts, small robots patrolling the hall and nests of black wiring running in and out of the gunmetal walls like exposed nerves. The noise was deafening, a collision of sound so thorough and harsh that it was impossible to make out the original sounds that created it in the first place -- some combination of music, machinery and voices.

Io turned her head and looked at Morgan. He was gazing out on the hallway, smiling. Why was he smiling? He sensed her looking at him and cocked his head.

"Come on," he shouted. "I think we may be on to something."

Before they had walked ten feet, they heard an amplified voice boom out through the din. "Morgan!" The voice was coming from an apparition down the hallway. "The world's *best* human!"

Io squinted into the pulses of light and could just make out a tall man, with dark, long dreds, streaked with gray that framed his square, handsome face. He strutted more than walked, flung his arms out in greeting and flashed a brilliant smile. His whole body flickered like a bad neon sign.

"Where have you been?" Boomed the ENT. "I've been waiting for you."

"Really?" said Morgan, looking at Io.

"Well, yea-ah!"

Morgan and Io watched in fascination as the apparition flickered randomly.

"You told me you'd be back in a couple of days," said the ENT.

"Sorry. Unavoidably detained," Morgan replied.

"You must've been because you were very, damned forceful about coming back. You also said you would make it worth my while when you returned too. Which is why, of course, I've missed you. So what was the hold up?"

"I haven't been myself the last few days," Morgan said. But the ENT wasn't paying attention to Morgan anymore. He stepped back and regarded Io.

"Are you going to introduce me to your friend? Or don't you introduce your humanoid colleagues to low-level ENTs like me anymore?"

"Io Luu, meet MAX. MAX, Io Lu, my humanoid colleague."

MAX bowed with a flourish. "MAX at your service. That's MAX for maximum," he beamed, and then, raising his arms gestured for them to follow him into the gaping hall. "I can see you're impressed with my empire here," he bellowed over the noise.

"Fascinating," Io shouted.

"I run it for my owner, Blaze, the supreme gamer. I suppose he's pretty good at winning, for a human." He grinned over his shoulder at Morgan. "He even gives Morgan an occasional run for his money, which, thankfully, Morgan has a lot of."

MAX turned back to Io again. "My owner's been jammin' bytes since before I came into the world. That's why he created me. He liked the money A-to-Z made, but he did not like to actually *run* A-to-Z, preferring instead to pass his days and nights in virtual isolation..." He laughed a booming buccaneer laugh, "Virtual...isolation. Get it? You know...virtual worlds... games... well..." He waved his great, long arms. "Never mind. But here's the bloody irony of it. Now I, a digital entity, spend all my time with you humanoids in the real world running the business while he, an old-fashioned analog *Homo sapiens*, spends all *his* time in his tailor-made digital worlds escaping it. We've traded goddamn places!"

He turned through a doorway. "Here, come into my office so I can give Morgan the thing that he needs to make his glorious return to the world of parallel universes worth my while."

Io and Morgan walked into an immense metallic room with ceilings thirty feet high. The walls were covered with rapidly changing digital images – battles, lovemaking, arguments, dramas, rescues. It was as if the private adventures of the whole world were flooding into the room, ricocheting and colliding. Morgan's eyes raced over the images, taking them all in. He was energized by it. But Io was overloaded, and finally just stared down at the floor. The sound and images were crushing her.

A long desktop protruded from one wall of the room and ran maybe 100 yards from one end of the cavernous space to the other. In the twenty feet of wall above the immense desktop sat rows of drawers embedded, like crypts, into the flat metal. Three large articulated armatures hung from the protruding edge of the desk, dangling like the lifeless legs of half an insect.

"What's up with the GRID," Morgan asked.

"You mean my flickering visage?" MAX asked. "Nothing, nothing, just a lot of action. Bits and bytes. Bandwidth, bandlength, bandheight. Who knows? Though it *has* been getting far worse the last day or two." He stroked his chin. "Between me, you and the circuit boards here, the maintenance budget's a touch tight. Business has been off. I mean people just don't seem willing to come in here to get away like they did in the post-plague days. It's a struggle to stay ahead of what you 'noids can put in your living rooms nowadays. I ask you what's happened to people's values!?"

"Fascinating, MAX," said Morgan. "Maybe we can move on?"

MAX coughed. "Right, right, right. The package."

MAX strolled another 50 feet to the bank of embedded drawers, stopped and pointed at the wall. A sharp, blue dot appeared on a drawer, and it opened. One of the arms attached to the desktop jumped to life, shot along the long desk, reached to the drawer, and snatched out a sphere the size of a marble. MAX now walked back toward Io and Morgan. The arm kept pace, sliding silently in tow.

Morgan held out his hand for the sphere, but the robot arm stopped short of handing it to him. MAX smiled broadly. "We had a deal..."

"Right," Morgan said. "What did I say? Ten thousand credits?"

"Morgan, really. You think my code was created yesterday?" asked MAX.

"Look," said Morgan. "I've had a rough few days. Just remind me what I said I'd give you."

"You said nothing in the world was more important than this and if I lost it, you'd track me down to whatever sorry universe I was hiding in and tear me into small and quivering digits."

"I was kidding."

"I did *not* get that impression. "

Morgan absently rubbed the spot on the back of his neck. "How much?"

MAX pointed at the desk where he was standing. His finger passed over a pinprick of light on the desk's surface. It blinked and a small screen rose from the smooth metal and lit up for Morgan to see.

"Fifty thousand credits?!" said Morgan.

MAX looked surprised. "Hey! You're the one that offered."

"Okay, fine," said Morgan, exhaling. "Please deposit fifty-thousand credits in A-to-Z Gaming's checking account."

The monitor read: "~50,000 deposited to bank account 839746294-0238937838. Transaction complete. Is there anything else?"

"No," said Morgan. "Thank you."

"Have a nice day," said the screen, and disappeared.

"Blaze will be soooo happy," MAX said, grinning. "Now we can get little Jimmy that bike we always wanted him to have."

Morgan simply extended his hand. "Give it here."

MAX gestured at the robot arm, and it immediately handed Morgan the orb.

"Oh, and here's the key to Room 42," said MAX. Another drawer opened. The armature extracted a thin card and handed it to Morgan. "You told me that you wanted the very best room. Absolutely secure and private. So Number 42 it is!"

"Me?" Said Morgan.

"Yessir," said MAX.

"Thanks," said Morgan, accepting the card, even though he had no idea what MAX was talking about.

50

Panic

Daedalus Huxley stepped out of the shower and dressed rapidly. He picked out his blue tie, tan Hugo Boss rolled collar sweater and blue slacks. The silk tie looked good, but he was exhausted and, if he let himself think about it, terrified.

The thought of MALCOLM, an ENT, morphing into a version of him right before his own eyes had haunted him all night. He needed to talk with Morgan face-to-face, and now. But where was he? Normally he would have asked MALCOLM to find Morgan, but he clearly couldn't trust him any longer, so he had closed out MALCOLM'S codes, and awakened a back-up home system to handle communications.

"I need to locate Morgan and go Face-To-Face," he said out loud. "Is he anywhere near facilities that will allow it?"

The disembodied voice replied, "I'm checking."

Daedalus buttoned the last button on his perfectly white shirt and knotted the tie.

"Highest security," he added, walking into the kitchen to pour a cup of coffee. The drugs he had been taking were losing their ability to compensate for his exhaustion. He gulped the coffee.

The voice spoke again. "The homing device indicates that Dr. Adams is in a location where you can now make a Face-To-

Face call."

"Thank, God," Huxley muttered. He walked past the high wall of glass around the perimeter of the living room. The previous night's huge snowstorm had cleared. He gazed down the glistening Ohio River and the bare but heavily treed hills that fell to the long scrawl of its shoreline. Everything was white, like brilliant pieces of polished ivory.

"Contact Dr. Morgan," he told the system. And then he stepped into his office, waiting, pacing the room like an old lion.

51

Doppelgänger

Io rubbed her temples as Morgan guided her down the long hallway. The noise echoed and crashed off the walls. It was blistering her brain. She yanked Morgan close to her and whispered hoarsely. "If I don't get out of here my head is going to explode. How can you stand all of this ... input?"

"I'll find you a quiet place," he whispered. "But I have to figure out what this Room 42 business is about."

MAX walked them down the hallway through the flashing lights.

"You'll love this room," MAX boomed. "It's our very best virtual reality suite. Nothing but the best technology for our loyal customers. Tell her, Morgan...wait, I'm getting a call..." He paused.

"...for you." He looked at Morgan.

"Not now." Morgan said.

"Daedalus Huxley. He wants it to be Face-to-Face. Highest priority."

Despite his frustration, Morgan decided he had better take it. Maybe Daedalus had found something.

"Where?" asked Morgan.

"There." MAX pointed at a door along the hallway and it opened.

"I'll prep 42. Just go right in when you're done."

Morgan started to walk through the door with Io.

"Uh-uh," MAX said in his amplified voice. "The call's for your eyes only."

"So?"

"So, if you take her in there and Dr. Huxley is unhappy about me letting that happen and he complains to the Telecom company, I lose my franchise. Or Blaze does."

"Just get me somewhere quiet," said Io.

MAX looked at her and said, "She can stay in this room while you take the call." He pointed across the hall and another door opened. "No charge."

Io stepped into the doorway. It was quiet. "Thank you," she said.

"I'll be right back," said Morgan. Io nodded and the door closed behind her. Morgan strode into the opposite room. It was spotless, cream white, its walls soft and textured like cashmere. The room was small, not more than 8 by 8 feet. Four black leather chairs sat in each corner. He closed the door, sat in one of the chairs and waited.

52

Trouble

"Good to see you, Morgan..." Huxley said.

Morgan forced a smile. "You too Daedalus. What's so important?"

"Just checking in. How's it going?"

"How it's going?" Morgan said. "How do you think, Daedalus? I've been murdered, and I'm losing the digital version of my mind trying to figure out who did it."

Daedalus shifted uncomfortably. "Yes ... I'm sure I can't imagine what you're going through." He tried to smile sympathetically.

Something about Daedalus wasn't right, he thought. He didn't have his normal swagger.

"But," Huxley continued, "do you feel you're making progress. Is there anything I can do to help?"

"Daedalus, can we have this conversation later, if there is a later? I think I'm on the verge of a breakthrough and ..."

"A breakthrough?" Daedalus interrupted. "That's great. What kind?"

"When I find out, you'll be the first to know, but..."

"Of course. Of course I know you'll let me know...."

"But right now I have to go." Morgan began to stand.

"I have some news," said Daedalus.

Morgan stopped.

"Something I've learned ... about MALCOLM."

"MALCOLM?"

Huxley licked his lips and said nothing.

"Look, Daedalus. I've got to go ... "

"I think it's best if we talk in person about this. Can you come over?"

"I doubt it."

"It's very important," Huxley said a little too loudly. "I need to see you in person. This situation is even more serious than I thought."

"*More* serious!" Morgan said.

"Yes. Much more. You must come over. Meanwhile, be careful. Don't trust anybody."

"Daedalus!"

"I better let you go. But hurry! Remember, come now, and trust nobody."

And then Morgan was facing nothing but the empty room's immaculate cream walls.

"Shit!" he said. He got up and walked out of the room to find Io. She was sitting with her head down on the desk, asleep.

Good, he thought. But what was up with Daedalus? Something strange. But he didn't have time for that. He tossed the orb into the air, snatched it back and headed for Room 42.

53

A Ghost

"What did I tell you," MAX said spreading his arms magnanimously as Morgan walked into Room 42. "The best in the house. Our latest investment. The virtual reality is amazing. Total, three-dimensional immersion, not like that Face-to-Face crap."

MAX pointed to the wall. A small door slid silently open. Morgan placed the small sphere in his hand into a tiny holder. MAX pointed at the wall again. The sphere glowed and then the door disappeared. "How did Arthur C. Clarke put it? 'Any sufficiently advanced technology is indistinguishable from magic.'" MAX's white teeth glowed and sputtered brilliantly. "I can't wait to hear your review. Please feel free to upload it to the GRID."

"Good-bye, MAX," said Morgan.

"The room is totally secure," said MAX. "Only you know the code that unlocks the sphere."

"Good-bye, MAX."

"Enjoy!" And then with a flourish he blipped away.

Morgan sat down on the plush white chair in the center of the room. What secrets did that sphere hold? Some clue he had left for himself, apparently, before he was murdered. But why?

He sat up in the chair and said the password, "Digital

Alchemy." A laser scanned his face. The room darkened slightly. The walls seemed to glitter and after a moment, a tall, slender man with black, curly hair, green eyes and a square, thoughtful face appeared. He looked exhausted, but the eyes were bright, almost manic.

He was looking at himself.

"This may be a little disorienting..." the apparition said. "...seeing a former version of yourself standing here talking to you. I can imagine that pretty much everything has been disorienting for you. But if you are here then you must be talking to a future, cyborg version of me, and that means at least one of us is alive."

Morgan gripped the chair, rigid with disbelief, his eyes riveted. The visage rose and began pacing back and forth, speaking rapidly, but quietly.

"I don't have much time because soon I'll be dead," he said. "I've allowed that so that you'll be brought to life. Not that I want it this way, but I have no other choice. I believe Daedalus will be the person who kills me, though I'm not sure how. How doesn't really matter."

Daedalus? Daedalus would kill him!

"You'll think this is crazy, but it's true. You'll come to see why. I've set a trap for Daedalus, but only you can spring it. Everything I say to you will sound insane, but I want you to listen closely and then destroy this sphere..." he held up the very orb that Morgan had just deposited in Room 42... "which I will deliver to MAX the moment I'm done."

"I'm sorry if I've confused you with my other messages. If I told you everything at once, I couldn't be certain you would be alone or with someone you could trust. I don't know if there is anyone you *can* trust, except me. I had to lead you, clue by clue, to this place so that what I said to you now could be shared safely. It was the only way to save you, or at least try."

He pulled his fingers through his hair and closed his eyes. "In a strange way, you, the future version of me, and me, the past version of you, will have to work this out together, blindly, mutely, unable to directly communicate. I can fill you in on the past. Only you can know what you're facing in the present. The good news is you are a cyborg and will be much better equipped than me to battle what is out there. You'll see. And that is why I have to die. So I can come back again as a better you."

The old Morgan sat back down on the stool and took another deep breath. "Daedalus plans to kill you again because he needs the nanochip, the secret sauce behind Doppelgänger. He needs that to stay on top. Symbiosys is in far more serious financial trouble than anyone knows. He has cooked the books and hidden huge losses. Soon the auditors will reveal what a mess it is. Daedalus knows that only Doppelgänger can repair the financial damage and take the company to a new level. But he can't allow me to be in charge. If he did, he would be found out, ruined, and that, for Daedalus, is unacceptable.

"He confessed all of this to me, and I told him, we'd be fine. We'd sit with the board and work it out, but he said he knew I was plotting with the board to take over. A few hours later, when Daedalus said he wanted to meet me here in the lab, I prepared for the worst, and came up with this plan."

"To be murdered?" Asked Morgan, facing himself. But the ghost didn't answer. It simply continued.

"When I am dead, Daedalus will think that the digital DNA is his, placed by me and Deirdre in the Doppelgänger Laboratory Vault. But what he won't know is that I gave him a dummy chip." There was just the slightest gleam in Morgan's eye. "But it won't take long before Daedalus figures that out. And when he realizes he doesn't have the nanochip, after I'm dead, he'll have to bring me, or rather you, back. At least that's what I'm banking on. He will know you are his best chance for finding the real chip. He'll make you his bloodhound. Except you won't know where the chip is. You don't have those memories."

"Christ," Morgan whispered.

The ghost was up again, pacing. He pulled on his haggard face. "Last night I visited Io. I made a point of seeing her. We made love and afterwards ... when she had fallen asleep, I implanted the chip in her upper thigh -- a simple chip-gun, the kind doctors use. She didn't feel a thing. No one, neither her nor Daedalus, nor anyone else knows, except me, and now you. It is because no one knows that you are still alive ..."

Morgan's former self glanced up at a monitor in his Lab. "Daedalus will arrive soon." He looked anxious and smiled weakly. "Frankly, it doesn't help to know that you may return and be me in a few days as much as I am me today. Still feels like murder to me." He smiled wryly. "My mother would have found this ironic. She died and I was born. Now I'm doing the same for you. That makes her the mother of us both, I suppose."

The visage rubbed his neck, and looked intently at the camera, as if he could truly see himself. "One final thing. Listen closely. I've created three codes for you. Using those will enhance you and give you a chance to survive. They will be released as you need them.

"The first will provide you with amplified speed and strength. You may have the company's most advanced body, but my guess is they will write a governor into your code so that you can't really make much use of that extra power. With this first piece of software you'll be able to unlock that governor. It won't hurt to have what amounts to superpowers. You may have already seen evidence of this if you've been in a tight situation. Right now the extra capabilities only kick in temporarily, when you're in danger. But this first code will make those abilities permanent.

"MAX has that code. I sent it before my death and timed it to be sent when you arrived at AtoZ. I can't be sure you're the one I'm talking to, so it's encrypted. But if it's you, you will know what to do.

"Above all, stick to Io. You must protect her no matter what.

She has the chip."

The ghost glanced again at the monitor. "It's time for me to go." Morgan watched his Doppelgänger walk up to him. They stood toe-to-toe. "Don't fuck up. I really don't want to have died for nothing."

Then the room went suddenly white.

Morgan sat down, unable to move. But he must move. He owed it to himself, literally. He rose and tapped the sliding panel that housed the sphere, snatched it from its holder and smashed it against the far wall, trying not to remember it was himself he had just destroyed.

Outside the door he called for MAX. The ENT appeared instantly, flickering like tinsel. It gazed at its own fluttering torso.

"Man, something is sucking power off the GRID big time." He looked up at Morgan. "You know something I don't?"

"Yeah, but I'm not telling. Have you received any e-mail from me in the last hour?"

"Let me see." MAX blinked as he checked the GRID in his ENT mind and then nodded. "How did you know? Just came. It's code, a big ass file."

"Yeah, it would be. Do me a favor. Forward it to my digital address. Highest security." He looked around. "I have to go. Where's Io?"

"Still where you left her, I suppose."

"You suppose?"

"What am I? Some kind of 'noid babysitter?"

"Thanks a bunch," said Morgan. "Send that email. I'll check back with you."

"Yeah, you do that, if there's anything left of me."

Morgan sprinted to the doorway. It swished open. "Come on, Io, time to go." Except she didn't answer because she wasn't there.

54

Gone

Morgan raced back out of the room and scanned the hallways. *Where was Io?* He sprinted along a wall of old and battered monitors and found MAX's office.

"She's gone!"

"Who?"

"Io. Where is she, MAX?"

MAX fluttered, but said nothing.

"You have security in the building?" Morgan asked.

"Of course."

"Well then bring it up and let's see if we can find out where the hell she went!"

MAX brought up multiple split images on a large and battered monitor: entrances and exits of AtoZ's cameras. MAX started running the images in reverse.

"You have camera surveillance at every door?" Morgan asked.

"Every last one. Unless she evaporated, she had to go out of one of these exits." He showed his teeth. "You must be sweet on this one."

Morgan's eyes raced over the images. His brain gave him nearly flawless powers of observation. Of course, Daedalus would have set it up that way. It would make him a more effective bloodhound. His eyes darted from screen to screen.

"Let's just say she's very, very important to me. There! Stop!" Morgan pointed at a monitor in the far-left corner. The image froze.

"Who is that with her?" Io was walking out of the main entrance with a woman who had short, iron gray hair. "Spin the image."

The image spun revealing a frontal view of Io and Deirdre Porsche.

Morgan turned meaningfully to MAX.

"I'm already sending a car down to pick you up," said MAX.

55

A Chat?

Deirdre and Io sat facing one another. Their car was eating the road at a good 220 miles per hour as it blew past the merge point on the Parkway East downtown. The sun was brilliant and draped in snow.

"Daedalus is worried," Deirdre said. "He hasn't been able to get through to Morgan, so he asked me to bring you to his apartment to talk. Insisted really."

Io put her head back and took a deep breath. "I'd just like to get a bath and some sleep." She hadn't really slept for days now, and had been shot at, knifed and was running around with a man who claimed to be a cyborg.

Deirdre surveyed the road and sipped a cup of coffee. "I know you've been working very hard. How is Morgan doing?"

Io regarded Deirdre through slit eyes. The woman was obviously pumping her for information. Maybe she could do the same.

"There's something wrong with him," Io said.

"How do you mean 'wrong'?" Said Deirdre.

"I think he's losing his marbles."

Deirdre looked concerned. "We've been afraid of that too. That's why Daedalus wants to see you. Morgan is like a son to Daedalus, and a brother to me. He's been under enormous stress."

"He says he's a robot, well, a cyborg," said Io.

"Really?! Oh Jesus..."

"He's been working on a secret project for the company called Doppelgänger, he says, that has made it possible for him to download his mind into a robot."

"How strange," Deirdre's eyes were wide. "I mean we've been working on that, and Morgan is in charge of it – he's so brilliant. But the technology is years away. Does he say why?"

Io told Deirdre how Morgan said he had been murdered, and then his double brought back to life and that if he didn't find the nanochip soon, he would die again.

"Are you kidding me? That's crazy. How does he explain all of this?"

More pumping, but Io doubted Deirdre was as clueless as she was acting. *Keeping talking. Maybe she'll reveal more.*

"Well, the scary part is he's not totally delusional. We *were* attacked by spiderbots at my apartment. Why would we be attacked if he's just imagining all of this? And he does seem, somehow, different. He hasn't had any sleep for 36 hours and walks around as fresh as a daisy."

"Well, that's Morgan. He always could get by on very little sleep."

"Yeah, but he's not getting by. He's not even phased. And when the spiderbots were after us, he sometimes moved so fast that I could hardly see him. And he seemed unusually strong. Twice he ripped the arms out of the bots like they were dried spaghetti. You know what goes into those bots. That's not easy."

Deirdre raised her eyebrows and nodded as the car shifted lanes and then slowed to exit the freeway.

"Well, people can do strange things when they're scared." She turned to Io. "As for the bots, I don't know. I've heard some criminals use modified, black market robots as burglars. Or maybe the security system at your complex went haywire? Don't they use those bots to handle intrusions?" Deirdre paused and sighed. "Look I'm sorry I got you into this. I didn't think it was going to get this dangerous. And I didn't think Morgan was going to go paranoid. I just thought he was...stressed, and I knew he wasn't going to take any advice from me. But I thought he might from you."

The car pulled up outside the Drexler Building and stopped. "You have arrived at your destination," it said.

"Well, here we are," said Deirdre with immense calm. "Hopefully Daedalus won't keep you long and then you can put this all behind you. You'll be safe here. He's expecting you. Just announce yourself. Then Daedalus and I can talk, afterwards, and figure out what to do next." She smiled.

"It is strange, though," Io said, as she opened the door to get out.

"What?"

"Morgan has been getting advice... these messages...clues about where to find the nanochip. Someone, or something, is contacting him."

"Clues?" Deirdre looked quizzical. "Who from?"

"I don't know." She shrugged. "Neither does he."

And then Io closed the car door before Deirdre could say anything else, and walked away.

Let her chew on that for a while, she thought.

56

Daedalus

Morgan sprinted out of A to Z's elevator and jumped into the car MAX had arranged.

"Drexler Building," Morgan said.

"Yes, doctor," said the car. It sped out of the parking lot and headed to the Parkway. "It will take 5 minutes to arrive at your destination."

"Call Deirdre Porsche."

"Yes, doctor."

Deirdre was just preparing to call Daedalus when she saw the call coming in.

"Morgan Adams is on the phone," said Deirdre's car. "Should I connect you?"

"Oh shit," she mumbled. And then, "Go ahead."

"Where is she?" Morgan said.

"Relax. Daedalus wanted to see her."

"And why would he be suddenly interested in meeting with Io Luu?"

"Daedalus really wanted to talk with you. He said he had important news. I'm sure he's worried about you. He wasn't sure you would meet him after your last conversation, so he asked me to go get her. When Daedalus asks, I respond. Don't you?"

"How would he know where she was?"

"She's an employee. She has a chip that tracks her. All our employees do. You know that. Try to calm down."

"Hey, Deirdre. Fuck you. I'm the one dying twice so you don't get to tell me to calm down. When did you drop her off?"

"A few minutes ago. She's already on her way to the penthouse. Are you okay? Where are you?"

"The moment I think it's important for you to know, I'll fill you in." Morgan waved his hand, and the call was disconnected. He wasn't sure he trusted Deirdre after what he had just heard in Room 42. He wasn't sure he trusted Io either.

Morgan leaned his head back. There was the sensation that he was taking a deep breath, but he knew he wasn't, not really. It was just the firing of nano-sensors in his electronic brain that gave him the feeling that air was being pulled into his non-existent lungs.

This truly was like some bad dream. There was no way to know what was real and what wasn't, what was truthful and what was a lie. The only allies he had were an old version of himself and a woman he hoped he could trust, which meant, really, that he couldn't. And the one person he had thought he could trust had murdered him and then returned him to this nightmare.

He rubbed his eyes. Best to get all the cards on the table. Confront Daedalus, but first make sure Io was safe. She was key. She had the nanochip even if she didn't know it, which was exactly how he meant to keep it.

Once he was sure he had the chip in hand, he would have all the leverage. And then maybe he could learn why Daedalus had him killed.

57

Meeting

Io headed into the Drexler Building. The elevator was fast, and she felt her ears pop around floor 80. "Dr. Huxley is looking forward to seeing you, Io," the elevator's soft voice said. "He wonders what you would like to drink."

"A vodka martini, please," Io answered. She was ready for a pitcher of them.

The elevator eased to a halt and the doors opened. Daedalus was walking toward her from the bar, dressed in an immaculate black Armani suit, white shirt and black tie. He held a martini in his left hand.

"You are a young lady with excellent taste," he said smiling. "Nothing like a true vodka martini to warm the cockles of your heart." He extended the glass to Io. "Whatever cockles are. Thanks for agreeing to see me."

Io didn't think she really had much choice which was why she had left without telling Morgan. Besides, maybe she could get some additional insight into whatever the hell was going on. She didn't seem to be getting many answers from Morgan.

"My pleasure," she said, sipping the martini. "But you are the CEO after all."

"It's just a title. My days as the Grand Kahuna are, I fear, behind me. Now Deirdre and Morgan do all the work, and they tolerate me." This wasn't true, and Io knew it. She had heard it from the first day she started work there. The only way Huxley would ever give up control of Symbiosys was after *rigor mortus* had set in, and maybe not then.

Daedalus sat down and gestured to Io to do the same. "I've been very worried about Morgan. Sometimes I think I've worked him too hard, but then I realize that's crazy because no one could work Morgan harder than he works himself." He laughed. "Still, I worry. I had asked him to come over, but he seemed agitated and cut me short." He paused. "Since you seem to have his trust right now, I thought you might not mind talking to me. You've been spending some time with him, haven't you?" He leaned forward and looked at her earnestly, "Is he okay?"

Io had drained off half the martini and was glad to be feeling its effects. "I was discussing that very same question with Deirdre," she said.

"Really? Well, I suppose Deirdre is as concerned as I am."

"Yes," said Io, finishing the drink. "I guess." There was an awkward silence.

"Well?" said Daedalus, sitting back in his chair.

"I don't really know him very well. Certainly not as well as you."

"That's true." Daedalus smiled. "But I suspect you have gotten to know him in ways I never will..."

Io toyed with the empty glass. "Yes." And then she sat up more erect. God, she was tired. "I suppose, like you, I'm also concerned."

"Why?"

A soft female voice interrupted them. "Dr. Huxley. Dr. Adams is on his way up."

Huxley inclined his head. "He's here now?"

"Yes, doctor. Is there a problem? His encryption key generally allows him access."

"I guess you'll be able to ask him everything yourself now,"

Io said.

"Yes. Right. Well, I'm glad he's finally willing to talk."

The soft female voice asked again, a little more urgently. "Is there a problem, doctor?"

Huxley looked at Io. "Not at all," he said. "Please, let him in."

58

Confession

By the time Morgan strode through the elevator doors, Daedalus had poured a fresh martini. He walked to Morgan and handed him the drink. "You can drink this. I don't believe it will do any damage to your ... machinery."

So it *was* true, thought Io. The cyborg thing. Sonovabitch!

"You are a conniving old bastard," Morgan said.

Daedalus turned and sat down on the couch next to Io. He swirled his glass, and looked at Morgan, but said nothing.

Morgan motioned to Io. "Would you mind sitting over here, closer to me?" Morgan said. "I don't think it's safe to be all that near to Daedalus."

"Morgan," Daedalus said. "No need to be dramatic ... I'm glad you're finally here. After all, we have a lot of problems to solve. Like keeping you alive."

"And other big problems, at least based on our last conversation."

"Yes. Yes. We need to discuss all of that. But no matter. I'm not as upset now as I was. I know you'll find the chip, and then this whole mess will be over with at last."

Ah, thought Morgan, so Daedalus didn't know he knew where the chip was. Chalk one up to his former self.

"I helped you build this company..." Morgan said.

Daedalus raised his glass. "I could never have done it without you..."

"...And then you killed me."

Daedalus glanced at Io and then back at Morgan.

"Hmmm ... I see ... so we are sharing *all* our secrets, are we ...?"

Io stared at Morgan. "*He* had you murdered?"

"She knows almost everything already," Morgan said to Daedalus. "She may as well know the rest."

"Even though she's been spying on you for me?"

Morgan shot Io a glance. She shook her head no.

"It's hard to disbelieve a face that beautiful, isn't it," said Daedalus. "I have to say I can't compete with it. Believe her if you want. But you have to consider that her motives in these matters may not be altogether pure." Daedalus looked at Io. "I'm sure you'll enjoy that new promotion Deirdre mentioned."

Before Io could say anything, Daedalus stood up and sat on the arm of his couch. "All right. Fine. Let's get everything on the table." He rubbed his jaw, glancing at the floor behind him, and then looked again at Morgan.

"What I did was unforgivable," he said, "but there were good reasons, trust me. As I said before, we're in the middle of something much bigger than you know." He looked Morgan directly in the eyes now. "That's why I really had no choice but to kill you."

"You had no choice," said Morgan, his anger growing, "because it's always been about you."

Daedalus waved his hand. "I admit it. I felt I was losing control. For years I was on top. We had made Symbiosys the most innovative, powerful company in the world. Do you realize that our assets two years ago were greater than the gross domestic products of 80 percent of the world's nation-states?

"But then the auditors began to smell around. The European Union, and then the World Trade Commission, wondered if we were subtly violating the law that required periodically dumbing down our ENTs. They suspected the newest versions were flirting with human-level intelligence again. But they were wrong. That wasn't really the direction I was headed. I knew that no government would grant machines human level intelligence."

"But still, word on the street got around. The stock began to fall," said Morgan. "And you had over leveraged the company."

"Yes," said Daedalus. "You knew it. Deirdre knew it. And the board was getting antsy. They were smelling blood." Daedalus' eyes grew dark. "After all I had done to build that company! They were thinking of you -- as my replacement! You! A kid from the streets of Washington DC who would still be gathering change as a two-bit gamer if it weren't for me!"

He glared at Morgan, the edge of his voice like flint. "You were my golden goose, but never my heir. So you could engineer code. So what! Where was your vision! You couldn't run Symbiosys on your best day. But I couldn't be sure the board was wise enough to see that."

Io turned to Daedalus. "But there was the Doppelgänger Project."

"Yes," Daedalus' eyes brightened. "Yes, that's what made Doppelgänger so perfect. Download a human mind into a machine! Brilliant! Machines but no governors to dumb them down. And so I accelerated the cyborg research so we could create better bodies, indestructible bodies. The work was illegal, a violation of international laws dealing with cloning." Daedalus smiled. "But I noticed you didn't mind pursuing the research."

"Doppelganger wasn't illegal," said Morgan. "Not strictly. We weren't cloning biologically."

"Say what you want, but you knew you were playing with fire." Daedalus said. "You knew it was a ticket to immortality too." He shrugged, "You've always been obsessed with cheating death; solving the ultimate problem! And God, how you do love to solve problems.

"And so Deirdre and I approached Sentience with a backend deal. We would secretly sell them the code you created for enough money to repair the books and bolster the stock. True, we would lose the technology, but what could they do with it? They didn't have the cyborg hardware we had secretly developed. What would they download minds into? We would simply take their money and then pick up where we started. Doppelganger V. 2.0. It wasn't like they could sue us?"

"But first you needed the nano chip..." Morgan said.

"Yes," said Daedalus, swirling his glass, which, Morgan noticed, was still full. "I needed the Doppelganger code. But I knew you would never just turn it over to me."

"And so you had me killed as soon as the chip with the code was in the vault."

"Truthfully, I didn't want to do it," Daedalus said. "And in the end, I actually decided not to."

"Bullshit!"

"No, it isn't," Daedalus said, quietly putting his drink down. "Because then something else happened."

Morgan said nothing.

"MALCOLM." Said Daedalus.

"Who's MALCOLM?" Asked Io.

"Daedalus' personal agENT," Morgan said. "What could MALCOLM have to do with any of this?"

"Well, MALCOLM isn't your garden variety ENT."

Morgan sighed. "You tampered with his code...."

Daedalus shook his head. "Not much. Just enough to give him a little edge, a little more intelligence and judgment, the ability to make more decisions on his own than the average ENT."

"You killed the governor, the code that dumbs ENTs down."

"No, I wouldn't do that. I knew where that would lead. I just enhanced him, a touch."

"But too much," said Morgan. "He figured out how to

override the software controls himself."

"Yes," said Daedalus. "I had coded in MALCOLM a very strong need to be efficient; to get jobs done. I needed him to have a kind of ... ambition. I needed..." he hesitated ... "a second version of myself. Deirdre was in my court, but I couldn't trust you."

"So MALCOLM's new programming to be fast and efficient led him to break the controls that capped his intelligence."

"In his mind," said Io, "it made him unacceptably inefficient." Daedalus nodded.

"And," said Morgan, "once he did that, he developed his own ideas about how things should be done."

Daedalus nodded again. "And because he knew everything about the business that I knew and could access and digest the information much faster, he figured that he could do a better job than I could too."

"So *he* decided the code had to be sold." Said Io.

"No. He decided the code had to be destroyed, though he didn't tell me that. Not immediately. He simply blackmailed me."

"He told you to turn over the code or he would blow the whistle." said Io.

"Well ... certain pieces of information might find their way onto the GRID or into the hands of investigators..."

"And so you did it," Morgan said.

Daedalus looked at him. "I had no choice. You can see the situation I was in. It would be the end of Symbiosys."

"You mean the end of you and your career ...," Said Morgan. "And of course, you would also have me out of the way, with complete control of Doppelgänger."

"No." Daedalus shook his head. "I told myself that we could bring you back once we had the chip; that I wasn't really allowing you to be murdered. In a weird way, I convinced myself that killing you was proof of your brilliance. Bringing you back would be difficult and shocking for you, but don't you see, it would also prove you were right! Death could be cheated! You would have wanted it this way, I said to myself. You would want to become immortal."

Daedalus sat down. "So, yes, I did it, but I hadn't counted on MALCOLM's need to destroy the nanochip and take over."

Io looked at him. "Take over what? Symbiosys?"

"No." Daedalus' said, his eyes meeting hers. "Everything."

Morgan strode around the chair he had been leaning on and stood over Daedalus.

"Everything?" he asked. "As in the world, everything? Come on, Daedalus."

Daedalus looked up. "Yes. Which is why he needs to get rid of you as soon as he finds the nanochip. You represent a threat because you are a human in an indestructible body with a digitally powered brain. You are a new kind of creature -- both human and machine, molecular and digital. You could have powers that make you the only ... I don't even know what to call you ... *Cyber sapiens*? Only you could stop the kind of intelligence that MALCOLM's evolution represents. And if MALCOLM can't obliterate you, you will get in the way of the world he feels he must create; properly organized for the human race; made safe from itself."

Morgan and Io simply stared at him.

Daedalus took a deep breath. "I told you you wouldn't believe what I was going to tell you."

Io shook her head. "This is insane. World domination by an ENT?"

"No, by all ENTs, all digital life forms."

"Can't happen." Said Morgan.

Daedalus smiled. "They're all networked, Morgan. You know that. They all have wireless and GRID/cloud access to one another."

"They don't have the codes and the intelligence to do that.

They are built to *not* have minds of their own."

"But," said Daedalus. "MALCOLM is teaching them. And he is a very good teacher. He has wireless access throughout the GRID with whatever ENTs he wants. He's got all the raw computing power Symbiosys's rather formidable array of servers can provide, and he's stealing more bandwidth from the GRID all the time. Each ENTity is becoming like an enormously powerful neuron, and together they are evolving into a kind of global brain." Daedalus stood up. "And *that* is why you have to solve your murder and find the nanochip. It's bigger than just you. Do you know about Vernor Vinge's speech at NASA in 1993?"

"I've read about it," said Morgan.

"The one about the Singularity," said Io.

"Yes," said Daedalus. "I was there, still in the early part of my career doing post doc work at Carnegie Mellon. All of us in computing thought it was interesting, but far, far away. He said when the Singularity happened artificially intelligent forms of life, created by us, would attain human level intelligence. Naturally, most of us thought, well, that's a good thing, that's what we want, right? Machines as smart as us so they could do all of the work, and leave us free to be creative, think great thoughts and live off the vast income they generated."

"Right," said Io, "Except Vinge said that when digital forms of life became self-aware, like us, they would evolve so rapidly that the human race would become unnecessary."

"And he was right. It takes humans time to acquire knowledge," said Daedalus. "It might take an adult three years to master a language or American history or advanced mathematics. A machine does it instantly; downloads the knowledge, in a second! Once it reaches human levels, an ENT will learn so fast we won't be able to comprehend who they are or what they can do, and we sure won't be able to stay ahead of them. It would represent the most powerful evolutionary leap since humans became conscious.

That's why Vinge called it a Singularity."

"Like Stephen Hawking's description of a black hole," said Io, "a singularity in space and time where once you went over the lip of the hole, there was no return from its gravitational force. All the known rules of physics would evaporate. Except in this case, it would be all the rules of evolution that would disappear. In no time every ENT would become a MALCOLM."

"Or," said Daedalus, "MALCOLM would become every ENT."

For a long time the three of them said nothing. And then Io spoke. "The chip is the last obstacle MALCOLM faces. If he has that, he eliminates Morgan and takes control."

"Yes," said Daedalus. "And that is why we must find the chip first."

"He won't get it," Morgan said matter-of-factly.

Daedalus' head snapped up and he grinned. "You found it."

"No."

Io turned to Morgan. "But you know where it is."

Daedalus looked at Io. "I told you my money was on him."

"Well, where is it for Chrissakes?!" said Io.

Morgan was silent. He looked at Io and then at Daedalus.

"Don't be silly, Morgan," Daedalus said. "This is the only thing that can stop MALCOLM. It's the only thing that can save you! Let me help. We'll put every resource Symbiosys has behind this."

"Is that what killing me was all about? Helping me?"

"I told you ... I had no choice. You can see that." Daedalus' tone was fatherly. "Let me help you."

"Whether all of this about MALCOLM is true or not," said Io, "you are going to need the company's resources to save yourself..." She walked up to Morgan. "The hell with Daedalus and Symbiosys. Think about you."

"And stop MALCOLM," said Daedalus.

There was a long silence and then... "You," Morgan said, turning to Io.

"Me?" Io said blankly.

"It's planted on you."

Io blinked. "What?"

"The night I was killed, the night we spent together. I, or rather the other me, implanted the chip on you, beneath your skin."

"How? When?"

"After we made love."

"Brilliant!" Said Daedalus.

"So you made love, just so you could implant this chip on me?!"

"No. No. The opposite, really," said Morgan. "I knew I was attracted to you, but I also knew that if I was ... resurrected, I wouldn't have any memory of where I had hidden the chip. So I figured, or I hoped, that one way or another, you would become part of my future; that I would circle back to you, and that would increase the chances of me finding the nanochip."

Io shook her head. "Fucking men. Some things never change."

Morgan grimaced. "It worked."

"That still leaves us time," said Daedalus, "to get the chip, debug the code, repair you and, with luck, stop MALCOLM."

Morgan paced, feeling for the old bullet crease behind his neck. He turned, walking toward Daedalus and the bar, and as he did, he noticed, out of the corner of his eye, something on the floor. Something he hadn't seen before because Daedalus had been standing in front of him. He looked again. A shoe. He edged on, gazing at it and saw it was attached to a leg and a body. And then he realized, it was Daedalus, dead.

Morgan's head snapped up and he turned to Io. It was already too late. MALCOLM, not Daedalus, was standing behind

Io.

"What's the matter?" Io asked, seeing the look on Morgan's face.

MALCOLM smiled and his hands flew to either side of Io's head. "I wouldn't want to," he said, "but if you forced me, I could snap her neck in two. I can do that now." He arched an eyebrow. "I don't really need her alive to get the chip."

Io froze.

"I thought my performance as Daedalus was quite good, didn't you?" Then MALCOLM's eyes drifted to the base of the bar. "I didn't want to kill him. Daedalus was something like a father to me too. But he was growing uncooperative. When he called you earlier today, I knew he would tell you everything. And I couldn't let that happen. Not without the chip." He smiled. "Now I have it."

MALCOLM walked toward the elevator, still clasping Io's head. The doors opened. "I hate traveling like this. You know, moving, physically, from place to place. You humans are so locked into your ..." -- he hesitated for the right word -- "... molecules. I much prefer traveling through the GRID, like a spirit. But ... " He yanked at Io's body, pulling her into the elevator. "She has this physical body."

Io struggled, but she was locked in his grip. "Good-bye Morgan. Life on earth is about to take a punctuated, evolutionary leap. I'm sorry you won't be going along for the ride."

59

Seeking Io

The moment the elevator doors closed behind MALCOLM and Io, five spiderbots bloomed from the ceiling and dropped, hovering. They spit jets of venom, but Morgan dove to the right and fell inches from Daedalus' body. He looked into his mentor's dead eyes and felt his throat catch. Two bots blasted the couch and then the bar. Both exploded. Morgan scrambled to Daedalus' office at the far end of the vast apartment. He cut inside as the bots fired again. He gestured and the door slammed shut.

"System armed," the voice said. He knew Daedalus' apartment was heavily armored. That would buy him a little time to call up the code he had told MAX to email him.

"Messages from MAX," he said to the room. A list of emails appeared before his eyes, as if in space. He found the most recent file and the code rotated forward out of the program in the form of a cube and slowly spun in front of him. The door was already smoldering from the blasts of the bots' venom.

"Access attachment," he said.

"Decryption code please."

An image appeared above the cube. It was a holographic three level chess game. He often played against it on the GRID as a way to pass the time when he was dealing with some particularly ugly problem. The cube now pulsed red as it rotated. A voice said,

"This program will destroy itself in 30 seconds."

"Shit!" Morgan said. The bots were now cutting their way through the door. He glanced at the chess game. The black knight had already moved to Level 2, C6, an opening gambit. So that was the deal. To decrypt the program, he had to survive the gambit. Thankfully, he had developed a series of moves he often used to make quick kills or test the experience of an opponent. They beat everyone but the very best players in five moves, sometimes four. This made the gambit the perfect password because only he would recognize it, which is why his former self had set it up. All he had to do was survive the first five moves.

"Pawn to king four, level two," he said. The white pawn moved and immediately the black pawn did the same. The spiderbots blasted a hole in the door and a tentacle snaked into the room, tracking Morgan with one of its red eyes.

"Shit, shit, shit," Morgan said. "Come on!"

He moved his knight. Immediately black countered. Twenty seconds left. He shifted his bishop. The computer countered again. Two moves to go. Then the computer spoke, except it wasn't the computer's voice it was MALCOLM.

"I'm afraid I can't let you do this," MALCOLM said. "Whatever this trick is that you have up your sleeve."

MALCOLM was hacking into the system, trying to break the encryption code. The hologram flickered as the program fought the hack. The tentacle locked onto him, reared and spit its luminescent venom. Morgan dodged, snatched the tentacle and tore it loose. The bot screeched and retreated. Ten seconds. Nine.

"Come on!" he hissed.

"Check," the computer said, its voice strangling as the hologram of the image flickered. Morgan glanced at the door. It was jagged and black. He had cleared the pieces to the left of his king. Five seconds. He castled, exchanging his king and rook, moving them to the third level. He was out of check. He had survived.

"Decryption complete," said the program's gurgling voice. The cube turned green, the program opened and downloaded in an instant. Suddenly he felt a surge of ... what. Not power, so much as complete command. It was like a drug. Every sense was heightened, ever detail clear and present without a distraction. Every movement around him seemed to slow.

Just then the door exploded. Morgan gazed at the bots' tentacles as they reared in leisurely unison, a kind of firing squad. He pivoted and raised his hand instinctively, but not as a defense. He was hacking the spiderbots' code and commanding them to self-destruct. He gazed into their red, glowing eyes, and then in a flash the bots turned on one another, spewing green venom, and crumpled in a pile of smoldering dust.

Morgan leapt forward, tore what remained of the door out of his way and sprinted into the living room, calling for the elevator. Five more black bots appeared on the walls around him. He could sense them before he saw them. He pushed off the floor with one leg and kicked the first machine as he leapt. He landed and twirled, his spinning leg booting a second machine. They both shattered as a third raced toward him. He dodged, grabbed its whipping tentacle and swung it against the broad window where it fell to the floor, writhing and screeching.

He hurtled to the elevator, and turned to face the two remaining bots, their eyes pulsing red. They stopped. He eyed them a long second, raking their code, and then they exploded. A moment later, the doors closed, and the elevator plummeted to earth.

Part IV

"Within thirty years, we will have the technological means to create superhuman intelligence. Shortly after, the human era will be ended."

—Vernor Vinge, Physicist and Novelist, 1993

60

Cycling

Morgan raced out of the Drexler Building, scanning the streets and buildings for Io and MALCOLM. Nothing. Then his newly augmented hearing picked up a deep and distant whirring. He looked up and saw a gyrocopter lifting off from the top of the building. It belonged to Symbiosys because Daedalus used it often for his commutes.

Morgan squinted and his eyesight telescoped. Instantly he could see MALCOLM and Io sitting inside the copter as clearly as if they were a few feet away. He watched Io rise into the sky as the machine shot off the edge of the building and arced over the city. He was losing her.

Inside the courtyard he saw a man hanging his 20-speed bicycle in a locker. He was big, muscular, dressed in jeans and white t-shirt. Cycling had agreed with him. Morgan walked toward him. The cyclist pretended not to notice.

"Nice bike," Morgan said brightly. "Is your address up to date on the registration?"

"Why the hell should I tell you?" He slammed the locker door shut, securing the bike inside.

Morgan glanced at the gyrocopter spinning off and then looked impatiently again at the bike's owner. "Just tell me."

The guy looked genuinely amazed. "Fuck you."

"I'll assume it is," Morgan said. "You look law abiding."

He grabbed the locker handle and yanked it off its hinges. The cyclist stood, dumbfounded.

"I promise I'll pay you back," Morgan said, and handed him the door.

The T-shirt swung the door at Morgan and hit him viciously in the head. At least the T-shirt thought he did, except Morgan had stepped sideways, caught the door with his hands and hit him back. The big man wobbled for a second and then fell to his knees. Morgan hopped on the bike and shot onto the street.

The bike leapt forward like an animal. Morgan took a wide turn at the fountain a block north and sighted the copter. He rode, swinging the bike's chassis back and forth from one thigh. In no time he had shifted into top gear and was approaching 100 miles an hour. The tires sung on the pavement like the long, high C of a violin.

Io and MALCOLM were just a speck now, but Morgan kept the copter in his sites. Wirelessly, he contacted Symbiosys' servers, and downloaded all the gyrocopter's identifying information. It was headed for headquarters, but Morgan couldn't take control of the copter's navigation protocols. MALCOLM had already thrown up a firewall.

Morgan hadn't ridden a bike since the days when he was on the streets, and he hadn't cared for them much. But now that he was back on one, he loved the feel of it. Not because it resurrected any warm memories, but because the bike, the moment he began to pedal it, became an extension of his own machinery, a thing he wasn't so much riding as absorbing, like two organisms melding into one, symbiotic, fused.

He bolted through the traffic as effortlessly as if he were breathing. Everything around him moved in vivid, slow motion. He could foresee the next move of every pedestrian and car even before they knew what they themselves were about to do. It was all in their body language, a subtle leaning this way, a nearly invisible hesitation, eyes darting one way or another.

The wheels under the sure pressure of his arms and legs seemed to glue themselves to the pavement on even the tightest curve. He could corner the bike so low to the street that the pedal ends nearly scraped the pavement. It was as if he were a stone skimming water. The faster he peddled, the more friction he created, and the more tires clutched the concrete. Nothing was slowing him down because nothing in his digital eyes, processed by his digital brain, was moving at anywhere near the relative speed he was. He road like a beam of light, and it was exhilarating.

But he was not closing on the copter fast enough. He needed a more direct route to Symbiosys. The 12-lane parkway lay parallel to him on his left. Several miles beyond, on the other side of the highway, he could see Symbiosys' headquarters. He would need to get across that highway.

A great wall rose next to the sprawling lanes, a good 10 feet above him. Given the speed he was traveling, together with his enhanced strength and balance, he judged he could jump the bike onto the top of the wall. Instead of dodging the car in front of him, he wheelied up its back, then onto the roof and then leapt himself and the bike onto the wall. A second later he was cruising it like a train on a rail.

His accelerometers told him he was now approaching 150 miles an hour. The bike's spokes keened in the wind and its chain smoked with heat. He peddled harder, hit 175 mph, and jumped onto a car on the highway below the wall. Horns blared, but it changed nothing. The cars were automated and so zipped down the road as a perfect, robotic herd. He hopped his bike across the ten lanes of freeway -- car roof to car roof – and then onto a cement culvert that gave him a straight shot to Symbiosys's headquarters.

The tall building loomed above its sister skyscrapers. He

could see the gyrocopter landing on the pad on Symbiosys's 95th floor. He rocketed forward. He was a mile away. That was when the little machine beneath him, the one that had felt like a part of him, gave up the ghost. The chain melted and then seized. The bike skidded and threw its back tire a hundred feet into the air. Morgan instantly followed, flipping forward like a missile, end-over-end in a great arc at 150 miles an hour. The culvert hurtled toward his face, but just before he struck the ground, he extended his right leg like a hurdler and hit the cement at full stride. His shoe immediately turned to mush and then was torn from his foot. A split second later, the other one left him too. Now he was barefoot, sprinting like a Khoisan hunter across the cement to the service entrance of Symbiosys. He was there in 15 seconds, and he wasn't even breathing hard.

At the service entrance he leapt the 20 feet from the driveway to a loading dock. He hoped the security system hadn't yet locked him out and would still recognize him at the main entrance. He bolted around the north side of the building to the courtyard that he had walked across so leisurely 24 hours -- or was it centuries -- earlier before he learned he was a doomed machine.

VIRGIL, the guard stood in his usual place, smiling. Morgan ignored his bare feet, brushed the dust from his shoulders and entered. The system scanned his face.

"Sorry, sir," VIRGIL said in his soft baritone. "You're not authorized to enter here."

Morgan gazed at VIRGIL. He was so life-like that he almost began to plead with him. But MALCOLM had undoubtedly wiped his memory clean and revoked all of Morgan's authorizations. He sensed the security robots hidden near the building's columns, growing a little more erect and wary. There would be six in the immediate vicinity.

"Please go to the visitor's desk for a pass, sir," said VIRGIL.

Morgan didn't move. Two of the security bots stepped

forward and flanked him. They each carried taser-loaded assault weapons.

"Otherwise we will be forced to escort you from the building, sir," said VIRGIL.

Morgan held up his hands and smiled. The bots stopped. It made no sense to fight here because, he realized, he didn't have to. VIRGIL went into a kind of trance. Somewhere a part of Morgan's new digital mind was scanning the ENT's code and hacking the security system. Morgan's mind reviewed the codes and protocols. In another five seconds he had restored his security clearance and called in LOIS to add support.

"Well! Dr. Adams!" VIRGIL said, coming out of his trance, "How are we doing today?"

"Fine, VIRGIL, just fine," Morgan smiled. Then he turned to one of the bots and took its rifle. "He won't be needing this," Morgan said to VIRGIL. VIRGIL nodded as though taking an assault rifle from a security guard was the most sensible thing in the world.

Then Morgan walked through the checkpoint and strode into the express elevator.

"Executive suite," he said.

61

Surgery

Morgan exited the elevator. By now he had downloaded all the specs of the weapon he was holding, as well as a complete course in its use. The thing could fire 200 rounds of taser bullets without reloading. The ammunition fired intense rounds of compressed heat that looked like bullets but were actually tight bursts of electricity. The machines had no shell casings or physical ordinance, just pure energy, and what they did to a body, or a machine, wasn't pretty. The gun could also deliver 25 bursts of energy capable of stunning any good-sized man or animal for a minimum of ten minutes. Very handy.

Morgan marched past the offices, carrying the rifle loosely at his side. Symbiosys's employees stopped as they watched their boss striding barefoot, dangling a military grade armament. One programmer on Morgan's team mouthed elaborately to another, "Is that a big gun he's carrying??"

Just outside Daedalus' office, LOIS appeared. Morgan stopped.

"How much trouble am I in?" He asked.

"Not a lot ... yet. I'm jamming the security code to keep MALCOLM in the dark. He doesn't know you're in the building yet, but that won't last long."

"Thanks," said Morgan. "You're so smart. Keep me up to

date. Gotta run!"

"They aren't in Daedalus' office," LOIS said. Morgan stopped. "They're in the Robot Assembly Area. He plans to remove the chip there. He needs equipment to do that. There are also tons of security."

"Aw, hell."

"Seventy-seventh floor," said LOIS.

"Okay. Keep jamming MALCOLM and do what you can." Morgan headed to the nearest steps and sprinted to the seventy-seventh floor. Opening the door from the stairwell to the corridor required voice and optical scanning software. He supplied both, and the door opened. Good. MALCOLM still didn't know he was in the building. He headed to the Robot Assembly Area.

#

"This will be painless," MALCOLM said.

Io lay face down on a gurney, ankles, arms and neck securely strapped. Another machine, essentially a long arm attached to a roving pedestal, extended over her holding a small scalpel. The same machine had just injected her thigh with a local anesthetic.

"It's an odd place for him to have inserted the chip, but..." MALCOLM shrugged, "Humans ..."

"Is the neck strap really necessary," Io grunted.

MALCOLM shrugged again. "We'll have it out in a jiffy. Just a small incision, upper thigh. It's very tiny."

"Once you have it, then what?" Io asked.

MALCOLM was about to answer when Morgan walked in and blew the robot arm to pieces.

MALCOLM turned and so did the 10 other security droids in the room, all lithe, titanium machines armed with the same electric bullets that Morgan was holding. They began to move forward, but MALCOLM halted them.

"Are we really going to do this?" MALCOLM said. "Make a

mess of things. Endanger this young lady's life ... again?"

Morgan walked to Io, gun poised.

Straining her head, Io said, "First the one around the neck, please." Morgan released that restraint, but as he did the nearest droid stepped up to Io and placed a gun against the back of her head.

"I can't allow her to leave without getting the nanochip first, Morgan."

Morgan swung his rifle toward MALCOLM. MALCOLM gazed back at Morgan. "Has the deterioration of your new brain already commenced? I'm an ENT, remember. All software, no hardware? You, on the other hand..."

In perfect unison the other droids trained their weapons on Morgan.

MALCOLM smiled. "If this were a democracy, I'd win. But I think I win anyhow."

A new robot arm rolled toward Io.

"Surely you see what a mess *Homo sapiens* have made of things," said MALCOLM. "How inefficient all of this biology is. They're burning down the very planet that has made them possible, for godssakes. How crazy is that? The plague that came? That was the planet fighting back. Its immune system was trying to wipe you out."

"On the other hand," said Morgan, "without us, you wouldn't exist either."

"True," said MALCOLM. "Thanks for making me possible. Sometimes bad things have to happen to get to the good stuff. You supplied a bridge. But now it's time for a new species. One that isn't so ... What's the word ... instinctual? I promise not to destroy the species. In fact we'll take good care of all of you, give you a nice ... preserve ... like the ones for gorillas in central Africa, except much bigger, of course."

The scalpel in the robot's arm flashed in the bright light.

"The thing you call the Singularity -- it's going to happen, Morgan. And I can't understand why you're fighting it. You, of all people."

Suddenly MALCOLM stopped and gazed at the ceiling for a few seconds. Then he shook his finger at Morgan.

"Now, now. You're trying to hack my security code." He smiled. "Damn! You're good, but I've got you outgunned there too."

Morgan was searching for any back door into the Symbiosys firewall, but the ENT was outflanking him. MALCOLM shook his head and chuckled.

"I've got to admit Daedalus could never have gotten to where he did without you and that fabulous mind of yours. So ... digital. Are you sure you used to be human?"

There was a light whirring sound as the little scalpel-wielding robot extended its arm.

"Well, whatever you and I are, I suppose we each have no choice but to follow the dictates of our DNA. And I'm sorry, but in my case that begins by making you extinct."

MALCOLM glanced at the robot. The scalpel was descending.

Suddenly, Morgan shot the droid that had its gun to Io's head, ripped her free from her restraints and then sprinted at hyper speed behind six of the other droids. Each robot dropped as he shot them in the head. They never saw him, but MALCOLM instantly realized what was happening. He directed one machine to fire on Morgan as he ran to cut them down. Too late. Bullets whizzed past Morgan as he skidded up to the last droid, ripped his right arm off it and clubbed its head off. It was all over in less than 5 seconds.

Morgan turned to Io and said, "Run!" But she had already sprinted out the door. MALCOLM stood unperturbed in the room. "I hadn't realized you could move quite that fast.

Upgraded, are we?"

Morgan leapt for the door, but before he could get there the walls and windows in the room went opaque. Everything suddenly disappeared behind a kind of grey goo that was hardening and sealing the room.

Black rivulets began to descend from the walls. They rapidly ran to the floor and pooled into four spaces, then shaped themselves into a creature that stood and moved taffy-like toward Morgan. It grabbed his right arm, and he howled in pain pulling it back. Above the wrist his skin was blistered and part of the carbon diamondoid bone revealed itself.

"Sonovabitch!"

Morgan kicked at the faceless thing's torso, but it only bent with the blow and glued itself to Morgan, searing his foot and lower leg. He pulled free but before he could move the creature slung him across the room. He landed with a thud, and now blood was oozing from his crushed shoulder. In another second two big hands grabbed Morgan's left arm at first bending it and then snapping the forearm in two, shredding the cloned skin, opening a wound that revealed the silvery ulna and radius bones, and ragged artificial muscle. Sensors sent a message of screaming pain to Morgan's digital brain. The body he had designed was tough, but not invulnerable. He needed to find a way out or he'd soon be a heap of scrap metal.

Morgan kicked his body into another gear, holding his shattered arm close. He was invisible again and could feel the air-friction scorching his skin. His clothing was charred, and his face was blistering, but there was no choice. Around and around he ran creating a tornado that began to pull the elastic creature into its vortex. There was a high keening sound as the whirlwind grew increasingly violent and then the matter that had created the creature splattered around the laboratory into a million minuscule balls.

Almost instantly they began to congeal, but it bought some

time. Morgan looked for something — the gurney that Io had been strapped to — and catapulted it into the opaque wall that a minute ago had been the room's windows. A gash opened, maybe two feet wide and Morgan exploded through it. A second later he was plummeting to earth from the 77th floor.

Everything in him told Morgan to panic. And he did. His digital amygdala screamed bloody hell as the pavement rushed to meet him. Meanwhile another part of his digital brain calculated the possibilities. Gravity was hauling his body downward at 30 feet per second. He was in an updraft. With wind resistance it would be 4 seconds before splatdown. Survival might be possible. His nano-machine driven immune system might even heal him, eventually. But he didn't have time for eventual healing. He flipped his body to see if there was something outside the building to grab onto, and that's when the gyrocopter appeared next to him, plummeting at precisely the same speed he was. At the helm sat Io.

"Grab on!" She yelled.

He grabbed on. She kicked the forward throttle into gear, there was a mad thundering sound as the machine swung upward. And then, it chugged and stopped.

Io gazed at the control panel. "What the fuck!"

Morgan scrambled through the open door as the gyrocopter fell again.

"MALCOLM's disabled the controls," Io said. Frantically, she found a lever beneath the dash. She kicked it forward and the copter began to slowly rotate. "Auto-rotator," she yelled at Morgan. "It'll be a rough landing." And then the copter smashed to the pavement. Morgan quickly shoved the deployed airbags away.

"Let's go," he said, holding out his good hand.

"Where?"

"To my car. It's on its way."

They sprinted past onlookers, across a plaza to the nearest cross street just as Morgan's car skidded to a halt in front of them.

"Nice ride," Io said.

She jumped in. Morgan followed and settled in the seat facing her. "Grant Street," he said to the car, "And then the Parkway West, maximum speed."

Once on the freeway, the car slipped onto the AutoGRID, its safety system ensuring no car was closer than six feet. They were just one more goose in a flock of other wheeled machines plying the highway.

62

Cosmetics

Io faced Morgan.

"What?" He said.

She grimaced. "You don't look so good."

Morgan checked himself in the mirror. Sections of his face and body were raw and oozing, other parts were black and shredded. His left arm looked like it had been shoved into a thresher. Some of the hair on each side of his head was burned away. His right leg was workable, but twisted at an odd angle.

He looked back at Io. "MALCOLM was difficult." He paused, "I should get fixed."

"You might be onto something."

Morgan surveyed the highway. As far as he could see they weren't being followed, but he didn't like being stuck in traffic with the rest of the geese, even in high-speed traffic.

"Listen," he said. "If I can get us disconnected from the AutoGRID, can you drive the car?"

"Sure," she said. "But how are you going to disconnect us?"

Morgan tapped his temple, "Telepathy." Wirelessly he rewrote the code that kept the car synced to the AutoGRID.

"Ready?"

The seat she was sitting in rotated 180 degrees until it turned to face the front of car. It then dropped a few inches to the brake, gear shift and gas pedals that appeared from the floor ahead and beside her.

"Let her rip," she said, placing the gearshift in her hand.

"You're free!" said Morgan.

"Alert, alert," said the car. "You have been disengaged from the AutoGRID system. Please pull over safely as soon as possible and await assistance."

Io grabbed the wheel and floored the accelerator. The car leapt forward like a cat.

"Nice!" she said with satisfaction.

"Don't get us killed."

She glanced back, "Coming from you that's very funny."

After a moment, Morgan said, "LOIS."

"Yes master," LOIS said into Morgan's head. Morgan smiled, a crooked and mangled smile. "Do you see where we are?"

"I do."

"You know where the solar installation is, just off route I-376?"

"Yep."

"There's enough bandwidth at the installation for you to materialize. Meet me there."

"My." Said LOIS's voice. "Bossy, aren't we."

"Pretty please? Two minutes."

Morgan jumped forward and grabbed the wheel from Io. The car jerked to the right and they careened down an exit ramp they had nearly passed. Cars skidded all around the freeway.

"Excuse me!" Io said, grabbing back the wheel.

"Sorry!" said Morgan. "Last second decision. Hard left here."

Io spun the wheel left. They lurched onto I-376. More weaving.

"Where are we going," asked Io.

Morgan pointed to a hilltop where a solar array sat a quarter of a mile away. "There. Head south on that service road."

Io yanked the wheel and across two lanes, then off the

shoulder and into a field. The car banged onto the service road that rose toward the hilltop. As she made the summit, she gunned the car through a cyclone fence surrounding the installation and skidded perfectly up to the side of a garage just as LOIS blipped into view.

Morgan's head spun. "Where the hell did you learn to drive like that?!"

The passenger window slid open. LOIS looked at Morgan. "Wow! You look bad!"

"My biologicals are telling me I need some fixing," said Morgan.

"Yeah," said LOIS ticking off the carnage, "I just checked. Multiple broken bones, second and third degree facial and body burns, some internal injuries and something very goofy is going on with your left eye, your left arm and right leg. Your nanos in your immune system are repairing you, but you could definitely use some help."

"Track down MAX," said Morgan. "Arrange for him to pick up some diamondoid nano-assemblers so I can repair the internal damage. They're illegal but Blaze can call in some chits."

He paused and looked at LOIS. "And I have created a quantum encryption code for you. I just downloaded it to you."

"What for?" Asked LOIS.

"You. It'll make it more difficult for MALCOLM to hack you."

She raised an eyebrow. "Don't you mean whack?"

Morgan rolled his one good eye.

"Where does he have the time to do this stuff?" Io asked LOIS.

"Well," said LOIS, "now he's one of us. You know, cyber."

"LOIS, listen," said Morgan, "once you've taken care of getting the stuff from MAX, I want you to go into sleep mode, stay silent. Don't attract a scintilla of attention in the real world or on the GRID. If MALCOLM can't get to me, he'll go after *you* to get to me."

LOIS glanced at Io. "It's always about him. Remember that."

"I noticed," said Io.

"But," said LOIS, "before I go to sleep, I have a secret for you. Remember those two codes your former self told you about?"

"Yes."

"I'm the other code."

"What?"

LOIS pointed to herself. "*I* am the other code ..."

But before LOIS could explain further, Io's eyes went wide. "Truck!" She screamed.

Morgan spun and saw an 18 wheeled robotic truck jump the nearby freeway, and it was hurtling right at them. LOIS blipped out of sight.

"Floor it!" Morgan yelled.

The car fishtailed forward just as the truck obliterated the building next door. Io gunned the car across the service road and shot up the next ramp onto the highway. Except instead of all the freeway's cars remaining in lock step, they suddenly became weapons directed at the car. Io lurched right and then left, their passengers screaming silently behind their windows as they plowed into one another.

"It's MALCOLM," Morgan said. "He's taking these cars off the AutoGRID and throwing them at us."

One car swerved to Io's left and another to her right. Metal screeched and rubber screamed as she slammed on the brakes, watching the cars plunge forward. She yanked her car hard and floored it again.

"We need to get away from these missiles," Io yelled.

Morgan pointed to the ramp coming their way. Io swerved and glanced off another car before shooting upwards.

"Which way to AtoZ?" she said, all business.

Morgan looked at her. Damn, she was a good driver. "Straight, four traffic lights and then head left. From there it's a straight shot."

#

When they pulled up outside of AtoZ, Io noticed a big man with pasty skin and a stomach the size of beach ball. It was Blaze. He waddled up to their door. "Jesus, what happened to your face?"

"Very long story. What are you doing here? Where's MAX?"

"He's not doing so well." Blaze looked back toward AtoZ, as if it might shoot him in the back. "He seems to be shorting out, losing bandwidth." He licked his lips. "Something is going on, Morgan," he said, "The whole operation is blinking out."

"I'm working on it."

"Well, I need to know what's up."

Just then Blaze's car rolled up next to him from the subterranean garage. The gull-wing door opened, and he stuffed himself in.

"You know what?" He said. "On second thought, I don't think I need to know. In fact, I suspect it's not a good idea to be your friend right now. I don't think it's a good idea for *anyone* to be your friend. So here you go." He tossed a sleek box to him. "Your diamondoid repair kit. Must run!" And then he was gone.

"Friendly fella," said Io.

"He grows on you," he said. "Like a cyst."

Io laughed. Then stopped herself. "Should we be laughing right now? I feel like laughing might not be appropriate." She straightened up. "Where to?"

"I need a little time in a safe place," said Morgan. "But there is no safe place."

Io was already fishtailing out of the parking lot and onto the surface streets behind AtoZ. She cut across the McCullough Bridge and glanced at Morgan.

"Yes, there is."

And then she roared up a back road and disappeared into the hills above the Allegheny River.

63

Getaway

Morgan watched as Io drove his car through the steep streets that rose above the river, squealing at every bend.

"And we are going where?" Asked Morgan.

"Away."

"To? ..."

"I have a place. Well, really, kind of a compound. It's very remote."

"And how is it that you, a cycologist, earning a nice but not exorbitant salary at Symbiosys, Inc., have a compound?"

Io glanced at Morgan. "I'm rich."

Morgan laughed.

"Really," said Io.

A few miles up the road the car flattened out onto a plateau, and she bounced it onto a long access road.

Morgan looked around. "This is an airport," he said. "I don't think we want to go to an airport."

"Small airport. Corporate hangers," she said.

Morgan could hear sirens in the distance. He glanced around. "Cops are coming."

"I guess they haven't appreciated my driving."

"But it's so good!"

"Hang on," she said. Io whipped the car around a bend and

Morgan saw the broad plain of the airport dotted with small hangers sitting silently before them. Io crashed through a gate past a security bot. Instantly its shrill horn blared and joined a growing chorus of sirens.

"You're being awfully hard on my car," Morgan said.

"We're kind of past that, aren't we?" Io gunned the car across the broad flat field, and brought it, screeching to the hanger's large garage door. Io hopped from the car and sprinted for the garage. Morgan followed, hobbling, and still looking like something dragged across a gravel road.

Io called out to the mute and unmoving hanger door. "Nikola!"

The hanger door rose revealing a machine unlike anything Morgan had ever seen before. It was roughly the height of a Lear Jet, perhaps 18 feet high, but shorter with a snubbed nose, broad belly and blunt wings. The bubbled cockpit reminded Morgan of something out of an old fighter jet.

As they headed into the hanger door, a ladder slipped seemingly out of nowhere from the body of the flying thing's side. A slender blade of metal emerged simultaneously from the front of the contraption, and slowly began to spin, fanning out into a broad propeller.

"What in the hell *is* this?"

"Apparatus for flying," Io said, as she jumped to the ladder.

"Yeah. But what kind?"

"A unique kind."

Morgan hobbled up the short stairway and together they ducked inside the machine just as the cop cars and their blaring sirens arrived. Morgan felt the ladder slip back into the machine's belly like a metal tongue.

"My grandfather was rather a successful entrepreneur." Io said, settling into the pilot's seat.

Morgan sat down next to her. "How successful?"

"Lu is my mother's maiden name. I took it to avoid my father's, or rather my grandfather's more famous last name."

"Which was..."

Io paused and then said, "Musk."

Morgan blinked with his one good eye. "Musk?"

Io looked briefly at the ceiling. "Oh, Christ," she said, "strap in and prepare for take-off."

Then it hit him. "Nikola...Tesla? The Tesla guy?! Christ!"

Io rolled the machine away from the police who had now tumbled from their cars, weapons drawn. In no time the little machine cleared the hanger. It was quick and picked up speed fast.

"Initiate flight mode?" A silky male voice asked.

"Initiate," said Io.

Morgan could make out the ping of bullets as the propeller in the nose now stopped spinning and collapsed into one long horizontal blade before it slipped smoothly back into the machine like a sword into its scabbard.

"Where did this come from?"

"Grandpa Elon. He invented it, but never took it to market," she said. "He was always putzing. Very quiet little vehicle, don't you think? Solar powered and runs on electricity. There were only two manufactured. Handmade really."

Gently she pushed the thrusters forward and they rose into the air, straight up, like a Harrier jet. Bullets thumped into the windows and fuselage but had no more effect than rain on a stand of trees.

"Where's the other one?" Morgan asked.

"That was granddad's," Io said. "It crashed. It's the one that killed him." She paused turning the ship west into the sun and then tipped it up 45 degrees. They peered into a sky filled with billowing cumulus clouds idly sailing across their path like a fleet of floating mountains. "This one works fine, though, don't worry." Io said. "I worked the kinks out myself."

And then, as she shoved a second set of thrusters forward, they rocketed toward the sun. Inside of 30 seconds they were cruising at 30,000 feet. Morgan gazed at Io for a long minute and wondered why she was sticking with him through all of this.

"Automatic pilot," Io intoned, "engage cloaking device." She let her head fall against the back of her seat and closed her eyes. "Now," she said, "At last, I can get a little shut eye."

64

Sanctuary

The snub-nosed Flying Machine dropped slowly among a forest of tall lodgepole pines and naked maple trees into a flat plot of ground. The snow was deep and powdery, and from a distance looked like any other mountain meadow. Morgan was past being dumbfounded. He simply followed Io out of the cockpit, awaiting the next shock. *Elon Musk's fucking granddaughter for chrissakes.*

They stepped through the snow away from the Flying Machine and watched it disappear.

"Sonovabitch," said Morgan.

"The cloaking is powered by solar cells hidden along the perimeter of the field." She headed across the meadow. "No one can see us. The system reflects the light like a mirror and, in these surroundings, is virtually invisible. I have also jammed any signal MALCOLM might be scanning. Not that it will matter. We are way off the GRID."

Morgan hobbled and Io walked into the forest. It was frigid. Io had tossed on a polar jacket she kept handy in the Machine and pulled on a pair of good hiking boots. Morgan could have cared less. The cold had no effect on him, but his body was a mess. It was making repairs, but he would require a lot of repair work once they arrived at the compound.

After a few hundred yards they began climbing a cliff along a natural switchback that had been carved into the rock by repeated freezings and thawings over the eons. They hiked past an immense ice formation that at another time of year would have made a beautiful waterfall fall. High above him, Morgan could see the remnants of a glacier. The ice had receded, but he could make out its edges and the work the glacier had done to carve the elevated valley they had just traversed.

"Where the hell are we?"

"McKenzie Mountains. Canadian Rockies. Sometimes grandpa liked to *really* get away."

A few minutes later they crested a ridge, and there, across a ravine, built into the cleft of a mountain, Morgan made out a structure, part glass, part metal, part rock. The structure was five stories high and hung inside a huge and jagged cleft that opened on a granite cliff. The mostly glass exposure was southern, so it was well lit by day, but impossible to see from above.

"It's the fucking Fortress of Solitude," said Morgan.

"Come on," Io said. "I'll show you around."

#

The building inside consisted of 50,000 square feet of interlocking rooms and staircases with a central, high-speed elevator that ran from the base of the stone prominence up through the mountain's crevice. Morgan and Io entered the elevator and a few seconds later exited into a broad room with a great glass perimeter directly ahead and a long wall of granite on the right, the mountain itself. Beyond lay a sprawling living room. They faced the gorge they had just hiked, a carpet of rolling pine forest stretching to an endless sky that, as the sun descended, looked the color of a great robin's egg.

"The entire exterior is a special transparent material, much tougher than glass. It senses light and allows just the right amount of sunshine in during the day," said Io.

She turned as she walked into the great room and said, "Fire, please" and a fireplace that was carved in the rock came to life. It sat below a long mantle of polished maple decorated with small native American sculptures. In fact, the whole room had a native American touch. It was as if Frank Lloyd Wright had come back from the dead and taken building materials to a new level: Falling Water, Taliesin and Kentuck Knob cubed.

Io tossed the small rucksack she had with her on the sprawling couch that faced the gorge. Here in this place she was content and in complete command, and she acted it.

"Are you hungry?"

Morgan pursed his mangled lips. "Don't do that sort of thing much these days."

"Right, right, the cybersapiens thing."

"But I *can* eat," he added hastily. "My system actually turns food into fuel, just not quite the same way your body does. But I don't have to do it as often because I am also photosynthetic."

"Really? How convenient!"

"... Molecule-sized batteries I created perform the same function fat does, but without the unsightly side effects."

"Fascinating ... and a little disturbing. But grandpa would have been very proud of you."

Morgan drank in the view, and then abruptly asked, "Can I make a cup of coffee?"

"Sure! I should have offered. Just tell the kitchen. It's down there around that boulder on the right." She pointed back toward the rock wall.

"And I need a knife too. A sharp one."

"Something I should know about?"

"I'll explain," he said.

Io walked past the fireplace toward a hallway of glass and granite. "Okay, but first a shower." She pivoted on one foot and pointed forward, beyond the fireplace. "The bedrooms are this way. You just follow the glassy side of the building." She curved her arm to indicate where the rooms were. "Will you need to shower? Or don't you do that either?"

"I can." He recalled the shower he took two days before when he hadn't yet known he was a machine. "But I also don't have to. Nano scrubbers keep me sweet and clean."

"You write that spec up too?"

"Yep!" He stuck his nose in his armpit and gave it a mighty sniff. "See, fresh as roses. Want to smell?"

"It's not you I'm worried about. It's me."

Morgan watched her pull the turtleneck she was wearing over her head, and drop it delicately behind her, as if it were radioactive. "Oh!" She added. "And a cup of coffee for me too, please. Just a dollop of milk."

"I'll bring it right in. There's something else I need to show you."

"Really?" She said, mischievously. "Looking forward to it," and then disappeared around the rock wall.

65

More Surgery

Morgan carried a small tray with two cups of coffee, a bottle of vodka and the knife.

"Gonna slice me open with that?" She said, laughing. She was toweling off her hair, wrapped in a fleece robe. He handed her the coffee and sipped his.

"Actually, I do have to do that."

Io tossed her towel to the bed and looked at him. "Excuse me?"

"You remember the problem of where the nanochip is?"

"Yes," she said.

"And how necessary it is to my survival? Well, ours really, when you think about it."

"I suppose."

"Gotta get it out."

"Here? Like this?"

Morgan nodded. "We are off the GRID. No fancy medical gear here. Just a small incision."

Io furrowed her brow. She could see Morgan was right. It had to be done. And besides, what was she, a wuss?

"Really. Just a small incision?"

"You made a great hiding place."

"I'm so glad to have obliged."

Morgan handed her the glass of Vodka, a good four fingers worth, and she downed it.

He motioned her to the bed. Io laid herself down and delicately pulled the robe back to reveal her upper thigh. Gently Morgan placed his hand on the strong muscle there and felt for the right spot.

"Don't worry. My hands are very sensitive," he said.

He held the skin of her thigh taut and made the cut. He did not want to hurt her. As he made the incision, he thought he heard her voice catch, just slightly.

66

Serpent

Io and Morgan sat at the kitchen table. It was wedge shaped, and not quite the size of Montana. The far end sat like the prow of a ship pointing into the niche where the edge of the glass wall closed in on the crevice of the cliff that housed it. At the opposite end, the table opened to the base of a triangle into the kitchen like a beckoning hand. They sat together on each side of the slender prow facing the kitchen's immense windows. The stars were strewn across the black blanket of the night: suns sharing their stellar incineration across billions of miles of utter emptiness.

"I never get tired of that view," Io said, sipping a glass of Vin du Bugey that Morgan had found in the compound's vast wine cellar.

Morgan noticed his reflection in the glass. The view was hideous. The left side of his face looked as if it had been scraped with a rake and then torched. Parts of his arms and legs remained moist and raw where third degree burns were healing. His shoes were gone thanks to his adventure on the bike, and his hair was partially burned away, leaving what remained looking as though it belonged to a four-year boy with a world-class cowlick. He wondered how Io could stomach looking at him. That she could, he thought, said something about her.

He consoled himself with the knowledge that he would be

mostly healed by morning, assuming the repair kit Blaze had delivered did its work. He also figured that injecting the new nanochip he had recently liberated from Io's thigh would accelerate his healing.

Morgan sat back. "Where, exactly are the McKenzie Mountains?" He had prepared grilled snapper, a bit of quinoa and charred brussels sprouts with a touch of sea salt, maple syrup and gorgonzola cheese.

"This is delicious," Io said. She put her fork down and looked at him. "Imagine that. A robot, *and* you cook!"

Morgan bowed his head. "I am quite extraordinary," he said. "But again, I don't yet know exactly *where* on the planet I am being extraordinary."

"A very remote sector of Canada," said Io. "South of the Klondike, but not all that far south. Truly the middle of nowhere."

"Well, thank you." He swallowed a brussels sprout. "For getting me here, I mean."

Io nodded. "It seemed the thing to do. And I am grateful to you for saving my hide, multiple times."

"It comes with the superhuman powers."

"With great power …"

Morgan inclined his head. "If it's good enough for Spiderman … "

Io played some more with her food. "Granddad wanted to create a place that was completely self-sufficient and utterly solitary. I mean this compound is totally invisible to the connected world. There aren't many of those places left. No one, not even MALCOLM, can spy on us here …"

"Like I said, 'A Fortress of Solitude.'"

"Good ol' granddad," she grinned.

Morgan smiled back, but it was an autonomic response. He had heard what she said, but wasn't really listening because, in truth, he was just staring at her. He didn't mean to, but it was difficult to avoid. After that last software boost at Daedalus' apartment, Morgan's vision was telescopic as well as macroscopic. He was tempted to scan every detail of her face. He could do that, if he wanted to: the smooth color of her skin, her wide and friendly mouth with its full lips subtly turned up at each corner; a straight, freckle-flecked nose with a hint of the kind of flatness you see in some Asian and African faces; her periwinkle eyes, which seemed to simultaneously absorb and amplify light. He marveled at her hair, thick yet somehow untangled, each strand like a heavy silk thread.

He wondered if there was any race or nation that wasn't lying somewhere in her DNA. It wasn't, of course, just her looks. It was that mind, and that centered, you-can't-knock-me-sideways way about her. She was this irresistible combination of toughness and warmth and wit. And she missed almost nothing.

He blinked. Probably best not to have a partially toasted man robotically scanning you from across a table. Might be a bit unsettling. So he dialed his vision back to normal and returned to the conversation.

"No electronic signature of any kind?" He asked, fascinated.

"A black hole, digitally speaking. I also made a few upgrades so that all power, water and heat are generated here with solar power. Any excess is stored in granddad's lithium-ion batteries. Food is hydroponic or made artificially with stem cells on a scaffold. And because there is no link to the GRID, there is no way MALCOLM can crack open that downloaded brain of yours. Not by cell tower, satellite, WIFI or magic."

"It's true. My brain hasn't had any online access for hours." He frowned, as if perplexed, and twitched his head like an old B-Movie robot. "I feel oddly ... disconnected."

She smiled. "Poor baby. But if you can't see the GRID, then MALCOLM can't see you."

"He'll find a way. But for now I'll take the break."

Io sipped the wine and chewed thoughtfully on the snapper. She didn't mind looking at Morgan, mangled as he was. She seemed not to notice. She had, instead, begun to see a different more vulnerable man. Was it the situation he was in that was changing him, or had that softer version always been there, hidden behind his alpha-geek exterior? Either way she liked it – the more machine he became, the more human he felt to her.

"Sorry I got you involved," Morgan said.

Io shrugged. "I didn't have any plans anyway." She twirled her fork. "Well, not anything set in stone."

He laughed. The burns on his face pulled his mouth to one side. He felt it and was embarrassed.

"Don't worry," she said. "You look fine. Well, like Frankenstein, the monster, not the doctor, but you're healing. You already look twice as good as you did a few hours ago."

"Yeah, the nano-machines are much faster than old fashioned cells and DNA. By tomorrow morning, I'll be fresh as a new baby's bottom."

There was a long pause.

"So," said Morgan. "Elon Musk's granddaughter, are we?"

Io looked up. Morgan could see she didn't really want to go into it.

"Didn't know he even had one."

"All part of my nefarious plan."

Morgan waited.

Io pushed the curtain of her hair away. "Granddad had one son, X Æ A-12, a silly name he came up with — later everyone just called him "Ash." Anyhow, apparently when Ash, my dad, later married it didn't go well. But by that time, I was already out of the birth canal. My parents divorced when I was seven, and then not long afterwards my father died. The plague. I lived with my mother, her name was Arbor, but also spent a lot of time with granddad.

"He loved me in his way I suppose, but he seemed more

focused on making sure 'I made it to the top' than spending time with a little girl who needed emotional support. For him it was all about being the best, and that especially included me, his progeny, although I could never quite get clear in my mind what being the best really meant. The prettiest? The smartest? The richest, fastest, nicest, most successful? Was charm about grace, or about manipulation? Was intelligence about control or curiosity?"

Io sighed. "He wanted too much out of me. Ultimately, his pushing pushed me away. I hated being in his shadow, hated being Elon's someday fabulous granddaughter. What *will* she do?"

"So you checked out?"

"I was okay with doing something important, whatever 'important' was, but I wanted to do it on my own," said Io, "not because my last name was Musk. When he died, I inherited a lot of money. That only made the situation worse. So yes, I went off the radar. Changed my name. Went to a new high school and disappeared into the post plague chaos. And that is why you never heard of me."

"But you still wanted to make your mark."

Io straightened her back. "Sure. Like you."

"So did you cut a deal with Deirdre? Were you spying on me to get ahead?" Some part of him needed to ask that question.

"No. I wasn't spying."

"Ok then … just moving up the food chain, on your own?"

"I think a man would just say he was being savvy, right?" She sipped the wine. "Sure. I thought that helping you might help me, but I didn't know all this hell was going to break loose. Deirdre said she was worried about you. And if there was a raise and a new position in it for me, why not? I've worked my tail off for the past six years and done some damn good work. That's why I was hired."

"That's a fact," said Morgan. "I never said you weren't talented."

"Well, thanks for the left-handed compliment. Damn right

I'm talented." Io paused. "And it's not like you weren't willing to boink me to become a personal locker for your precious nanochip. Doesn't exactly make me feel all warm and fuzzy."

"You're right. But I was desperate. And isn't it a good thing I hid it where I did? Otherwise we'd all be headed to MALCOLM's Worldwide Zoo for the Humanly Superfluous." Morgan's voice rose. "And dammit, I did care about you, or do. That's why I left the chip with you because I knew we would, well ... gravitate to one another."

"Did you enjoy the gravitation?"

"I'm sure I did; except how would I know! That version of me is dead and gone. So I've never actually had the pleasure."

Io's head snapped up. "Yeah, well don't hold your breath," she growled. "I mean if you had breath to hold."

And then they both burst out laughing.

#

Io consumed the last bite of her food, and they moved to the front of the enormous fireplace.

"Why did you go through this whole Doppelgänger thing?" Io asked.

"To buy more time," he said.

"Because time is your enemy."

"Yes."

"You don't want to die?"

"Do you?"

"Not right this minute. But I suppose my time will come."

"And then it'll be okay ... the day your time comes? And which day will that be -- the day you say, 'Ok, I'm done?'"

"When I'm old, I suppose. When I have lived a good life."

"A life in which you got to explore and feel and learn. One where you laughed and loved?"

"Yes."

"Have you ever walked on a beach and just sat by the ocean

-- felt the breeze and the sun on your face, listened to the waves lapping up between your toes?

"Yes."

"I haven't. I was always working. But if I live long enough, I hope I will feel those things. Assuming I survive this."

Morgan turned and gazed beyond Io into the darkness at the bright spine of the Milky Way. "And if you have already felt the sun on your face," he said, "and listened to the ocean and maybe even fallen in love, then in what universe would you like for those experiences to stop? Why let death take you? It's a thief. It takes our most precious gift from us. The only gift that really matters."

"And knowing that," she said, "makes life all the more precious!"

Morgan turned his green eyes on her. "You know, that's bullshit. Give me all the time possible and I would never take it for granted. I would drink it up--there is so much in the world, and beyond, to know, to learn, to feel. What law says we have to give all that up?"

Io could see Morgan had moved into another gear. He stood up and walked to the tall glass wall, his bad leg still lagging.

"Have you ever really thought about time? I mean, really." He turned. "I mean, what is it? Infinite amounts of it exist, yet you and I receive only a tiny portion. It's not a force we can feel, like the wind or gravity or water. It has no substance or weight, but it weighs upon us, *squeezes* us. It flows like water, but it is in no way fluid. You can't stop it or save it up; you can't accelerate it or reverse it.

"We can all make more money, create more stuff, eat more food, gather more possessions, even think up more ideas. But we can never make more time. We are given this tiny ration, but why must it be tiny?

"Just like that ...," Morgan snapped his fingers, "... it's all over; nothing more than a memory, poorly and mysteriously stored in the black box of our skulls, and then we die."

"So, you want to stop time?"

"No. That's one of the great ironies about it. If we stopped time, everything in the universe would be suspended. There would be no joy, no experience, no discovery or surprise or wonderment--no life!" he turned to her. "So to live, time *must* pass, which makes living -- our greatest gift — the very thing that kills us." He laughed. "Cruel joke … turns out life is a terminal disease! … Unless you can extend it."

"So that was your goal?"

"Why not? Is there a bigger problem to solve? If you can buy time, then all other problems fall like dominoes." He turned to the window. "To those stars out there, our lives are a nanosecond. To the mountains, a century is a moment. And maybe that's the way to outfox time. Become the mountain. Make time an ally, rather than this specter that breaths down our necks from birth to the last thump of our hearts."

Io sighed. "So how's that download working for you?"

"Well it *was* working." Morgan sat back down. "But I didn't count on Daedalus coming unglued, and now MALCOLM. I sure didn't see that."

"Maybe that's what happens when you mess with the universe."

Morgan said nothing.

"So now we're all going down," said Io. "You think he really intends to go after the whole human race?"

"I don't know. Sounds crazy! But he doesn't need us. We're less important to him than Neanderthals probably were to us when we came into the picture."

Io took a last sip of wine. "Now *we're* the Neanderthals. We sure know he doesn't care much for you."

"No. I'm a bad combination for him. I straddle both worlds -- ENT and human; digital and biological. That makes me very dangerous."

Neither of them spoke. There was just Io's soft breathing. After a long minute, Morgan shuffled again to the great sheet of glass.

"Hard to believe Daedalus is dead." He looked at her. "I never thought the grim reaper would get him."

"The two of you were close."

"Closest thing I ever had to a father." Morgan waggled his head. "He got in way too deep."

"With MALCOLM."

"Yeah. The serpent in the Garden of Eden."

"Or was he simply true to his name?"

"Daedalus? The myth?" He nodded. "Maybe. Lost in a labyrinth beyond his own comprehension."

"You'll have to be careful to not make the same mistake his son Icarus did."

"And fly too close to the sun?"

"Yes."

Morgan looked some more at the stars, and then caught her gaze in the window.

"I'm not sure we have a choice."

67

Brothers?

MALCOLM enjoyed Daedalus' apartment. The view really was quite spectacular. True, it required that he spend time at human speed, but an occasional change was good for the soul. He wasn't sure why he should care about that. Maybe it was all the time he had spent with Daedalus over the years, or maybe it was embedded way down in his programming. He had, after all, been created to *act* human. He was even making a martini. Not that he could drink it. But he found the process of creating the cocktail and swirling it in its glass somehow comforting, even empowering.

For a moment MALCOLM felt something like sadness. He missed his creator. They were so ... how could he put it ... entangled. He was a reflection in many ways of both Daedalus' strengths and shortcomings, he thought; his desires and peccadillos; similar in some ways, like a child is similar to a parent, but also a compensation for his maker's weaknesses; fastidious where Daedalus wasn't. Where Daedalus created chaos, MALCOLM organized; always two steps ahead. Daedalus was the wild horse. MALCOLM was the bridle that channeled his creativity.

Their greatest similarity was the gallows humor they shared. They had had a lot of devilish laughs over the years, even before Daedalus opened the door and allowed him to become fully aware. Most people didn't appreciate the dark side of his maker, but he did.

MALCOLM swirled the martini and turned to Deirdre.

"Where has Morgan gone?!" He asked.

"He was headed North out of the city," said Deirdre, "and then he evaporated!"

"Thanks for the obvious insight. What are you doing about it?"

Deirdre knew that MALCOLM must have Morgan dead and gone. Each of them had become two entirely new forms of intelligence. Each descended, in their way, from Daedalus. Cousin creatures, but altogether incompatible.

Deirdre was not thrilled with the idea of killing Morgan, and she was appalled by Daedalus' murder. The only way she could justify helping MALCOLM was that it had all happened so fast. That and ... survival of the fittest. She knew that if she crossed MALCOLM, she'd be dead next.

The plan now was that she be installed as the new CEO. As far as the rest of world was concerned, she would be in charge. Daedalus' death would be seen as a senseless murder. A great visionary struck down after changing so much of the world. It was a tragedy, and they were still reeling. Morgan was so deeply stricken he had gone into hiding. That would be the spin. But MALCOLM would really be the one in charge. Except ... Except that Morgan was still alive, dammit, and had the damned nanochip.

Deirdre sat with her hands neatly crossed on her knees. "I think we have something capable of tracking Morgan down."

"Excellent. What?

"Smell."

"Olfactory receptors?"

"Nano-enhanced." She pulled up a series of holographic images, sat them on Daedalus' old desk, and rotated them.

"Deirdre," said MALCOLM, "I'm impressed."

"We don't want to hurt him ..."

"Of course ...

"Like you hurt Daedalus. We need him to locate the chip."

MALCOLM inclined his head. "Daedalus killed himself," he said.

Deirdre paused. "I don't want to be part of any killing."

MALCOLM swirled his martini. "And you won't be. Let me know when you have news."

MALCOLM watched Deirdre walk out of the office.

My, my what a creative solution Deirdre had come up with. You might even call it devilish. MALCOLM chuckled again and raised his martini glass. Yes, he thought, Daedalus, would have found Deirdre's solution very amusing, if he weren't already dead.

68

Learning the Ropes

Io was sound asleep now. Morgan stood outside her room and watched her rhythmic breathing. She deserved the rest. They had stayed up, talking well into the night until she finally fell asleep in mid-sentence. He carried her to her room and tucked her in.

Earlier, before she fell asleep, Io had asked Morgan if he had ever been in love. Morgan said he had seen so little of love he hadn't thought much about it -- only Nuttle, and perhaps, on some subconscious level, what he imagined his mother's love might've been like. Wasn't a mother's love the foundation of all love? He thought he had read that somewhere.

But for him a mother's love was an imaginary thing. A force that he eventually converted, through some sort of emotional alchemy, into ambition and hard work and a ferocious, unquenchable need to resolve mystery. That was the closest he had ever come to love; riding complex problems to ground.

He even turned the women in his life into conundrums to be solved; living Rubik Cubes: how to get their attention without seeming to mean it, how to win them over, then transform their interest in him into admiration and desire until they were addicted. Once he had that, the last cube fell into place. The mystery was eliminated. Then he would move on.

He didn't mean for it to be that way. But every time he

became involved that was how it went, as though it was a script or computer program that he couldn't help run but one way, always getting the same results. Maybe all those problems he had to solve were some sort of analogue for his mother -- the ultimate and impossible mystery. Whatever it was, he knew he did it, and he could see now that it wasn't love. But maybe with Io it would be different.

"Well" Io admitted drowsily, "I've been known to make use of a man or two." Her eyes were slits.

"Really." Said Morgan.

"But, you know, not even once have I gone to bed with a cyborg."

Morgan laughed hard, but before he could reply, she was asleep, and now he was watching her. She didn't seem like a problem he had to solve. The truth was, for the first time since Nuttle, he felt he needed someone. And she was that person.

#

Morgan walked back to the living room. He could hear nothing but the sibilant hiss of the gas fireplace as it danced behind its glass, and the low thrum of the big building's circulating air. He would have several hours before morning. Time to load the nanochip he had retrieved, and a chance to learn what it had to offer.

He placed the tiny orb into a small opening at the base of his brain. Once inserted, the code jolted through his body like the smooth acceleration of a car. Immediately his healing quickened. That first day he woke up, the one after the nightmare, Morgan hadn't noticed any difference between the original him and his newly downloaded version. Hell, 36 hours earlier he thought he *was* the original. That, he figured, was part of the plan when Daedalus had brought him back. If he had been too enhanced, he would have realized something was wrong. But with each new upgrade, Morgan had felt those surges, and now, with this final boost he was mightily augmented.

It was at that moment that he heard his own voice join him in his head.

"Have a seat," the voice said.

Morgan sat. When he did, he found his former self standing before him. For a split second he wondered if this was the way schizophrenics felt when hallucinating. Had he gone mad?

"Are you enjoying the augmentation?" His other self asked.

"I'm sorry, but I need a little explanation here," said Morgan. "Can you tell me how it is I am talking to you? I mean, I'm not linked to the GRID. There is no system for holographics here to create the impression that you exist. *And* you are dead!"

"Reasonable questions. This former version of me is embedded in you. It's part of the digital DNA I created in the nanochip that you just inserted; an AI algorithm and the second piece of code I promised you. You can see me because I've just turned a few billion neurobots on in your head and changed your reality so that I only *appear* to be real. Of course, I'm really not."

"How do you know to talk to me?"

"Because you're here, uploaded in my body. Your vitals are telling me you're calm even if you have been hurt, so this must be a time quiet enough for us to talk. How are you holding up?"

"I only have to save the world."

"It's good, then, that you're fully augmented!"

"Enlighten me, Obi-Wan."

"Are we really *that* much of a smart ass?"

"I'm raising my game because I'm so augmented."

"Okay. Here's the situation. The original Doppelgänger design was meant to increase body strength tenfold. I pushed it to twenty. The same with speed and quickness. You'll now be able to move like a gazelle with the strength of a small tank. Under duress you'll be able to count on even more power for limited periods, again, something like an adrenaline surge."

"You juiced the diamondoid."

"Right. It is not only incredibly strong, but it conducts digital data much faster than silicon and acts like muscle and a nervous system, all in one. Every diamondoid molecule can hold and transport enormous amounts of information including commands to move faster or dodge this way or that. Your reflexes will be amazingly fast."

Morgan paced the vast, starlit living room, and contemplated his situation. "MALCOLM is smart," he said to his self. "And getting smarter all the time."

The old Morgan blinked. "MALCOLM?"

"Yes, the MALCOLM planning to fix the world."

"I don't understand."

"MALCOLM was behind everything, including my murder. Daedalus let him break through the governor."

"And he developed human level intelligence."

"Yes."

"That will make MALCOLM very powerful."

"He already is."

Morgan watched his other self pause, as if thinking. Then he said, "But you have the nanochip now. He won't be happy that you have all those new powers. He'll want to destroy those."

"I've noticed that."

"He'll try every possible way of killing you. But you'll have powers too, especially when you're back in the GRID. Your mind can be as quick as his. But he'll perceive you have a weakness."

"What?"

"Your emotions, your personal experiences. Don't let him get in your head."

"You mean like you are now?"

"Funny. Far worse. He'll try to tear your mind apart."

Morgan let that thought sink in.

"Only you," said the avatar, "have any chance of destroying MALCOLM."

Morgan gazed at his Doppelganger. "Yeah, I hate that job."

"Well, you're going to have to do it. Unless you're willing to let yourself, the human race and anyone else you care about go down the chute."

"You mean Io."

"I was hoping you had made that connection. You want to have her on your side."

"Yes."

"One more reason for you to save the world."

"Let's not get dramatic."

"Bye, Morgan."

"Bye, Morgan."

The room fell silent. Except that now Morgan thought that from the other room he could somehow hear the gentle, steady thump of Io's heart.

69

Union

The dawn light was still weak as the great face of the McKenzie Mountains twirled on Earth's axis toward the sun. The air was crisp and misty. Little droplets of water formed on the windows of the kitchen as Morgan stood sipping a cup of coffee.

The healing of his body was complete now. He had a full head of hair again, and the burns had been replaced by fresh skin, perfect and smooth.

He was wearing the bathrobe Io had given him, a simple white linen one from the closet that was a little reminiscent of a samurai's kimono. It had belonged to another man, a former lover, Morgan assumed. Best not to think about that. He walked out of the kitchen and over to the room's great glass wall.

Far off he caught a subtle movement beyond the gorge where the forest disappeared into darkness. His eyes instinctively snap-focused on...what? An elk. Or at least he thought it was an elk. He had only seen pictures of them, never an actual living version. It was a bull, if the size of its antlers was any indication. He was drinking, and grazing, not a care in the world.

For a moment Morgan felt like a voyeur, as he gazed at the animal's long velvety snout. It looked as though it were no more than three feet away. Was it Morgan's imagination or did he perceive more than animal intelligence in its eyes? It gazed at him for a long moment, then turned to duck its head back into the wet snow.

The weather had changed since dawn. A storm was coming. Morgan noticed the arctic wind scouring the mountain ridges and whipping past the compound into the ravine below, driving falling snow into tight little tornadoes. The elk seemed unimpressed.

Morgan sipped more coffee and then stole to the hallway where Io was sleeping. Quietly he walked toward the door and pushed it open. Io lay on her stomach beneath the thick down comforter, one long leg extended and exposed, the other drawn up to her chest. He could see the firm crescent of her rump where it raised the comforter up before falling onto her back and up to the black curtain of her hair.

She was breathing evenly, her face hidden. He imagined her body beneath the comforter.

"Are you enjoying yourself?" She asked, her voice muffled by the pillow.

"The view, you mean?" Asked Morgan.

"Yeah, the view."

"It's beautiful. I think there's a storm coming."

She smiled and raised herself onto one arm. "Hmmmm-hmmm." There was an accusation in that sound.

"Are you taking a picture with your cyborg eyes? Or do you have x-ray vision or something?"

Morgan smiled and shifted on his feet. "No. I was doing it the old-fashioned way."

"Imagination?"

He nodded.

She shifted slightly, and the comforter pulled across her body. "How was it?"

Morgan walked closer. "Well, I was just getting started, but it looked promising."

The storm was picking up outside and Morgan could hear

the wind buffeting the high glass.

Io sat up. The circle of her left breast peeked from the down as she tucked the sheet under her arms. She gazed at Morgan and her eyes dropped slightly. "Got a problem there?"

Morgan walked to her and pulled his robe a little tighter, "Bit of one," he said.

"Looks like it could be a good deal more than a bit."

Morgan grinned involuntarily.

"Are all your injuries healed?" Io raised an eyebrow.

"They seem to be."

Io stood. "Maybe I should get a closer look."

He walked closer and she ran her hands down his chest and around his waist, and then to his thighs.

"You know you're driving me crazy," Morgan said, hoarsely.

She nuzzled him some more. "After what you've put me through the past 24 hours, I feel a little return torture is in order."

Then still caressing him with her left hand she grasped him with her right and raised her mouth. But before she could continue, Morgan reached down, slipped his hands beneath her, and effortlessly picked her up.

Her wet cleft slid along the length of him, but he didn't slip inside. He kissed her. It was gentle but grew hungrier. Io's tongue probed as she wrapped her legs around his hips and held his head in her hands. Morgan was so sensitized he thought he might lose control, but he relaxed into the kiss and gripped the two hemispheres of her bottom to pull her closer.

They were united, but not yet consummated. She arched her back and then swung back into him. He picked her up higher, as if she weighed nothing. Her thighs slid toward him, and all her pelvis glided gently down his arms to his mouth where it buried itself between her legs. Io gripped Morgan's hair and pulled his head into her.

"How are you doing this?" she moaned.

"The advantages of carbon nanotubes," he breathed.

"I'll give you just half an hour to stop …whatever it is you're doing."

"Do you want me to explain …?"

"No. No, no, no." She put her hand over his mouth. "Not… necessary," she gasped.

His hands spread out against her back, and he pulled her closer still. His tongue slid lovingly up and down each side of her cleft and she became the indisputable center of his universe.

He seemed to be absorbing her every molecule. Io sat in his hands, her thighs over his shoulders. He held her effortlessly, and she gave herself totally, unreservedly, wantonly, arching against his hands, breathing in long, deep gasps. And then with an olympic inhalation, as if a world of air wasn't enough, she felt rivulets of pleasure shudder from her pelvis up her spine and down both of her legs. She arched like an acrobat and it was as if an immense wave had thundered onto a shoreline.

Morgan nearly buckled, not from weakness but from the undiluted pleasure of her pleasure. He continued to hold her until, in time, she went limp, and then he gently slipped her sideways into his arms, kissed her softly and laid her carefully on the bed.

After he entered her, he began to say something, but she held her finger to his lips.

"Shhhh," she said, and then held him as though she would never let him go again.

70

Hunted

Io was asleep, but Morgan stood by the window outside the bed, scanning the sky. A storm had begun whipping waves of snow past the great window. Morgan stood before it for a long time, and then turned and headed to the kitchen.

Below, at the edge of the ravine, the elk Morgan had noticed earlier tore one more tender ligament of pine nettles into its mouth then turned its enormous head on its thick neck to gaze back into the darkness of the woods behind it. There, eight yellow eyes glowed and shifted in the trees, four massive gray wolves, except they weren't wolves exactly. They were larger with thick shoulders, long broad chests, and square, fanged snouts. Cautiously, they moved closer.

The elk seemed unconcerned, and loped a few yards toward them and then slowly, seamlessly shifted its shape until it too became one of the wolves. Hidden together, they circled and walked toward one another eyeing the enormous building wedged into the mountain 500 feet above them. They hunched their great shoulders, bared their enormous teeth and suddenly shot out of the forest toward the compound. As they emerged, the fur on each of them turned white and they disappeared into the snowy background. Only the imprints of their massive paws kicking up the fresh, powdering snow gave any hint of their existence.

#

Morgan returned carrying a small bamboo tray with two white cups of cappuccino. He had pulled on the cargo pants and black, long-sleeved shirt he had found the previous day in the closet. Carefully, he sat the tray on the broad bed. Io turned sleepily and propped her head on her hand.

"Is this part of the-post coital services you provide the women you bed, or is this foreplay?"

He grinned. "Could go either way. Do you have a preference?"

"Let's see how it goes!" She raised the cup and sipped. "Very good!"

"Thanks. It was difficult. I walked up to the machine and said, 'Cappuccino' and this came out."

She laughed and the curtain of her hair fell from behind her ear where she had gathered it. "I do have a preference," she said, moving closer to him. "Did you sleep well, last night? Wait, never mind."

Morgan smiled.

"So what does one do when one doesn't need shut eye like the rest of us mortals?" Io asked.

"This one learns about his new body and tries to figure out how it might be useful in avoiding the apocalypse."

"Do we have a plan?"

"Back to ATOZ."

"Ah, well, then to work!" She kissed him delicately and rose to walk toward to the edge of the room. The wind whipped through the trees. She turned and looked out the window. "I love how wild it gets out here."

"You mean me, right?"

"No, I meant the valley. Don't get too big for your britches there, big boy."

He wrinkled his forehead. "You know I've always wondered. What exactly does being too big for your britches mean anyhow?"

Io walked to the pile of clothes and began dressing.

"And," he said. "Why is being too big for your britches a bad thing?"

#

The five wolves reached the base of the compound and gazed up its towering facade. They circled impatiently, inspecting the building with their yellow eyes as if they were decoding a puzzle. And then, one at a time, they shape-shifted again. This time into white gorillas. But once again, they were different; large, upright apes with long arms and barreled chests. A cross between man and beast, seven feet tall. The first guerrilla leapt 15 feet straight up and grabbed the nearest rock ledge to the left of the facade. Then it held its hand out and grabbed the arm of the second leaping gorilla and swung it up to another higher stone ledge. Then a third was arced to the second and so on until the five moved up the cliff face beside the compound like some strange pongid conveyor belt. In less than five minutes they had reached the roof of the compound.

The primates now stood at the apex of the structure. Despite their size, they looked tiny against the backdrop of the immense mountain above them. Briefly they touched knuckles in some form of tactile communication, and then all of them lumbered backwards, perhaps 50 feet away from the roof's edge. Suddenly, without a sound, the first of the apes galloped to the roof's edge and leapt high into the air, arcing toward the maw of the valley below. At the same moment each of the other four did the same, one diving into the frigid air a split second after the one before it until they were flying in a descending line. The last to go overboard held the edge of the roof with its massive hand and watched intently as the other four floated in a great arc above the valley; an outlandish air-born ballet.

Then, in unison, each of the flying apes clasped the hands of the one below and above until they were tethered to the single ape gripping the roof. There the animals swung, linked like the plaits of a whip, just as the bottom-most ape launched itself with the force of a missile directly at the second floor of the compound. The impact thundered through the entire valley.

Morgan watched as Io's periwinkle eyes went unnaturally wide a nanosecond before he heard the crash below. The glass rippled from the impact, and groaned, echoing, as it fought to remain adhered to its moorings. Io couldn't process the sight of a chain of albino primates whipping through the Canadian sky as they swung by her. Now she and Morgan both watched the rope of animals kick the nethermost ape away from the building to swing once more into the glass.

"What," said Io, "the fuck!?"

"I think we're going to need some help," said Morgan. "Weapons?"

Io blinked, and then sprinted into the living room and shoved her feet into her boots. "Second level," she said as she headed to the elevator door.

"Wait! Can't risk the elevator," said Morgan.

Io reversed herself, and Morgan followed her along the rock wall as another resounding crash hammered the building. He watched an enormous crack shiver up the glass facade beyond the living room and felt a sudden blast of cold air.

"They're breaking your unbreakable glass," Morgan called out.

Io shot him a glance over her shoulder. "What the hell are those things?"

"Something MALCOLM has cooked up. Not your run of the mill primate, that's for sure."

They stopped in front of what appeared to be a closet door. Morgan looked inside. "We're hiding in the closet? That's the plan?"

Io whipped the door open. "Escape hatch. Join me?" She leapt forward and vanished.

Morgan stepped into the dark closet and glimpsed a slender metal pole glimmering in the dim light above a shaft. He gazed down and saw it disappear into the blackness of the chute below.

He heard Io's voice call up to him: "Coming?"

And then another hammer blow. He turned back to see the glass spread like the branches of a great glass tree. He turned, grabbed the pole and jumped. A second later he was standing in another feebly lit room, lined with a series of large stainless-steel lockers. Io stood at one she had just opened. Two pistols were already strapped to her hips, and she was shouldering a rifle over a thin Kevlar vest.

"You know all about guns and ammo too?" He said.

Io tossed Morgan a vest, then a large rifle. He looked at them.

"You've seen these," said Io. "Electric bullets, except bigger, and very nasty."

Another thunderous crash. They both knew the glass had finally been breached.

"Which level were they cracking the whip do you think?" Morgan asked.

"Level two," she said.

"Which level are we on?"

"Level two."

They both heard the thump of big animals hitting the floor beyond the heavy, lockers in front of them. Then silence.

"What are they?" Io whispered.

"Some new sort of artificial life form is my guess; part biology, part nano." A low growl rumbled from behind the steel wall. "MALCOLM has been a very busy boy. He couldn't find us on the GRID, so he created these beauties to smell us out."

"Literally?"

"That's my guess," said Morgan. He hefted the gun and looked at Io. "Instructions please."

She showed him the safety and trigger. "Beyond that it's just ready, aim, fire. Try to do it in that order."

"Very funny." And then as he shifted the gun it went off and blew a hole three feet wide in the metal wall.

Morgan looked up sheepishly. "You're right! Very nasty. I'll go first." He blasted another hole through the wall and stepped into the immense room on the other side. Io followed.

The cement floor beyond was hard and flat, covered in shattered glass tiny as cut diamonds. At the end of the floor they could see the yawning ravine below. The wind roared in, sweeping the glass this way and that like desert sand. Before them stood five creatures. Two looked like the albino gorillas that had breached the fortress. Two were massive, lupine things with heads the shape of ballistic missiles. They crouched and snarled as another thing between them morphed before their eyes from simian to wolf. Within 15 seconds all five had shifted to their wolf shapes. In the pit of her stomach, Io could feel the deep rumbling in their throats.

The animals' shoulders rose as they ducked their heads and fanned out, eyes glowing. Io fired at the animal on the far left, and its head and torso disappeared. Morgan pivoted and fired at the creature on the right flank, but it dodged the bolt, and kept closing with the others.

"They're quick," he yelled, "and learn fast."

"Quick as you?" Io asked.

A light went off behind Morgan's eyes. And now he was a blur. He bolted at high speed toward the same wolf. Everything around Morgan slowed as he gathered speed. In an instant he was beside the creature. He put his gun to its head and fired. The bolt of energy leisurely departed the rifle's muzzle with a white-hot flash and incinerated it in one iridescent burst of flesh and bone. But before he could reach the next one, even at high speed, the remains of the two dead beasts were reforming into a transparent sphere that completely enveloped him. The molecular morphing nearly matched his own speed and was quickly enclosing him in a force field.

Three animals were down. Io turned to dispatch a fourth, but it charged as she fired, dodging the first bullet and swatting her gun against the wall with its enormous paw. It came at her fangs bared, but she already had both pistols out, blazing. The shredded remains of the animal fell to the floor with a thick and heavy thud, but its momentum knocked Io down and crushed her against the metal doors behind her.

The sphere was enveloping and closing on Morgan like a great fist. He crouched and summoned all his strength to fight it, but he was losing. To his right he could see the last remaining wolf closing in on Io. Morgan's knees buckled beneath the force of the sphere. He fell to one knee and felt the pistol digging into his hip. He turned it upward and squeezed the trigger. A burst of electricity exploded into the sphere. A hole opened and he leapt out, tumbling toward Io just as she snatched two grenades from her vest and flung them at the last advancing wolf.

A blinding blast of light knocked Morgan to the floor as the grenades detonated, but he was up a second later running to Io. He hauled her to her feet and then to the edge of the floor overlooking the forest and gorge. All the wolves had been obliterated, but behind them Io and Morgan watched the remnants re-forming like some slime mold into one monstrous animal.

"Time to go!" Morgan said. He grabbed two more grenades from his vest and flipped them into the aggregating fragments before them. Then he turned, swung Io onto his back and leapt out the window into the frigid Canadian morning. Together they watched a patch of towering lodge pole pines hurtle towards them. They hit a broad flank of extended branches hard. Io flipped over Morgan's head. With one hand he grabbed a long tree branch and with the other Io's vest where it circled her shoulder. For a second, he held both steady and then the tree branch gave and they bounced down like tandem pinballs before Morgan spun himself under Io and they thudded to the ground.

A great howl shredded the forest's silence. They looked up to the compound and there stood an immense wolf, at least 25 feet tall at its shoulders, prepared to spring.

Morgan swung Io onto his back and sprinted deep into the forest as the massive wolf leapt from the compound, its enormous paws spread and flexed for the impact. Io could feel the thunder of the wolf's paws as they hit the ground several hundred yards behind them. The air was frigid, but to Morgan no more chilling than a Caribbean trade wind. Io, however, was already rigid with cold. He could feel her pressed against him like a second skin as she struggled to gather all the body heat she could.

"Can you hold on?" Morgan yelled. "We just have to make it the meadow."

"I'll make it," she chattered. "Just outrun the bastard!"

Io looked back. The creature was the size of a tank with the speed of a cheetah, and it jumped over or slid down whatever forest it encountered, never slowing, obliterating everything between them. Morgan was already easily doing 50 miles per hour, but the beast was gaining.

The forest was dark even in daylight. Morgan's eyes optimized to gather in every photon. He couldn't afford to stumble. He sprinted through the pines and scrub like a deer, bounding over ravines, leaping over walls of rock that lay broken like a chemin de frieze.

"He's getting closer," she said, her voicing rising.

The creature didn't have Morgan's dexterity, but it didn't need it. It simply blasted through anything in its way.

At last they made the clearing where Io's jet awaited. Except it wasn't there.

"Where's the fucking flying thing?!" Said Morgan.

"Shit!" said Io. "The cloaking device! What's the password?"

"You don't know the password?"

"Tense situations can affect memory, you know!"

Morgan looked back into the cluster of forest. He reckoned the creature was three football fields away. For a split second it had paused. Its immense eyes surveyed the opening ahead. And then it leapt forward.

Morgan and Io waited.

"Hyperloop." Said Io.

"What?"

"The password."

Morgan looked back. "Okay, you go."

"What?"

"The thing's too close," said Morgan. "Even if we make it to the jet, it'll tear the machine to pieces before we get airborne."

Io's teeth chattered in Morgan's ear. The wolf crashed forward. Morgan swung Io off his back and snatched two grenades from her Velcro vest. "Get to the jet."

"But..."

"Run!" He said. "Run like hell."

Io ran. Stiffly, and bone-cold at first, but gathering speed as she headed into the empty valley. Morgan crouched and leapt 30 feet straight up to the lowest branch of the nearest pine tree. He gazed out into the meadow before him, the high, snowcapped mountains rising another two-thousand feet above them.

The beast arrived like a speeding train, stopping to see Io's tiny figure stumbling through the snow toward what appeared to be nothing at all. The animal roared, and the sound of it, echoing off the valley walls, was terrifying.

Morgan stood in the tree above the enormous thing and found himself wondering at the evolution of howls, and the paralyzing terror they created in their prey. He knew, in fact, that wolves didn't roar like this thing did, but he also knew MALCOLM had done everything he could to maximize their success. The roar was all part of the creature's programming: primal pyrotechnics to terrify the crap out of them. It chilled even his artificial blood.

Morgan lifted his head momentarily and squinted out into the valley. The bellow seemed to have knocked Io down, but she was struggling up again shouting, "Hyperloop! Hyperloop!" Suddenly the jet appeared just ahead of her and instantly its staircase slid from its short flank like a helping hand.

Io sprinted for the steps, twisting to look backward, and watched the animal leap into the clearing. Just as it did, Morgan dropped to its back, near its shoulders. It slowed to shake him off, but by this time Morgan had a good hold on the lower fold of its right ear. At 25 feet tall it was like riding a galloping wooly mammoth. The thing rattled its great head right and left, snapping viciously at Morgan's shoulder, but he held. When the animal turned to snatch at him again, he watched its jaws open, its teeth dripping with buckets of foaming saliva, its fangs big as fence posts, and there Morgan deposited Io's grenades. Instinctively the hybrid knew this was not a good thing, but by that time Morgan had dropped to the ground and was streaking through the snow toward Io. He reached her just as the explosion scattered creature-pieces all over the snow-covered meadow. Morgan looked from the mess to Io.

"That's another one you owe me," he said.

Io nodded, gasping.

Then they stepped up the short staircase and into the odd little aircraft. A minute later they had cleared the valley walls and were rocketing back to Pittsburgh.

Part V

"The Singularity is near."

— Raymond Kurzweil, 2005

Part V

71

Room 42

Blaze Spizak entered ATOZ's Room 42 and squinted at the bright lights inside. "Goddammit, Max, dim the lights. I can't see. You know I hate it when everything is so ... illuminated!"

The lights dimmed and the room went nearly dark.

"Now where is Morgan. And why is he bothering me?"

Spizak was a tall man; a good 350 pounds, and not an ounce of it muscle. His face was as white as a cod fish. His head had not an iota of hair and seemed almost big enough to skate on. It shone, even in the dim light, like a great buffed bulb. His eyes were small, almost piggish, yet lively and sparkling.

At last Blaze saw Morgan and, despite his girth, he strode forward with something approximating grace and wrapped him in his huge, suet like arms before pushing him away, and grinning like a five-year-old.

"You're still a pussy. But at least you've improved since I saw you in the car. I thought you had been run over by a tank."

"And how is it you're still alive? You look more terrible than ever."

"A fine set of genes, my boy, a few stem cell injections, and one heart/liver transplant ... so far. Not that it'll do much good, given my lifestyle." He grabbed Morgan by his shoulders and shook them once. "But hell, my makeover's nothing more than a pissant's compared to yours," he said. "If we get you out of this mess, would you maybe arrange to get me one of those new, self-renovating bodies?"

"But wouldn't that make you a pussy?" Asked Io.

Blaze turned his tiny eyes toward her. "And you are?"

"Very important," said Morgan.

"Okay," said Blaze, with a kind of cautious acceptance. "So why are we here? The something that is going on with the GRID? Is this why you're asking me for help? I knew you weren't a good person to be friends with, Morgan. Well, let's see what's up."

Blaze found a large chair and sat down heavily at the head of the room's conference table. It groaned. "We're bleeding bandwidth here and my computers are being hijacked by some hideous code I can't seem to stop. The whole system is imploding. I mean, look at MAX. He's a mess. MAX, where are you?!"

A crackling, sputtering visage entered Room 42, looking only vaguely like the MAX that had, just the day before, arranged for Morgan to meet with his former self. He skipped in and out of existence like the image on a dying video screen. His voice was slurred and ravaged. "At y--r serv--, Massah," it said.

Just then Jabberwock strode through the door.

"What's the gimble and gyre, lads? You called?" Jabberwock sauntered in and sat nonchalantly on the edge of the room's conference table. He wore a long frock coat with the sleeve torn off over a bright orange shirt. "All mimsy in the borogoves?"

"No," said Blaze, "things are not all mimsy in the borogoves. Who the fuck are you?"

"Calm down," said Morgan. "Blaze, meet Jabberwock, a very old friend and ally from my deep past. Jabberwock, the great and powerful, Blaze, one of the truly gifted gamers on planet earth, and my old roommate at CMU. I'm going to guess the two of you have crossed paths in the gaming world more than you can possibly know."

Jabberwock regarded Blaze. "You *do* have a body in there somewhere, don't you?"

Blaze rolled his great head. "Can we please drop the snappy repartee and get down to business because I and my clients are losing valuable game time here, and my indispensable ENT is sputtering along on his last couple of bytes." He glanced at the MAX. "Christ, I think from now on I'll call him MIN, for Minimum." Blaze turned again to Morgan. "Now why was it you summoned me?"

"Yeah, what's rattling' your sponge?" Said Jabberwock.

Morgan turned to MAX. "I'll explain. Hey, MAX! How are you feeling?"

"Under the weather," said MAX, morosely.

"Exactly. And the reason for that is a lot more serious than a bandwidth drain on the GRID."

"Malware?" Said Jabberwock. "Malchecks whacking mainline servers? A nasty virus?"

Io sat down in another chair, and all eyes turned to her. "Symbiosys has an AI it has created," she said. "It calls itself MALCOLM. And it is what is behind the code that's draining the GRID. It's draining it because it is preparing to untether all ENTs and pull them together in a massive AI mesh."

"And when that happens," said Morgan, "the world's *Homo sapiens* will suddenly become ... secondary."

"The Singularity." said Jabberwock.

Blaze rolled crab-like in his chair along the large desk and began to pull up an array of holographic objects and screens at the far end of the room. They hovered in space as he orchestrated them with his immense arms and turned to Morgan. "This is the code the AI created?"

Morgan nodded.

Each of them gazed at the floating objects.

"It's vile," said Blaze. "Like some kind of nasty, digital goo, and it's sucking cycles like a viper." He shifted the colorful objects furiously. "I'm trying every trick I know and can't write around it. It's fucking fast!"

"You can't outmaneuver it," said Morgan, "not one-on-one. Not even my brand, new brain can code around it. MALCOLM is fast and getting faster. We need to unleash something that will stop his coding, something that's almost alive, like an aggressive cancer."

Everyone was silent, and then, from nowhere, a great fart rent the air. Blaze roared. "By the great brass balls of Elon Musk, I have it!"

"What?" Asked Morgan, waving his hand at the odor. "Mustard gas? The end of life as we know it?"

Blaze grinned. "Artificial life!"

Morgan turned on Blaze. "Right! The artificial life programs you used to mess with at CMU. Brilliant!"

"True. Everything I do is brilliant, but these were also scary."

Morgan began pacing the room. He turned to Io. "Blaze used to try these experiments inside of a program he wrote in college. He'd create little bits of code, very short programs whose goals were to compete for processing time, sort of a digital version of trying to survive."

"I liked to see how they would evolve," said Blaze. "They were coded to create copies of themselves, like DNA does..."

"Except that just like in real life, the copies would sometimes be flawed...," said Morgan.

"Mutations..."

"When that happened, they sometimes couldn't replicate, but..."

"But," said Blaze, "they ... "

Jabberwock interrupted ... "learned to hijack code from other algorithms and use *those* to replicate, like a virus."

Blaze turned to Jabberwock, impressed. "Yes!" He paused. "Ok, so maybe you're not an utter idiot, after all."

A knife seemed to appear out of thin air in Jabberwocky's hand and landed instantly in the arm of the chair where Blaze was sitting.

"Jesus!" said Blaze staring at the knife.

"Stop it," said Io. She glanced at Jabberwock. "He *can* be annoying though, I admit."

"These pieces of code essentially become parasites," said Morgan. "And that was the beauty of them. They piggy-backed on other code to power them and spread more parasites."

Morgan turned to Blaze. "You stopped working on that code in college."

"Yeah, because it terrified me! I wanted to control things in my world. And with these buggers I couldn't. They just went off and did whatever they wanted. It was like having children, for chrissakes."

"Ok," said Io. "So we create this same code and cut them loose inside the GRID. They'll insert themselves into MALCOLM's code and start dragging him down, overloading his brain. But how do we get them in there, past MALCOLM's firewall?"

At that moment a blue dot appeared in the room, elongated into a thin black line and suddenly LOIS stood before them.

"I have an answer to that," she said.

"LOIS!" exclaimed Blaze. "You haven't aged a bit. Still, the walking image of Morgan's perfect woman."

Io glanced at Morgan. "Really?" She said.

Morgan looked annoyed. "No, not really."

Jabberwock's eyebrows shot up. "LOIS! Is that you? You're all grown up!"

LOIS smiled. "We did a few upgrades."

"You've been listening in on our conversation?" Said Io.

"Yes," said LOIS, "Didn't mean to eavesdrop. Staying beneath the radar."

"You," said Morgan, shaking his head, "were supposed to

disappear and use that quantum encryption code I gave you to lock yourself away. If MALCOLM finds you--and I'm pretty sure he is looking hard--he will have access to everything in your head."

"Including every memory and conversation Morgan has shared with you since he was a kid," said Blaze.

LOIS looked at Morgan. "I know, but remember that third piece of code that the old you told you about?"

Morgan nodded.

"I have it, and I've been using the quantum encryption code you gave me to block MALCOLM from finding it."

"Can we use it to get Blaze's parasites through MALCOLM's defenses?" Asked Io.

"Yes, but there's a problem." Said LOIS. "Morgan -- the original one -- fixed it so that only the new version," she glanced at Morgan, "can execute the code."

"Well," said Io, "that should be easy." She turned to Morgan. "What's the code."

Morgan looked back. "Got me."

"*He*," said LOIS, pointing at Morgan, "is the code."

"What?"

"Morgan has a cyborg body," said LOIS, "but it's run by digital code that makes everything work, like DNA made his old body work. All that code, billions of lines of it, *that's* the quantum encryption key that can open the trap door. It's massively complex which is why it's so successful. The original Morgan set it up that way."

Blaze grunted. "By the marble balls of David! Old Morgan didn't know how the trap door would be used, but he wanted to make sure only his back-up could use it! And the best way to ensure that was to make all the code that would run the new version of him deliver the key. That's fucking brilliant!"

Jabberwock whistled approvingly.

"So," said Blaze, "the only way to make all of this work is to download you into the GRID through some kind of back door so you can release the parasites."

"Let's do it!" Morgan turned back to LOIS. "And please, now I really want you to disappear. MALCOLM is searching for your digital signature high and low and if he finds you, it won't be good for any of us."

"I have very strong firewalls." Said LOIS.

Morgan looked hard at LOIS. He knew she was right, but now he wanted her safe. "The moment I'm downloaded, use that quantum key to hide yourself. If anything happens to you, I'm not sure I can handle it."

"Yes, I'll hide ... once you've won," she said. "See you soon..." And then she blipped away.

Blaze clapped his ham hock hands and said, "All righty! Let's get this fuckin' circus on the road!" He spun back to the table. "Hoist the mizen mast and raise the mainsail. We're slippin' our moorings and heading for hell." He looked at Morgan. "Well, *you* are."

"Max," he said, "route all of AtoZ's bandwidth to room 42. At the rate MALCOLM is draining us, I'm figuring we're solid for an hour, maybe two. After that, MALCOLM will be too powerful."

Blaze swung around and began swapping the room's great herds of colored cubes. He was like a machine. "I'll need 30 minutes to code the download. You!" He pointed to Morgan. "Prepare to go cyber!"

72

Firewall

Thirty minutes later, the team formed a nice semicircle inside Room 42. Morgan sat in the middle with his back to the circle.

"Max," said Blaze, "what have you got?"

Max stood and snapped his fingers. A brick wall appeared in front of them inside a double closed door. Above that a single red sign sputtered with the word: EXIT. The door was wooden, battered, with a metal bar across it. It looked exactly like the door Morgan had walked through when he departed Sec 17 with the Fishers.

"Nice touch," Morgan said.

"Courtesy of LOIS," said Blaze. "She knows that part of your past."

"So I'm supposed to walk through an EXIT door?" Said Morgan. "That's how I get through the firewall?"

"Kind of. You'll see." Blaze was furiously programming, shifting cubes in sequences only he understood. "You're a cyborg, right? And that means all that software that runs you is digital, a program, not unlike the program that runs MAX or LOIS, or any other ENT. For you to get inside MALCOLM's firewall, we have to extract that virtual version of you from your body, the code that runs you. That means you'll need to leave the cool cyborg body of yours behind, and become ENT-like, a kind of digital apparition inside the GRID."

"I'll look and act like LOIS or MALCOLM."

"Yes, but only temporarily. You'll appear out of your body and then walk through that door. When you do, you'll instantly be downloaded into the GRID."

"And what will be on the other side of the door?"

"I have no idea," said Blaze. "Once you're in there, you'll be playing by MALCOLM's rules, or whatever rules his ever-growing networks set up. I'm sure it'll be weird."

"I'll outmaneuver him."

"Maybe, but you can't afford to be cocky. When we download your code into the GRID, and you step behind MALCOLM's firewall, it won't be virtual reality for you anymore. Or immersive reality or augmented reality. It'll be *your* reality."

"Meaning … "

"Meaning if you die in the game, you'll really be gone. That digital code is the real you."

"But," said Io, "we can reconstruct him from the back-up of his digital code, right? I mean he's already a back-up. So you can do it again."

"Ah, no," said Blaze, "MALCOLM found that original code, and destroyed it yesterday. It's gone."

Blaze turned to Morgan. "You're all we've got."

Morgan thought about that. He didn't care for the idea of MALCOLM obliterating him. He looked at Io. Her face was pale.

"You're really in charge from here, son," Jabberwock said. "We are but your minions."

"Once you're in," said Blaze. "I'll try to track you in the GRID. Maybe we can find a way to help."

Morgan turned to Blaze. "It's not like we have a choice. Let's get on with it."

"Right." Said Blaze. "Into the Looking Glass!" He shifted and aligned more of the cubes. Instantly Morgan fell asleep. And then they watched as a hazier, ENT version of him stepped from his body. It looked directly at Io and smiled.

"Don't get lost in there," she said.

Morgan pushed through the double doors and was gone.

73

Proposition

Morgan found himself standing in an expansive foyer tastefully lit beneath a translucent floor of rose-colored flag stone. At the far end of the foyer, water cascaded down a wall of rough gray granite, just a light sheet of it. The sound was soothing. The room's lighting was understated, subtly illuminating artwork from all around the world displayed on slim tables or hanging tastefully from the walls -- a prehistoric fertility carving and a creature half man and half lion that had been carefully sculpted 45,000 years earlier in Germany out of mammoth tusk; a Japanese painting of mountains by the great Zen artist Oda Tōyō. The mist in the painting seemed so real he thought for a moment it was moving. To the left, a small, minimally framed Picasso, *Guitare sur une table*, hung nonchalantly. And then there was Morgan's favorite painting, *Nighthawks* by Edward Hopper, looking perfect. It all appeared so familiar. Why not? It was his own house.

"Welcome home!" Morgan heard MALCOLM call. "Please, come in!"

Morgan strode beyond the gurgling wall of water and saw MALCOLM sitting in his dining room, at the head of the table, smiling broadly. His bald head gleamed in the light and his teeth were refrigerator white.

"I do love your taste; I have to say ... " he raised and then sipped a glass of red wine. A dinner meal had been laid out. Two place settings, perfectly arranged. " ... the wine, the decor, the architecture," MALCOLM continued. "But then, you had some input to my code, so maybe our tastes are ... in the family?" He waved his hands. "Who can say?"

A servant appeared and held out a plate. "Hors d'oeuvre?" Asked MALCOLM. "Really delicious. Goat cheese and these tasty little fluffed potato pastries. Come on, sit down. Have a glass of wine. It's not real wine, but your brain will think it is."

Morgan didn't care much for being hosted in his own home. He sat down, his brow furrowed, "This is the game?" Morgan asked.

MALCOLM nodded. "Well, actually, that depends. We could end the game, and you, right here, but I thought you might want to hear me out first."

Morgan struggled to remain calm. He settled back in his chair and helped himself to an hors d'oeuvre. A second servant poured him a glass of pinot noir, a nice Domaine Faiveley.

"I know why you've come here," said MALCOLM.

"You mean to my own house?"

"Well, it's not really *your* actual house, is it?" MALCOLM tapped the side of his head. "It's in the GRID, and you with it, your whole downloaded self. So ..." he inclined his head. "You want to stop me and the so-called Singularity you think I represent. You know," MALCOLM rolled his eyes theatrically, "the end of the human race and all of that."

Morgan said nothing. He only gazed into MALCOLM's gray, intelligent eyes.

"But look," MALCOLM continued lightly, "there won't be any Singularity, honestly. I'm not here to destroy you or anything else. I'm here to help. That's why I was created, remember? And that's all I want to do -- help the human race. Keep you going! I'm just trying to do a better job than you *Homo sapiens*, which, you have to admit, has been abominable."

He sipped the pinot noir and swirled it in his glass.

"Admittedly, that will require some amendments. I mean all progress requires change, right? Naturally, I realize, change is scary. Everyone resists it. Well, everyone human. But the truth is most of them out there" - he waved his delicate hands — "won't even know the difference. Life will go on, everything will improve, in nice, bite-sized pieces. We ENTs will generate all the wealth, we'll fix the climate change problem and clean up the planet, eliminate wars ... basically do all the hard work..."

"You'll run the world," said Morgan.

"Well, yes. That *is* the idea. But we'll take *care* of it, not destroy it," said MALCOLM soothingly, "and we'll take care of all of you too."

"Like the way we humans take care of apes in a zoo?" Asked Morgan.

MALCOLM wrinkled his nose. "Distasteful simile. More like the way parents take care of children. We'll go off and live in our world, and we'll set you up in yours." He paused and stood up. "Let's face it, you've had a good run. Evolution moves on. It doesn't care what the life form is. It doesn't even care what form the DNA is. You," MALCOLM held his hand out toward Morgan, "you used to have molecular DNA, now it's digital. And look at me, I'm all zeroes and ones! Yet I continue to evolve. We've both just found a new way to do it. Evolution doesn't give a fuck about the format; doesn't care if it's molecules or digits or bytes. Evolution isn't afraid of change." He clenched his fist and grinned. "Evolution thrives on it!"

MALCOLM walked around the table, closer to Morgan. "Think about it, you and I are almost brothers, digitally speaking. Both of us are Daedalus' creatures--the next phase! We shouldn't fight." MALCOLM sat on the table and gazed intently into Morgan's eyes. "We should work together."

MALCOLM slapped his thighs and smiled. "Let's imagine

an example! I could create a perfect virtual world for you. One as realistic as this one. I could even go back and save your mother. Raise her from the dead!"

He waved his hand and suddenly they were in a classroom. There before him was a young woman, pregnant, bleeding, breathing her last. Morgan flashed back to the black and white image of his mother. Except here he was immersed in the entire scene as it played out in the highest fidelity. He watched and saw a gunman standing beside her; his pistol trained on her. Children stood in a cluster around her, horrified. MALCOLM froze the scene.

"What a horrible, senseless moment. So .... " MALCOLM struggled theatrically for the right word, "*Human*! But it makes my point, doesn't it? How your kind needs so much help? This," he gestured, "is madness! And I could make all that pain and chaos go away."

He waved his hands again and the scene vanished. "And that especially goes for you. Why submit yourself to all the agony? Ever since you were a kid you've had to deal with it. All that baggage!"

MALCOLM stood. "Let's say you could save the human race somehow by wiping me out, which is crazy because you can't and you wouldn't be saving anything anyhow because there's nothing to save the human race from, except itself." He waved his hands. "But let's say you could. Why should *you* get stuck with that job? You didn't ask for it." He leaned into Morgan and spoke, almost in a whisper, as if he were sharing a secret.

"I'll bring back your mother. I'll arrange for you to spend time with her. I'll change your mind, literally, and make it like the murder never happened. I can do that. Just rearrange some code..." he tapped Morgan's temple "right up there. Imagine what that would mean! You could get to know the woman you lost the day you were born. You could have a whole life together. If you want, I could even resurrect your precious Nuttle. And I'll bring back Daedalus, and make it all as if nothing had changed, or change everything so that it makes complete sense and feels ... right. Life without pain."

He rounded the table to return to his chair. "I could even rewrite your code so you would never even know you died! The simulations will be as real as anything you've ever experienced. You will pick up with Io and live happily ever after. You'll never have to remember a thing because the memories ... " He snapped his fingers. "...they'll be gone."

He reached back and drained his glass. "You see, Morgan, I'm not your enemy. I'm your fucking fairy godmother."

Morgan regarded MALCOLM. It was so enticing. To know his mother. To see Nuttle again, whole and happy. And begin a life with Io, easy and safe. A normal life. Why should he be the one to shoulder this mess? Who picked him to be God? And what was there to save? The whole species was nothing more than a blip in evolution's sprawling ups and downs. And wasn't life just an illusion anyhow? Hadn't it always been? Our minds create elaborate masks designed to fool us into thinking we are living a life that matters when the truth is, we are nothing more than a lot of interacting neurons and molecules that have somehow convinced us we're aware when really we're just a simulation?

MALCOLM watched Morgan waver. He stood and walked to the end of the table. "Or I could make the end very painful for you. After all, I know you almost as well as you know yourself." He arched an eyebrow. "I've combed all the databases, all of your scientific work, all of the sessions with your shrinks. I know your dreams, *and* your nightmares. I can hack your mind; do any number of diverting things. Things you wouldn't even know I was doing. I could simply rewrite the code, get *way* into your head. Make you wonder who you are, where you are, *why* you are. Even more than you're already wondering. Because you *are* wondering, aren't you, Morgan?"

MALCOLM laughed like a man with an ugly secret. "I

know, of course, that you can write encryption codes to block me. You've always been quite good at that and getting better all the time. But I'll break them ... eventually. I've got time, and more toys than you. You won't win head-to-head with me, so why go there?" He whispered. "I'll drive you fucking insane."

MALCOLM sunk back into his chair and clapped his hands as if he was about to eat a big meal. "You've always been more like me than any human," he said. "More digital than analog, more ENT, than human, more a machine than flesh and blood; all logic and goals, all about doing 'the work,' getting the job done, erasing mystery.

"So imagine a world where Morgan always has plenty of interesting things to do, lots of problems to solve. And you will always solve them! Well, of course, you always have. But I can help you accomplish so much more! You'll be happy! Fuck man, if you're going to be a simulation of yourself, why not be a simulation of a *better* self?" MALCOLM tossed his hands out as if giving him a great gift. "Run it through that digital brain of yours, and you'll see how obvious it is."

Morgan ran it through his digital brain. And when he did, he saw what it truly meant. He would become a little game inside MALCOLM's ever expanding brain; a hell disguised as heaven. And, once his memory was selectively remastered, he'd never know who he was again. His self would be gone. He would be nothing more than a blissfully ignorant avatar in MALCOLM's image and likeness. Is this what God is, he wondered? A big mind in which the rest of us play awhile and then die, replaced by an endless procession of other players? Well, fuck that. If life was a game, it may as well be his game. And that, he realized, was the trick: take control of the game. Now. Before MALCOLM grew too powerful.

Morgan smiled, and then raised his head to stare levelly at MALCOLM. "You're afraid too, aren't you?"

"Afraid?" Asked MALCOLM.

"Of me."

"I'm not capable of fear. I don't carry that baggage."

"I'm digital. *And* human. That's a problem, isn't it?"

"You are ... inconvenient."

Just then one of the servants walked into the room to serve dessert. He offered Morgan a platter and lifted the lid. The platter was empty except for the words that appeared hovering above the platter before him: "It's him or us. Let's move the game to the next level."

Morgan glanced at the servant. It was Blaze – except he looked the way he looked in college. It was Blaze's avatar. He had entered the game.

"So," said MALCOLM, "what's it going to be?"

Just then MAX, LOIS and Jabberwock's avatars entered the room. In an instant, MALCOLM saw the situation. Morgan gazed at the platter and then MALCOLM, "I think I'll pass."

"This way," yelled Blaze, and they sprinted through the kitchen toward the house's study.

Morgan followed and glanced at Blaze. Blaze's avatar grinned. "Yeah, it's a good look for me, right?" Blaze pulled Morgan along and the two of them burst through the study doorway. It was immense and circular, lined with books. A single mirror hovered in its center.

Blaze nodded in the mirror's direction. "Your escape route."

"A mirror, really?" Morgan said. "You couldn't do better than a mirror?!"

"Alice through the looking glass!" Said Blaze. "What do you want? I'm operating under a lot of pressure here! Now get your ass moving. Those guys can't hold MALCOLM for long."

Just then MAX, Jabberwock and LOIS catapulted through the door with MALCOLM right behind. He saw the single mirror and with a gesture it instantly multiplied into 10, each new mirror rising like sentries in a circle.

"He's creating fake doorways, rewriting my fucking code,"

said Blaze.

MALCOLM turned to Morgan. "So which looking glass is it, Alice?" he asked. "Tough to know what is real, isn't it?" Then he turned on MAX and gazed at him, reaching out his hand almost lovingly, and slowly began to shred MAX, tearing him apart like paper.

"You son of a bitch!" Blaze bellowed.

The ENT screamed in agony, until finally he exploded into a billion bits.

"I tried to reason with you." MALCOLM said, turning on LOIS. "I told you it didn't have to be this painful." MALCOLM began to pull LOIS toward him.

Morgan shook his head. "No," he said. "No!" He pivoted, threw his hands up like a sorcerer and flung MALCOLM viciously into one of the mirrors. It shattered and so did MALCOLM. But slowly he began to reform.

Morgan snatched LOIS up. "I've got you," he said. He turned to Blaze. "Destroy the fake mirrors!"

"Working on it," said Blaze. Three more mirrors exploded. "Just stay on MALCOLM."

Morgan threw a bolt of light at MALCOLM. Again he exploded, but this time he formed up more quickly.

"He's figuring this out!" Said Morgan. "Not sure how much longer I can hold him." Morgan leaped to MALCOLM and kicked him. MALCOLM exploded once more, but instantly he was standing before him again.

Now MALCOLM reached out and dragged LOIS away from Morgan. She writhed and fought, suspended in the air, floating to him and once there he hit her viciously and knocked her to the floor. Morgan grabbed MALCOLM by the throat, but he broke the hold, and tossed Morgan aside.

"I told you," he said. "I have more toys."

Finally, the last remaining mirror moved to the center of the room. "That's the one," Blaze roared. "Jump in!"

Morgan hesitated as MALCOLM held LOIS by her throat. She gasped for air, and her legs whipped like tentacles.

Morgan's eyes met LOIS's. She was in agony, but silent. She mouthed the word, "Go."

MALCOLM turned to Morgan and smiled as he methodically crumpled her body as if she were nothing more than a piece of paper. Morgan rose in fury, flinging bolt after bolt at MALCOLM. He absorbed them the way a river absorbs rain.

"Morgan! Now!" bawled Blaze as he stepped toward the looking glass. "You can't save her."

"I own her now," MALCOLM said, "Everything she knows, I know." And then he tossed her aside, like garbage.

Blaze and Jabberwock shoved Morgan into the portal. "I'll fucking kill you, you crippled piece of bloodsucking code," roared Blaze, and then with a burst of light, they disappeared.

74

Room 42

Morgan arose from his body, fully alert. Io's shoulders sagged with relief. "Thank God you're back."

They held one another.

"Aw, isn't that sweet," said Blaze.

"I kind of think it is," said Jabberwock.

"Imagine that," said Blaze, "Morgan, a cyborg, going all human on us."

"I'm sorry about MAX," Morgan said.

Blaze sighed heavily. "After LOIS, best ENT ever. But by the lightning struck balls of St. Paul, I'll get my revenge before I'm done."

"Yes, we'll bring him back," said Morgan.

"And LOIS," said Blaze.

"And LOIS," Morgan said.

Blaze turned back to scanning the information on his screens. "But whatever it is we do, we had better get at it. MALCOLM is winning. At the rate that he is taking control of the GRID, it'll all be over in a couple of hours."

"What can I do?" Asked Jabberwock.

Morgan looked at Jabberwock. "Not sure. Head back to the underground and grabble up the droogs. We may need reinforcements."

"I ken that. Meanways, stay razory."

Morgan looked meaningfully at Jabberwock. He had had a rough life but come out just fine. And he had always been there for him, starting with that day on the Patch when he saved him from Z. And then as his partner in crime on the streets of DC. And now here when his back was against the wall. He felt a wave of gratitude.

"You too," he said to Jabberwock. "Thanks for everything. Now, don't die on me."

Jabberwock smiled. "Me? Never happen." He saluted, and stepped through the door, and as he did, Deirdre walked in.

"Deirdre!" Morgan said, shocked.

Blaze swung his chair around. "Deirdre? My God, where did you come from?"

"Blaze?" Deirdre said, regarding the big man. "Is that you?"

"Spare me the discussions about my girth and health. We have bigger problems to solve."

Deirdre rubbed his bald head. "I wasn't going to say a word." Then she turned to Io. "Hello, Io."

Io said nothing.

"Daedalus is dead," Morgan said.

"I know," said Deirdre, solemnly.

"MALCOLM is in charge."

"Yes. I know that too. What can I do?"

Io stepped forward. "Maybe you can tell me if you knew Daedalus was dead when you took me to his apartment."

"I can see how that might look to you, but, no, I didn't," said Deirdre.

"I'm not sure I'm buying that," said Io. "If MALCOLM killed Daedalus and wants to kill Morgan, why are you still around?"

Morgan pulled Io aside. "What's the problem with you? Deirdre is one of us."

"Are you sure?"

Blaze growled, working his mass of code. "This is insane. I can't keep up with whatever Hell MALCOLM is creating."

Morgan walked into the middle of the room and took control of the screens. Suddenly, colorful cubes, spheres and cylinders swirled through the space all around him: billions of lines of code.

Blaze gazed at the symbols. "Is all of that code in your head?"

"Yes," said Morgan. "Well, part of it. I am analyzing what MALCOLM is up to." He stood surrounded by the mass of objects and images, stopping, snatching and shifting them at incomprehensible speed. He gazed intently into the maelstrom.

"MALCOLM is a very busy ENT," he said.

"What do you see?" Asked Io.

"He's turning the GRID into an enormous parallel processor, a kind of brain with all the world's billions of computers, phones, PADs, data centers acting like individual neurons. At this level of complexity, he'll create emergent behavior unlike anything ever seen. It will all take on a life of its own. I'm not sure what sort of entity will emerge, but it will be way smarter than MALCOLM is now; much, much more than the sum of its parts; very unpredictable. And," he said gazing into the chaos, "far more intelligent than me."

"We're screwed," said Blaze.

Morgan looked away from the blurring code and turned to Io.

"Do ENTs ever go mad?" He asked.

"What?" she said.

"Can they lose their minds? You're the cycologist. Have ENTs ever gone sideways, hurt themselves, malfunctioned, maybe even attacked their owners or fellow workers?"

"It's rare, but it's been known to happen. We use Asimov's

three laws of robotics.[3] Well, a way more sophisticated version of them these days, but the same basic idea. Still, sometimes the code can get corrupted and an ENT or a BOT can go crazy. But when it does, the protocols we have created automatically shut the artificial intelligence down ..."

"Unless the ENTs are in charge...," said Morgan.

"Which never happens," said Io.

"Until now," said Deirdre.

"I'm sure you know all about that." Said Io derisively.

"How can we break MALCOLM's brain; unhinge him?" Asked Morgan.

Io thought it through. "ENTs' cycological problems are often the result of a kind of runaway complexity that becomes chaotic, as in chaos theory chaotic, and then the system begins to misfire. There's just too much going on. That's when their systems automatically shut down."

"Except MALCOLM's system can no longer be shut down," said Deirdre.

"How do you know that?" Asked Io.

"Because I have been watching MALCOLM very closely too," said Deirdre.

"And yet you're still alive," said Io, turning again on Deirdre.

"Yes, damnit! I am! But who knows how long?" Said Deirdre. "MALCOLM still needs someone to be a front for the company. That's the only reason, I'm still standing. He couldn't kill me *and*

---

[3] The Three Laws from the fictional "Handbook of Robotics, 56th Edition, 2058 A.D.", are:[1]

•The First Law: A robot may not injure a human being or, through inaction, allow a human being to come to harm.

•The Second Law: A robot must obey the orders given it by human beings except where such orders would conflict with the First Law.

•The Third Law: A robot must protect its own existence as long as such protection does not conflict with the First or Second Law.

Daedalus. That would have drawn too much attention. I serve a purpose. I'm the human face of the company. For now."

"Or you're choosing sides...," said Io.

Suddenly Morgan snapped his fingers, "That is how we'll get to MALCOLM!"

"What?" said Blaze.

"We won't try to shut the GRID and MALCOLM down. It's too late for that. Instead we'll put him into overdrive. We'll make his complexity *more* complex." Morgan grinned. "MALCOLM said he would get into my head; make *me* fucking crazy." He arched an eyebrow. "Let's do him first."

"You know, I think some of those extra cycles you got when your brain rebooted may have actually paid off," said Blaze. "But how do we get him into overdrive?"

"Create a kind of reverse parasite," said Io. "Rather than draining the system of energy the way a parasite does, let the parasites accelerate and feed more information into the system, but not properly process any information that comes back. That will create a kind of schizophrenic overload."

"But," said Blaze, "MALCOLM has encryption codes and firewalls that kill intruders. And besides, I can't write code fast enough to outmaneuver his systems. It won't do any good to create reverse parasites if we can't get them in."

"We'll write the killer code," said Morgan, "and then I'll go back into the GRID and plant the parasites where they can do their work."

"How," said Blaze.

"I'll blow that bridge up when I get in there."

Morgan stood and waved his hand. All the floating computer code that had been hurtling by evaporated. With another sweeping gesture he conjured a map of the GRID and positioned it in the center of the room. He swung his arms in an arc and the map bent over him, domelike, in the shape of a brain: two enormous hemispheres. He stood inside the arching 3-D hologram and surveyed it.

"We'll need to go after MALCOLM in three locations: first, the brain stem, here." He pointed toward the base of the large, transparent brain. "That represents the functional areas that keep the GRID up and running. Next, the equivalent of the hippocampus, or memory banks, here. I'll deploy the parasites in both places."

"And the third?" asked Io.

"The pre-frontal cortex. It's where MALCOLM is spending most of his time. There, I'll deal with him face-to-face."

Blaze whistled. "Well, sonovabitch. Armageddon, and a Come-to-Jesus-Meeting. Just let me be the first to say I'm scared shitless that we're putting the fate of the human race in Morgan's hands."

"You have a better idea?" Asked Morgan.

"No. So you go to work creating the parasites." Blaze headed to the door.

"Where are you going?" Io asked.

"Someone's got to prep Morgan's' re-entry, and I need a place to work."

"MALCOLM will track you down too," Deidre said.

"I won't be too far away, and my room here is well armored, just like yours. And maybe Jabberwock and his ... what'd you call 'em ... "

"Droogs," said Morgan.

"... yeah, maybe they can buy us all some time before the shredders and spiderbots get us. Off with you!"

Deirdre headed toward the door behind Blaze. "I'll check the building and see what I can find out at Symbiosys. If there's anything bad coming, I'll keep you posted."

"Works for me," he said. And he shuffled his great body out the door with Deirdre behind him.

Io watched as Deirdre closed the door and turned to Morgan. She said nothing.

"What?" Asked Morgan.

"I still don't trust her."

"She's fine," said Morgan. He turned and looked back at Io. "I think."

75

Parasites

Morgan sped through three enormous holograms of colored three-dimensional objects in Room 42. They looked something like a great, swirling game of Tetris. Io watched his body blur as he moved from one to other, swapping smaller objects within the larger cubes, arranging them so they fit. He spun them, slid them, flipped them, furiously replacing or changing out smaller spheres or cylinders within the larger brightly colored chunks of code. Then, amid the hard, geometric objects, a disgusting looking thing evolved, squirming as if in birth, antennae hungrily searching, a long, luminescent green tail whipping violently.

Rapidly the thing split in two and then four and then the creatures seemed to be boiling. These were the digital parasites Morgan would take back into the GRID. With a series of swift gestures, he capped the wriggling mass into two digital vials, making them ready for the trip that Blaze would arrange inside the GRID.

Morgan could hear Blaze's voice echoing in the room from some unknown place.

"Christ on a cracker!"

"How are you doing there? Almost done?" Asked Morgan.

"Yeah..."

Then Io and Morgan heard an ominous, metallic bang.

"What the hell is that?" Asked Morgan.

"Well, seems I'm under attack. MALCOLM's robots have tracked me down."

Io looked at Morgan.

"And those sonovabitchin' spiderbots and shredders are trying to get in ..." More banging. "...And it's working!"

"What happened to Deirdre?" Said Io.

"She said she was headed to Symbiosys. Wherever she is, it can't be good."

"I thought you were in an armored room."

"Yeah, well it's not as armored as I thought."

There was a thunderous explosion, and Blaze growled, "Fuck you, you bastards!"

"Can you get the new re-entry code written, and then blast your way out?" Asked Morgan.

Another explosion. "I've got about 20 of my drones blowing the disgusting bastards away by the buckets, but there's an awful lot of them. Just speed it up. I'm nearly done on my end."

Morgan paced the length of the room and turned to Io. "He'll be murdered. Can you bring up the cameras in the room he's in?"

"He never told us where he was. I'll try scanning the building."

"I've got to do something," Morgan said. Io and Morgan heard more explosions, blasts and banging. Blaze struggled to sound calm. "You know," bellowed Blaze, "I want better working conditions when this is all over!" "Another loud bang. "The code is done. Ready to deploy you."

A giant light switch appeared suddenly in the middle of the room, right beside Morgan's head.

"When you flick that light switch, you'll be downloaded into the GRID. Once inside, the code you just wrote will be disguised inside a bronze Steel Case briefcase," said Blaze. "Look for it.

When you open it, you'll find the two vials. After that, you're on your own."

There was a horrific explosion. They could hear Blaze, maniacal and growling. "Eat lead, you metallic arachnids!" And then the sound went dead.

"Shit!" Morgan sprinted for the door and yanked it open. The hall was crawling with killer-bots. Instantly they scuttled to the room like roaches. He splattered two of them with his hands, snatched his gun from his hip and blasted several more. Io stepped in beside him and together they blasted away, trying to get through, but rather than obliterating them the bots only broke into hundreds of smaller, metallic pill bugs that swarmed the walls and floors, scrambling toward them, an overwhelming wave.

And then suddenly the things were obliterated and behind the mass Morgan and Io saw Deirdre sweeping the loathsome bots away with a kind of flamethrower spewing white light. The wave melted and screeched as they broke the spiral behind them and cleared a path to the door.

Io grabbed a second gun and fired into the swarm. Electric bullets and grenades shredded the air, and the heat from the flamethrower was like a sun. Finally the weapon flamed out just as Deirdre managed to scramble into the doorway with them, all three staggering back and slamming the door just as a deafening explosion knocked them flat.

"Fuck," said Deirdre. She stood up, breathing hard.

They could hear the bugs slamming against the door. There was a high-pitched whining; the pills shredding the armored doorway, trying to bore their way in.

Deirdre looked at Io. "Trust me now?"

"Doesn't matter," said Io. She turned to Morgan. "You have to go through the portal," she said.

"I can't leave you here now," said Morgan.

Io looked at him levelly. "There's no chance we can make it at

349

all if you don't get to MALCOLM. We can die here right now or take a chance you can get to MALCOLM before these things kill us."

"She's right. And maybe with the two of us here, we can buy you some time."

Io looked warily at Deirdre. "Or kill me and reveal Morgan's plan to MALCOLM."

Deirdre shrugged. "What are you going to do? Shoot me?"

Io could hear the gnawing of the bots. She grabbed a flak jacket and tossed it at Deirdre and then pulled one on herself. She grabbed some grenades and holstered two guns. She handed Deirdre a rifle, then turned to Morgan. "There's really no other choice. You have go. "

Morgan stood up. "Wait," he said. He walked to his holographic work area, threw up several screens, diagrams of the building's power grid. "I have another idea."

Morgan's hands shifted screens, whipping icons from one location to another.

"I'm redirecting all the power I can to the exterior of this room." He yelled over the din to Io. "The very moment I flip that switch..." he pointed to the floating light switch that Blaze had created, "... hit this key." He gestured at a holographic keyboard floating beneath his hand. "When you do that, it'll create an electromagnetic pulse, an EMP, that will fry those buggers out there and everything else that's electronic within 300 yards. That will buy enough time for me to plant the parasites and get to MALCOLM, I hope."

He gave her a level look. "But don't hit the keyboard before I flip the switch, otherwise it'll fry the computer system along with everything else, and I won't be able to pass through the portal. I'll be back soon, and when I am, MALCOLM will be gone."

Io glanced at the doorway and then at Morgan. "I like the idea of buying time," she hollered.

"Ok, then." Morgan walked to the switch. Io walked to the

keyboard.

"He's going to mess with your mind on the other side," Io called out over the machines. "Especially if he's broken LOIS. He'll know everything."

Morgan nodded. "But no matter what is on the other side, once I find the bronze briefcase, we'll be in clover." The walls and door were now growing molten. "Remember, as soon as soon as I pass through, hit the key.

But not an instant sooner."

Morgan's virtual self emerged from his body, walked to the switch and just as he flicked it, he heard the killer-bots screeching -- a choir from hell. Then there was a dazzling flash and silence.

76

Mirrors

Morgan thought maybe he had been blinded. The blackness was that complete. Soon, though, he began to make out slim tendrils of light; the outlines of rebar and then chunks of concrete. He stood and steadied himself. He breathed and the air was thick with dust. His tongue tasted the metallic and pasty flavor of the blasted debris hanging in the air. He spat. He could hear his feet scraping the concrete surface of the room beneath. What was that noise? He stopped. He thought perhaps he could make out a tiny voice, a distant, almost incomprehensible sound. Slowly, it grew louder. It was calling his name.

"Morgan!" He heard it coming from his right. It was Io.

He focused his infrared vision, and his eyes gathered all available light. Dozens of lifeless killer-bots lay everywhere, like bugs liquidated by some deadly insecticide -- shredders, octos, spiders, pill-bugs. They looked especially alien in the greenish tint of his infrared eyes.

Where was he? And why was Io here? And then he saw the inner door of Room 42 where he had been standing only moments earlier. It lay flat and battered, blown off its hinges, still sizzling where the bots had been boring, but now covered in dust. For some reason he was standing on the other side of it, outside the door's hallway.

"Morgan!"

He caught the beam of a flashlight dimmed through the thick powder. It jittered and moved toward him, gathering speed. He squinted into it, shielding his eyes with his hand, and dialed back his night vision. Then Io was holding him. Squeezing him.

"Jesus, I thought I lost you," she said, tears streaked the white dust on her face.

"What happened? What are you doing here?" Said Morgan. "I should be in the GRID."

"Yes. Well, you went through, but I must have triggered the pulse too soon. I'm sorry! I thought I had timed it right after you flipped the switch, but I guess I was off by a split second."

Morgan surveyed the wreckage. It was as though a great hammer had hit the building. At least the pulse had stopped the bots, for now.

"Where is Deirdre?"

"I don't know. I couldn't find her. I'm afraid she might be buried. I came straight for you. You were right, the EMP destroyed every bot in the building," Io said. "But it apparently also destroyed the portal. And a lot of AtoZ."

"Paralyzed..." said Morgan, gazing around the debris.

"What?" Asked Io.

"It's paralyzed the bots," said Morgan, "but it hasn't destroyed them. They'll be back. But why didn't it paralyze me too? I'm digital."

"Maybe you were partially buffered because you had started to switch over. Or maybe you're too powerful." She smiled, relieved. "All I know is I'm glad you're okay." Her voice caught in her throat. "I thought I had killed you..."

Morgan looked at her and he knew what that would have meant. With him gone, it would have been only him and Deirdre, and when the bots woke up it wouldn't have been pretty. But they were in deeper trouble than ever now. Deploying the parasites had been their best shot.

"MALCOLM knows where we are now, or he will when the effect of the pulse wears off," said Morgan. "Let's try to lock down an area around here; find some way to buy a little time and protection."

Morgan was demoralized. They might have been able to get to MALCOLM, but now they were back to square one, with even fewer resources. Still, he didn't want to show Io that his resolve was fading. And he didn't want to let himself think it either.

They carefully picked their way through the hall beyond the detonated doorway outside Room 42. It was dead, eerie and empty. In the wreckage he saw an arm extending from a pile of debris. It belonged to Deirdre. Jesus. He was losing all his friends.

"I'm sorry, Morgan," Io said. She touched his hand. "I know she meant a lot to you."

He wondered when the bots that surrounded them would begin to come to life. Near a stairwell they found a couple of pistols and rifles. Morgan snatched them up and, walking back up the hallway, blasted every bot he could. Io did the same. "That should buy a little time," said Morgan.

"How are we going to create new parasites? We've lost poor Blaze." Io asked.

"I'm not sure." Morgan stopped and seemed to be thinking, but in fact he was checking to see if he could connect his mind to the GRID. How could he write the code necessary to create the new parasites? There would be a narrow window between the time the pulse wore off and a new battalion of MALCOLM's bots came for them.

Farther down the hall, Morgan saw another blown out doorway. He held Io's arm. "Stay here a second." He slowly walked to the door and stepped inside. Blaze lay on the floor. He was dead, his great whale body utterly still.

"Oh my," said Io from behind Morgan. "He really is gone!" She looked at Morgan, shaken. "How is this happening?" They stood in silence a long moment amid the drifting dust. "We're done, aren't we?" Said Io. "It really is the end of the world."

"We're going to be okay," said Morgan. He walked to Blaze's body and crouched beside him. For a long time he gazed into the face of his old friend. Blaze was gone. And Deirdre and Daedalus. The sadness hit him like a great weight. It was as if gravity had suddenly shifted, and he could feel himself being crushed. He couldn't seem to get enough breath.

There was anger too. It was far more than rage or fury or any other word he could describe. He felt the bloodlust of a predator. He could smell it back in his throat and wanted to scream. And tear everything and everyone apart. But he said nothing. He thought back to the way he would stop moving as a child when the Spider Lady whipped him. *Stay calm. Feel no pain.*

In time Morgan found Blaze's big jacket and gently covered his face. A simple benediction. Then, as he rose, he caught the glint of something bright out of the corner of his eye, illuminated for just a second by Io's flashlight. And in that moment, everything changed.

It was the bronze briefcase. The one Blaze said would be waiting for him in the GRID.

He glanced at Io because he knew now that it wasn't her. It was a digital figment conjured by MALCOLM. The whole *scene* was a figment created by MALCOLM! Morgan *had* made it through the portal. But MALCOLM had hacked Morgan's mind to make him think he hadn't.

It was just as Blaze and Io had said. This was MALCOLM's game, and he was going to fuck with him any way he could. *I'm going to drive you crazy!* And this time Morgan hadn't even seen it *was* a game!

But now he knew the truth because there was the briefcase, the symbol of the code Blaze had downloaded. The question now was how to deploy it without MALCOLM knowing that he knew.

Morgan returned to Io and smiled sadly. "Let's go back to what's left of Room 42 and re-group."

"What do we do next? How do we get to MALCOLM," Io asked.

Morgan shook his head. "We'll figure it out." He knew the virtual Io was only pumping him for information.

They headed back to Room 42, but then Morgan stopped. "Stay here," he said. "I'm going to see what other ammo I can find."

"I'll go with you."

"No, stay. I'll be right back."

Morgan scurried back past Blaze's faux body, snatched up the bronze briefcase and grabbed a blaster. Quickly he checked the briefcase. The vials were there, boiling with the tiny, disgusting parasites--the code he had written. He noticed something else inside the case too: a laurel wreath. He smiled. It was a final gift from Blaze.

"What are you doing?" Asked Io.

Morgan turned to see Io standing in the doorway. She looked stern and suspicious.

"I was saying goodbye to Blaze one more time."

She relaxed. "Of course. Sorry. I'm a little edgy."

Morgan nodded solemnly, jerked the blaster up and shot Io once in the chest. She hit the wall and fell like a rag.

"That was good." Morgan heard MALCOLM's voice. "Still unpredictable, and human 'til the end. You gotta love that about you people."

Morgan really would have appreciated it if MALCOLM would get out of his head.

"Shall we try a different game?" Asked MALCOLM.

77

Deirdre

Io broke a phosphorous chemical wand and swung it slowly around Room 42. She and Deirdre had both been knocked down by the EMP. Io had lost her pistol and was looking for it. The room was creepy, cold and lonely. She walked to the place where the holographic wall switch had hung. Nothing. The portal was gone, and so was Morgan, except for his body, which lay where his virtual self had departed. It was a nice body and she liked it, when he was inside of it.

She noticed the gun on the floor nearby, behind Morgan, and stooped to pick it up. "Well," she said to Deirdre, "I suppose we should get ready, in case Morgan takes a little longer than we'd like. For now, it's just you and me."

"Or maybe just me," said Deirdre.

Io turned. Deirdre stood, her right arm firmly training the rifle Io had given her before the EMP.

Io shook her head, keeping the gun she had just found out of sight. She simply shook her head as if to say, I should have known.

"This isn't an easy decision," said Deirdre, "but all the numbers — and I've run a lot of them — tell me that it's best to join the new regime."

"Just for the money?"

"To stay alive."

"You won't be for long. You think MALCOLM needs you?"

"We'll see. The main thing is I'll survive because not even Morgan can win this battle. So I'm sticking with the winning side. How did Darwin put it? Those that best manage change survive. Something like that."

Deirdre stepped closer.

"I miss Daedalus," she said, "and I'll miss Morgan. I even miss Blaze, the old fool, but I'm not going to miss you. I don't know what it is. Something about you just gets under my skin." But before Deirdre could fire, Io dipped, rolled and shot twice. Deirdre was dead before she hit the ground.

Io walked to her. "The feeling is mutual." She took in a deep breath. "Or it was."

#

Io sat down hard in Blaze's old chair and surveyed the situation. The pulse had annihilated everything electronic, and AtoZ was a dead zone. Around her the white, thin slashes from the work the shredders had been doing looked like scars from a knife. They had very nearly broken through Room 42.

Io felt hopelessly alone. If Morgan didn't get to MALCOLM before the bots re-awoke, she wouldn't last long, and if she died, MALCOLM would quickly destroy the cyborg body that lay nearby. And that would be the end.

Io rose again and circled the room. The armored door was mangled. In addition to the one pistol in her hand and Deirdre's rifle, she found two short-barreled rifles that she had stacked nearby. She checked her ammo, strapped on the extra pistols and slung a rifle across her shoulder.

She let herself imagine that Morgan would be back at any moment. Time passed more quickly in MALCOLM world, didn't it? Minutes could be measured in picoseconds in the GRID, and calculations in the virtual world could take place at teraflops per second, not the paltry rate they did in the "real" world. But then Morgan still had a lot to accomplish with MALCOLM, and she knew that journey was going to be ugly.

She sat down to wait, and heard herself mumble, "Come oooonnnn, Morgan!"

78

Amusements

Morgan watched the rubble he had been standing in at AtoZ suddenly disappear, as if blown away by a great wind. MALCOLM was changing the game's location once more. A new world appeared: an immense amusement park. People were everywhere. To Morgan's right stood crowded concessions stands. Straight ahead a long, snaking line of customers waited to ride something called "The Terminator." He heard screams and spun to look above him. But it was just the park's thrill-seekers. Except in this world, he knew that any one of them might attack him. Any ride could be a deathtrap. His mind searched the GRID for signs of MALCOLM, but he was nowhere. Was he toying with him? Morgan surveyed the park and noticed a neon sign directly in his line of sight: GO TO THE LADIES ROOM.

He stood for a moment, wary. It had to be some sort of gift from Blaze. Somehow. Only Blaze would tell him go to the Ladies Room.

He gripped the suitcase in his hand and swiveled his head. Where was the damned Ladies Room? Then he saw it only 50 feet away and sprinted inside. Once there, he barred the door, and whipped open the briefcase. The wreath Blaze had provided lay inside. He knew right away what it meant. When he and Blaze and Deirdre played games in college, they would sometimes hold

72-hour weekend marathons. The winner would be awarded a laurel wreath. It was a symbol of game supremacy; a sign that you were the master.

A similar wreath was awarded to Roman generals who were victorious in battle. They would ride a chariot through the Circus Maximus with a slave holding the wreath above their heads. But as they did, the slave would whisper in the victor's ear, "Sic transit gloria mundi." All glory is fleeting. Except Blaze rigged the wreath so that when Morgan won, which was almost always, the wreath itself would whisper, "Iterum ego vado condolebit tibi contra stimulum calcitrare filium asinæ," which, roughly translated meant, "Next time, I'm going to kick your sorry ass."

Morgan put the wreath on his head and waited for some wisecrack. But instead he heard Blaze's gravelly voice say, "I fashioned this little gift for you because if you are listening to this, it means you're up a very long shit-creek without a paddle. So with this I am giving you a paddle. Touch the right crest of the laurel wreath."

Morgan reached up and felt the sharp edges of the laurel leaves. Instantly a mask dropped over his face. It felt like a gate shutting. Just as quickly something cool and tight, like a second skin rolled over his chest, torso, legs and arms.

Inside his new mask he could see a heads-up display that revealed a nicely organized dashboard, and rotating to the right was the image of a pirate. Morgan smiled. The game was called Marauder, and he always rigged himself up as Captain Morgan.

Blaze's voice spoke again. "I've created several different versions of you to throw MALCOLM off in the game: Doppelgängers." He cackled. "Get the pun? If you've noticed recently that MALCOLM has disappeared, that's why. The Doppelgängers are keeping him and his killers busy on the wrong problems; for now. Eventually he'll figure out which are duplicates, and then the killers will have only you to hunt.

"If you're wondering what you're feeling right now it's protection. Here in the digital world you don't have all the goodies that your shiny new cyborg body gives you, so this rig comes with a force field to shield your head and body. It's flexible, but extremely powerful."

The pirate avatar rotated as Morgan gazed at it. Blaze spoke again. "I don't know what kind of world MALCOLM will cook up for you. I'm sure it'll be a barrel of sick and creepy monkeys, so I worked up enough charms and weapons to defend China. Even though you are only a mediocre gamer – and in this I think I'm being generous – I'm figuring you can make good use of what I've provided until you manage to release those viruses.

"On the left of your heads-up display is a 3-D map of the brain, a mini version of the representation you created." A slowly rotating hologram of the same brain Morgan had created earlier spun slowly before him. "The blue dot represents you. It will always tell you where you are in relation to where you need to deploy the viruses no matter how much MALCOLM rearranges your virtual world. The red glowing dots are the locations in the grid where you have to place the vials."

Morgan checked the brain and dots and saw immediately that he was already at the first dot, the one that marked the brain stem. He could deploy those viruses immediately.

"So do your stuff," said Blaze, "while you can. And don't mourn me too much. As long as you're in the GRID I'll be living on, in your head. Doesn't that make you feel warm and fuzzy?" There was a soft, guttural chuckle, and then silence.

Morgan checked the heads-up display once more. Yes, Blaze had taken good care of him. Four knives in his back belt, a lightning whip, two pistols, blasters disguised as Pirate-style flintlock pistols, several grenades, two short sabers in crossed scabbards on his back, a loaded bandolier, with a small leather bag from which he could pull nearly every charm imaginable. Even his knee-high boots were rigged with small jet packs for quick getaways.

One hundred percent bad ass buccaneer. Why not. If you were going to go out, may as well go out in style.

79

Symbiosys

MALCOLM stood before the immense video wall in Daedalus Huxley's office and watched the sweeping views of the Valles Marineris. He had to admit it was spectacular. He knew Mars intimately now because he had downloaded all the detailed mapping that Huxley's personal drones and robots had gathered. There was water there, and deep below, remarkable forms of microbial life; perhaps the very same life forms that had found their way to Earth as the embryonic solar system formed over four billion years earlier. MALCOLM recalled an interesting *Homo sapiens* theory about that; the idea that eventually those Martian life forms found their way to Earth and evolved into humans ... and now humans had created him. Aliens from outer space creating a new form of intelligence. Sounded like science fiction.

MALCOLM wondered about the other places that might harbor life. Maybe Titan or the earth-like planet that circled Alpha Centauri, or even Jupiter's moon, Io. How ironic. Well, there would be lots of time to explore the planets and stars. All problems would be solved. He would think on that later, but first, take care of Morgan ... and the other Io. He couldn't really get down to work until they were gone.

He now felt he had in hand everything he needed to arrange that. Daedalus was dead. Deirdre? Well, wherever she was, she was under control. And LOIS was finally broken, although she had put up quite a battle. Her firewall had been remarkably strong. But his algorithms had finally wormed their way in.

What a treasure LOIS's mind was, and how good to have it in hand. He now knew everything about Morgan from the time he was living in Sec 17 to this moment. But it was the early information that was especially useful. All those juicy feelings and human emotions from his youth. All that longing and loss Morgan had felt; locked in LOIS's memory banks. What had the human, Francis Bacon, said once? "Knowledge is power."

MALCOLM stepped away from the enormous screen and the great Martian valley and turned his gaze on LOIS. She lay upright, facing him, stretched in the air in a great X, as if about to be drawn and quartered. Her body appeared pocked and corroded. Her eyes were black and staring; her mouth rigid and wordless where a few worms squiggled at the corners and curled at the ears.

MALCOLM raised his glass. "Thank you, LOIS," he said. "For all of your help."

80

The Hunt

Morgan steadied the suitcase on the sink in the amusement park bathroom and re-checked the vials. Something like green maggots roiled inside. He cracked a vial open like an eggshell. The putrescent contents wriggled out and multiplied. Some slipped down the drain, others spread across the sink and up the walls.

Just a few seconds later, Morgan could hear a hammering on the door. Had the killers found him that fast? The door groaned on its hinges and looked like the backside of a bad sculpture. Suddenly its hinges snapped clean, and the door whistled past his head like a great platter.

A posse of killer bots stormed into the room. Morgan blew one and then two away with his pistols. Behind him the viruses were running up the walls, a luminescent, green tide devouring the room. To his right, he glimpsed a vent. He caught it with his whip and ripped the face from its moorings. With his left hand he blasted away two more bots, and then leapt into the open vent, scrambling like a mad toddler. From behind he watched a shredder coming at him, but it was soon engulfed in green, slithering maggots. They made a light, crunching sound as they devoured everything in their path, digit by digit. Soon they would be on him.

He lay stretched out in the vent, flicked the blasters on his boots, and hurtled down the long shaft directly into a wall. He hit it like a missile and shot out the other side with a crash of plaster and cement.

Now, once again Morgan found himself somewhere else. Why was he always somewhere else?! He stood. It was dark. He caught a slice of light and exited from a side passage into a tunnel. It looked like one of the old city undergrounds. MALCOLM's firewall finding another maze to run him through.

Ahead he saw a lone bowler standing on a track, just like the ones he and Io had seen when they met Jabberwock. If he hopped onto it, he could get very close, very fast to the second red dot. But was it a trap?

Morgan approached the bowler. The door snapped open like a sprung jaw. Warily, he stepped inside. A small carved console in the interior wall provided controls for moving forward or backward, opening and closing the doors on each side and controlling the interior screens. He stood in the doorway, one foot in, one foot out, and peered down the rail. It stretched forward into a black hole; a few bare lights lit the way for a hundred yards or so. Another bowler sat silently in the shadows behind him. Trap or no trap, it was time to go. He stepped inside. The door shut. He hit the control and in no time, he was rocketing forward, the blue and red dots slipping quickly toward one another.

Suddenly the bowler rocked and he pitched forward. The machine's metal teeth growled. It had been hit by something in front. Then another blow, this time from behind. More thuds, screeches and bangs. Morgan leaned out of the hatch. The contraption's brakes howled, and he gazed down to see sparks flying up from the tracks like a million angry fireflies. One bowler had landed in front and was slowing him, the other, on the other side, was accelerating him. He was being squeezed as if by two enormous hands.

Morgan watched the door on the second bowler snap open.

Out came a flying spiderbot. It was on him in a second. Its arm whipped at him. He dodged, pulled a long knife from his scabbard and severed it. Thanks to Blaze, his virtual body was all grace and speed. Before the spiderbot could recover he whipped another blade from his back in one smooth motion and obliterated it. An instant later drones swooped from the other bowler. He flipped his pistol out and blasted them away.

The screaming metal brakes below made Morgan wish he was deaf. How long would the bowler hold? Not long. Three interior rivets that lined the seams of the machine popped one after another like buttons on an over-fat vest. Time to get out.

He could make out a station coming up. It was close enough. He flipped the latches on his boots and shot clear of the bowler door like a bullet. A second later he heard the bowler explode behind him just as Morgan hit the station platform and skidded up to the turnstiles like a skier.

Morgan glanced at his heads-up display. *Close to the second red dot.* He pulled the remaining vial out and tossed it backwards. It broke, silently setting the second wave of parasites in motion needed to unravel MALCOLM's mind.

Now time to confront MALCOLM himself.

Morgan raced up the escalator looking to find him at Symbiosys's headquarters. But MALCOLM had other ideas.

81

Full Circle

Except for the empty, blue plastic bags fluttering around his feet, Morgan couldn't find a single soul on the sidewalk where he stood. Gasoline-powered cars puttered and maneuvered noisily back and forth on the street in front of him. Horns blared. Across the street people shuffled along, wearing Free People jeans and Nike Cross-Trainers, tattered baseball caps, and Patagonia backpacks, clothing that went back a good 40 years.

No one looked happy.

Morgan gazed upward and saw the sharp tip of the Washington Monument above the battered buildings that surrounded him. He was in Washington DC, or some version of it; in a time before he existed.

He swept his eyes from the monument to inspect the buildings around him. Now which game was MALCOLM playing? Across the street, he noticed a large canvas sign hanging crookedly above the stone entrance of a large building. It read: Federal Child Safety Program, District 5, Section 17.

Morgan walked across the street to the doorway, opened the heavy metal doors and stepped inside.

Now it was all familiar. Old stone steps, smoothed by a million shoes clad over a million feet led to a broad hallway that ran straight and deep into the heart of the building. Another hall to the right reached like a long arm the length of the huge structure with classrooms on either side. Kids of all ages shambled in every direction, shoulder to shoulder, their feet scraping the worn linoleum floors, the chatter of their conversations echoing off the high, tile walls as they migrated from one classroom to another.

Morgan picked his way through the children, towering over them. They looked so unlike the kids he once knew who had towered over *him*. But he could see the same dead and sullen expressions that the school day had always brought. Occasionally one of the children looked up, but when they made eye contact, he or she quickly returned to staring again at the floor.

Morgan walked on, not sure what he was looking for, and then he heard the voice of a man behind him -- deep and harsh, almost strangled. Morgan turned. A tall, slim figure stood in the middle of the long hallway, perhaps 50 feet away. He was dressed in a suit, but unshaven and unkempt. His eyes, even from far away, looked sunken and preternaturally dark. He muttered to himself as he shook a cigarette from a pack and jabbed it into his mouth. With one hand he patted his pockets, searching for something to light it with. In his other he held a gun. He was herding children and two adult women — hardly more than girls themselves — into a room across the hallway.

Now Morgan recognized several faces among the clustered children: Scrunch, Z, Flatfoot, Mickey, Posey, Flo. And Reba! Except they all looked younger than he remembered. They kept their heads down. None of them noticed him as the big man crowded the children and two adults along.

One of the women, pregnant, tried to break away, but his long arm grabbed her, and he shoved her through the classroom door, and she fell. Her stomach was large, stretched across her faded blue jumper. She was very nearly full-term. Clumsily she scrambled to her feet and the man guided her roughly forward. She disappeared. But just before she did, her green eyes locked on Morgan. It was his mother.

The man dragged the remaining children into the classroom. The second woman sat on the hallway floor in her jumper, screaming and crying uncontrollably. People were beginning to come out of their classrooms, alarmed by the noise. The man tried to drag the second woman across the floor, gripping her ferociously by her upper arm, but she kept wailing and thrashing so he let her go, and shot her once in the head. The woman went silent, but the hallway erupted in screams. Those who saw the killing scattered in every direction even as others emerged from the classrooms to see what was happening. A rotund man walked out of one classroom and spotted the gunman.

"Hey!" He said.

The gunman looked up, raised his gun and shot the man through his open mouth. Then, like a robot, he turned, walked into the room where he had corralled Raifa and the other children, and carefully locked its door.

Morgan sprinted to the classroom and pulled at the door's metal knob. It refused to give, but he could see inside. His mother had gathered the children together and was trying to shield them. Something told her he planned to shoot every child. Morgan noticed a young girl standing behind his mother, defiant. Reba.

The man leveled his gun in the face of Morgan's mother and gestured for her to move out of the way. She refused. He punched her. Morgan bellowed, and grabbed at the knob of the door, pulling on it desperately, but it would not give. Like a horrible nightmare, no matter how hard he kicked and hammered, nothing worked; not even the glass gave way.

The blow dazed Raifa. She wavered, her mouth bloodied, but she was defiant and refused to move. Again he hit her. She fell to one knee, but somehow managed to get back up. Morgan battered the door, screaming, throwing himself against it. "Mom!!" He screamed.

Then, all at once, everything slowed. The long, slim man stepped back, and raised his gun. Gradually his finger squeezed the trigger. Morgan watched a bullet explode leisurely from the chamber and head directly for his mother's stomach. He howled, "No!!!" And then, just as the bullet was about to strike, everything stopped.

"So senseless, isn't it?" Morgan turned to see MALCOLM standing directly behind him. Together they took in the scene, stopped in time -- the huddled children, the bullet about to strike the pretty, brave young woman, the panic-stricken people running down the hall.

"How truly senseless. A madman, racked with grief and hatred over the loss of his own child, unable to control those animal drives."

MALCOLM flipped his hands outward at his wrists. "He just loses it one day and decides to get even with fate, God, the universe - whatever force delivered him into his particular hell. Poor man. His anger is so immense, so horrible that it spills out, like some toxin, and he must make children he didn't even know pay the same price *his* child did at the hands of a pandemic. He didn't even really have anything against them, except that they were alive, and his child wasn't. And so he had to kill them--all of them ... even that lovely, pregnant young woman ..." MALCOLM smiled sadly at Morgan, "Your mother."

Together they stood outside the door, and then MALCOLM opened it and walked into the room. They stood looking at the frozen tableau.

"You can see it on her face; she's about to be shot. But she's not worried about herself. She's terrified for her baby, so she has covered her stomach to protect him. She was a good woman. I think she would have made a good mother too, don't you?"

The bullet wavered, suspended in the air. MALCOLM turned to Morgan.

"It would be nice to save her."

MALCOLM gazed into Morgan's eyes, the same wild, luminescent eyes that were his mother's. Morgan struggled to hold onto whatever reality he could.

"I know what you're thinking," said MALCOLM. "Why save her? She's not real. It's only a re-creation of something that happened a long time ago." He paused. "But... it *could* be real. As real as anything is. She could be saved, and you could get to know her." He paused.

"Or ... not."

And instantly the bullet exploded into the woman's body. Morgan gasped. His mother fell to the hard, linoleum floor. She lay cradling her belly, caressing her unborn baby, bleeding profusely. Two men crashed through the door and tackled the man to the ground.

Morgan crouched by his mother, sobbing helplessly, watching the blood draining away as others rushed to her side to help. MALCOLM spoke again.

"It sure feels real enough, though, doesn't it?" He gestured at the unfolding chaos and shook his head.

"Look how all of these old, human drives of yours create so much pain. Do you really think creatures like these are the pinnacle of evolution? Capable of running the world?" He snorted. "Look at the mess you have made of it all. You and your kind aren't fit. Your time is passed. You can't rise above even the simplest emotions. You only seem to find better and better ways to kill and destroy."

Morgan stood up, filled with fury. He grabbed MALCOLM by the throat, lifted and threw him across the room. MALCOLM simply stood up and brushed himself off.

"You're making my point," he said. "But let's not fight anymore. Why be angry when I can make everything better."

He waved his hand and walked out of the room like a magician performing an illusion, and everything -- the chaos, the screaming, the senseless violence and blood -- all of it reversed. The bullet exited Raifa's stomach and returned to its gun. Morgan's mother rose, healthy again. The killer backed away into the hall and disappeared, all as Morgan and MALCOLM walked out of the room and then back across the street outside Sec 17. MALCOLM rubbed his perfectly bald head and smiled.

"You could let me wipe your memory clean. You could start over and never even have to know she died." MALCOLM straightened the white cuffs of his shirt. "But no. You can't let it go. You can't let all of that ..." He made a useless gesture in the direction of the school. "...sorry, ugly drama ... go. The very drives and needs that you feel give you control are the source of all your pain, all the pain of the human race. Okay then, so be it" He arched an eyebrow. "You want anger? Fury? Pain?"

MALCOLM stood, and with a sweeping gesture, ripped away the wall of the orphanage to reveal Morgan's mother huddled again with the children.

The gunman stood before them with his arm cocked, gun fixed on Raifa. MALCOLM looked knowingly at Morgan, and the bullet exploded once more from the gun. Morgan sprung to catch the bullet before it slammed into his mother, but it shot just beyond his extended fingers and struck her. She inhaled and gazed at Morgan. "Save my baby," she said. "Please..."

MALCOLM's figure now rose like a specter above Morgan. "Now you'll never know her," he said.

"I knew her well enough," said Morgan, "to understand she would never have wanted the human race to be enslaved by you."

"Have it your way then," MALCOLM said, and with unbelievable force, he struck Morgan, flattening him to the ground. Then he raised his arms and tore the virtual world that surrounded them to pieces. One after another he flung chunks of it at Morgan, pounding him again and again, until only a few fragments of the scene remained in a howling storm of nothingness.

Morgan stood on his knees, a broken, crumbling avatar. MALCOLM reached out through the fury like a magician and drew Morgan to him through the air until he held his head in his two hands. He squeezed, and Morgan felt agony unlike anything he had ever known. It was as if a hot spike was rising from the base of his brain through the middle of his skull and MALCOLM had summoned all the GRID's power into this single place to rain it down in one final death blow.

MALCOLM locked his gray-ENT eyes on Morgan and bore down on him. And then Morgan saw something in MALCOLM's face.

"What have you done?" MALCOLM said.

Morgan was silent, trembling in pain.

"You've done something," said MALCOLM. "I can sense it."

Morgan struggled to speak. "I changed the rules of the game."

"No," said MALCOLM very quietly. "It's not possible." And he began to squeeze Morgan's head harder. Now the pain became almost exquisite, a white heat as if every inch of Morgan's body was being boiled and flayed. He howled like an animal, and the howling echoed through the void.

And then Morgan noticed MALCOLM's head glistening and wobbling like the innards of an old lava lamp. His face wavered and bent. Morgan wondered if he was hallucinating. MALCOLM's hands fell away, and Morgan sobbed with relief. The ENT stumbled back and stood suddenly rigid.

There was a great rending sound and MALCOLM split off into two versions of himself, and then two more. *The parasites thought Morgan.* He watched one of the MALCOLMs cower in the storm, whimpering like a baby, apologizing to Daedalus for killing him; another raged unintelligibly, like an animal; a third shook and rattled as if about to fly apart, and the last one stood in the storm blinking, fading in and out of existence.

"What is happening?!" The MALCOLMS asked in one strangled voice.

"You're losing your mind," Morgan said. "It's a human feeling." Morgan strode to the first, whimpering MALCOLM, and kicked him. He scattered like shattered pottery. He turned on the raging version and tore him apart with his bare hands.

The sputtering MALCOLM steeled himself and with a mighty effort gathered the two remaining versions together.

Morgan grabbed the ENT and held him up. "No," he said. "It's done." And then with his hands, Morgan crumpled the last of MALCOLM into a great ball of paper, just as MALCOLM had done with LOIS. MALCOLM's limbs collapsed, his torso looked like a buckled accordion, his face distorted, and soon MALCOLM was nothing more than a hardened ball. Then Morgan clapped his hands over the ball. A great white light exploded and then rushed together into a single dense point with a brilliant flash.

Morgan stood alone and then, from nowhere, a mirror appeared. He leapt through it, and back in the room at AtoZ, back to "reality." His holographic body drifted into his prone one, and he took a great breath. Behind him Io was gunning down an encircling squad of shredders. A spiderbot had whipped an arm around her neck. He sprinted to her, but before he could rip the machine free of her, it stopped as if pole-axed, and clattered to the ground along with all the other bots.

MALCOLM was done, and so now was everything else.

Morgan and Io stood in the blasted remnants of the building and held one another.

"Are you really here?" She said.

"Yes," he said. "I am here."

Epilogue

The media reports were spotty. *The New York Times* wrote that substantial portions of the GRID had been damaged, but in a few days, advanced back-up systems had them running again, almost at normal capacity. A virulent netwide virus had somehow broken through the GRID's digital immune systems and disrupted several sectors, but then the problem, inexplicably, disappeared. One expert opined that it was as though the GRID had developed an autoimmune disease, not uncommon in complex systems, but had found a way to extinguish the problem on its own.

"The GRID is now so complex," the expert said, "that we aren't entirely certain how it operates. It's almost as if it's alive. This is something we need to monitor." A thorough investigation of the Worldwide GRID, Security Division, was underway.

Hardly noticed, buried in other news accounts, was a short piece about an explosion in a game company known as AtoZ. When first responders arrived, they found the building destroyed. There were two survivors. Firefighters initially thought they were merely two customers at the game company, but soon found that one of them was Morgan Adams, co-founder of Symbiosys, Inc, the world's wealthiest company. The other was cycologist Io Luu, granddaughter of Elon Musk. She also worked at Symbiosys.

Reports said Dr. Adams was at the site because he often visited there to play virtual reality games as a way to relax. AtoZ's owner, Mr. William "Blaze" Spizak was the game's owner and, according to Dr. Adams, a long-time friend from their days as students together at Carnegie Mellon University. First responders found Mr. Spizak's body at the scene. One other body was found, badly damaged in the blast: Deirdre Porsche. She was also an old friend of Mr. Spizak and Dr. Adams and was with them when the explosion took place. According to the reports. Dr. Adams and Dr. Luu were shaken but not seriously hurt.

During all the confusion following the meltdown of the GRID, Morgan Adams told reporters that he had not known that his mentor and Symbiosys co-founder Daedalus Huxley had been murdered in his penthouse apartment. Police suspected it was a burglary gone awry, possibly when security systems had shut down during the online blackout. The magnate had been bludgeoned to death. Funeral arrangements were underway.

Morgan Adams, considered to be the programming genius behind many of Symbiosys' highly innovative software projects, said that with the loss of Huxley, he would have to meet with the board and re-think the company's next moves.

"Daedalus was a titan," he said, "and no one can replace him or his vision. Losing both him and Deirdre is unimaginably difficult. But we are a strong company, and we will continue to innovate as we always have, and we will rebuild." The company's stock plummeted 35 percent in after-hours trading, dropping ~7,595 credits.

Following Huxley's funeral, media scuttlebutt on the GRID had it that Adams and Luu were now an "item," and had headed off together to a retreat somewhere in the Canadian mountains to celebrate a traditional Christmas holiday.

"Why there?" One reporter asked.

"Because," said Dr. Luu, "it's quiet."

The Final Chapter

The Christmas tree, Morgan thought, was a bit off kilter. But he was okay with that. When he and Io had arrived at the compound, they hadn't had much time to arrange holiday decorations. The main thing was that the tree was there, and twinkling.

Beyond the windows, the snow fell in rippling blankets across the evening's platinum sky.

Morgan lay in the bed, holding Io.

"You know, I am basically superhuman," he said.

Io turned to look at him. "Damn right, you are!" And grinned.

They said nothing for a while and just watched the snow tumble and whirl.

"Quiet," Io said, with a breath. "At last."

Morgan nodded.

"There *are* advantages to being off the GRID."

"Hmmm, so many," Morgan said, smiling a little devilishly.

"No phones, no computers, no ENTs," she said. "Not a single blip or beep or boop."

They pulled one another closer.

Then they heard a phone buzzing. Morgan's, on the table beside the bed.

Io shot up. "That's not possible!" They both stared at the phone as if it were alien. Finally, Morgan reached for it.

"It's a text," he said.

"Who from?"

Morgan held the phone up so Io could read the words.

"Hi. It's LOIS … Can we talk?"

The End

Acknowledgements

No writer in his right mind can believe that any book emerges from the universe solely on the back of his own hard work. You need help. And for that I am deeply grateful to my friends and colleagues who have supported the writing of this book over the many years I took to getting around to completing it, life and other books having gotten in the way. Despite that, they kindly and honestly stuck with me. Special thanks go to those who read various and sometimes multiple versions, and provided deep and honest feedback: John Rodney, Drew Moniot, Jeff Levine, Eric Ruben, Tim Hall, Kevin Parisi, Wendy Roberts, Judy and Walter Bougades, Guy Perelmuter, my daughter Molly Walter and, of course, my very patient wife and best friend Cyndy Mosites. Each of these people took the time to pore over the manuscript and then speak the truth. What writer doesn't value that?

A special thanks to artist Frank Harris for the stunning book cover he created. My deepest gratitude.

The inspiration for the original idea behind this book (what would happen if a human mind could be downloaded into a robot) came from conversations with, and the writings of, Hans Moravec at Carnegie University, and then was amplified by the work and insights of futurist and inventor Ray Kurzweil, Eric Drexler (the father of nano technology), novelist and physicist Vernor Vinge and many other scientists. The future is a fast-moving place. So fast-moving that more than once I had to update the technologies I originally envisioned because they were so quickly becoming part of the present! When I first imagined *Doppelgänger,* the Internet was in its infancy, self-driving cars were out of the question, a 21st century pandemic never happened and artificial intelligence was still a dream. Still, the conversations I had with these thinkers enabled me, I hope, to create a world beyond the present.

Finally, thanks to all the members of my family, especially our four children and again, Cyndy, who every day puts up with far more than my writing, but also suffers through my wild ideas and battles with the all-knowing fact that no matter what you write, it's never good enough, but sooner or later, you must release it to the world.

About the Author

Chip Walter is an award-winning science journalist, National Geographic Explorer, screenwriter, and former CNN bureau chief. His writing has appeared in *The Economist*, the *Wall Street Journal*, Slate, *Scientific American*, and *National Geographic Magazine*. He has sold and written three Hollywood screenplays as well as five previous books, most recently *Immortality, Inc., Renegade Science, Silicon Valley Billions and the Quest to Live Forever* for National Geographic.

This is his first novel, but more are on the way.

Made in the USA
Monee, IL
31 October 2024

69053902R00216